D1603897

"*Lamb* isn't just another novel.
It's a fast-moving adventure story
that exposes the hidden forces that rule the world.
The secret organizations
and covert government programs exist, and dominate our
lives. You will be captivated by Zeph Daniel's
descriptions and multiple story lines.
I recommend his book without reservation."

Stanley Monteith, *author* — Brotherhood of Darkness,
Host of Radio Liberty

"Zeph Daniel's book, *LAMB,* will be like Nathan the prophet,
exposing the reality of radical evil. It will help victims verify their
pain and see there is a way out, the only way —
THE LORD JESUS CHRIST"

Russ Dizdar
Sr. Pastor: Calvary Community Fellowship
Director: Shatter the Darkness

LAMB

ZEPH E. DANIEL

Elderberry Press
OAKLAND

This is a work of fiction.
Any resemblance to locations, organizations, or individuals, living or dead,
is purely coincidental.

Elderberry Press

1393 Old Homestead Drive, Second floor
Oakland, Oregon 97462—9506.
WEB: www.elderberrypress.com
E-MAIL: editor@elderberrypress.com
TEL/FAX: 541.459.6043

All Elderberry books are available from your favorite bookstore,
amazon.com, or from our 24 hour order line: 1.800.431.1579

Publisher's Catalog-in-Publication Data
Lamb/Zeph E. Daniel
ISBN 1-930859-31-7
1. Christianity——Fiction.
2. God——Fiction.
3. End Times——Fiction.
4. Prophecy——Fiction.
5. Prediction——Fiction.
6. Conspiracy——Fiction.
I. Title

This book was written, printed, and bound in the United States of America.

I dedicate this book to the Lord God Almighty,
and to my "patient," talented and lovely wife, Patricia,
a Holy Spirit woman if there ever was one.

ACKNOWLEDGMENTS

To my editor, D. W. St. John, who kept me in bold mode. To my text editor, Victoria Giraud: your talent, dedication, exactitude and amazing eye is hopefully not in vain. To my readers, Vicki Anthony, sister in Christ, who tested the message; to Gard Hollinger, the ultimate motorcycle guru; Robyn Wing, a friend; and to Ken Unger, who reminded this brother that first drafts actually do need editing—8 months later, Ken...all I can say is, Amen. To the pastors who read, got a'feared and ran. Hey, it's only a work of fiction. To George Oja, a top notch writer and missionary to the mean streets of LA, "who knows where the rubber meets the road." Thank you for helping me seek the unction of the Lord; thank you for praying for those battalions of angels to stay by me during the process—you're the one-man Gideon's Army. To my mother, who always encouraged me to write.

Special thanks to my glorious web people: Ross, Rodney and Art. To Esther, book cover designer and web artist extraordinaire...thank you for www.zephreport.com. To all those who believe in the prophecies of God.

And to His lambs.

To the mysterious angel who inspired me, and to the Holy Spirit, who made me get up at 4:00 AM daily to write and Who told me He had the outline...well, this is a continuing thing.

For behold, the day is coming,
Burning like an oven,
And all the proud, yes, all who do
wickedly will be stubble.
Malachi 4:1

Beloved, now we are children of
God; and it has not yet been revealed
what we shall be, but we know that
when he is revealed, we shall be like
Him, for we shall see Him as He is.
1 John 3:2

And it shall come to pass afterward
That I will pour out My spirit
on all flesh;
Your sons and daughters
shall prophesy,
Your old men shall dream dreams,
Your young men shall see visions.
Joel 2:28

Those who survive will escape
and be on the mountains
Like doves of the valleys,
All of them mourning,
Each for his iniquity.
Ezekiel 7:16

one

A ndrew Wexler's pale body was lying on the street. The corpse was laid out, drained of blood, yet strangely at peace. As if there were no struggle. As if he might have even caused it to happen.

Puncture wounds in his wrists and feet indicated he had been ritually killed. It was a sacrifice, a satanic rite—Bauman had seen it before.

Bauman knew Wexler from the news media—he was a mogul of sorts, a famous man. A multi-millionaire who dealt in business ventures—everything from electric shavers to basketball teams. The whole thing seemed impossible, Bauman thought. The homeless men who lived in this seemingly random stretch of the forgotten San Fernando Valley street were the only witnesses and had told LAPD officer Sergeant Bauman that a woman, probably Wexler's wife, had been kidnapped by the occupants of a Caddy SUV.

"The prophet told us he was crucified upside down," Shep, the spitfire eighteen-year-old who had grown up on the streets and was determined to stay, interjected.

"How do you know he was upside down?" Bauman asked as the dispossessed men, the usual eyes and ears of Bauman, gathered around, staring at the bloodless body. They had already reported that the perpetrators seemed (and perhaps this was the booze talking) invisible.

"He spoke words we hadn't heard, like they were from the Bible. He was like, you know, like confident, man—powerful. Told us this guy was crucified...upside down," Shep said in an awed tone, wondering why Bauman seemed so slow.

John the Apostle, the resident man of God who laid claim to a certain wisdom, added, "He had long gray hair and a beard, and I'm sure he was an angel of the Lord since he spoke about God without moving his lips, in a different language. But I could understand that he was talking about grace."

Reports of the strange man floating above the ground when he spoke were alarming, especially since Bauman heard the same account from independent sources. Even more alarming was the fact that no one really *heard* his voice—he spoke to their minds.

"Oh, yeah," said Shep. "Grace. Definitely. Anything else you want to know, Bauman?"

"Nuthin' else, kid," Bauman answered and couldn't stop himself from some fatherly advice, "But you've been on the street too long. I'm sure your brothers here would like to see you make something of yourself."

"Yeah, sure," Shep replied. He'd heard Bauman's advice too many times.

"We seen him, the prophet, over at that church too," John the Apostle butted in. "He's in disguise as a gardener."

Bauman cared more for these homeless friends than this murder of a millionaire, and he wondered if they actually saw more than they were letting on. He knew he could not bring them in, could not expose them to the state authorities if he could help it. They seemed to him like wild, free horses. He heard a voice in his head. At first it was a distant voice in his thoughts; it grew closer despite his medication, "Don't touch these little ones. They are all right."

Frustrated and knowing he would not be solving this one, he said to the boys: "Come on, this isn't Oz—a man was drained of blood. And okay, it looks like some weird crucifixion type thing, looks like no struggle. You guys were in the area, and some gray-haired guy you call an angel knew all about it, and he floats in the air and speaks a strange language, and that's all you know, right? You know what—" Bauman concluded, "—you know what? You tell me when you're ready to tell me the whole thing. By the time the suits get here, I'll be gone anyway."

Shep would not meet his eyes, neither would the others, many of whom Bauman did not know by name, if they even had a name anymore. It was clear that they were afraid of something. Perhaps retaliation. Bauman, with his 5'8," withering, ex-bulldog frame and fading blue uniform, put their minds at rest with his own silent body language. No, I won't bust you guys; yes, I'll look out for you; yes, I care for you. When he was in the area, he'd usually give them a five dollar bill to share.

They were good kids, he thought, and there were a lot of them on the street. They looked so strong and established with their hair blowing in the hot, dry wind.

"You know there's a place for you, over at…" He was going to say the Mercy Rescue Mission, where Big Fred and Dr. Louis Denney, brain surgeon-cum-missionary, waited on the Lord, waited for their prayers to be answered with more souls coming to Christ.

"It's all over," Shep said, ignoring Bauman's words. "This is the end. That's what *he* was saying, man. And the clouds and the stars are weird, like I could see all these angels looking down."

John the Apostle (who refused to be called anything else) still avoided Bauman's eyes and kept staring at the pale body. "Something's changing—things are moving," he said softly. "I feel sick."

Alice Garcia, Bauman's youthful, invigorating partner stood by while he interviewed the boys; she knew he had a special compassion for them and didn't need or want her help until he asked.

When Bauman saw her smile at him, her smile was so beautiful it made him feel like smiling too, despite the strangeness of the crime scene. He liked her take-charge ways. She liked to drive the squad car, in fact usually insisted on it.

Other police vehicles began arriving on the scene. In a separate car, arriving last, was the Coroner—Aguillar. His morbid fascination for dead things would get a real boost here, Bauman thought as he watched him slide effortlessly from the van. Without any fluid left in the victim, Aguillar wouldn't need to drain his blood in the lab. Tissue samples would provide information on blood type, time of death and other items of information, useless at helping solve the case.

The winds began picking up—the Santa Anas, sometimes called "the devil winds," which brought hot and dry air from the California desert. As Bauman watched the palms swaying and swooning like big rubber hoses, he kept thinking of it as the City of the Lost. The Loss of Innocence. Lost Children. *Los Angeles* meant *lost angels*, or *lost angles*.

Even God was lost.

This wind was one of change—it was drier, it was hotter, and Bauman felt good about it this time.

Alice wondered why Bauman looked so distracted as they ambled toward the squad car. She knew he wanted to talk to her yet again about his daughter, Marta, and the continuing downward spiral of his own life. "Alright, Bauman, spill it—your wife and your daughter, go for it."

He picked right up where he left off the day before: "Her teachers give me the creeps, and Sheila is encouraging her to get involved in every liberal issue from abortion to tree preservation. Not that it's so bad being 'socially conscious,' it's that I want Marta to have her own mind."

She re-tucked her shirt in and quickly changed the subject. "This one's out of our hands, boss," she said. She lit a cigarette and added, "It's Ricky—it's just gang stuff. It's drugs."

"Don't you know who Wexler is, or was, Alice?"

"My hubby's been usin' again," she said, veering off the subject and shocking Bauman.

"What? Oh, Alice, oh, man…That's…it's just not fair, and it really hacks me—you want me to talk to Jimmy? You want me to scare him real bad?"

She laughed at Bauman; almost twice her age, as he would nearly always remind her and tell her again how he used to be quite a boxer in his prime, "which wasn't so long ago."

"Bauman, you're so cute," she said. She called him *Bauman* like everyone else. No one said *Phil*, his first name.

"I'm not cute. And it's…you want to get a drink or something, shoot the canaries at Jake's or—"

"I'm worried about my husband, okay? I don't know who Jimmy's dealing with."

"Alice, you're a cop—you can't tell me…"

"You know what I'm talking about."

He did. He knew that being a cop meant nothing. Being honorable meant nothing anymore either. Who would you go to; who would care? It was a chess game, no, it was checkers, and everybody wanted it all—all the world had to offer. And Bauman had to admit it: "I know, I know—I was using too. Remember when you first got assigned to me?"

"You stole my innocence, Bauman. No more Santa Claus. You did the barrio busts just to get high, and you set a bad example—you embarrassed me. But then you straightened up, and that was impressive," Alice Garcia said sincerely.

"But I found out it wasn't my fault. I'm bipolar. I mean, if the force found out...can you imagine if Max found out what you and I were doin' when we took Ricky's stash—oh, man."

She laughed. It was good to see her laugh. Yes, there was an attraction. She was the most beautiful, slightly pudgy woman he had ever seen; he loved the way her pants hugged her hips, but he kept his hands off her. She covered for him, and they became close friends.

He was a great man, Alice thought, the way he brought himself back from the brink. She'd covered him on the shooting in Burbank, the incident that pushed Bauman into permanent sergeant-ship. She'd make it up to him—after all, he saved her life and he never complained.

Bauman shooed away his street buddies—his *intelligence* operation—as the detectives approached and he and Alice returned to the corpse. Detectives were gathering around Wexler's Bentley Azure. "You know, Wexler owned a big piece of the Lakers, the XFL, and the Phoenix Suns," he told Alice. "He ran with...I don't know...He was into some sort of cult. The paper said he was a charitable guy and that he was involved in a satanic cult and then renounced it when he became a born-again Christian. You never heard of Wexler?"

Before Alice could answer, Bauman heard behind him: "Well, well, well," the voice of the hotshot they called Redfish, detective of the hour, who bypassed Bauman after the controversial shooting of a gang-banger drug dealer named Shady-3 outside Grady's in Burbank. "What'ya got for me?" Redfish demanded.

He really was obnoxious, Bauman thought. Nature's gift to women, always clean-cut and judgmental, and Bauman hated him for every reason Redfish justified and defined himself. But Redfish wasn't important; he was emblematic.

"We're leaving. You're the detective," he told Redfish. "You'll figure it out."

"Thanks for sharing, Bauman," said Redfish.

two

*T*ed Gunderson preached at the First Trinity Church on Sherman Way. His life was nothing more than a dipping reflection of a valley: It would have been much better to be on the mountain, where he could see clearly. Yet he loved all the straight streets, all the roads below sea level, the few roads leading out through narrow canyons. Keyword: narrow. He loved all the languages; his mission was the crossroads, and it was glorious. He was grateful.

Pastor Ted led a congregation willing to bake cookies and conduct Bible study once a week at Sharon Goldfarb's apartment. He was proud a previously orthodox Jewish woman like Sharon (the only one) had come to Jesus Christ. She was a personal answer to his personal vigil that all God's chosen people would one day embrace Christ, would one day fulfill Scripture, that the Messiah would return to save the whole world, Jew and Gentile alike. He knew that God was free to pass judgment on cities, principalities and nations, that before any prophecy of Tribulation, there might be worldwide strife—he did not often speak of this; it was just something that plagued him, especially when he'd watch the news or went online.

He knew from his study of the Book of Revelation, or Isaiah, or Daniel, or Ezekiel and in all the prophetic Scriptures, that the world would be brought low before any rise of the Antichrist. You could feel that this was the time, *that something might happen soon,* he would say in so many words to his colleagues and his wife, Sarah. She worried about the kids and he would vow not to bring it up again.

Despite all the projections for society's improvement, he knew that nothing had changed. There was no peace on the earth, there was no brotherhood of man; there was no fear of God. There was terrorism; there was war; there was depravity across the globe. He was what no preacher ever wanted to be...fearful—God did not spare the children of Israel when they rebelled, could he expect mercy for his mission? The answer propelled him to evangelize.

Pastor Ted was slipping, becoming sorrowful, was not being a good shepherd. The forms were present: plenty sung in the choir; they were adept at putting the good Lord's face on everything church-related, never missing the May bake sale, the Christmas concert, volunteering to answer phones during the cancer drive, praising him for his preaching, or donating what they could afford, no doubt about that.

And he hated that.

He hated the word *Churchianity*. Hated how narrow the gate actually was. Knew it and the hatred of it were both sins. But if he made it easier from the pulpit, if he institutionalized sin—would he be serving his flock?

Hate broke the second of two major commandments that Christ admonished his followers practice: 1) Love God and 2) Love each other. No room for hate in God's law. Jesus Christ was, is, and forever will be God. Only God can hate with perfect love, he told himself—a concept that he sometimes understood, but that place was where words could not go.

There was no courage to combat it or try something different, perhaps more *true* because he was afraid of losing his flock—and the tithe was barely enough to keep his meager staff of two. Sometimes a mysterious man, who supposedly lived in a trailer in an industrial park nearby, would come around and argue a Scripture or two while clipping the hungry hedges for a ten spot. No, Pastor Ted need not risk losing his flock by becoming *mysterious*. Though the enigmatic man had no apparent name, he respected and admired him for his accuracy on Scripture and his totally happy-go-lucky, if flaky nature. The secretive man's handsome, lithe features made him seem more cultivated than nearly homeless. "Still looking for that morning star, Pastor Ted? Soon," he would say while Ted walked past on the flagstone steps leading up to the hedged way.

"You keep looking for it, Dan," Ted would answer, using the name he thought was his, yet the stranger never corrected him, nor would he say when he would return. Pastor Ted even thought he saw the man floating above the ground, but dismissed it when he saw him walking.

While Ted was brushing his teeth one evening, his daughters Carole and Beth came running in: "Daddy, daddy, there was a rainbow in our room last night."

"Yeah, yeah. Just make sure your mom gets you ready for Bible study tomorrow," he said, covering the fearfulness he never wanted Carole or Beth to ever see, not ever.

"It's an angel," said eight-year-old Carole, with buckteeth and a cute face framed by blonde pigtails. He lifted her up. "Daddy, you're not fat."

"Thanks, sweetie, that makes me feel a lot better," he said, kissing her on the forehead.

"But you're getting a double chin!"

"How 'bout if I grow a goatee?"

"Eu gross!" said Beth, six, who was a touch "sophisticated." Her tiny hands patted daddy's face.

He tucked them into their beds; they had always shared a room in the modest two bedroom and a den house. The small house was filled with the nice aroma of cedar walls; it had a real beamed ceiling and a cozy living room, a galley kitchen that Sarah loved, and a couple of bikes in the yard. After he shut the door, he looked around to appreciate what he had and then he slipped to his knees and prayed for forgiveness, prayed in praise and supplication and thanks.

• • •

It wasn't a rainbow, not exactly, but a pulsing light that was under Carole's bed. Sugarplum, the cat, watched it wheel around like a spinning top. The light was bright but did not emit or radiate out away from its spinning center. Then it grew into white light and moved across the floor, transforming into a mist or a cloud-like substance as it slipped away under the door. Bored, Sugarplum hopped up on the bed with Beth and snuggled into her feet, purring.

• • •

Flying from Columbia was always treacherous, but the advent of Hurricane Willard made this the most awesome storm Cal Wilson ever encountered. He was carrying contraband, just like M-16s and C-4 for the CIA, like drugs for the cartels. After leaving the Air Force in the 70's, Cal had slipped into this dangerous, illegal lifestyle. He was now fifty-five with a long gray beard and wondrous childlike blue eyes. He flew with his pet parrot named Sam and his favorite Scotch in a flask. Shyly flawed, not proud, he was just flying another *last mission* so he could pay off the plane, save the house, and keep his ex from the poor house.

He looked through the whirring blades propelled by the massive Pratt & Whitney turbine on his de Havilland Otter, the most successful seaplane ever built in Caleb Wilson's opinion. Usually nothing could thwart the craft, but a sudden gust knocked him off trajectory and into a narrow, nearly out-of-control spin. Ahead, toward the Florida Keys, was nothing but pain. Another gust and he could feel the strain on the turbine—that sputtering sound no pilot ever wants to hear. The plane was silent; he wasn't using his radio. On a flight like this he had to be silent. It was bad enough that the plane made a dent on somebody's radar screen at all.

The only place he could make a landing would be either Cuba or possibly San Juan or maybe he could turn and head for the Dominican Republic.

"They're gonna kill me, Sam," he said to his beloved parrot.

The parrot looked around and said, "Cocaine kills."

"You bet it does, baby, you bet it does."

Rummaging through his memories, he recalled when he was a boy and all he wanted to do was fly jets—which he did in Viet Nam. When he lost it there, he was captured and held, tortured and starved. He was dying by the inch and he knew it. They all knew it—yet were in agreement that hatred could only go so far, and would not kill you if you did not let it. Hatred could not produce anything of lasting value; it would not make your body endure, especially when you're talking three years in some gook claptrap. Jerry, Syke, Bust, Tits and Scrub were falling into a weary psychosis, calling for the past, for other personalities, for anything—but nothing worked.

Only when he spoke of Christ, only when he quoted Scripture drilled into him from his Baptist mother since a baby, did it seem they were soothed. It worked. But it worked because it was the only thing that offered hope.

Now that things were rapidly diminishing on his plane, he was suddenly reminded of that thing he blotted out from the camp, that thing he could not know that proved that God was right here and right now—something that made him want to run from God. That was when Syke started quoting Scripture while staring at the mold-crusted ceiling. Psalm 22, for instance. Syke would utter strange words, then suddenly in the middle of the night he would start speaking: *"All the prosperous of the earth will eat and worship; all those who go down to the dust shall bow before Him, even if he can't keep himself alive."*

Then Syke, tall, slim and uneducated, who would be more fearful if he wasn't a man of service, fell asleep—in fact he slept silently. Before reciting Scripture, he would be whimpering. They would tolerate the sounds; they knew he was a simple man. He was tough enough, but deep down he was the baby, the terminal child.

"Syke, do you remember last night?" Cal would ask, and Syke would answer, "Cap'n, something strange is goin' on. I feel at home."

"Well, you're not! This can never be home! You got that!" Cal yelled at him.

"Sure, Cap'n. Yes sir. This is hell, sir."

"We're going to get out of here, gentlemen," Cal would say, but they were all waiting for night to fall to listen to Syke, with the dim hope that he might speak from some other realm once again.

Sure enough, the next night he spoke in some Middle Eastern dialect, which no one understood, and then:

"Every valley shall be filled, and every mountain and hill brought low; the crooked places shall be made straight, and the rough ways smooth..."

"Hey, Scrub, get him to do it again."

"I didn't do nuthin', Cap'n," he said to Cal.

"That was from Luke, I think—"

"The Bible?"

"Oh, yeah. It's...it's impossible," said Bust, pulling out another tooth from his beating a few days before.

Yes, Syke did it again, and again, speaking in what Cal knew to be a form of *tongues*, at least he knew that from a Pentecostal uncle. But the Scriptures, there was no way that Syke, or anybody for that matter, could, or even think of doing such a thing!

They were all afraid. Cal led them in prayer. They were tortured even more because they seemed to be doing "better," and that meant that they were sane. The guards shot Syke when he tried to walk out the front gates, waving and laughing.

No one could stop him. Cal tried to forget, but could not, could not ever get that look erased from his mind. Syke, tall, lanky Syke, arms akimbo, looking back with love in his eyes—staring at the Vietnamese guards as if they were long-lost brethren. His eyes glowed like fire, and his face had the countenance of a child. He had been delivered; Cal had understood but never fathomed it. He could not really understand the depth of it, and if depth was truth, he did not know it; he knew that much.

Caleb Terrance Wilson would forget the whole thing, would never look back again. Would not even acknowledge that they all had perished. Unwelcome everywhere, hating the church from then on, hating himself and everything but a few animals and a few pleasures, fleeting but real. Fleeting but understandable. Fleeting was just fine, was more than good. Was finite and full of color, dexterity and form. Full of time and circumstance—so all of it got put behind him all right.

Nothing at the University of Florida ever taught him anything about this experience, not anthropology or comparative religion. Anyway, it didn't matter now. "It's all mind! That's what it is, Sam!"

Nothing from the bird. Who would soon be free. Nothing from Sally Anne, once a sweet dove, later overtaken by blow and bottle, but that was life—it was bitter. Money made it sweet; flying made him alive. None of the beauty of the ocean or islands ever made a difference. He liked how a set of new gauges looked, a braided fuel line, pontoons with more ballast, Barbados rum, Caribbean women; the beauty of things everlasting were the things of alligators, of himself. Constitution was nature, and the key was to think like the animals, to never look back, never look ahead, to rejoice in knowing that your enemy will or won't kill you, to help the weaker people, help the poor, like fixing Theresa's rusted tin roof. Some materials, a couple of willing men and voila! Simple. She is happy; he can get drunk with a glad heart. Life was really quite simple and total when you thought about it.

He was complete.

He looked at his gauges. Fuel was sparse enough as it was just getting to the swamp and Ingo's airboat. That wasn't going to happen this time. The clouds virtually locked around the Keys, while up the coast both sides were already socked in from a northern storm.

If for some reason he didn't make it, he could deal with the government; in this case it was their contraband, it was their dope. If for any reason he did not land at the proscribed area, he would be a marked man. He could see Syke's face with that smile, something he never understood, but now that he could see it again, he began to *know* something—something his mother told him when he was a baby.

"You have to have hope; there's no excuse for giving yourself to the enemy."

He had to try. He had perhaps enough fuel to get the Otter to the coordinates at the Glades. If he were fortunate, he'd land it right in the eye of the bloodsucker.

Cal told himself and all the holy angels that if he ever flew contraband again, they should simply cut him down.

three

*T*he Greyhound was halfway across Kansas when Katarina woke up. The methadone pills had worn off, but not the bruises on her face, not the past, nor the present. The passengers would stare at her and she would smile and then withdraw. She'd get off at the next rest stop and have a cigarette. She promised herself that she would not befriend any young men. There would be no more men in her life; she would get even one day, not now, and certainly not on every single man in creation.

The withdrawal. Going badly. Going nowhere. No dream or vision, disconnected, no participation—she would need protection.

She began speaking with a mechanic named Stephen, "handsome *Stevie*," she tried to call him but it didn't stick. He told her he used to be "Steve" and even "Stevie," but not for a long time, that he was in his early twenties, and he hadn't settled down to one job but kept transferring from one job to another in Arizona. She liked listening to him talk about his mother. How would it be to have *homemade* apple pie, she wondered? What was it like growing up in your daddy's business? Was it difficult when his daddy died? Stephen J. Petchick, a clear-eyed handsome gentleman, had all the right answers, *she thought*.

And he was kind.

It didn't matter that when Stephen fell asleep they would stare at *her*, Katarina. Stephen never stared at her bruised face; he never asked any questions.

He escorted her to the restroom at the bus stops, a true gentleman. He covered her with his Harley Davidson jean jacket. He was sweet, thought Katarina. He would make a great husband. But a mechanic? Motorcycles, boats, cars, he talked about all of it—but how could someone of Katarina's "worldly stature" live in Arizona? Better a temporary lover. She would be comfortable with that.

"So where are you headed, Katarina?" Stephen, the mechanic, asked.

"I got a cousin in California. I'm going to art school out there."

"Cool. Art school."

"Design."

"You mean, like cars and stuff?" Stephen said excitedly.

"Well, clothes."

"Oh. Sure."

She had forgotten that she was wearing a slightly tattered, three-day wrinkled dress, a soiled T-shirt underneath it, high leather boots, carried a purse and had no luggage. It didn't make sense and she knew it—but he did not press it.

"You believe in God, Katarina?" he asked.

"Sure. I believe in everything, like you."

"I mean, do you believe in God, in Jesus?" he asked politely.

"I love Jesus, I love him so much. I'm just like Magdalene."

Stephen looked away, end of conversation. "Sorry, I didn't mean to pry."

"No, I'm sorry. I'm just not used to people talking to me like a person," she said, drawing demonic-shaped heads on a thinning legal pad.

"Here's my card."

"A mechanic with a card?"

"I'm thinking about moving out to California. There's a motorcycle franchise that pays pretty good for mechanics."

"Great. Maybe we could have a date."

He looked away again.

She started crying. "I'm just so...I'm just so...I'm a child, I'm lost, I'm...I hate these people on this bus, I hate the—"

"—the guy who beat you up?" Stephen finished her sentence, he had noticed after all.

"No one beat me up—what are you talking about? I was in an accident."

"Okay. Look, let's just ... keep going."

"It's a very good idea to keep going. Keeping going is what I do best," she said.

He said nothing further. She wondered whether he wanted his jacket back right on the spot. She suddenly felt the contraction, the dry heaving, the cold sweat, that sicker-than-sick running empty through her veins. She pretended not to be sick, of course—but her condition alerted Stephen, who rescued her.

Because she needed to be saved.

"Bus-driver, stop the bus!" He rang the emergency buzzer. "Sir, she's sick! She needs off."

The observant bus driver could see stopping was the best choice. The passengers agreed vocally; hopefully she would not come back.

They were just a few miles from a place near the Oklahoma panhandle called Liberal, Kansas. The driver pulled up next to a gas station and watched Katarina's departure; he couldn't help admiring her long legs as she briskly but gracefully headed toward the dirty, side bathrooms.

"Now look, son," he said, "I'm not gonna wait more than about five minutes—we're late. I got a bus of very tired people here; we're headed for Phoenix and that's what I intend to do today."

"She'll be alright. Cut her some slack—the lady's had a hard time."

"Lady?" he chuckled.

Stephen hopped off angrily then strode purposefully after her.

Twenty minutes later, the retired policeman/bus driver opened the luggage doors. "Which one's yours?"

"Katarina! Hey!" Stephen yelled outside the bathroom. Nothing. "Katarina, you still in there?"

Finally, "Uh...yeah. Sorry. Are they all mad at me?"

"No, ma'am," he said. "Not anymore." He prayed for her. He prayed for himself. He prayed for the world. All he could think about was the dryness of Arizona, the Camelbacks, the hot strip, the broken air-conditioner at Tri-City Cycle, the money pouring in from yuppie Scottsdale riders, the rides up to Flagstaff, his barely legal '62 turquoise Electra-Glide, which was stolen years ago. But he still remembered. There was nothing for him in Chicago. Uncle Freddy's shop was going under anyway. It was empty and he needed something. He'd spent his money; Cheryl Bingham wouldn't marry him and move to Arizona. He'd moved out and he knew he shouldn't have lived in sin. Furthermore he shouldn't have hidden the fact that he was a Christian from the rest of the world—he denied Christ and he knew it, but he wanted to fit in. He'd forgotten the Ugly Duckling story; he was not cut out to run in the disco crowd, out of his element, unable to make sense—unwilling to indulge in peace, double-speak, unwilling to call sex love, gone from dope. The world did not understand. He would not embrace life; he was separated into eternity. He did not run with the Jesus riders; he did not run with the Hell's Angels, did not do well with crank and Coors, had not voted for anything. He'd fallen through the cracks; he had a few tattoos, fixed teeth, broken nose (set straight), and a broken body healed by a miracle.

He did not fit into the life of the acceptable Christian—but he knew God loved him...because His Spirit rescued him, because he was set free by Him. Because he was cast out, he knew he was right.

But that was a few years ago—easy to forget.

He was lifted up once when the accident crushed his body and he could not move, and it had made him a virtual quadriplegic. When the fever made him see things, when he begged Jesus for help, when he saw his room spin and a couple of men with long white hair and eyes of gold looking down at him from above, when he'd been caressed by a mother figure who was not his mother but had told him that he would heal. He cried for joy because he knew from that moment on he would be walking again. He knew he'd be healed. And in a few months he was riding again.

He could feel himself quake when he heard a familiar praise to Jesus song; it made him cry because once the Holy Spirit spoke to him and lifted him up, dried his tears and made his father seem alive again.

They were both in eternity. Jesus did that.

• • •

Perhaps the storm wasn't as powerful as Cal first thought. Until he encountered the wind shear that bounced him down a few thousand feet like an air ball, then he got the picture.

"Okay, so I only have to make it to the drop point, then that's it—I'm retirin', gettin' out, sorry jerk-losers, think they can buy me, think they can make me do things because I'm hard up, because I lost my money in a real estate venture up in Lauderdale? I don't need this! Right?" he said out loud.

Nothing from the parrot, who could usually read between the lines: f-e-a-r.

A friendly cloud turned out to be masking another torrent—down three thousand feet faster than falling. It was no use; if he tried for the drop point, he'd lose it. Which is just what you're supposed to do—if you can't make it, then you'd better die because you will be killed.

As he was hurtling toward his final resting place, he noticed that the gauges had stopped working. He noticed the rain had stopped; it was black as night. Then he saw the sun rising from a distant cloud, as if all was okay.

When he looked down, he no longer saw the Florida coast as he had assumed, just open sea. It was as if the plane had been thrown, rather than a simple descent. Besides, he seemed to have plenty of altitude now, and he could see a small ship on the water. This time he opened up his radio. What would it matter? He wasn't going to make the drop and so he could not go home again anyway.

"This is Delta Star Q-three-oh-seven, en route from Bogotá to St. Lucy over?" (It seemed a great idea to head to St. Lucy, where he had flown guns for a hotshot outfit some decades ago.) Anybody read me out there?"

The scratch of static was not wholly unexpected. He needed fuel; he couldn't see the gauge, but just knew that it was basically flying on yesterday's fumes.

Confirmed when the starboard engine went out. Though the winds were so calm, the weather suddenly so good, just enough sunlight, as if the sun were permanently stuck at four o'clock.

"Dear Lord, I've been mad at you for so long I can't remember—I'm not mad anymore. Okay, Sam?" he said to his beloved.

The parrot responded, "Okay, Captain!"

"Don't you know what kind of trouble we're in?"

He looked at the parrot, prying open another peanut, happy, joyful, eternal.

Tears welled over the bright baby blues, he scratched his beard, looked around—a tiny island harbor, off to the right. "Sam, you movin' land masses around, girlfriend?"

"Guns and butter, good for what ails ya!" Sam said happily.

"Sam, you know I love you, right?"

"I love you too," she croaked.

He knew just how to handle this one, as he spiraled the plane down gently before his engine went, though he thought he could probably coast from where he was.

It was the island of St. Lucy—and it was the Lamont Harbor, seemingly abandoned. Not a soul in sight.

"Sam, how could we be over the Keys one minute and five hundred miles away the next?"

Not a choice. On descent the fuel was spent, the other engine gone, and the descent effortless—seaplanes need a little something, or they sink like a stone, but not this time. He sailed down and hit the water right near the harbor—he'd need a tow, but what the heck, this was...gliding. And his plane was anything but a glider, ballast yes, glider no. But this time it glided.

Through his binoculars he could see the harbor, but where were the people? Or the cruise ships, the drug runners, the DEA and their Coast Guard ships? He knew for sure from Sable and Doc that the tourist industry was booming this time of year—the robber barons were prospering—that is, the Brits who stole it from the French, including all the displaced Africans the French brought with them.

• • •

She just can't be like I thought, Steve told himself. Let's get it straight. Her name probably isn't Katarina; it's Cathy or Katherine. She's not from some podunk little ice house on the north side of Chicago; she's no debutante; there would be no courtship; she was not as wealthy as she had gone on about earlier. She had eyes, eyes that could reel him in, could make him jump off buses and lose destinations—at the end of the world and still in the station.

"What happened? He left? Bummer, man—how am I supposed to get to LA without transportation?"

"You sure you're okay?"

"Yeah," she said, brushing her black hair around with her fingers, smiling happily.

"You look better."

"Thanks. I feel great."

He was puzzled. He looked around—then saw the Skinheads in the station.

"You high?" he asked.

"Sure. Who isn't?"

The station attendant and two other young bald, pierced and

tattooed men were watching and laughing.

"Thank you for waiting, Stevie."

"Just Stephen, please."

"Just Stephen, cool. Well, Just Stephen, buy you a drink?"

"Katarina, I want to apologize. I have to get to Phoenix to-night—so I'm going. You look like you're alright. Keep the jacket."

"I don't need it." She handed it back to him and walked away while the farmboy-to-strip-trash-junkies were having a good old time watching the woman who serviced them, while the square guy waited dutifully, none the wiser.

When she walked on, shooting them a smile, her wrinkled, now putrid, slut suit, shone in the sunlight.

He could smell the slaughtering houses; the wind was strong that day. She made her way toward the Holiday Inn.

He looked down the strip of local businesses—he knew there was a bus or a train he could get; he had enough to make it back. He should not and would not pursue this woman. So he turned and walked down the street. The fumes of slaughter houses the only thing abounding. She walked away without looking back but looked a fright.

• • •

"And so, my friends, let me share something with you. Without the Spirit of God, no one can ever learn the Bible, and you're not a Christian without the Spirit of God. Just standing up here and say-ing you believe in Jesus isn't enough! The world does not under-stand the Bible, and they never will, not without the Spirit to teach you. That's the end of the sermon. It you don't like it, take a hike." The pastor walked away from the pulpit, went to the restroom and smashed his fist into the mirror. Then sunk to his knees and wept.

"I'm sorry, Lord. I'm sorry. I'm sorry, Father. I'm sorry, Jesus, oh God I'm sorry, I'm sorry, I...I can't just keep...lying. I don't know what makes you real, I don't know your Word, I don't know You. I don't know and I quit! Okay! I quit! I—"

The pastor's anguish was abruptly interrupted as he noticed him standing in the doorway in silence. His long beard and angular face was alight in the darkness, was the calm in a storm, was the counte-nance of peace.

"Hi," said Pastor Ted. "Come to watch the meltdown? This is what happens to fallen pastors."

"This is what happens to mortals." The reserved stranger—who had yet to reveal a name—entered calmly. At once he was lifting the pastor up and then he was sitting on the floor, legs crossed. His beard parted his chest; his long gray hair was no longer braided but hung loose and white against his bony but firm shoulders. His blue eyes were bright as the shimmering sun in the overhead skylight. Ted thought he might have to squint.

"They're waiting for you. The second service."

"Don't you see? I'm through—"

"Your daughters are out there, your wife. You could just chalk this up to a bad moment, a bad day; they'll forgive you. Look, let me show you something." He stood Ted up and angled him toward the cracked mirror. "You want to see the Spirit of God, Pastor?"

"*What* are you—?"

He placed Ted's hands on the mirror—all went blank, all disappeared, the sun was forgotten, as Ted understood his ancient memory, that spirit means present time—and blots out the memory. He opened his eyes and the mirror was smooth, not cracked. He looked back and Spright, the elder, was urinating while whistling.

"'Mornin' pastor. What's the good word today?"

"Jack, thanks for coming."

"It's almost nine—gotta take my seat."

"Nine? It's eleven!"

"No, sir—you jokin' with me, Pastor?"

Portly Jack Spright washed his hands, dried them and turned to leave. "God bless you, Pastor—without your preaching I'd never have made it after losing my wife. It's a privilege to be an elder in your church; I just want to tell you that."

He turned back to the smooth mirror, then ran out of the bathroom. The worship team played *Unto the Lamb*, and he saw the clock in the hall—sure enough: 8:58 A.M.

Unto the Lamb, be all power and glory, and honor...forever, and ever, and ever...

He ran into the parking lot, looked at the smooth hedgerow. Was it the stranger? A dream? He saw someone walking away in the distance with a jean jacket on, gray hair. "Hey—hey, you!"

But no one answered.

"Good morning," Pastor Ted opened. "Let's...let's start with the

Lord's Prayer. The congregation immediately recited the perfect humbling verses. And he went on, "How many of you believe in miracles?"

A few hands went up. Jack Spright's especially.

"How many believe in angels?"

No hands went up. Except for his daughter.

He stared at her incredulously.

"How many have ever witnessed something that you would call *supernatural*?"

No hands went up.

"Well, I'm here to tell you that there is a conspiracy on this planet because you have all witnessed supernatural things. One, when your life changed after coming to the Lord. When you admitted that you had nothing but broken wings, that you were nothing in yourself, that you had nothing to offer the Lord. Isaiah 25, verse 4. Romans 5, verse 8. That you were nothing by yourself, but you became something in Christ. You transformed your life at that moment of believing that Jesus was God, who became man to destroy your sins, then was resurrected into heaven, residing as Lord. When you believed *that*, something changed."

Amen, pastor.

"Amen?" he asked for more to join him in agreement.

"Amen."

"Good Word, Pastor."

"That's good preaching, Pastor," said another who came from the Charismatic end of things.

"When you turned left instead of right, avoiding certain death because of an oncoming truck, when you beat the cancer, when you got the job and saved yourself from bankruptcy. You didn't do that—only by grace did that occur. Only by grace does this planet revolve at just the right speed, only by grace is the earth just the right temperature."

"That's good preaching, Pastor," reiterated the handsome, happy woman in the back row.

"Amen, Brother," came from Raul, the tattooed ex-con in the front row.

"And your history changed when you started walking with the Lord—there became no history."

The flock got uneasy.

"You know, I'm not quite sure what I mean by that."

Laughter easily broke the tension in the modest four hundred-seat chapel.

He looked toward the back of the room. There was a man wearing a black trench coat, wearing what looked like clown makeup or lipstick; he didn't quite seem real. He stood up. The pastor looked around; no one seemed to notice.

And then the Trench Coat—now armed with a semi-automatic pistol—stood in point blank range and fired five shots into Pastor Ted's stomach and chest. It was like instant slow motion. The room was spinning; Alf Blicky, a blond surfer-boy elder, was looking over him. Both his daughters were screaming; his wife yelling at everyone, 'Stay back! Get back!' Alf and the other four elders ushered the three hundred or so out the side doors of the chapel.

Soon there was an ambulance. He passed out before they could strap him down to the bed. He watched it all go silent and he finally felt at peace. He could see everyone, but no one looked at him, and he was not alone anymore.

four

"Hologram," that's how he described it. "I might die for you," that's what Justin Kincaid told his band mates as they woke up. The bus kept going like a trusty clock.

"Hey, man, the crank got you on that God stuff again? Time to knock it back a blow or two, mate," said Anton Duffield, the homesick manager, slugging down the first cup of coffee.

"You do not understand," said Justin, the charismatic lead singer with an innocence that all could see—though no one really believed in innocence anymore. "I can't sleep because I don't want to lose the...the... well I don't know what it is, but it talks to me, and I'm figuring out lots of stuff. I think my parents really messed me up, and I think this world is...a lie. It's a hologram—one person can make a difference! It's like the movie—look, I don't need you to *unbelieve*, man—truth."

"To *disbelieve* you, mate. Didn't you learn your grammar, or is it brain damage?" Anton asked, chuckling.

"Look, mate," Justin said sarcastically to the Brit, "you don't have a clue, brother."

"And neither does anybody else! Hey, the lyrics kick, but the drugs, man—got you by the shorthairs," said drummer Jeremy, tall and lanky, with thick brow—the Handsome, the Hip. "You never sleep, do you?"

"That's because I'm figuring it out for all of us, including you, Anton!" Justin said enthusiastically.

Anton headed up to the front to help a woman named Roebuck

"drive."

Over all this, the bus made its way across the flatness. Roebuck, the bus driver, who was heavy-set and tough enough to take any of them in a fight, was chewing tobacco as she drove. She'd been married and divorced; she'd been happy once.

The roadies followed in three trucks that carried lighting, sound and personal equipment. A modest entourage for a new hit single metal band. Half the tonnage but more substance, Anton Duffield would tell them when he wasn't warning Justin about doing too many drugs and not getting enough sleep. The whole reason for the success of the band, everyone would hate to admit, was its front man, Justin Kincaid—even though he was incapable of balancing a checkbook, balancing on one leg, or balancing impulses which sprouted like marvelous weeds on a scissor-clipped lawn.

"It's not drugs—it's a special dispensation," he might say. "It's special because I'm special. It's about God, and He's leading me, feeding me—he's my source now."

"Just don't make yourself out to be Jesus Christ," Rope, the lead guitar with porno tattoos and the black leather fringe, said.

Jeremy, the drummer, added: "So, why would it matter if we play Kansas City again? It wouldn't."

"It did matter, and you stank," Rope said angrily.

"Sorry, dude—you're the one who forgot what we decided on the tempo of *Jail Bite.*"

Rope retorted at 6:00 A.M: "Let's get drunk." He opened the Jack Daniels and swilled away. Handed it to Justin, who passed it to Jeremy, who slammed it. They laughed and listened to the live tracks where Justin was so off-key that Roebuck threatened to shut the bus down for the day. Next stop, Phoenix. Phoenix above all others, teenage girl heaven.

June in Phoenix was better than anywhere east of the Mississippi. *Strange Muumuu* had been on tour for three weeks too long; the band was faltering—it was getting old trying to hold up to the one American hit. A lark, put together from spit, lies and good looks. It was never supposed to be *real*.

And then it was.

Their tattoo artist, Sibyl, was hypnotized by the dancing holographic display on her computer—she had been looking at it for days. But no one sought to ask her about it. She liked getting high on meth and it just seemed that this was a meth experience, why worry? As long as she could still draw a skull or a devil head, all was right with the world.

But soon Rope began to watch it too. Booting it up on his laptop, it came with music, some kind of Indian ambient dance beat, a sort of tribal New Age disco thing.

"Rope...Rope! Hey, we gotta go over the new tune, dude."

"He's just staring at the screen," said the bassist.

Sibyl defended him, saying: "Exactly! That's exactly what I thought—don't you see? He's translating immortality. You can't be in two places at once."

So Anton Duffield, the manager, the old guy, the parent, the chaperone, the cop, the enabler, jumped in, looking at the big hole where all paychecks check out. "Rope, can you hear me? What is this, Justin? That weird stuff isn't—"

"—I didn't do it, man! He's like...catatonic."

"Over here, Anton!"

In the back of the bus, Sybil, the tattoo artist, sat glued to her screen—both she and Justin were immovable.

The bus slammed to the side of the road. The trucks kept going on ahead, Anton knew how to manage that.

"It's all a lie!" said Justin. "These people are more real than you, Anton!"

"Okay. Then I guess you're running the show now, is that right? I guess I can just sort of hop off and let you handle yourself tonight in Phoenix."

"Forget Phoenix, praise God!"

"God? If you're not on that stage and absolutely electrifying, then I quit. Okay, I quit."

All were silenced. He had never said anything about quitting before. He did not seem to be a quitter—he'd always been the one who kept it together, who held everybody's hand. But Anton did understand that things had moved to the critical stage. He understood the same thing when he toured with every big name since the mid-70's, and he was well-respected as a man who could keep and impose order, therefore the record companies loved him. He understood what to do here. He had always been the person who understood. God was never necessary, and would not be now.

• • •

Captain Cal, of white beard, ponytail hair and a tattoo of a heart and a cross, stood on his pontoon; Sam the green bird from *Nag*, or simply parrot to the impossible, was sitting on his shoulder. Just outside the ghost town of Lamont, which was impossible. On the island of St. Lucy—also impossible. Filled to the gills with co-caine—which he could care less about. He fantasized he was trans-porting brand new M-16-B rifles for the freedom fighters some-where in the world. But there were no more freedom fighters, and probably there never were—all rhetoric, but at least he loved to believe in such things. In freedom, in mankind, in a bright future, in a better tomorrow.

Out from the harbor came a small fishing boat manned by sev-eral locals. He did not sense danger, although the thought of selling somebody the drugs and changing his identity did cross his mind.

"Hello! Hey!" Cal waved and the boat drew nearer.

Perhaps they were cops—three locals with the patois talk, black, young—and not Coast Guard coming his way. "Ahoy, mates," Cal said fearfully.

Looking grim, they pulled up alongside the plane. They had M-16s and an AK-47 and were wearing berets and epaulets.

But they were fearful. The patois went on, as Cal picked up on a few French words.

"Sah, who you work foh?"

"Me? Nobody," said Cal Wilson.

"Not a doctor?"

"No...I'm a, I'm, but I can get a doctor if you need. What seems to be the problem? Where is everybody?" Cal asked worriedly.

They looked at each other, puzzled.

The leader, who was the tallest and youngest, looked earnestly at Cal. "Here da line, mon."

The older, bearded military guard (for that's what they were) hoisted a tow rope, which Cal retrieved without difficulty and hooked to a ring just below the engine.

Other than these few men, Cal could see there was no one around. Not a single soul. Not in the buildings, not on the docks, not up in the infamous police station. There was no life, anywhere. Not a soul. There was no electricity either, and most of all, for Cal, there was no cogent or even elastic explanation as to why or how he got there. He should be elsewhere, several hundred miles elsewhere.

On the other hand, Syke should not have been quoting Scripture.

His plane was the occupied vehicle in the Lamont harbor, home of pirates from this era and beyond—corruption brewed hotter where the climate boiled on occasion.

They were telling him about a witch doctor on the other side of the island, *who caused all this.* There was just no way of knowing what to expect. No one had ever prepared Captain Cal—who had been a captain of the U.S. Army 43rd Infantry—for what to expect. He had, after all, seen death. He thought he knew everything there was to know about it. It was painful, it was painless, it was bloody, it was bloodless, it was living, it was dead, it was a portal. It was a dead end, his memory.

He thought he knew what to expect. First, a queasy feeling, the sort of deep root acknowledgement that you too were vulnerable, that death can happen to anyone, that it should be expected, even though no one believes it.

He had known strangeness, though he knew nothing of magic. He knew nothing of witchcraft, let alone voodoo, which some on the island had apparently been practicing from the first days off the boats from Africa to gain the advantage over the European empires. He had known poverty, but nothing like he had seen in Bombay.

The rusted crew cab, driven by a Rastafarian with long dreads and a focus that the other two did not have, made its way along the impossible roads, most of the second lane washed down into gullies where Cal could see the remnants of past cars, even buses. As he looked below, the mountain was littered with 4-wheel drives, even a motorcycle or two. They told him of more than a few tragedies involving women and children who were traveling to the windward side of the island to the town of Soufrière.

He knew how to fight, whether hand-to-hand or with any rifle make. He knew something of survival, thought of himself as an expert in the "one match" theory of survival, long before the genre had become popular. He knew which bugs and which twigs and which leaves would sustain him. And he knew how to fast, even on very little water. This had worked in Viet Nam, in Columbia, in the Middle East, even on that utterly disastrous attempt to kill the North Korean Premier.

He feared God, or so he thought. Still felt a twinge of guilt when taking His name in vain, knew the difference between battle and savagery, knew about repentance a long time ago.

Yet as he surveyed the field, all he could think about was his mother—how he loved her and how he had not been there when she died. How he had not cared enough for his brothers, how he deserted his wife, who was childless when he caught her cheating—how he was so full of regret he created more to regret in avoidance.

There were bodies, lifeless and bloodless, in neat rows like fallen corn stalks or rotting bananas, the local failed crops. There were women weeping—perhaps all the women on the island. For it was the adolescent boys who were dead. The *males* specifically. The older men wept with the women—the white priest led the prayers and he was the only white person besides Cal.

"We need your help. Help from United States, the world," said the chief of police named Clarence, a short, well-fed elder, the kind of cooperative sort of chap that he'd seen many times before.

"I can't help you," Cal said defensively. "I'm just a freelance pilot."

"But you know."

"Look, far as I'm concerned," Cal began, "I'm still in bed in Jupiter Beach, my girlfriend's not even thinking about making coffee and I'm never flying another mission again."

"But can you help?" d'Auville asked, his countenance of corruption fading into pathos, succumbing to the sight before him. "We arrested all mambos, witch doctors, we took in the drug runners, even political adversaries."

Surrounding the field were banana groves, all of it overlooked the windswept cobalt Caribbean Sea. The sun began to set, rendering the incomprehensible loss complete.

"You are the hope we have been waiting for," said Father Anthony, the priest.

"What are you talking about?" Cal asked as he turned to see what they were all looking at.

Framed in banana trees with the church steeple in the background, a tall, bearded black man named Gabriel stood quietly, watching from a secure distance. He had a walking stick and his clothes were loose. Like Cal, he had not shaved in a long time. His salt and pepper beard set off his diaphanous long shirt, which billowed in the breeze, revealing Gabriel's lanky and skinny frame.

The survivors of this atrocity looked up fearfully as they saw Gabriel standing alone.

"He said you would come," the priest told Cal.

• • •

The gig was gone—all had fallen apart, thought Anton, as he paced around the emergency room in Albuquerque. Things had been getting worse for a long time now, no sense seeing decay in everything. No sense lamenting about what might have been if only he had become a lawyer in the first place.

The doctor told him there was no explanation—technically. Except too much methamphetamine and the need for rest. A psychotic break like this is easily handled with Xanax, and that is exactly what he gave them—and they talked and slept and ate and Anton was relieved.

"Anton, you're a genius," said Rope, seconded by the others.

"All he needed was his rest."

"Look, he's a great artist; it can happen. Kansas City sucked, and he sort of lost it, so he got wasted and tried to shake it off, but it bit him. That can happen," said Roebuck, the den mother.

The band was ready for the last leg to Phoenix. Sibyl felt so good after her Xanax and egg breakfast (and she was still hopped up on crystal) that she started a new tattoo for Justin while he slept. "I know he'll love it—we were communicating."

• • •

He was thought to be dead and then he was not. No one could have sustained so many bullets to the chest without hitting at least a vital artery or even the precious heart. A punctured lung could heal, could be re-inflated, perhaps even transplanted, but not in this case because, despite the trauma of taking several direct hits, there was no damage; in fact the 9mm slug barely caused any internal bleeding.

They never caught the assailant. There was no ongoing investigation. Wife Sarah and daughters Carole and Beth became the prayer warriors, leading the church in a round-the-clock vigil sustained by the mysterious stranger-gardener, who someone said was "Daniel," and Alf Blicky, the elder, now pastor-stand-in who once had a prison ministry. It was reported in the papers, and the church thought collectively that it was nothing less than a supernatural attack. Others dismissed it as some deranged or disgruntled transition—but after the investigation all leads simply evaporated.

After Sunday school class, Beth and her girlfriends were playing around the side of the church while the gray-bearded homeless man they called Daniel was watering and taking care of the plants, avoiding too much pruning. Beth could tell he had his eye on her, with his winks and a nod, quick little smiles, and a few chuckles.

"You want to see me do a cartwheel?" Beth asked jubilantly, knowing her daddy would soon come home.

"Sure," said the longhaired man with the blazing blue eyes. He marveled at her ability as she did two, then three...

"Yahoo!" he cheered.

"How come you don't cut your hair?" she asked him.

"Against the code," he said.

"Code?" she asked, skipping around him.

"I'm one of those guys who lives by a code."

"Cool," she said.

Beth playing with the stranger did alert a few suspicions. He knew the eyes of the gathering were upon him, and though he had a task at the church, he knew that just playing with a little child, especially if you were a stranger and an enigmatic one at that, never looks right to some people. Two ways to look at enigma: one, admire it; two, hate it. Usually it's just "crush it."

"I know something you might like to know," the stranger said.

"Is it a secret?"

"Well, *I* know about it."

"That's okay," she said, now intently staring at his shining face, a face that did not seem old; it was like a child in an old man, one to be trusted.

He said: "I know about the lights in your room."

"What lights?" she asked.

"Under your bed," he said.

"Are they Jesus?"

"Beth, you are a very special girl, your father is alive, and when he comes home, you might want to share with him about the lights too," he said.

"Okay, you sure?"

"Sure am, sweetheart. I think he would really like it."

"How come you didn't tell me if it was Jesus or not?" she asked, skipping around him again.

"Well...do you love Jesus?"

She nodded happily.

"The Lord's moving through this church and all around the City of Angels—do you believe in angels?"

She nodded happily.

"They're real, ya know."

"I know—is that what the light is under my bed, an angel?" she asked.

He said nothing, but his eyes twinkled.

Suddenly there was an interruption.

"Hello, Mrs. Gunderson," the stranger greeted her.

"My husband hire you?" she worriedly asked.

"He did."

"Well, I don't think he's around to pay you today."

"Praise the good Lord for Pastor's recovery," he said politely.

"Come on, Beth," said Sarah, pulling Beth to the eleven-year-old Volvo station wagon.

Her bright long skirt swayed despite her stiff walk; and though her hair had been done on Friday, it still had the tousled blonde look and bounced optimistically.

• • •

"The things of death and life, I told Pastor about them once," said the homeless gardener to the policeman named Bauman at the precinct.

"How long you been homeless?" asked Bauman.

"Heaven is my home, officer, and you know me—I've seen you around the church patrolling, that's what you do, patrol—when Pastor Ted is there."

"Look, I don't make the rules. Somebody said you were harassing the kids—now that I can't have, no sir."

"Oh, no. Do you know the way to Endure?"

"*Endure*? What are you talking—?"

The homeless man stood up, paced around the desk.

Officer Bauman did not stop him. Instead he broke into a sweat and coughed uncontrollably.

Memory: Endure, a drink. Nutrition. Mom drank it.

He looked into the strange man's eyes, saw something that felt like an end and a beginning, though he did not understand this feeling. Something like a *finish* in the *start*.

A memory. Pain.

Bauman sat back, denying it with a half-grin. He scratched the top of his head, felt his pocket for the Merit Lights, glanced at the clock and wondered where everyone in the precinct went suddenly. "Guess it's just you and me, huh...what do I call you?"

"Daniel."

"Oh, well," he began sarcastically, "why the hell didn't ya say so. Just call me Bugs."

"As you say, officer."

Exasperated, Bauman looked at him, struck up the chewed upon cigarette—cupping it when the secretary walked past the desk.

But *Daniel* continued on: "I want you to know, officer Bauman, that the past is quickly falling out of fashion. It can be changed and you would not even remember it."

"You got any place to crash tonight?" Bauman dutifully asked.

Daniel looked around at the empty desks. Bauman offered him a cigarette (for the road). He was so moved by that he looked back at Bauman with tears in his eyes.

"That was a real gesture, a kind gesture, sir."

Bauman looked around nervously. "All right, Daniel, let's not get carried away. You know, being a Jew I can certainly relate to the Old Testament prophets, and come to think of it, that's what you look like."

"You're not a Jew," Daniel said.

"What are you talkin' about? My name is Bauman; I'm Jewish. Look, Jim, Daniel, whatever your name is, you worry about Daniel, or is that Mr. Daniel?"

The stranger smiled.

Bauman continued: "You worry about Daniel, I'll worry about Phil Bauman, clear? Look, man, I don't want you going over to the church again until the Pastor's out of the hospital, okay?"

There was wind outside, there was mystery in the air which gave Bauman the creeps; he was happy to be rid of the stranger, but not his memories. Who was this homeless vagabond? How could he know anything about *Endure*, Bauman wondered? Coincidence, it had to be. But there was something else. Something he wondered about. He got up and tried to follow the man, "Daniel."

He exited the station and caught just a wisp of gray hair turn the corner at the end of the block. "Hey, Daniel! Hey!"

The usual press of pedestrians shoulder to shoulder, the red glow of orchestrated traffic lights on Van Nuys Boulevard, the porn outlets and production houses, violent surge shooting through him as he watched, waiting for a response from someone who knew. Bauman wasn't perfect; his partner Alice was the fifth partner in as many years. All the years of substance abuse and the guilt over being half-Jewish and half-heathen (which Daniel could *not* have understood!), half-bred and half-baked, all the memories of nothingness, happiness in blank walls, in the lack of *bar mitzvah*, in secularism, in regularity, in white lights, in stasis, order and congeniality, of manners and protocol, *of rules*. Of borrowing people, of following others, tears of unknown origin, big dreams lost in lousy hamburgers and overpriced coffee. Where the hell was *he*—Daniel? He who knew *something*. Accused of vagrancy. Possible perversion. No way, a ridiculous thought, Bauman said to himself.

He strode down the alley looking, calling, not quite satisfied that all the questions he wanted to ask were completely answered.

He even went to Reseda Presbyterian Hospital to meet with, or rather, to visit Pastor Ted Gunderson. Room 2112, he was told. His partner waited outside, needing to solve a few sticky points in her messy divorce. Messy because her teenage boy, Freddy, would move with her soon-to-be ex-husband to Europe. Germany to be exact. She knew Freddy didn't hate her. Not really.

"Mr. Gunderson?" Bauman began.

"Yes, officer," he answered, looking straight at Bauman with the confidence of a man completely healed.

"You up to answering a few questions?"

"God bless you, officer. Thank you for looking after the church. You'll find my gardener or, as he is called in my dreams, 'Daniel,' to be a gentle, helpful, Godly man. He would not hurt one hair on my daughter's head. He would not hurt one hair on my head, if you want to know the truth."

Bauman was taken aback. This was a man who survived several rounds to the chest, which somehow missed his vital organs or his aorta, or his bones even. It was nothing short of miraculous. "Sir, I'm sorry to bother you, I want you to know that the church is in good hands with—"

"—Let's get to the point, officer..."

"Bauman, sir."

Ted continued: "There are some things which cannot be understood, would you agree with that, officer Bauman?"

"Seriously?"

"Officer, after what I have gone through, everything is serious, and everything is a joke—they co-exist."

Bauman thought the man was delirious from medication, from trauma.

"—Hi, daddy!" the voice of eight-year-old Carole interrupted them. She was followed by Sarah, Pastor Ted's confident wife.

"Hi, sweetness," the Pastor said as Carole accidentally fell into the bed before she was corralled by her mother.

"Carole! Watch it—"

"It's okay, honey," Pastor Ted said, "I don't feel any pain."

"Hello, officer," said Sarah, to an increasingly shy cop named Bauman. She now seemed less strident and a bit more fearful and reverent. "Praise God," she said.

Bauman left after speaking with Dr. Shofar about the pastor's condition. Shofar looked at him or through him, bristled and said: "It's not normal—he looks like he'll be home tomorrow. Hell, he looks like he can run a friggin' marathon, know what I mean?" Bauman thought he did not sound like the kind of doctor he would ever want.

•   •   •

"Can we just go over there for a minute?" Alice asked, staring out the window of the squad car. She did not expect him to comply, and she did not expect to see him distraught. In fact, Bauman was always the rock, always the counselor, always the critic—never the one in need. Never the one to have "problems."

"What do you think it means?" he asked distractedly.

"What are you talking about?" she answered, concerned. She checked her eyes in her compact, gave herself a touch of lipstick, then saw the vehicle and looked back. "It's Ricky and Jiggo again! There goes the drop! Nice wheels, man!" she said, admiring the Cadillac SUV, which appeared to either drop off or pick up something known to be narcotic, either coke or smack, from Ricky, an adolescent who dealt mainly to grade schools in his spare time. He'd been up and back a few, and no one ever thought he'd make it to eighteen, let alone straighten out. Too many people had too many hooks into him and even if he wanted to stop, he just couldn't. It was his way out of poverty in a hurry.

Bauman U-ed it quickly, causing the tires to screech loudly. "I'm going for the customer!" Bauman exclaimed to his astonished partner, who was watching Ricky and Jiggo run away.

"We had them both right there! Besides, that's probably their dealer, man!"

"Either way, we win," Bauman exclaimed.

The vehicle was a new Escalade with trick tires and heavily blacked out windows, probably bulletproof, which he dreaded. Or perhaps a wealthy customer. "We can always go for Ricky again," Bauman said.

"Yeah sure, but I would've...." She cut it off right there.

"It's okay," Bauman went on, "you can tell me it would have been better to go for the kids, but we never got close to their sources. Besides, they would rather go to jail than spill the garbanzo. I always wanted to bust me a rich customer."

They caught up to the Caddy, doing about 40 on San Fernando Road. Alice leaned out the window, pointed, indicating for them to pull over. Bauman flipped on the lights and punched a blow of the siren. The windows were so dark, they couldn't see inside—no telling who was in that car. Whoever it was slammed the pedal down hard, slightly lighting the tires.

Then the Caddy slowed down, and Bauman easily caught up. The window zipped down and the "customer" was wearing a Halloween mask and was armed with a 45 acp Glock, aiming it at Alice Garcia's face. "He's armed," she cried out. Bauman slammed on the brakes, careening off the curb, spinning, then rolling, the "past from the beginning," as Daniel had said, the windshield shattering just before they righted the squad car, landing on all four wheels. "You okay?" he yelled toward Alice.

She answered sarcastically: "Fine, you?"

They began to laugh—especially after looking around and seeing that no one was hurt. Thank God Bauman backed off when he did, she thought. Thank God they were cops and not drug dealers, thought Bauman.

"You know, Alice, I wasn't listening; you wanted to go see your ex-husband. Forgive me for being insensitive."

He noticed immediately that there was a crushing silence from his partner's side of the vehicle. When he looked, he saw what Alice was looking at—a shotgun against her neck, a mask on *his* face, the black Escalade in neutral to his right. Before he could react (and it would later appear that he was in some kind of shock—they both were) *Alice was gone.*

He would tell them that they dragged her kicking and slamming her fists into their bodies. In answer they pistol-whipped her, they slugged her, they cocked the shotgun and held it against her neck. He would say that he thought there was a second gunman on his left, but he was not sure of that. He knew now that he had been speeding. He thought he caught up to the buyers, or at least he thought they were buyers, that's what Ricky had been selling, smack, speed, coke, crack—the usual stuff. But this was different he told Captain Moss; this was something akin to hunting, setting the trap, the advent of decoys and mistaken identities.

"Alice Garcia is gone, Sergeant, where she is, or why she was taken in the first place is highly puzzling, the subject of this investigation—i.e., you are under suspicion, Bauman," Moss, the high blood pressure, high fever, high temper, high-stepping captain of the Van Nuys precinct, said.

"I just think you have to connect it up—it's got something to do with Daniel, or uh....this homeless guy."

"And furthermore, Sergeant Bauman, you're relieved of your beat, suspended with pay pending the results of the investigation."

When Bauman left to drive home, he found a note affixed to his Toyota truck...from Daniel? From Alice's husband? The note read:

> OFFICER BAUMAN
> THIS IS THE BEGINNING OF LIFE AS YOU DO
> NOT KNOW IT

He tucked the note into his pocket, folded neatly, and drove out from the parking lot.

When he got to the corner, he saw a tall man with long gray hair and beard and was certain it was Daniel. He pulled over and started to follow him. This time he would not announce himself; he would simply follow. And he would do it to the elimination of any other activity.

five

Cal walked with Gabriel. The tall bearded man drank warm water and honey. Gabriel claimed he knew what kind of plague had devastated the island; it had been a demonic attack. Gabriel told Cal he felt that every single person is known to God, but he understood that the earth and the stars had to pass away.

"I come from far away; I'm not a native of St. Lucy or any other island," Gabriel said gravely. "I can change my appearance and my manner of speaking to suit whatever place I am sent by the Spirit. There is no death, you know, only judgment."

Cal knew this was all a crock. "Look, as far as this tragedy goes, have you had the young men inspected by a medical examiner?" He was trying to dissuade himself from the delusion that what he was experiencing was nothing short of a nervous breakdown. He knew he was off-course, had thought he was near Florida when in fact he was no further than the West Indies; there just had to be a way to get his mind around that. There had to be a way to clearly see the truth. Everything has a cohesive explanation; he would not dive into a bunch of foolish talk just because some native mystic drank too much elixir. But he kept walking with him anyway.

"American man, you have yet to understand. Some of us walk the earth," he said, opening the church door for Cal. They were followed by the guards, who were strangely nervous. Cal hadn't figured out who the guards were, exactly.

In the church Cal saw DEATH. Bodies were piled on top of bodies. He inspected one of the boys and found no visible marks of

violence, of disease, of trauma, of stress—nothing but peace on all
their faces. Several hundred were piled in the aisles, on pews, on the
altar of Christ—right in front of the Catholic crucifix!

Why, he asked himself? Why? The others prayed. Cal would
not pray, but he fell to his knees and wept. Sam stayed on his shoulder, oblivious to the whole thing, it seemed. The animal would soon
fail him.

He felt sick and was taken to a crumbling French estate called
St. Remy, a failed banana plantation but in times past the place of
aristocracy, of robber barons, pirates who had made good, fugitives,
drug lords—familiar territory, or it should have been.

They were met by Fred and Leoni, a couple who cared for the
estate owned by a so-called baroness named Lady Angela Spencer.
The couple had connections to the drug-slave-gun trade, which had
become a business of sex slaves. Involved in wars of illegal trade,
they had given the United States special ops the run of Lamont
harbor, so the U.S. "cartel" (a collection of mercenaries from the far
reaches of wealthy society) could steal the drugs from Columbians
and import them to Europe and the U.S. with impunity.

Was this tragedy perpetrated by DEA, Cal wondered? Coast
Guard? US Navy? UN? Was it something he could pinpoint and
say, this is it, or that is it? He didn't think so. Today it looked like
DEA and Coast Guard, but that could mean anything—a front, a
label, old as time.

The power of the world, Cal knew, was divvied up by a few
powerful families—Cal's employers. Everything was cash and carry.
He knew the Spencers, and Fred told him that they had deserted
the island and all their holdings, which meant that Cal's mission
was completely unclear. Irrelevant.

Gabriel took Cal aside to explain that certain people knew the
secrets of prophecy from millennia ago, from the beginning of time,
which was only about 6000 years ago. Cal studied the strange emaciated man and wondered how he had the name of an archangel; he
did not seem like an archangel at all.

"There was a time when we would feed the hungry," Gabriel
explained. "There was a grace period, a time when God would tolerate selfishness and vice, but that time has ended, my friend. Perhaps it should be extended."

"All I want is some more fuel for the plane and—" Cal, who was
uneasy, changed the subject.

"—you run your dope, Caleb Wilson, just one more so you can

feed your widow, whom you have yet to bury."

Cal started to run; there was no stopping him. He ran through the banana fields, for miles it seemed, searching for his stray parrot, searching for anything familiar.

Just outside the town of Soufrière, he stopped right on the beach and looked at the quaint and colorful clapboard storefronts and broken streets; the sun was hanging terminally at 4:00 and nothing was moving. He was free! He would leave—pay someone to take him back to Castries, inform Walter about the mass cult suicides and go about his business, deliver the drugs, get his 100K, go back to Jupiter. Take care of his wife, ex-wife, Sally Anne, just out of the hospital in Lauderdale, though there never was a divorce, not technically. He moved away—*temporarily*—that was it. She was alive; let's get that straight, he thought he had said to Gabriel, whom he could not mistake for anything other than a crazy guy who must have talked to one of his employers, the deeply hidden military people.

The nightmare on the island in the middle of the hapless ocean was nothing compared to Nam, nothing like a gook prison, nothing like scud missile attacks or biological weapons wiping out or making forever ill many Gulf War buddies. The only reason he wasn't dead or afflicted, like them, was because he...he would never admit this to himself, but under his breath in the middle of the night he might call it luck. One hundred percent luck. Luck too good to acknowledge. Luck where no luck could be found.

He had to get that straight. It was only luck. Dumb luck at that.

He washed his hands and face in the ocean, one klick from the main street of Soufrière. He tucked his work shirt into his khakis, washed the dirt from his beard and looked at his face in the four o'clock reflection of the sea. He did not look worried. It was much worse in Nam. This is nothing. Counter-terrorism was worse too, come to think of it.

He did not look crazy, he thought, wondering if his face was dirt-ridden, for he could not see so clearly in the reflection; it mainly sparkled, obscuring what had once been a beardless, shaved, and pleasant face.

He did not look worried. Did not appear deluded or nervous, his eyes were like familiar movies, but he had to turn away. Survival, if it could be done at all, relied on familiarity, on delusion, if that's what life would ultimately turn out to be. On self-reliance, none of that hocus-pocus—it would ultimately rely on that which is unfortunately termed "the survival instinct."

Maybe he would write about it, perhaps he would write a memoir and cash in. He could *out* several politicians; he could vet the CIA, he could make their hair stand up on end: mass executions, whole towns, even islands, like this one. He had to face it: he lost it in the air, flying around in the clouds his instruments failed, his sight, his health, his greed, his hatred, his gloating and his carelessness, his failing to take advantage of every God-given opportunity—his callousness, his memories.

They were all dead in the bar. Many slumped over in their barstools, frozen. The bank, the post office, the pharmacy, the church, the police station.

Back at the St. Remy, he confronted Fred and Leonie for the last time. "So why are you people still alive?" he asked, pacing around the creaky wood floor.

"We were with Gabriel," said Leonie as she genuflected, indicating her Catholicism and that she might even believe that this was Gabriel the Archangel!

"It so you could come, sah," said Fred. "This is da world, du monde, oui? C'est du Jour of the Lord—the judgment. I am very frightened."

She explained his struggling words: "Bad things now," she said, in shock.

"What, you think this is the whole world? I got news for you," Cal pointed out. "This is some sort of military situation—I just don't know what it is yet. How long this Gabriel guy been hanging around?"

"He always around," Fred answered, startled.

"Come on," Cal said incredulously.

"No," said Leonie, "he walk the earth, he raise the dead. He know many things, American."

"So where did Gabriel go?" Cal asked.

They both looked up then started crying.

"Please help us, American. Please help us understand," Leonie said, wrapping her arm around the trembling Fred.

"They are all dead in Soufrière," Cal pointed out.

"He said you would come, sah; he said you had a key," Fred told him.

"Look, he's not anything strange—you know him, don't you?

You made him into some sort of folk hero or something like that, and as you can see, he can't seem to find his way out of this," Cal pointed out reasonably.

"Please help us, American—please!" Leonie said as she dropped to her knees and wept, her arms were wrapped around his calves.

Cal did his best to lift her up, but her eyes were clearly leaving this world, constantly looking up.

"Help us, Lord Jesus—please," she said.

"He been on other islands too. He be him a good man, sah. You need anything—Leonie? I take care of her now, sah. She very good cook—she cook for you."

"Is the whole island like Soufrière?" Cal asked, almost not wanting to know the answer if one should come.

But Fred had the answer: "It iz, sah. Trés mal. Very bad, sah. I listen to short wave—nothing. Maybe every island the same."

Cal stared from the verandah to the setting sun over the sea beyond the banana groves. In town, it was males. That was it everywhere.

The rains had washed out the road to Lamont and back to the plane. He had no alternative but to try and find his parrot once and for all. Sam had flown into the jungle, spooked by none other than Gabriel. He wondered if Sam could fend for herself, and he wondered about reality itself—was it sane?

The first thing was to bury the dead. No, the first thing he would do would be to find this Gabriel and confront him, outing him as an operative involved in heinous crimes—he could then leverage what he had seen; it would buy his way home and then some. Yes, the government would and could be blamed, some would be scourged, if Cal had his way. But that was unlikely, and finding Gabriel was not an easy task since the people would only point upwards to the sky every time Cal would make even the most casual inquiry.

•   •   •

It wasn't that Stephen wanted to please Katarina. She told him she would make it up and she did. Two new tickets to Phoenix. He had been a gentleman; he had cared for her and she was deeply appreciative, in her own way. He wasn't like the others, but he could drink, and she loved seeing him like that. She did not want him to know this, however, because he did not feel his best when drunk. In fact he was apologetic, which was delicious, better than sex, an apologetic man. Then again anything was better than sex but nothing better than love, which she thought she'd had once. A memory that fades, a night gone forever.

An abandonment. A denial.

They did not mean to miss the bus in Tucumcari. It was, after all, costing twice as much to get to Phoenix and then Los Angeles as previously arranged.

None of that mattered. He would not have sex with her and instead read from his well-worn, poured-over, best friend Bible, a New King James. She had never been to a motel room and had the Gideon's Bible read to her, let alone a real one. But it made sense because this man was a fundamentalist Christian, probably all his life spent in the shelter of Jesus and the angels, probably never knew anything cruel or unkind, she thought. He was therefore narrow-minded, bigoted, intolerant, and needed desperately to be saved— delivered into the flesh for once in his life!

That might have to wait. She stuck her thumb out on Highway 666—both felt they could more easily get a ride with a trucker. When she saw the highway sign she shouted for joy! "666, awesome! Know what that is, Steve? Home!"

"Oh, your home is hell?" he asked.

"Ever heard of AC-DC?"

"Sure," he said. "I used to listen to them before I got saved, and that was quite a while ago—I hear they're grandfathers now."

"You did *not* get saved, my dear Stevie. What's your last name?" she asked.

"Petchick," he said.

"Stevie Petchick."

"Stephen," he corrected her again.

"Steve Petchick, a used car salesman," she said, trying out the name and making it fit.

"A motorcycle mechanic."

"Oh, right," she said.

By now he was wondering what the Holy Spirit was up to.

"You did not get saved, you got deluded, you got stupid, you got greasy—you did not get saved," she said.

"How would you know?" he asked politely.

"You were weak—what happened, your girlfriend break up with

you? Lose your job? Past trauma caught up with you?"

"Look, I got saved, lady! And I don't need this!" he nearly exploded, then briskly walked on ahead of her. How he failed and he knew it, but he could not help it.

He walked further in front of her, faster.

She smiled, victorious. Then quickly got a fast ride in a dirty old Ford truck with an unshaven drifter who was only heading to the next town. But it was enough for her—the final capitulation.

Stephen grabbed his duffel and turned his back on her as she went by, but he caught a glimpse of her beautiful smile and a peace sign, which she waved and held and kissed.

He found a clearing just off the road and sunk to his knees. "Dear Heavenly Father, please help me. I don't understand Your ways. I have been a rebellious son, I have strayed from the One I loved—and that's You, Jesus. Please Lord, show me that way. I want to come home, but I don't know where that is. Like you, I have no place to rest my head, but I'm not complaining—you have always taken care of me...but for what? This? I need help—I'm sorry for what I did a long time ago, Lord. Even though I'm not supposed to pray about this again, I am; I am sorry for what I did."

Then he looked up—and the setting sun shone on his face, and he felt the peace he felt the first time with God. It washed over him and pulled him up and he laughed, joyful and ever-reassured! He wanted to throw himself back down into forever and never leave. "Don't leave me, Lord—I'll stay with You, I love You—You're the only One."

He looked up and broke into a huge smile—a kind of invincible absorption. "Thank you, Lord. Praise you, Jesus! Thank you for everything You've done for me. Please keep Your hand on Katarina. I'm not sure why I'm...why I care. But You do, and in Jesus' holy name I ask for You to forgive her. Amen."

He walked and the rain clouds missed; he was wondering about his mother's asthma (it was always worse than she said, and it was an optimistic thing to call it asthma when in fact it was lung cancer). Spanning the whole history of lies, salvation was the most real thing, the first truth, but was he truly saved as he claimed? The satanic voices would come around every time something good occurred, every time progress was made, each time he could barely hold on, could barely keep God's commandments, could not see the eternity in the box of broken toys called youth.

It had happened in prison, serving three years for car theft. The

[51]

day he fell, Stephen J. Petchick had been lucky, as he used to put it, since he was sixteen. He could always rely on his mantra: there is not a vehicle made that cannot be stolen by him—he was gifted. There was not a lock that could not be picked, there wasn't any security, there is no such thing as love, only mother's love—which is mainly instinct. His training went like this: *Don't get picked up by the minors, steal cars, don't make it as a drummer in a band, steal cars.*

Ask anyone in his neighborhood about Stephen—then "Steve"—Petchick and it was always the same answer—everyone just loves him. Especially the kids. He's such a great athlete, so multi-talented. He can play quarterback, pitcher and forward, all in the same year, and every college wants him, his mother, Anna, would proudly boast. Somewhere in the distance was a father who left and who was violent. But he could not think about that for too long. It just wasn't part of his world. There are no fathers, and that's a good thing because they are too drunk and violent.

He wasn't too good at schoolwork, but that was because he was in such demand by the athletic department of Forester High near downtown Phoenix.

He could remember the fast pay and how easy it was to pay cash for medical treatment—he was just a boy, sometimes pulling down thousands a week. Sometimes a couple grand a day. The future, the past and all points in-between were effectively handled by money.

Just before he found Christ, he was in the Yard defending his ex-boss, Sonny Lobo Jones, who in turn sold him to Fletcher for a few packs of smokes. But then Stephen became trouble because he would not sink to his knees in submission; he would not succumb to prison life, to the reality of being a cute twenty-two-year-old pretty-boy in the most gnarly and needy prison in Arizona, perhaps even the Southwest, and certainly more than any prison in New Mexico.

He would not even see Jesus Christ until after the fight that took him to death's door. He found the Lord where he had never known him to be, in his head, in a dream, pulsing through his veins, calling him, Spirit filling him, but he was still unwilling.

"I want to die, please, nurse, tell the doctor to stop," he would say, "please tell him I don't care about Demerol or Tetracycline or bandages or hemorrhaging or progress. Here's to you and your medical profession." He saluted with less than a dignified hand-signal.

In solitary confinement he became separated from the reality of flesh. Visions of chopping his father's head off with an ax filled him with excitement—he could lop their heads off and believe it would be so. He could practice killing the man who put him here with several nice parries to the gut, ribs and neck, but he missed the mainline, that incompetent jerk! Let him shudder in his sneakers; let him worry that I might recover and take him down; let him worry because I am no longer scared; I am no longer worried, no longer a kid, no longer stupid, no longer foolish, no longer do I make a wrong move, a false statement. I am a viper, a lion, a predator, he said to himself. The scars seemed to evaporate, what he might have told Katarina was the result of a motorcycle accident, a stomach operation. Childhood cancer, battle scars, something not to hide. He was alive in solitary.

One hundred pushups, two hundred sit-ups, fifty pull-ups on the window sill, jumping the fake rope all day and into the night—killing, a warrior to kill.

He can kill now because he did not break, so he will be feared.

Walking step-by-step back to the cell, the beard and hair marking the madman—silence on the block. Silence from now on, no one can say a word to him. Jones would just hide at lunch and hang behind Clap and Devil Face, and he had the blind support of the much maligned and feared Aryan Nation.

"Just stay away from me, you're nobody's squat—let it go, man," his cellmate said.

"Come on, man—let sleeping dogs lie. Hey, Lobo wants to be your friend. Hey, no one will mess with you now, man," another "friend" said.

"What are you gonna to do, white boy, kill your pimp, man?"

"Don't push it butterboy, you upset the apple cart here, you get a real love letter," the guard told him.

"You need me, Petchick," Lobo-Jones pleaded. "Look if you kill me no one will protect you from the Crips or the Mexicans—we could have thrown you to the wolves."

He saw the fear in Lobo-Jones' throat, the sweat on his nose, the beating of his heart in his jugular vein, the cringing of his tattoos. There was no turning back, even if he was being used again. His superior athletic skill made it all very routine. Lobo-Jones tried to defend himself, but Petchick got him in a headlock, began punching him about the nose and teeth, kicking ribs into misbegotten matchsticks. Lobo-Jones crumbled easily—the knife superfluous.

"Do you see this?!" Petchick screamed, ripping off his T-shirt and revealing the scars. Scars so freshly healed as to appear pink, like a newborn baby, scars that healed in one way, but remained open wounds, vigorous and vengeful. Give me one good reason not to waste a good shank on your dumb guts—"

"—I'll tell you! I'll tell you who did it! It was...it...it was..." the pain and spitting of blood and teeth made it almost impossible for Lobo-Jones to deliver that one juicy detail to turn all others obsolete. "Petchick, man...I'll tell you, bro."

"I'll kill you anyway," said Petchick, but Lobo-Jones did not believe that. Good information is always worth something, at the very least, despite the cheapness of life. It meant time. And time was eternal in prison.

"It...it was Dicky," Lobo-Jones strained and got out. "DICKY! That's yo' man, bro! Now let me go...please. I'll look out for you— you're nobody's woman, I told you that."

The knife slid in easier than Petchick had previously thought. Easier after the first thrust, ten, twenty, he lost count—it had to be fast jabs, decisive and clean, because you had to get the shank back out. It was about twelve inches, a sharpened piece of plastic—the point was noted to be sharper than any hunting knife Petchick had ever owned. It easily lodged in Lobo-Jones' heart, where he left it, a proud stake, a claim on freedom, respect, love, honor and heroism. A tomb-maker, blood covering Petchick's face and stomach and legs and even his shoes; blood spilling out all over the floor, blood bringing back his reason. What if it wasn't just him...what if it isn't his will at all, but someone else's?

The rest was easy. No one confronted him. As he waited to be brought up on charges, instead there was silence. He stared at his hands soaked in blood, even though he'd washed them a thousand times; still there was blood and it kept flowing, filling up his thoughts, the room, splattering his cellmate, Lazy-J, and flowing all over the guard's shoes, then up in the cafeteria, and over into the yard. He'd wear yellow shades while lifting weights, even on a sunny day, because it made the blood go away. There would not be an investigation. He stared at his hands, soaked in blood, knowing Lobo-Jones had died for something else, that he had fallen, that he was used, that there would never be an investigation, would not ever be any inquiry. They knew he would not say anything, and they had him for as long as they wanted. Stephen Petchick was silenced by the blood.

Would never be free again, the avenues of freedom gave way to unspoken alliances and shady dealings. A big man could command a pack of cigarettes, drugs, women, men, anything he wanted. The blood made him a hero and how many were involved? How many had a stake? Who really spilled Lobo-Jones' blood in the laundry room? A guard looked the other way; two more sneaked him out in the towel bin, three more moved the body and cleaned up the blood. Another made up the story, one more to corroborate, to be a faithful witness, another to look the other way—the executioner walked on, feared, famous, and bound. He would not ever enjoy another moment of living; that became clear: the big man in prison is the smallest man on the block. The blood endless, it spanned time and space, history and future, the story of every single person on earth. It was futile to fight it anymore—yet it was the only logical thing he could do.

The only solace, next to the law boys in the library, was the crazy killer who got saved by Christ and became a pastor they all called "Preach," who did not preach, at least not in the yard, or if he did he had a funny way of doing it. He mainly hung with the most violent criminals, the class-A guys who could look at a guard and make his jockeys fear their own whiteness. They all hated each other, all had killed for sport, all were there for life, *and they listened to Preach*.

"Look, Preach, I had to do what I did, or I couldn't show my face again," Stephen had said.

"Petchick, you done yet?" was all Preach, the one who himself had killed abortion doctors, said.

"What do you mean by that?" Petchick asked, or he'd say something like, "Why are you hurting me?"

Preach would laugh crazily—no explanation given. But he knew *something*, and that was something no man could shake once it got inside, a virus of eternal proportions.

"But you still killed after..." Petchick struggled for words that would not come.

"It's a process—don't expect it all in one day. What am I talking about, Stephen Petchick?"

"I don't know."

"Exactly."

"You're...I don't understand you," Petchick once said.

"You done, Petchick?" he said over and over. "Because if you're not done, I got nuthin' more to say to you, man, except God bless you. He loves you."

There were no more visits and there were nightmares. He wondered if he had truly begun again, a new life in living red; the truth, whatever it was, had long ago been crossed off as an option. There would be no way to return, no way to reconcile, no way to wash himself, ever again.

"He doesn't love me," Petchick told him.

"He also hates," said Preach, again with crazed laughter. "Oh, boy does he hate! It is truly awe-inspiring how much our Lord hates sin!"

"What?" asked Petchick, sure now that Preach had made some mistake.

No answer came, that would have to wait. That would have to endure a certain lifestyle of disobedience. A certain attitude of survival, of the sort that makes one live and at the same time anger God.

He had learned that when he started working on bikes, when he joined a church with the help of the owner of the repair shop, when he first said "no" to the newest theft ring, the good 'ol boys of cell block eight, when he understood that he was broken and beyond repair. He understood his life did not, and would not, ever amount to a smile or an act of kindness, let alone thirty pieces of silver, as Judas got. He needed God now that God was at his door. He quit—and only then did he quit it all—he would always have to go step by step, as Preach said.

It was grace, and nothing of his own, that truly convicted him—not the judge or the jury. He admitted that he lied, that he stole, that he killed, that he was everything vile and nothing worthy. That he was anything worth saving, or that he could be self-reliant, that he could handle things or had earned his stripes was now a complete lie, and only Christ could have made his insides bearable.

Only God could handle *his* memories.

Only the Blood of the Lamb could wash the blood he had spilled away.

He walked alone down the two-lane highway, the passing sun the reminder of all things past, of all things he must do now. She had not understood anything about him. She did not know why he was different or closed-minded, conservative, narrow in all ways, without history, and he could not show her either. Long ago he had fought his parents, had fought in the playground and up in the mountains at the Flagstaff Fireman's Camp, then down at the bars and even around the bikers. When he got to prison, he still had almost all his teeth, later replaced by a couple of nice crowns, thanks to his mother's insurance policy. As he walked along the highway in New Mexico, he had enough anger to propel him to Mexico City. So he stopped and prayed again, and the anger went with the Lord. Some did not like him in their church, and he was plenty of bad even if the spirit beamed out from his eyes, shouting: I LOVE YOU.

Now he was fighting a stranger named Fallen, on a mission from what he hoped might not be Temptation. He had to laugh. There was a reason to be joyful.

six

lease help us, American—they all dead in Soufrière," Leonie had said to Cal, and now it was a slogan, a sort of island policy. He found the chapel filled with black women in mourning; the few men left living were down at Spider's, pouring beer into a hole that was bigger than space. There were no bodies lying dead on the bar or slumped in their stools—it was just drunkenness.

"This is not the way to investigate this tragedy," Cal told them. "Look, you help me get my plane fueled up, and I'll help you. I'll call my friend in the CIA—they'll look into it, believe me; they've got a big stake in your island."

The chapel was simple clapboard on a dirt foundation, raised adequately for the rainy season, which lasted for months. Surrounded by mango trees and rusted, broken-down cars, but enough space to gather the locals in. Inside, the pews were wooden, some rotted at the edges, and there was a large cross over the altar and a statue of the Virgin. All the candles were lit; the procession of grieving women continued to light another and another, but they could not match the tears. Did not anyone think it was strange that all the young males and a good number of older ones were dead—the *Herodian* nightmare, as Cal remembered a Scripture vaguely—but these were spared? Truly, this was not the world of yesterday, and yet the people were as before, simple peasants under a monarchy of independence, with no freedom but lots of hope, with radios and cable TVs in dilapidated huts. They would not question anything because they believe in God, he told himself, unable to find the words for prayer.

Hold on to the military demeanor: keep one step in front of the last, one word followed a second word, no conclusions, just reconnaissance.

Hold it back! She is alive! She did not die! Your wife. Is. Okay. NOW.

Cal ran out. He stole a Suzuki jeep and headed around the long way; he would make it to Lamont, he would call Williams, Jennings or even Schlage, perhaps Allison McCarrow—no, he would not do that. Not to alert the world, not yet.

The rusted 4x4 ran out of fuel in the rain forest. This time of year there would be no tourists passing through this way, even though the roads of St. Lucy are deadly the other direction; they would rather save an hour or so and risk their lives. Tremendous courage in a funny kind of way, like young soldiers who have not been wounded yet.

The rain felt sticky, thicker than water somehow.

At nightfall he found a shelter underneath a waterfall. A few wild bananas, some mangos, nuts, all ripe on the ground. Soon there was a star-struck moon shining its light upon him, three-quarters and strong, the lullabies of tree frogs, the serendipity of sustenance. Only Sally Anne filled his mind; was she a ghost? Had he been feeding her spirit? Was this a paranoid delusion—all of it?

Reality. The one mutable substance truly worth bending to one's liking. But this situation was beyond most imaginings save what he knew about the black-ops folks, back in Maryland. It was easy to see: the males in the population were the guinea pigs in a covert science project, the kind of *poindexter-al-shenaniganzo* he had seen before, in Lebanon, in Iraq, in Africa. Any kind of spiritual mumbo-jumbo, fear-based conclusion would render him no better than the ignorant peasants on that bankrupt banana plantation, where the white slave owners were absentee dictators and the law was cocaine traffic.

It made sense to Cal that someone made a mistake and that there must be some sort of blackout. How he might have gotten off course was the subject of his next inquiry. No problem. Instrument failure. He flew in a wide circle and after several hours arrived back over the West Indies, in a case of the worst timing in history, or perhaps it was divine misguidance, punishment, he thought—busting him for the cocaine run. He would get back, call the Drop named Frank, explain what happened, arrange for another drop, take his money and...

He would pay off the plane, use it for charters; he would help Sally Anne again. She probably needed some help, he thought. She had had a breakdown, and she was not dead. He spoke to her just last week—flesh and blood. But his parrot named Sam would not be coming back, he concluded.

The dried palm fronds made a nice cover, while the dead mango tree leaves an exquisite bed. He could survive. He always had.

The morning was glorious—everything lush, bristling with life. The pond was next to a stream with fresh water and a kind of bass or perch. He was only halfway up the volcano peak of the island. There were terraces upon terraces, natural plateaus, waterfalls, mango groves, pools, wild palms and coconut groves—the primordial paradise, the way things looked before the advent of man, of progress and tourism, of foreign policy and independence movements that propped up the few landowners and destroyed all economic hope for the masses, of corrupt might and war machines. He had never seen such purity! Suddenly never felt so free. Knew what it was to be lost and liked it. As he climbed the mossy hillsides, spurred on by sunlight and rain, nurtured by sky and harmony, he tasted true wealth. It was not in the plane; it was in nothingness, and yet poverty stained the towns and drunkenness filled the streets. Perhaps the men were better off dead than drunk and sad, perhaps a revolution might help—music had failed.

He climbed higher, just out of the rain belt, into the more rocky places. The ocean was distant and no road led to it. He heard dogs below and knew why he had started climbing—not simply to get to the leeward side of the island more quickly by going over the volcano mountain then through the ranches on the sunny side. But because there would be some sort of pursuit, probably from the police, either because of the car, which they probably had found already, or because they now needed a hostage, someone to be blamed, a way to explain something only science of the supernatural could explain. Most likely it was the US military or British intelligence, or both. And those folks would kill the whole island if there were any possibility of talking to CNN—i.e., any witnesses.

Higher, happy distance. The dogs were no longer close, but fading into the sound of the birds chirping, or a Mynah bird or two. When he looked up, he saw a bright green flock of wild parrots, screaming, screeching and squawking as they flew to the next large tree. Was Sam with them? Was she now free? Was this her final deliverance or a drop off for dead? Was she able to go wild and join in or would she fly alone as he was doing now? With all that food it would seem that she might be happy. She would definitely find the situation to her liking—she was the native, not man, especially not *this* man.

Especially if they were looking for a scapegoat, once the fear of magic wears off.

He arrived at the top, the summit, co-equal to clouds and serenity. From here no dog dare bark, no human voice was heard, and the idea of hunting something to eat brilliantly cast aside any and all lingering doubts. He laughed heartily and jumped up and down. "Think I'm some sixty-year-old outta shape infantryman, drunk and slow? I live! You are all pathetic! Anyone can beat you!"

He danced his own Caleb Wilson Jig, reminiscent of his days at Florida U. After winning the state football championship, or even while drunk down at Fresco's in Miami, drunk as a skunk on the eve of Nam, where he also won. "You're all a bunch of pathetic morons, you make me laugh—come and get me! Make me pay for your plight! Make me a hostage before your true ruler, the crowns or the presidents or the dictators! Make me the devil incarnate! Try to get me to pray, why don't you—I am beyond prayer, because I do not need it! I live and I'm happy—I always live no matter what circumstances! Everybody dies! I live! I beat you, but you're too drunk to admit it! You will never see me in prison, hanged, confiscated! They already tried it, suckers! In Nam! I lived, they didn't—I beat all of them. Hey, I'm sorry if they were on my own friggin' team, okay? But that's what happens when you—"

WHAP!

It sounded like something whooshing through the air, like something natural, the flapping of wings, of helicopters in slow motion, something supernatural, like passing through time and space and not fully remembering the blow to the back of the head.

• • •

Stephen arrived in Phoenix at 12:38 on Sunday afternoon. He knew it because that is exactly what the clock said in the bus terminal. He had been fortunate enough to receive money from a grandfatherly driver from whom he had hitched a ride. The bus trip took him up to the Four Corners, then it was simple to get back to Phoenix, just twenty-two dollars, which left him enough to buy some joe and smokes at the Abstract Café, two blocks from his mother's house on Slater Street.

He got there. She had been sleeping. He took the cot in the second bedroom. When he saw the medicine cabinet, he knew.

It had been a long, protracted and painful disease. When he had his own place, he had prayer groups assembled for Anna Petchick, who had hidden her "asthma" for a long time, who had taken care of Steve and his brother, Silas, even when Silas was on heroin.

Even when Silas, ten years older, was thrown into prison and killed for double-dealing.

Stephen never admitted going to prison because he didn't have to, though he always felt that the asthma probably resulted from her knowing all about his personal troubles, because of her absent husband and the father of her two bad kids, who would only come around when drunk; and having to live on welfare checks.

The house itself had fallen into utter disrepair, something Stephen vowed again and again to fix. He had made a pretty good start on it while he was working as a mechanic, and it was time to start again. Just as soon as he got another job.

"Stephen, you look so thin, let me see you," she said upon his arrival.

"Just workin' out at the gym," he said cautiously.

"Your father was here, gave me some money, which I told him I didn't need, but I took it—prescriptions are so expensive these days—" and she started coughing before she could finish, then took her medicated mist. A jar next to her bed was full of phlegm and blood.

He knew that his father had not been there, but he would not, as was his policy, tell her this.

After he'd seen her, he called the doctor, who told him that there would be no guarantee how long she might live. "Mr. Petchick, she could pass from us any day now. No need for the hospital until or unless she has another attack. Besides, her insurance only covers the hell-hole type of care."

"Why didn't anyone tell me?"

"It's good you're there—we were sending social services to look in on her—so impersonal," the doctor told him.

"Mom," Stephen said, "I've been lost."

"You're with Jesus aren't you?"

How he had failed Jesus, he thought.

"The good Lord will help you find your way. He told me something. You want to hear it?" she asked, furrowing her brow and focusing on her son's eyes.

Her face seemed to have an angelic countenance, a look of surrender; the lines had gone. He was enamored. He did not understand completely, though it was familiar to see her like that. "Sure," he said, "I'd love to hear it."

"He told me that there is no such thing as death—only spirit and flesh."

"I don't understand," he said.

"I don't either, but I hope He's right, because I don't want to die."

"I don't want you to die either, Mom."

He had to walk to ease it. He walked to the Grace Church on 86th Street then walked further. He sat on the bus bench and noticed a poster for the band Strange Muumuu, playing downtown at the Chelsea Theater. He thought about going; in the past he always used to sneak in. He also could set up full concert halls—he knew how to run generators, lights, soundboards, but motorcycles were a bit easier. He thought if he hung around the concert bands that he'd get his chance as a fledgling drummer. Now all that seemed silly since he felt his purpose was what the Lord wanted to do with him. He would no longer try and do it his way: he remembered prison and that kept him humble.

He walked toward downtown, and he didn't like the band, even that song on the radio, "Fallen Hero," but it lured him and his legs had to keep going—it wasn't too far. Mom was sleeping, after all, and she did not need him pacing around the living room or watching TV, though he sensed that she wanted him near. He'd do the unthinkable if he had to—he'd steal again to get her the money to pay the doctors for a nice hospital room. A grand or two a day, he could make five!

It bothered him that the doctor simply wrote them off as trash, that he didn't think they'd ever be able to afford quality care. That he probably thought they lived on the wrong block, too close to downtown, not up in Tri-City, not up in Scottsdale along Camelback, where all his previous Harley customers lived—not a fancy kind of family, the Petchicks. The doctor obviously did not understand that the Lord will provide for those who are His, Stephen reasoned.

. . .

Justin passed his tests, as did Sibyl. The main thing was that they had broken out of the collective stupor that had plagued them on the bus. Anton thought how grueling it was to have his whole life wrapped up with the fate of a couple of people in a successful band (though fading no doubt). If they weren't successful, his children might not eat. The band was just the sort of thing that Anton, who was from England, promised himself he would not get into stateside. In fact, he promised himself he wouldn't go into music in the first place, and that he would never do something against his family, namely, hold back on funds.

But all was forgiven by show time, and it seemed that Justin was well enough to sing again, and that was the main thing. Justin and Sibyl shared a sort of *folie à deux,* what a shrink might call two people sharing the same insanity.

From Albuquerque on things went splendidly, since the pair did what they had to do. They did what no one else could have done—recovered in their minds and then acted accordingly, as if for the first time they would turn on to music, to drugs, and to sucking in all the vitality the world had to offer: the audience, the money, the pride of life, ego and lust...maybe even fame.

Justin exuded the perfect physical presence, Anton thought. Whatever Justin might have been without the stardom, however fleeting it might have been, was something truly scary to behold, thought Anton, something truly *derelict.* But therein lies the appeal, of *not needing* success. Of not caring about it in the least. Of not being aware of pressure. A free spirit beholden to no one, and certainly not a record company. A threat to society, his drug-induced bravado, stemming from a life of privilege, no doubt. Those who truly need a job, who need to care what the other person thinks, who need to make an impression; those who have a family to feed, as Anton did, do what they need to do to make ends meet. Anton hated Justin for all the reasons Anton needed Justin. Truly, Justin would be nothing without his willingness to be nothing.

The crew was frustrated trying to set up at the old Civic Auditorium in Phoenix. It had inadequate power, lights that were ob-structing the band's laser lights, a small stage—nothing like the arena when they backed up Sphinx.

Anton was on his cell phone at the Scottsdale Hyatt resort, which featured massage, faux beaches, and a good deal of pampering. Sipping worry from the planet or at least from his life with a Marguerita (he planned to have a Bloody Mary later on), he was sunning himself while talking to Persimmon, his wife of twenty years. "Fine, love. We just got here...sure. How's Bobby then, still hurt? Well, let's hope he's back on the field by the time I get back. We finish in Los Angeles."

"We all miss you, daddy, you know that," she said. "But we need the money if we're going to send Major to the University."

"I think this is my last run, love. We can always retire in Spain, or on my uncle's chateaux *nouveau* in the south of France. Right, see to it that Matthew gets back to his football. Tell him if he's very good—I met a promoter in Los Angeles—he can play out here. The lads here don't know much about football, or love, or ... how did we lose the war again?"

"Funnay, you are, dearest. Miss you, daddy."

"I love you, Persi. I love you, you know that."

"Just don't have too good a time."

"I won't. It's not so good here anyway."

When he hung up, he saw Sibyl and her new "friend" swimming. With a few hours to show time, he didn't like to see anyone wandering around the hotel until after dark.

The crowd around the pool watched the two young women, who were immediately too familiar, embarrassingly drunk, flaunting the girl-girl thing and laughing at complaints. The stranger wasn't as obvious, Anton thought, but definitely Sibyl was. Sibyl, who was more like a gunslinger than a wench, who was just simply wired male, she told them, though Justin told her she was wrong. She had been hooked into some frequency that no one understood; it was the same with Justin, which was strange.

"Refill, Mr. Duffield?" came the voice of a slender waiter with a dark-brown beard and dark hair piled into a hat. Quite a departure from the clipper class appearance of the true corporate luxe resort.

"Sure. Bloody—"

"I understand, sir. But do you?" the waiter said, and his nametag read: "Michael A."

Anton looked around with astonishment. All the customers had disappeared; those in the background were too far away, as if he'd swum out to sea and looked back at the shore, with no one knowing if he had drowned. "Sorry?" he asked.

"You're marked," the waiter said.

"Are you talking about something I should understand?"

"Not by me, but others. Just a friendly warning." The waiter strode easily around the pool to the open bar.

Temperature: 105, and the gaggle of voices was spiraling all about Anton, increasing in volume, increasing his disturbance. He wanted to complain. The girls were gone.

A young woman brought his drink. She was blonde and cheery and shallow and reminded him of his daughter, Serena. "What happened to the chap with the beard?"

"With a beard? No, that's not allowed," she said.

"The chap with the beard, I'd like to know what happened to him," Anton insisted.

"Was he tall?" she asked.

"No, short. Or, no, he was...very, very medium."

"Short, or thin?"

He suddenly realized that he could not really remember the waiter's appearance at all. "Have you always been my waitress?"

"Of course, Mr. Duffield."

Both turned to look at Sibyl and her friend, as a drunk Sibyl chased her friend around the pool—it was embarrassing. He had thought a moment ago that they were gone.

"They bothering anyone?"

"No, sir," replied the polite co-ed waitress.

"I'll just have a word—this is a very conservative town. After all it's not South London."

"Oh..." The waitress finally seemed to get what he was talking about.

Katarina looked up at Anton with disdain and seduction. She looked like she'd never seen a man before. She forgot her new *friend*. For a moment.

"Look, I don't know why Justin has to have you on the tour, but that doesn't give you the privilege of embarrassing everybody."

"Homophobe," Sibyl said to Anton.

"You know what the root syllable of your name is? '*Ant*,'" said Sibyl's new friend.

"What's it tell you, Sibyl, when this...this—" Anton tried.

"Go ahead and say it," said Sibyl's friend. "HO," she said.

"Shush, come on," Sibyl interjected. "Anton, you're such a loser."

"You're taking up space—you're a bad influence," he told the newcomer.

"Justin had the same problem—but it wasn't a problem. We're all marked," the new girl answered in a strange tone.

He stepped back, dizzy in the midday sun, while Sibyl and her friend stood in the waist-deep water, cool.

He wandered into the bar. The suit-and-tie arrivals looked away, as if they knew something too. He ordered two shots of tequila and a Bud Light. He watched the news and ate pretzels. The bearded waiter turned from one of the other customers, who likewise stared at Anton expectantly.

"Another beer?"

"Look, who are you?"

The bearded bartender looked at the others with a knowingness that Anton could sense. "Michael," he said.

"Well, look, Michael, are you of a mind to say inappropriate things to people at poolside?"

"Sorry, sir?"

"You told me I was marked."

Michael said nothing.

"Yes, you did," Anton said as he slammed the shot, chased with suds.

"Have another?" Michael asked.

"Yes, two more," Anton answered indignantly as he looked around at all the people staring at him. "So what are they looking at?"

"Sir?"

"Friends of yours, no doubt. Whoever you are."

"Here," the bartender said, handing over two more shots of some sort of Don-something-or-other, fancy five buck-a-pop tequila. "Now you listen to me," he said after gulping a shot and chasing it with freezing draft, the likes of which he had never tasted before, "That is—icy! I'm going to report you for harassment—harassing a foreigner. I can call the consul too, have you brought up on charges— anti-tourism or something, report you to the Better Business Bureau of the United States of America. Or you're a terrorist."

The drinkers in the bar were sensing by now that Anton had managed to achieve a state of total drunkenness. The critical looks on their faces conveyed their mutual opinion that drunken behavior was very uncivilized in the afternoon when *activity* was the key—getting drunk occurs after sundown.

"I'm sorry, Mr. Duffield, if I offended you."

"And my real waitress, who reminds me of Serena, so sweet and innocent—"

"Yes..." the bartender said, as if *knowing* all about it.

"Now there you go again!" said Anton. "I'm not sure I like your attitude."

"*My* attitude?"

By now the customers had cleared out, going to their tennis matches, golf tournaments and massages.

"Yes, *your* attitude. You didn't think I was talking about someone else's attitude, did you? Because if you really thought that, you'd be a twit of the first order."

The bartender turned around and took off his hat, revealing a waist-length braid. "Is that part of the dress-code, sonny?" It was clear that Duffield was a mean drunk.

"What I told you was this, Mr. Duffield..."

"It's Anton, sonny."

"You're marked. This is the case...leave the hotel now. God loves you—submit yourself to Him and He will save you. He'll show you the truth. When God says, 'Come and see,' go and look. If you know what's good for your eternal situation. You know who He is...Jesus. His Name is Jesus."

Anton noticed that the bartender's eyes beamed at him—shot through with a kind of light that didn't quite seem real. Originally, perhaps they were light brown, but they became windows to something Anton did not want to look at, and he looked around again for any sign of a rescue. In the distance, people were playing, arriving. He could still see Sibyl in the pool with her friend, flagrantly fondling and playing.

"The abomination of desolation," said the bartender.

"You've driven me to drink, you know that, don't you?"

"You're a witness. But a temporary one."

"I'm no witness—I'm trying to support a family. I'd like to get out of the rock and roll racket; I don't like the hours, and I need to dry out."

The bartender forked over a few pills. "They will help—perfectly safe. Sober you up."

A moment after popping the little pills that reminded him of saccharine pellets, he felt better, though not high.

"A form of manna," Michael the bartender said.

"Well, I can't go all day being drunk—got to sober up some time. Thank you, sir. Sorry for saying that you were the cause of my drunkenness, since I've been drunk every day."

"Everything comes from God."

"Now there you go again," said Anton, feeling suddenly invincible, sober and on top of things.

"Even you—you who think you're cut off," Michael said.

"Cut off? Laddy, I have never believed in any God."

"Sure you have. When you were a little boy, your father took you to St. Timothy's cathedral where you were baptized in the Spirit. You confessed your faith in Jesus Christ, the Lord of all things, and your sister was killed the next day on the Manchester Highway. You put a wall up, and you courted the Devil, who was also a reptile. You were very pleasing because you are a good servant, but that's not who you really are. You can look at it this way—no hiding behind any occult or devil worship will save you now."

He stared at himself in the mirror between bottles, convicted on all counts. To say, "Who are you?" or, "Why are you doing this to me?" or, "How dare you?" would be impossible for him now.

"He knows about the—?"

"The occult, your Druid ceremony—the fact that you killed—"

"Stop! Stop! WHY ARE YOU DOING THIS TO ME?" Anton screamed and ran from the bar. Those who had entered the bar stared and were seemingly unaffected as the wake subsided, and then ordered their drinks from Jim, the bartender, who was tall, fat, and a whiz at the stock market.

• • •

The theater was a nightmare, but the crew—now aided by a *canned genius,* who really knew some things—was working steadily on solving every single limitation. Not only was the stranger instrumental in solving the problem of the Civic Center electrical limitations, but he had found the acoustic shields as well, which could be electronically lowered from the ceiling by activating the servo drive found in the upstairs control room. The sound checks turned out to be pretty good.

Stephen J. Petchick had somehow, in the course of showing up and volunteering and within the first half-hour of his service, landed a well-paying job. Afterwards he locked himself away in a bathroom stall and prayed, while crying tears of joy. He had always, always been guided; he never had to take things into his own hands again, but often he would worry. He did not quite believe his good fortune—but he still couldn't help but worry about the care that his mother needed. The crew boss mentioned they had lost their best electricians and it looked like Stephen was just as good at rigging lights. And running the board. And fixing the trucks. The Strange Muumuu crew couldn't afford to do without him. He was no roadie, he was a master of all trades, jack of none.

Stephen did not quite know how he knew about the lighting rigs, the sonic baffles, the electrical mains, bypassing the breakers for the laser lights—he just knew. It was automatic, and he'd seen this sort of thing before—with motorcycles, with Harleys no less, fuel injection, carbureted, no matter what. He was walking in a bubble of protection; he could do no wrong, but he wasn't doing anything. This show was going to go on and no one was going to stop it now.

He had forgotten the fact that he was caught up with Katarina. He had surmised, or assumed, that he would not see her again. It was his mother, Anna, who needed him most. He would not leave her again.

"Where's Duffield?" Bernie, the crew boss, asked one of his boys.

"Haven't seen 'im, boss. Where's Paco with the Guinness, man?"

"Anton's always preaching to everybody else, but he's late a lot too," Bernie said to Petchick.

"Does he have to officially hire me or something?" Stephen asked.

"No, man—you're a Godsend. *I'm* hiring you. You got that? Starting out with what Kenny made, and then some—and if you want to head to LA with us, great. We'll take care of your mom under the band's insurance policy—it covers things like that."

Incredible, Stephen thought. Thank you, Lord God. Thank you, Jesus.

seven

Bauman had nearly given up. He spent a few days on his back, on the sofa, his precious daughter crying because, "Daddy's sick." Then laughing because he had a new tolerance that was refreshing, though his wife did not like it.

Sheila wasn't the sort of woman to complain, was not the kind of person who would lose sleep over the danger of her husband's profession. He'd been shot at, never shot, thank God. She had been a seeker—Judaism led to Buddhism, then Scientology. She had been sympathetic with the Rajneesh movement, often fantasized about leaving it all and living in a commune, her "kibitzing" was her Judaism.

Phil had always thought that by marrying a real Jew he might one day become one. But there was no getting around the lack of *mitzvah* and the critical scrutiny that he did not belong. There was no getting around that he had no spiritual home—but that didn't matter anymore.

The Valley was his beat—a place he had confidence in; he loved the heart of the valley when everyone else wanted to be on top *looking down*. Drug busts in the hills were beautiful, but prostitutes on Sepulveda were tawdry. The streets cried out for the mountains to disappear. People put themselves in a trap because it had an odd feeling of security—blocked from the West Side, blocked from the ocean, blocked from the desert, cocooned, sheltered—*nonjudgmental*. What was dawning on him he couldn't shrug, where his mind wandered indefensibly he could not escape.

Leading to, leading to...must not look back, can never look back, he thought again and again.

Sheila, on the other hand, was just interested in family—she wanted Marta to grow up with friends. He could see the fourteen-year-old was changing. If there was one more cheap silver ball or pin or club through her eyebrow or navel or ear, then he was prepared to go to counseling. Then she got tattoos, wore a skirt scarcely bigger than a napkin. She was beginning to look like Julie or Astrid, the prostitutes he'd pick up on next to the motel on Magnolia to get them out of harm's way—from other police. There was no counseling; he didn't judge. But he wouldn't want his daughter to be like them. No, he would never let that happen.

Sheila urged him to seek the fellowship of his brother officers. She thought it would help him more than the shrink who tattled. He didn't have the heart to tell her that his best friends were only to be found on the street. It wasn't what he did that mattered so much, it was because he was frozen. Isolated. An island in pain. And nobody wanted that to rub off on them.

He only felt true fellowship with a man named Daniel. He only felt fellowship with something indescribable that was pulling him toward the light, toward chaos.

She threw him out of the three-bedroom house near the high school. The lawn was not clipped that day, and the large Japanese maple was dropping leaves all over the broken driveway. His Toyota truck was rusted and it had never known harsh weather. He packed two suitcases and threw them in the back of his truck. He had progressed beyond needing sleep; he had no need of any accommodations but the back of his truck. Whatever it took to find himself again. If vengeance was in the picture, then he would have it. He would make his way with it—it would ease his burden. Vengeance could heal...everything, maybe. After all, Bauman did not make himself...he was made by others, formed by cruelty, by sheer hatred. Because he would investigate. Because he would *not* look the other way, not because he didn't want to help the other guy out, it did not occur to him. He never understood how to play the game. Indeed, he did not play well with others. No one ever told him he was a good man. Condemnation was his lot, but not anymore. Those voices were gone.

Still no word on his partner, Alice. But he knew he would find a way to solve it, now that he was driving his streets as a civilian. A newfound freedom, a bigger responsibility—he could do anything yet he'd have to check himself. He had gotten away, not reported to the high school as an irresponsible parent, not followed by the department shrink, not hounded by the Captain, no partner to own up to, no more sinful urges since he quit eating.

There would be no danger of tasting the bitter fruits of his bust or being a father figure to Angel, who reminded him of Marta. There would be no further transgressions because he was being led to something above and beyond his beat.

How many would love to be on this kind of adventure, he wondered? How many carry their briefcases, satchels and burdens to their prisons where they check in and are kicked in the face for excellent behavior befitting a prince while expiating the stress on the streets and hiding from the moon? Unchecked, dishonest, driven, misery circular and unwinding, checked out in all their sins, just like he was!

How wonderful it is to be on a *real* investigation! It's okay that no one understands. *Those voices were gone.*

Bauman couldn't remember needing the approval. Or the water cooler, the desk, he might as well have been stuck on the end of a pin under extreme magnification—he now knew who he was. Whoever was looking did not care what he did right or wrong. He was told he could do nothing worthy anyway. No way back, not now— he'd pulled up lame and the race went on. And yet he'd forgotten. *Those voices were gone.*

And so he was free!

And so he would be Phil Bauman, counselor to the wind.

He would simply be Bauman, the saint of the uncircumcised Jews.

He would be a Gentile, working stealthily for the establishment of the end of everything the world had ever known.

He could see it all now, and it was very good. There would be an answer to what can only be described as irrelevant, the atheists would say.

Daniel knew! Bauman was sure of it. He had to have known everything, and nothing was left to chance.

Ignorance was a good excuse. How could one believe in something they could not see? How can someone ever believe in anything in the soup bowl of unloving *kindness*? In the crush of competition for no one to see but the birds? For the family gathering at the end, saying, *Good job! What a legacy!* He won because he died on the (irrelevant) job?

Those voices were gone.

Now he knew he needed none of these friends. He could be an uncircumcised Gentile with the grace of misguided stereotypes—he was now chosen *and* justified. His journey was guided by something more real than his own face.

He could do it for Marta, for Sheila, for Alice—the women in his life that he would look back at from now on. He could do it for the seed of mystery that at once lived in the gutter more than the heart. He could do it, not for himself—he would reject their ways. All that backroom bull was nothing but a feeble attempt to hide ignorance, to justify the base in all, the card game of greed, the exposure of weakness, dominance, submission—a woeful pecking order.

All completely and utterly irrelevant, Daniel was telling him.

Daniel was speaking to him all the time. Probably speaking to him even before his birth. Step this way, Bauman! Go that way, Bauman! Be the driver today—go here, go there! Safe! It was Daniel who saved him every time. Wasn't it?

The testimony, the process that led to the clean air at the top of the mountain, was not something available to the strong fleshly monsters, the big suits or the flashbulbs.

Even as the broken truck ran out of gas, he just laughed, left it on the corner of the industrial section, grabbed his big duffel bag and left the trunk with all his shoes—he could stash those later. He knew this place was as good as any to pitch his small tent.

He had heard that Daniel lived here in a dilapidated trailer.

The bottom line was this—there was no trailer or even a lean-to. There isn't a soul here—but it felt like home. Rows of personal storage garages. He remembered his wife had a private storage garage here. No cameras, not like the new places, and furthermore, the security guard knew Bauman and would surely understand. He needed his garage as a place to live because the wife threw him out, and he scared the department after Alice was taken.

In fact the security guard known as Big Willy could be enrolled. What does a security guard have to look forward to anyway? What does he have that someone else wants? Or himself? He would surely join the team.

It was exciting. He hadn't taken his medication for two days now—phooey! He would be manic and he would strive for true knowledge now. And through God, who would surely bless him (always through Daniel, he was getting onto it now), he could figure out where Alice went.

The combination would not work—the lock would have to be cut. In the solitude of the private storage complex, down one of the alleys—two rows of concrete with metal sliding doors, the whole complex surrounded by barbed wire. He could hear Spanish children yelping in play outside. His gun was all he needed to keep the criminal element out, but he hadn't noticed much graffiti, always a good sign.

Gunshots were no big deal in this neighborhood, right at the edge of San Fernando, a straight shot through to the desert. That will be my escape route, he said to himself. Just another drug deal gone bad neighbors would figure, as the shot would resonate for a couple of blocks. A .40 caliber round was not something he should be concerned about.

He fired the weapon into the Master Lock, obliterating the combination dial. A piece of shrapnel lodged in his cheek, blood flowed like water. He fell to the pavement and felt very sleepy. In his heart was a scar of betrothal—to everything in the rear view mirror, the distant dedication. Oh, how he must claim it now, but he could not! He was dizzy and weary; it had been a long day. First of all, Bauman had to work out a plan, which required a lot of thinking. Second of all, he must allow his mind to obliterate, as it was only survival. He was being guided—by a force? An intelligent being? God? He was no longer being judged. By himself? Others? The world?

He could sleep it off. He wasn't wounded; he was protected. He wasn't brave; he was guided. He wasn't thinking; he was thought itself. The physical was the pavement—the cold floor of lies built on brokenness and fostered by the spark of a new childhood...a new day would dawn for Bauman. *Those voices were gone.*

eight

The Serin Institute was funded by the Compassion Society, which had its origins in Europe and an outreach in the Middle East, particularly in Turkey. Its stated purpose was to help those in need around the globe and to bring a certain harmony to the planet. Its most major influence was Descartes, primarily because Descartes, more than any other philosopher, believed that humanity's problems were humanity's to solve, and rejected any notion that some outside influence, such as God, would have any ability to govern the general flow of events. After all, his main thesis, which shocked the world and actually changed it, was: *I think, therefore I am*. If man is the *I am*, then man is God.

Psychiatry, therefore, would be paramount in any effort to civilize or bolster into opportunity those who have been left off the economic scale altogether, those who were in perpetual need and could not fend for themselves, and in this regard people such as Gandhi and Mother Theresa figured prominently. The Pope shied away from any endorsement, and certain liberal politicians might on occasion mention the good works, or work up one of their speeches to reflect the global vision of the Serin Institute.

Its leader, purveyor and chief architect, was Brand Kincaid, M.D. Dr. Kincaid had degrees in anthropology, psychology and medicine. He had practiced psychiatry in private practice in Manhattan for many years and had been teaching at NYU when he was named head of the psychiatric team at St. Mordecai. His stature and influence was, in private elite circles, as major as Descartes' was, so long before. Like Descartes, he believed that the problem with human beings resides in the mind, and its name is fear, though he still liked to refer to it as neurosis. The state of psychiatry today had fallen from its earlier Freudian stature, he felt, and what remained was a kind of beg-for-rich-clients-so-you-can-eat mentality, i.e. say anything you please, just keep them in therapy until the psychiatrist can figure out the next step. Or, "I'm okay, *you're not.*"

Psychiatry had become, in the last few years, a pharmacy. A medical doctor was required to write prescriptions for all the latest derivations of Prozac, for the Post-Prozackian Age, and the clever practitioner would set himself up as a drug therapy office, thereby garnering the elite, who could afford to pay. There was no quality control; instead there was devolution into feelings. A line of questioning might be a general inquiry as to how the patient was feeling. For example—whether they were having sex often enough, if they wanted more sexual prowess as a possible deterrent to depression, how the job was going, would they need some sort of tranquilizer in addition to the anti-depressant for the purposes of staving off the pain of aging, retirement and death? Of course, you've come to the right place.

Things were left unsaid. Never, under any circumstances, was the earth or life on it seen as impossible to bear. Life could not have features described as dark, dreary, horrific, insane, etc. Life was always seen as wonderful, and the patients who did not subscribe to this view were medicated until they finally grew into that beatific panacea of a good person in a good life: humanity was essentially good, and life depends on viewing reality as basically good. Indeed, anyone opposing this viewpoint was seen as malevolent, a possible terrorist; anyone not cooperating with the "group" was seen as dangerous to society. All agreed that man is a social creature—man needs to cooperate with the ways of man, and if not, he must be urged—without apology—to do so. In the future, Kincaid knew, the loner would be outlawed. The recluse, the independent artist, the free thinker, the unshaven critic of the new world, would not be tolerated. And he was ever so thankful for that. What a relief to have a happy society, finally!

The word *sick*, while not used as much as it had been in the 60's and 70's, was beginning to be employed again, on more of a social scale. That is precisely what Dr. Kincaid was excited about—the return of the medical practice in relation to treating entire cultures of people.

Funding was primarily a stealth operation. Washington power brokers made sure that the Foundation maintained a strictly hands off status as far as the IRS was concerned. For America, Serin was European; for Europe, Serin was the European Union, with no oversight. For the Middle East, Serin was partially Muslim, in so far as it was opposed to Christianity and had no policy with regards to Israel. Serin was involved in everything from helping flood victims in Turkey to fostering Islamic studies at the universities in Cairo and Tehran. The whole education team was basically dedicated to one thing: spreading the Cartesian doctrine and their humanistic hero, Carl Rogers, a psychiatrist who developed a certain "client-centered" therapeutic approach. Rogers fell short of the current doctrine of guidelines for sanity being strictly the private property of Serin and all illumined beings located throughout the planet.

There was a good reason why strict humanism could not be employed in modern psychiatry: some humans had beliefs, which were racist, narrow-minded, xenophobic, uneducated, or fundamentalist. Fundamentalist Christians, as well as orthodox Jews and zealous Muslims were considered dangerous elements in the world—mainly due to hatred and violence. Serin's *raison d'être* was to stamp out this kind of barbarism forthwith. This elimination was all Dr. Kincaid and his entire staff, as well as entities such as the United Nations and many other political foundations, were concerned with. Most universities had caught on—they were confident they would be able to eliminate entirely fundamentalist religious views in their lifetimes, and this was an exciting prospect. People with the proper stimulus, based on years of research, would naturally cooperate, love one another, feed each other, share fairly in the world's resources, stop torturing animals, destroying forests and natural resources; begin trusting governments as planners for the individual, rather than the individual fending for themselves in a hostile world. Indeed, it was the Wild West all over again. Kincaid and his staff thought life was to be tamed, was to be enlightened, and education was the key.

Not limited to economics or global order, physics also figured prominently. In Dr. Kincaid's mystical pursuits, even in his tepid worship of the goddess Isis and as a Freemason (though not a master), helped him to understand the laws of the universe. Understand what and who the adversary of human order truly is. All the disciplines would have to reflect these truths subtly, enough so that the human mind, as a unit, would be trained on one principle, one constant, ever-present drumbeat of unity; all cycles to reflect the perfect union with nature and Her majestic order, a reflection of the Divine Architect and certainly available for human control.

The human was a resource, no question, as he understood it. Dr. Kincaid had been initiated into the mystery schools, which spanned back to Pythagoras and beyond. He had seen what the One Principle is really all about—he had seen it in action.

He learned the proper method of sacrifice because he knew the ether of the universe was conscious but by no means untamable. He knew that man was on the verge of being the godhead-creator himself, but certain elements of their plan would have to be at least accommodating and certainly this would involve belief systems. With a media team comprised of some of the best minds from the finest institutions in America and Europe, most of whom had completely adopted the policies of order and tolerance, they would forge the group mind in a manner such as no other civilization in history—it would be a group consciousness focused on goals of worthiness and sustainability. *That* was what it was about, instant spontaneity of purpose. Brilliance to be rewarded. The electronic pliable media, a tool unlike any other, and Brand Kincaid had already had a great deal of success with the media.

His predecessors had been hard at work for several decades, and it had been even longer since the gods (meaning The Advanced) ruled the earth. He knew the earth was good, earth was necessary—earth cannot be seen as some kind of temporary housing. He knew where souls went, but Brand Kincaid, M.D. would never admit what he knew to anyone else. The soul, even the concept of it, is inscrutably unscientific, and it would be disaster for Kincaid to admit what he knew to those who have no need of the truth and to those he worked for, whom he hoped to meet one day.

In his private practice as a psychiatrist, Kincaid was involved with some of the wealthiest families, since he knew the Serin Institute was looking for candidates from a wealthy family, the highest in the realm, from the forefront—as their prophecies had stated. He would be born to privilege, but would renounce it because the Hand of God was upon him. He would be male; his very presence would be anathema to world order, to stability. Yes, born to them would be a traitor to world stability. Kincaid was confident—as all schools throughout the land were trained to keep an eye out for just such an individual. They would all visit the school psychologists to find: the artistic, the spiritual, the misfits, the loners. One of these, one of these in this season would be found. The instrument of God was nothing more than shame to his family and the world.

Kincaid looked for patterns: innocence (which he saw as reluctance) and an inability to join in certain physical activities without the guidance of certain counselors. Those who led must adhere to a strict code of conduct, and initiation is a matter of psychological normalcy. His entire life had been justified by these results, and results were always predictable. A child is born for certain duties, and when discovered by trained operatives posing as teachers, that child would be recommended for certain positions in the world order. Kincaid was nothing more and nothing less than a gatekeeper. He had been involved in the success of many young men who were raised to lead, who were raised to command authority, to administer the principles of civilization. It was baffling why so many had to be put to death.

Now there were prophecies, something he had thought wholly superstitious, except that the people who had trained him had never been wrong. The Dean of the Harvard Medical School fondly remembered things converted to the truth, away from the arcane religious precept of the Masonic forefathers, who seemed too apologetic. There was no way for the modern university to fit into the world without servicing the world. Service was the key, which Kincaid knew intimately well. Cooperation was vitally important.

Psychiatry was, if anything, the red carpet upon which modern civilization would flow. There were no mass murders or suicides; these were aberrations—executions—unconsciously motivated on the part of the unenlightened or uneducated. Kincaid supported the President's policies on education, all except for prayer in school. It was well known that the President had had misgivings about his own past, but that was no excuse to alter civilization just because of his own regrets. He was in need of counseling—or perhaps removal— and Dr. Kincaid knew very well that presidents do not, and will not ever, run the United States or any other territory in the civilized world. Knew all too well who owned it all—those who civilized it, of course. Knew whom he worked for. Knew what they expected and he would not disappoint them.

Kincaid's life was great—the three-story apartment in Manhattan, the upstate country home on Lake Placid with two docks and water vehicles, including a splendid fishing boat. His only blemish was his only son, Justin, who had dropped out and disappeared from the society scene altogether. He had been waiting for word from the private investigator, a report he received every Thursday about his son's rock and roll band.

Dr. Kincaid was an older child of the 60's and supported with great enthusiasm the music of old—all well-trained artists in directing the mass-consciousness of a generation to behave according to the principles of man, and not some distant Jewish God. The kingdom of What You Want was here now—all one had to do was break through to the truth. Why it could not have been forced more systematically was something he was looking forward to discovering. It was only a rite of passage, after all. The fact that it had to be lied about, be covert, hidden, was ridiculous—the whole point of Kincaid's career was to bring this all out into the open sunshine. The whole world cooperating and working in harmony! Naturally due to self-interest. Anyone found not cooperating was to be taken away to a labor camp or a science project, where they could still be of use and re-educated on the use of their own bodies for purpose of divine will. What was so wrong with fashioning the world collectively? Spirit was semen and not God. Intention combined with spirit created results. Imagine that kind of power in the hands of a true visionary, guiding the grunts and groans of the Mind. From the Mind came Things. As if by magic. But magic today is science tomorrow, Brand knew. Oh, how proud he was of all who had gone before him.

One common theme rang true to him: his beliefs were about civilizing the world, making the human sacred, tearing down traditional hypocritical institutions and erecting great monuments to the truth, which was held secret for thousands of years—more if he counted those, as he was taught once, who seeded the earth.

How he and his wife, Jackson Bertram Kincaid, would laugh at the misguided Christians whose idea of God and man started with Adam and Eve. Even symbolically, he knew the serpent, the symbol of healing and of the secret rulers of earth, was basically good.

But these sorry Christians were to remain in the dark; they had no idea of the complexity of the world at large.

Things had changed recently. His contact in the Council, for the first time in his thirty-five years of dealing with him, seemed terribly worried. If his mentor, Arthur Reddick, was anything, he was courageous. He did not spook easily, and Kincaid had heard reports that Reddick had seen what no man living today had seen after completing his initiation into the inner heart, the actual center of the tabernacle, beyond the inner sanctum. This process, known as *Felicitas-Mundi*, was rumored to exist after the death of Christ. It was the continuation of the blood sacrifices, involving what was known as the Lamb—or the consecration of the innocent. Jesus was the ultimate lamb and final sacrifice for Christians by none other than God Himself—by the blood—the actual blood taken from Calvary! New lambs could be consecrated in Christ, then sacrificed to justify worldly power; this was what Kincaid guessed, because he had never seen it. He had a skeletal understanding and an intellectual one at best.

He knew about the mind and how it was linked to the satellite system of the world, the entrainment of brainwaves through cell-phone technology. Those who engaged in cell phone activity should have known better—after all, it's called a *cell* phone. There is always a clue for the initiated, and that is precisely why Kincaid would not use a cell phone. He preferred a satellite device, which was provided by his Men's Group, who met at St. Amsterdam church off 5th Avenue every Thursday night. Jerome Spinks, the pastor, was always very accommodating—one of the few inner circle blacks who served as a dutiful watchdog over that part of the empire. Always aware of expenditures, his *forté*.

When Kincaid got the call, he knew something was dreadfully wrong.

"Listen, Brand, we're counting on you to see this Smith boy," Arthur Reddick began. "I want the best minds at the Institute to interview him—and of course we would like him admitted."

"Mr. Reddick—"

"—You may call me *Arthur*."

"Sir… (it made him extremely uncomfortable to call him anything else) about my son, I want to tell you it's under control. Besides, he doesn't know anything."

"I'm concerned about the Casey Smith boy—there is something about some…abilities that are anomalous. He also questions his parents and teachers in a manner qualitatively matching our requirements. This is urgent."

"*What's* so urgent, sir?" Kincaid asked, perplexed. (He'd processed many boys with similar traits.)

"He may be *the one*. I'm telling you this civilization of ours is threatened beyond its limits and resources. He supposedly talks to God. He wrote some things on the Internet, which alarmed us. Just check him out. We understand he's been admitted to St. Mordecai for some tests—dizzy spells, I believe. His parents don't know what to make of him—seems he's one of them."

"Okay, I'll...sure, I'll check it out," Kincaid told the faceless man whom he had never met, though he knew that Mr. Reddick was in Los Angeles.

"It just alarmed us. How can a child like him be born into the Smith family—Darwain Smith, of all people?"

Kincaid did not know what Mr. Reddick was talking about.

nine

When Cal woke up, he was not in pain. He was in a small wooden structure on a smelly mattress on a wooden floor—he knew there was a tin roof overhead because it was raining. He had been dreaming of flying, and whenever that happened something good would always follow. Hard to see how this might happen now.

Soon, a tall Rastafarian—or at least he filled the bill—entered with an MP-5 submachine gun pointed directly into his face. He said nothing, just motioned for him to get up.

"I think I'm..." was all Cal could say, as he moved outside and vomited.

Why he vomited was subject to debate, he thought. It was either because he was sick or because of what he had seen that he could not understand.

There, in the harvested marijuana fields stood a thousand young men, boys he had seen before, and in the same white clothes. Young men whose names along with their faces had been committed to a world beyond this one, young men whose lives amounted to nothing but mystery and pain. Here they were, many from the lower island, standing in the harvested, empty field—but not physically well.

He thought instantly—*voodoo*. It had to be that. He had heard about the death cults and this was nothing more or less than some sort of drug-induced state whereby the entire island would be incapacitated.

Cal thought of Jeff Jentz, Harry, or Dane—it had to be some experiment, some military maneuver or test.

"What do you think of the boys?" asked Gabriel, standing in a white robe. "Do you think we're all dead, American?"

"I'm ... I'm sorry, Mister...Gabriel, is it?"

"Yes," he replied.

"Look, I mean no disrespect, but this is either the biggest zombie ceremony ever held or one of our black ops is using the island to experiment."

"What do you think it is?"

"Devil if I know?"

"Promising," Gabriel said.

"What do you mean?" Cal asked, feeling the rather large lump on the back of his skull.

"It's more than natural—watch."

Gabriel unveiled a Gatling gun and one of the Rastas began firing, killing a thousand young men instantly. As they fell, Cal leapt onto the Rasta, pummeling him to the ground. As they scuffled, Cal was grabbed and hoisted up. And when he looked there were no bodies, just an open field.

"Pretty trippy!" he said and they laughed. He got up and looked around, and then he heard a lone parrot in the distance and felt sad.

"You got th' bends, my man," said the leader.

"You go down too deep, you don't get back up," said another.

"Where's that guy, Gabriel?"

"*Gabriel*? There is no one here dat name. What they do to you, American, down de're. They do somethin' t'you?"

"Am I a prisoner?"

"No, man—but you walk in our fields, we have a business to run, man, we don't know why you're here."

"Why did you shoot like that?"

"Why do you ask so many questions, American?"

"Because I think you know something—I think you know something about what I saw," Cal said.

"You saw nothing," the leader said.

"You have half your island slaughtered—mainly young men."

"What young men? You saw nothing, American."

"You don't know?"

"You saw nothing but what you wanted to see."

The Rastas retied Cal and told him that they would not use poison, which caused the hallucinations, to subdue him. The potent herbal blend used spider venom because of its paralyzing properties. Cal, who was losing his paunch and had not yet realized that his hair was white as snow, started to regain himself. Highly intrigued about the supply of cocaine from South America, they transported him to Lamont Harbor to their contact.

When they arrived, the town was bustling with energy—filled with people!

"When I arrived they were all gone...no one was here."

"You get high on your own supply, American. Now, where is this plane of yours?" the leader asked.

They could soon see it—it had been towed in and sat at the edge of the harbor, not two hundred meters from the American Coast Guard vessel, the joint collaboration between the DEA and the Coast Guard.

As soon as Cal and his captors got to the plane, a captain named Rains also arrived at the plane on his skiff, with two DEA agents.

The Rastas looked at Cal and smiled. "Sorry, dude," the tall Rasta said in familiar *American* speak. "You're under arrest for transporting half-a-billion dollars in cocaine from the republic of Columbia. You have the right to remain silent..."

Cal smiled at his arrest. This was a perfectly acceptable outcome. If he was busted by one faction, the other would—as they had done before—would make the evidence disappear and break him from prison.

"Remember," said the Rasta, "you saw nothing."

Cal saw the brig of the quick Coast Guard Cutter—he smelled the American quality! He felt the sadness of losing his parrot, but even that would miraculously be restored, all in time.

He would think well of his ex-wife, Sally Anne, how she had hit the bottle and dope, how he kept her in that shack down at Jupiter, and how she wanted for nothing, as long as he could make a quick run. He predicted that the run would soon end.

He checked himself, urinated without pain, felt his face, then sat down on the bunk and rolled into a deep sleep.

It did not last too long; there was a loud explosion and the cutter rocked, spilling Cal to the floor, rolling him hard into the wall. The *ratatat* of machine gun fire! Then silence. The boat was still in the water.

He would think of these facts as proof, but not today. He would think of it as final, but not now. It would be a sign and a wonder, which he had not experienced since the healing of Sally Anne in the revival church in Lauderdale that summer, when he and Frilly Martin and Baggs Ross and Sumner Phillips, Sally Anne Criswell (always the ex-wife) and Giselle Goldstein, and a few he'd forgotten all about except for their faces, went to hear some miracle preacher/healer named Buck Samson, in a tent in an open field at the beach. The tent was filled with poor superstitious people, Cal recalled, but anything was worth a try to cure his wife's cancer, Sumner Phillips' heart condition, and Frilly Martin's inability to walk.

Samson paraded around the stage like a dancer—his voice boomed low and prominent, then high as the tent poles when he would exalt his Lord and Savior, Jesus the Christ, and when he would exhort the lives of the saints, those who believed in Jesus. He had the Rolex, the gold chain and the entourage. He had the organist, the ushers who looked more like thugs with earpieces, and the loyalty. He had the crowd, and oh, boy was it thronged against that stage! He wore a purple jacket and tight black pants and a white ruffled shirt. Perhaps it was Giselle who said the preacher wasn't gay. He asked Giselle why she didn't seek the help of the local Rabbi, and Giselle responded with something like: "Well, he's not good enough."

He felt silly, until he saw the poor people on the stage, the sagging faces, the crippled children, the poverty, the regrets, the scourged humanity. He held himself above it all until Frilly went up there and started weeping like a baby when, supposedly, the Spirit was on him, put there by Buck Samson, who had total direction from God, a direct line to Frilly's entire existence. And Frilly got up, as if he would walk again, as if he would finally be able to overcome the plague of his stroke once and for all.

Then he fell. He fell on his face and broke his front teeth; he fell and Cal attacked the preacher, the false prophet, the true con man, the liar, the cheat, but he was stopped by some local folks who had no hope. They told him nothing else has worked, and they had seen miracles.

It was just that Frilly Martin fell and broke his teeth. That was the last time God spoke. He had decided to break Frilly's teeth, poor man; if he had anything left, it was his teeth, and now not even that.

Sally Anne went back to shooting smack, "to ease the *daddy-awful* pain," to ease the flesh out of its burden of holding back a soul who longed to soar. She'd say to him: "Honey, if I didn't have a body, I think I could fly high above that sunrise, high above those

stars, and I could walk with everyone, and I, I would just call everyone and tell 'em how much I loved 'em, like right now. I love you,
Cal. I love you, darlin' and I always will." He remembered she said
that.

He knew she was high when she felt good like this, but he fell in
love all over again. In fact, the divorce proceeding was irrelevant; it
only meant he'd live a hundred yards away with his parrot, and Sally
Anne would live alone and wait for him to call.

He'd push her blonde hair back over her ear and whisper: "I
love you, Sally Anne, always have. You know that, don't you?"

"Then why are we being so silly?" she would ask.

He would remember that she did not bear him a child, and he
wondered if he hated her for that. But he loved her even more than
he could ever hate, more than he could ever disdain anyone or anything. This love was the way to elevation, but he would not take it,
instead he would fly his plane—he would not be there when she
needed him. But she would not go with another, not after him, not
after forty years of love. Not since being schoolyard sweethearts back
at Joliet High, not since she waited for him to return from Viet
Nam. He came home to find that the burgeoning drug culture had
taken its toll, and then later he found out she was sick.

It was ennui, she had said, once. She was in a deep depression
and found it hard to work at the Dockweiler Restaurant over at the
marina. The heat made her cry. The rain made her laugh. The win-
ter was fine, but in the summer it hurt to see young couples arm in
arm, and she prayed for Cal all that time to come home, and by the
time he did, she could not care for him.

He had tried to help her. He had been more than a support, a
pillar upon which her life would crumble, not the rock she needed,
but no human could be that, she often said.

Still he flew the contraband, and still he was going to stop. He
had often said that he would only do one more run—and now at
last he knew it was over.

When Cal awoke, he was in a prison cell and not at sea. It was a
dream, perhaps, or some sort of hallucinogenic drug, or just plain
mind control—government's got all kinds of stuff they can do to
you if they want. He knew that from his years in special ops, psychological warfare training and just plain soldiering; he knew better
than to become superstitious, at least not at this point. He wondered if he had even flown the mission.

All that cleared up when two American men moved him to an

interrogation room. First, a doctor named Coates entered and performed a blood-pressure check and gave him a look-see. Everything seemed to check out. Cal complained about his head. Coates gave him a couple of pills and told him that the head wound was not life-threatening; he offered no emotion nor a bedside manner which might have assured Cal under better circumstances.

"I would appreciate you telling me where I am, Doc," Cal said wearily, still drowsy due to what must've been some sort of drug.

"Someone will attend to your head wound shortly," was all Coates said and then he left the room, his presence like a wisp. Cal forgot to ask him for a cup of coffee and a cigarette, at least he had had that in other, similar situations.

There was a small picture on the wall and Cal considered it might be hiding a camera. He looked it over—a portrait of a snow-laden house in the woods with a windy path leading up to it—Catskills, Rockies, High Sierra? He was just not sure. He wondered if he might be somewhere else in the country, but he did not recall travel. In fact, at this point, he recalled nothing.

Finally, a man who did not introduce himself entered. He looked like the typical company man, cropped neat hair, fresh shave, a dark brown suit and a notebook. On second thought, Cal knew this was no company man; he was some kind of technician, but he had no idea of what discipline.

"How are you feeling, Cal?" came a gentleman's voice.

"I'm... I guess I'm okay," Cal answered, "If you consider that I've been halfway around the world, seen all kinds of horrors, then wind up in prison, and I don't know what really happened to me the past forty-eight hours."

"What do you remember?" the professional man asked.

Cal told him everything. The man then looked at his watch and smiled. "What if I told you that you never left the United States?"

"I'd say you're about as poppycock as that locoweed down in St. Lucy," Cal said. "By the way, my parrot, Sam, she's on my mind—"

"Your parrot is safe at home where you left her."

"No, I was runnin' contraband, you know it, and I know it—I know what I saw down in St. Lucy. What kind of operation you boys scammin' this time anyway?"

"Do you feel up to flying your plane?" the professional asked, and Cal figured he was some sort of shrink.

ten

*J*ustin was everything the crowd could hope for, and then some. Never mind what had happened in New Mexico, he was a new man, and he commanded the stage like the showman Anton always thought he would or could be. He ran through the sets and no one messed up this time—that would have been great for Anton to see.

But no one had heard from Anton Duffield, the manager, since the afternoon.

Stephen Petchick thanked God profusely and asked Him to help him resist the demonic urges inherent in the talent and crew of this operation. He manned the board, fixed lights, troubleshot it all and assumed a leadership position; it was an indispensable position, a position that he had not had since running the mechanic shop in prison.

He had no idea what to do, however, when he saw her again.

It wasn't until after the show, because Sibyl wasn't in the habit of going to concerts. She'd seen them so many times, but she was always happy to attend the after-concert parties. She was also in charge of lining up the evening's liquor, babes and drugs.

Steve did not know what to expect until he saw Katarina in the banquet room in the hotel in Scottsdale. He had Jesus; she had survivor instincts. She had sex; he had dreams. She had sorrow; he had grace. She needed what he had and he did not need anything of hers, and the idea that Jezebels could be saved was not something he adhered to, or had even heard of.

At the same time he remembered that God forgave him of his sins, that no sin is unforgivable as long as a person repents of it. He had been changed from the inside out, and he was nothing but a lowly sinner, a murderer, a thief. But she was still Jezebel.

When he saw her, she was—impossibly, abominably—sitting on Sibyl's lap. After she recognized that Stephen was working the show, after she realized that he had saved the day, after fawning all over the players in the band, there he was, and she was filled with anger, which was couched in little kisses on Sibyl's mouth.

There she was. Forever past. Forever in the future and out of reach, at least that's what he wanted now. He begged God for the strength not to judge, and not to fall.

There they were, finally, at the window overlooking the faux tropics, overlooking the imported pools, sand, trees and waiters; there they were thronged between fifteen-year-old groupies and next-door pimps. She had not seen him in this capacity, around people like *this*.

That it was even possible was something she simply had to find out.

Not so easy because Sibyl was snorting line after line of crystal, powering champagne and potato chips, letting people see her tattooed private parts. "Lookie but no touchie!" she'd say. She had no intention of giving up what she had found, indeed what was *hers*.

Katarina thought that was rather silly—she had never felt the way that Sibyl had. Territory was one thing, upon which Stephen was encroaching, but possession of another would only lead to harsh disappointment. She was much more interested in Stephen's reaction. After all, she knew he had those possessive feelings, that feeling of being smitten. She could kill it in herself and conjure it in a man, no question.

She's got no idea who I am, he thought. "The Lord gives me strength. Who'd save you if not for me telling you about Jesus Christ?" he said.

She laughed. And she allowed Sibyl to fondle and kiss her in front of Stephen yet again, then gauged his reaction—but he turned away forthrightly and that made her upset. She'd never seen a man turn away; this was not possible. Of course he'd like to bed two women engaged in abominable sex! Who wouldn't? Only a loser, she told herself.

Of course he'll forgo his vows, just this once. Wouldn't he want to see some real action for the first time in his life, or was he just a mama's boy, from cradle to grave afraid of his own shadow, always following the rules, strait-laced and boring? In fact, arrogant and judgmental, hypocritical and cold—like a warden. *Warden Stevie*, she'd think of him. How dare he turn from her like that!

Or was she wrong? A couple of lines of drugs, a couple of cognacs and feeling her euphoria in her sex—which she would turn on big time for Stephen. And he would not even show her his tattoo, poor boy!

Oh, she would make him want her if it was the last thing she would do.

"Sibyl, darling, Stephen is so nice, don't you think?" she began.

Sibyl was slurping oysters and champagne, floating like a lost birthday balloon, and she looked him over. "What, you want to give him a little show, sweet cheeks?"

"He's so strait-laced. He needs to loosen up a little."

Even Sibyl realized that Justin had found a new friend in Stephen. Katarina could not understand how Stephen had chiseled into her action and had instantly risen to a status much higher up in the food chain. It was just cosmic torture and it would have to stop.

"Sibby, I want to do him in front of you," she said, kissing her, hoping her sensual nature would be elevated.

"No way—I found you. I thought you were like me!"

"I am, Sibby, I'm just, well he makes me mad because he's so holier than thou, know what I mean?"

"You do that and I'll throw you off the tour," said Sybil unequivocally.

Sibyl did not say that, did she?

If Katarina knew anything, she knew she would find a way. When she saw him grabbing some shrimp hors d'oeuvres in the corner, she took her chance. "It must be destiny," she said, all smiles.

"Hey, Katarina! It's great to see you again," he said, kissing her on the cheek.

"Yeah, just think of the odds," she said flirtatiously, while sipping from her forever full champagne glass, "me finding you and you finding me again—it must be destiny."

"Yeah," he said. "Thank the Lord I got this job—my mother really needs the money."

"Will you stop with all your...*being good*. Don't you do *anything* wrong?"

"What? I—"

She quickly interrupted him: "Look at me, aren't I beautiful tonight?"

She was stunning in her sleek new skirt but he looked away from the see-through silk top.

"It's...I'm sorry about, you know, the way it ended out there. I didn't, well it's great to see you again, Katarina. I'm...I guess what I'm trying to say is that I didn't mean to offend you," Stephen said.

She did not hesitate to wrap her arms around his neck and kiss his face, hoping for his lips, which he guarded. "You're so handsome, Stephen. Your body fits so well with mine," she went on, trying her best.

She wasn't wrong. He was the tallest, most fit, most handsome, most likeable, most notable, and most valuable—if you were the crew. He was an all-around leader, and people would look up to him, she feared. He had the countenance of peace. That would have to end, she thought, trying again for his mouth.

Embarrassed, he simply pushed her away.

"So what's with you—you need mommy's permission or something? You gay or something—a big sissy, is that it? Is love outlawed in the Bible too?" she asked.

"Love?" he laughed. "L-U-S-T, it spells lust, Katarina, with all due respect," he said confidently.

It was effortless for her to change the subject at this point, not letting his eyes wander even an inch. "So you're in with Justin now, huh?" she said.

"I'm not *in* with anybody," he said defensively.

"Think you're so hot 'cause you fixed some lights?" she asked.

"No, I don't think that. I'm grateful for—"

"Well, why do you hang out with Justin then?" she demanded.

"Hey, I don't. He wanted to talk to me, that's all."

"I see what you're doing, Steve. And it's totally un-Bible-like. I know *exactly* what you're doing."

To make matters worse, Justin strode up, limber and victorious. It had been a glorious night for him, three encores and a flawless medley at the end, leaving them hungering, lingering and willing to buy anything: T-shirts, CD's, tickets to the show in LA—it was amazing. They had failed in KC. "Stevinsky," he called him, which made Katarina's eyes roll back, "I know I'm supposed to talk to you."

"Oh," said Stephen. "This is—"

"Katarina, my lovely," said Justin, making her smile. "Sibyl's looking for you—you know how jealous she can be."

That sunk her and she answered: "I can see you gentlemen need to talk—can I get either of you a drink? Some more soda pop, *Stevinsky?*" she said, and by now her eyes were glaring daggers.

"No, thanks," Stephen said, unable to mount any defense of what he did not know. But Justin was drawn to Stephen. It was just a strange match-up, the closest thing to male bonding Justin would ever know—but it was more than that. Stephen sensed it; others were baffled. Justin was always *l'enfant terrible*; he was always out-of-sorts. He was always late, always stoned, always disheveled, always pampered, always the poet, misunderstood and uninterrupted, and this had started a long time ago. The princely stature of entitlement—Stephen had never known it; it did not seem human, but he knew the Holy Spirit was asking him to help.

"Stevinsky, you know about holograms, don't you? God's talking to me, and He says it's infinite from each point of view."

Stephen prayed in the bathroom about Justin, hoping to have the right words that might help him to Christ.

But all of this did not sit well with Katarina, who *knew* why she was there, and knew too that she could just as easily be gone unless perhaps...

But no, Stephen would not be able to help her; she couldn't rely on him at all, which made him an enemy, no doubt. This intrusion was not something she would have to let fall; survival was more important than heart—but the idea that Stephen was getting in good with Justin, saving the day, it just had to be put to an end. The idea that he was trying to establish himself as indispensable in every way, a temple priest, was outrageous. This was hers, hers and for no one but her.

"So, look at you, Stephen, so high above the rest of us," she said while cornering him on the way out of the bathroom.

"Hey, I thought a lot about you. I prayed for you," he said.

"Well, please don't ever do that again."

"So you and Sybil—"

"Don't be an idiot."

"Sorry."

"*I'm* sorry. I thought we said goodbye. I thought we understood—this is my turf."

"Oh," said Stephen, chuckling to himself, "it's *your* turf. It's God's—"

She turned and walked away from the impossible. She turned and would not turn back again. He wanted to talk to her alone, and just as he made his way back to where Sibyl was holding court—

"*Stevinsky*! Come on, dude, I need to talk," said Justin.

And Stephen listened.

"So, it's like, there's this, it's like *God*, man. It is God."

He listened to Justin as they made their round of the hotel property.

"Maybe it's God's Spirit—the *Holy Spirit*," Stephen said by the pool.

Justin looked away, then fell suddenly to the concrete by the pool. Stephen tried to help him back onto his feet, and Justin quickly snorted a few more lines of crank, then swigged his vodka out of the Stoli bottle, and he was filled with new inspiration.

"He says I'm going to die," said Justin.

Stephen laughed. "Yeah, man, if you keep on like you're doin'—"

"—No, by the hand of another—but it's bigger than me. Where do you think my manager went?" Justin asked.

"I don't know," Stephen said, wondering if he would ever meet Anton Duffield.

"Well, *I* know—*they* got him."

"Who's they?"

"I'm not crazy!" Justin yelled, shoving Stephen back into a plastic-strapped recliner. Stephen got back up and silently asked God for help. And God told him to stand in the gap.

"I'm *not*! I'm truth! You're a witness, and if you turn away, then you're not worth the salt in your light!"

Stephen did not need Justin (God speaking through him?) to shove him back again. The statement "*salt in your light*" was shocking coming from a non-believer who had not read the Bible. "What...what'd you say?" Stephen asked plaintively.

"We're both salt and light," Justin said, not knowing that he was quoting Matthew 5, verses 13 and 14. Stephen knew this because that was one of his favorite passages.

But again, Stephen did not believe it was the Holy Spirit, or that it was miraculous—not completely. "Justin—"

"Call me *lamb*," he said, gazing at the moon, at another person.

"Where did you hear about 'salt' and 'light'?"

He looked right at Stephen and said, "Have you *no* faith at all?"

Dear Lord, if this be a demon, please help me, Stephen thought silently. If this is a trick, please give me the strength to fight.

"You are the light of the world, righteous one! I am fallen. But

He talks through me. When we were in the hospital, I hid every-thing. Sibyl is my stumbling block—tied to what I do and say, as if to destroy me by imitation—but it fell away in Albuquerque. That was the meaning of Albuquerque, Stevinsky. You are the Witness. Understand?"

"I'm...I'm not sure I do," Stephen said, trembling.

"He's looking through my eyes right now, Stephen J. Petchick," Justin said. "He's looking at you for the first time and he's saying that you don't let Him in, and without Him you will fail at your task, which is to prepare the Way for God's judgment to protect the lambs. Jesus is The Way, The Truth, and The Life; that's what He's telling me now. They kill innocence to power their world, their 'light'—but that is darkness. God hates that!"

Stephen thought of his abject neglect of his mother, Anna. He thought of the scourge of prison life, and no one would ever know now that the Holy Spirit *almost* transformed him into the man he wanted to be—but tonight he knew he had fallen far short.

Justin said: "I am the one you cannot escape. A key will turn a lock, a seal will break, another will come and the Lord God will judge, and maybe after that Jesus will come back. I don't know. I am just a little person—but God screams in me! Oh, I'm sick! You see? I'm sick! You are the salvation of *this* tour, which is stupid, worthless and less if it doesn't glorify the true God of all! See, if I were Him, I'd destroy everything, but I'm not."

"He's your God too, brother."

Justin welled-up like a child when Stephen called him "brother," the tears streamed and he started weeping, but then he said: "I am not here, Stephen. Only God is here with you now. Katarina is what you say, and yet she is also a witness. Everything I say is one hundred percent correct, and pardon Justin's manner of speaking—he has limitations," Justin said.

Stephen wanted to sink to his knees and pray for forgiveness. He knew Justin was speaking a form of Tongues, but he, Stephen J. Petchick, could not or would not help him. He was a failure, and ashamed. "I am so sorry, Lord. Please forgive me, and please help my brother Justin to sleep and rest. Justin, He's with you, got His hand on you, man, and I failed you, all right? Like I failed my mother. Praise be to God, who can help both of us tonight. Come to Christ, Justin—He died for your sins and mine, and He's the only answer, okay?"

"I do not need sleep," Justin said. "Let me tell you the truth," he began.

Stephen felt a seeping dread move around and through him.

"I was born of Satan," Justin began. "But God made me a lamb. You might call me a Trojan Horse. My people worshiped the beast for breakfast. All institutions are satanic, every school from the tree, every doctor, every lawyer, every success in the last moments of this ridiculous amalgam of evil, man. Do you hear me, Stevinsky! Am I getting through to you?"

Do you hear me, Stephen?

"I need to pray," Stephen said fearfully.

"Pray then," Justin said.

Stephen began to pray out loud. "Dear Heavenly Father, dear Lord God, please forgive me. I have sinned; I have been selfish; I neglected my own mother; I was ambitious, and thank You for saving me from myself. I didn't want to steal again—but I felt I had to make it up, just one more time to make up the money, and that maybe I could help her. I thank You for the forgiveness I do not deserve. And now I pray for my new friend Justin—he is possessed; he is talking falsehood; he must be. Please help him come to know You, to know Your love, to feel the regenerating power of You through Jesus Christ our Lord and Savior. In Jesus' name I pray. Amen."

"Thank you," said Justin. "He loves you, Stephen. He's never going to leave you—you'll be a leader one day; that's what He says to me now. You're right about my being possessed—by God, my friend, not by a lie."

"Okay—I...I feel you need someone more experienced—"

"Nonsense! I don't need anything, I want you to be a witness! Okay?"

"Okay," Stephen said.

"Listen to what He says, and you tell me if I'm possessed. Your mother is Anna and she needs you. You need to learn from her, you are *not* her healer."

Stephen, trembling, said: "I, uh...I never told you her name."

"You think I'm Satan, don't you."

"I—"

You think you're in a nightmare, don't you? And you think you know everything about Jesus Christ, don't you, he thought Justin was saying, but Justin was not saying anything, because his lips were not moving.

"You think that all this spiritual stuff is for church, or a good pastor, like you had in prison."

"Oh, my Lord, help me."

"Like it was when you were left for dead, and raised again...for what! So you could be some misbegotten roadie on a trip to hell along a highway of sixes? So you could finally wind up with the fallen angels on the coast and lose your Christ, and lose your soul? You know, when He looks through your eyes, the only way I know Him, when He speaks through you, when you are His vehicle, when you're His Way, His Will—then you're gone, he's got you. Then you're like, over."

Stephen could not utter a sound.

"So why is this guy, bombed to the blizzards on Stoli and crank, saying these impossible things? He's just gotta talk because he *has* to? *That it could not be God, that it could not possibly be Justin letting God use him to talk to Stephen*! No, it's gotta be demonic possession, that's definitely it."

Nothing from Stephen.

Justin rolled right on after a gulp of air: "And all the rock and roll parasites—whoever made any money, including me—had to profess a love for evil. Don't you see? The rebellion wasn't rebellion, it was allegiance," Justin went on. "And that allegiance led to certain perks and prizes, and those prizes led to decadence because the evil one doesn't care about us, but he'll reward those of us who do for him to a certain extent and then he'll use someone else, all for his own glory. His plan is to do away with us, and that is why I was successful, and I'm here to tell you that my success has nothing to do with talent. I am the *talentless* one. But I am not who I am—I renounce Justin Kincaid! I renounce my father's way. I renounce the *miseducation*. Even this hotel—even this hotel is damned for eternity, that rock, that sand, those cactus plants, the bar, everyone you see..."

Stephen looked at him earnestly; he wanted to help.

You are the one who needs help, Stephen.

He did not understand; it sounded like Justin was speaking truth, or possessed with truth, but the idea of the Spirit filling him or using him and then the drugs and drink, and all he was spouting, it was all false, wasn't it?

Trust the Lord, son—open your ears. I am the Lord God; I can do what I want.

Despite the Voice screaming in his head, Stephen refused to listen. After all, Justin could have found out Stephen's credentials from the other crew, he could have guessed about prison, but he could not have known his mother's name. That he could not have known. That he did not even tell Katarina.

"In Los Angeles I'm going to make a splash," said Justin. He got up from the poolside chaise, brushed himself off, looked at Stephen as if he did not know him, as if there were no recollection of what had just transpired. Then Justin Kincaid strode deliriously, desultorily toward the entrance of the hotel.

Stephen walked around the main pool by the small faux beach, curving toward one of the hot tubs. There was a peace at the pre-dawn time of night, and by now he'd dispensed entirely with Justin's speech, his knowledge—or guess—of his mother's name, something he could have gotten, perhaps, from the manager. Or flat out demonic possession; sure, demons can know stuff like that.

A streak through the sky, a warmth over his body now—he had escaped the den, had escaped the notion that he needed further conviction, had escaped failing God. Had done his best, not good enough, never good enough, but he could smile. He in fact laughed. He leapt for joy and jogged hard around the pools singing "The Saints."

"Lord God Almighty! Who was, and is, and is to come!" Praising Him who made everything. Praising and not forgetting. And then he came to the hot tub.

He noticed someone, or something—was it floating? A sack? A toppled garbage bin?

As he drew closer, a cascading chill moved the air around him, and he felt the noise of dead space like a vacuum, invisible, pervasive, surrounding him. Sinking to his knees, gasping for air, he was trying to find the voice to call out.

That's when *she* arrived behind him. "Oh, my God," she said, horrified.

He could not move. "I just got here...I just—" He had no words to describe it. She looked at him suspiciously.

Someone was in the shadows, someone he saw out of the corner of his eye. Someone he knew was there, but it had never really registered.

"Did you do it?" she said callously as they stood over what in the increasing early light was the body of Anton Duffield, the manager.

"Of course not," Stephen said. Soon there were police on the scene, a blue and white Coroner van, and Katarina kept on with a story that she believed Stephen killed him because he wasn't going to help Stephen's mother out as he had promised, gossip that she had in fact heard.

"Ridiculous!" Stephen said. He went home just as the sun was peeking out from behind the trees. He crawled into bed, careful not to disturb his mother, careful to pray hard on his knees for everything to change.

"Stephen...wake up. Stephen!" Anna stood over him. When he opened his eyes, she was healed! She was victorious! His prayer was answered!

"Mother, you look wonderful!" He leapt up to hug her lightly. For she still seemed weak, frail in fact.

That's when he looked behind her and found something that he promised her she would never see again. Two uniformed officers.

"Mom?" he asked. Tears flecked her face and she left the room.

"Stephen Petchick, you are hereby under arrest for the murder of Anton Duffield. You have the right to remain silent..."

She was back in her bed, and he was allowed to say goodbye to her, as one of the officers named Brill stood at the doorway, on his guard.

"Mom, it's not true this time."

"I know, son. We must pray now—only God can help us," she said, and he kneeled down while she whispered: "Dear Heavenly Father, please care for my son in this time of persecution. He loves You, Lord, and keeps Your commandments. He is a good son, since You raised him up. He loves You with all his heart, with all his soul, and with all his might and mind, and he won't let You down. In Jesus' precious name I pray. Amen."

He looked at her, amazed. "You believe me. You know the truth," he said with a comforted smile.

"Yes, my son. He shows me the truth. Be sure to take your Bible. I'll call Jeremy, and if I can get someone to drive, I'll come visit."

He only took his worn New King James Bible, and he walked lightly, happily with the officers. "My mother knows the truth," he was saying to one of the policemen, who remained steadfastly silent. "I'm going to help her when I get out," he said.

That night, while reading Scripture, Anna Petchick turned out her light, rested her head on the pillow, shut her eyes and died peacefully.

eleven

r. Kincaid was called to the Serin research center to observe the questioning of the teenage boy who had demonstrated certain unique abilities. His full legal name was Casey Burns Smith, and he was a member of the well-to-do Smith Appliance dynasty, who had sold their company to Consolidated Electric some years back, dedicating a portion of the proceeds to a foundation which contributed to the Serin Institute. Casey was chosen because he had undergone a conversion experience at a Christian summer camp, where he claimed to be in touch with a spirit, which he claimed was God, and affirmed Jesus as not only the Christ, but God. The family had gone to church for weddings and funerals, a baby baptism or two, but had never really seen their son change his beliefs until he claimed to be *born again*, a term which his mother, Elizabeth Smith, hated. She knew in her world there was only one true belief—and this was rebellion, which was an embarrassment and obvious to all.

Upon the much-anticipated arrival at the Institute in northern Arizona, in an underground facility that government scientists had used for genetic engineering experiments a decade earlier, Kincaid and his group were busy rebuilding the subterranean town, or *resort*, as Kincaid liked calling it. Above ground, there were dorms for patients; it was a functioning psychiatric facility of the highest order, but not known to the world because of its renown as a research facility, and that's how Kincaid would keep it. The psychiatrists here, as well as the rest of the staff from aides to nurses to secretaries and accountants were well paid because they had to live "in the middle of nowhere."

There were things that had to be given freely, like one's passion, and that had to be accommodated, had to be nurtured. The Institute was a place for honing skills and was a place of inquiry of the highest order, inquiry into the unanswerable things, such as the nature of the soul, man's relation to God, or more specifically, man's religious nature.

There were times when all this inquiry seemed to hinge on whether or not experiments on the human psyche—hence consciousness itself—was ethical. New standards would have to be developed, Kincaid felt; these experiments were a far cry from cult deprogramming, Kincaid's specialty in the 1980's.

Kincaid was not privy to certain information, like where some of the patients were eventually transferred. It bothered him, but he had always known that in order to achieve what was necessary to transform the world into one of peace and cooperation, which is why he was paid in the first place, there would have to be a decidedly new world view based on the greater good. Norms such as national pride, corporate identity, cult identity, the media and especially Christianity were under comprehensive study and scrutiny. The media experiments were a fabulous success in the 1980's, and this was how Kincaid had distinguished himself and had appropriated a higher order of responsibility, thereby being initiated into a greater understanding of the mystery tradition that had spanned the ages.

He only knew it as benign and agreed wholeheartedly with its purview, its philosophy, its scope and purpose, and its divine aspiration: that there is a Godhead, from which man is supposed to harness his beneficent power. He agreed that nothing is separate from God, which was established firmly in all institutions worldwide, except in the churches. Man is God per se, anointed from birth, and man on earth is nothing new, as man has been everywhere throughout the galaxies (secretly, of course). The earth was to be a slave planet for the purpose of something he would learn one day; it was somehow evolutionary and was gratifying. He'd learned about their reaches into space when dining with a friend named Betfloeven, who indicated that not only did the Order, or "Brotherhood," as it was called, extend off this planet, but that Betfloeven himself had traveled to a distant star system where he saw another, more advanced civilization that somehow got there through an ancient tradition and the blood of Christ.

When time becomes timelessness, it does amazing things to God's prophetic clock—like stopping it. This concept was beyond Kincaid's grasp—how could you prove it? He responded to Betfloeven with laughter and skepticism. Yet his next degree of initiation verified the tradition of the blood. From Jesus' crucifixion onward there had been a *cultivation* of the blood, a use of the blood for the purposes of those he loosely deemed as *the rulers,* those individuals of a dimensional and interdimensional constitution who claimed by tradition to own the earth and many other things. The blood could be rekindled through genetic manipulation, by DNA, in order to create more like Jesus, so that they could be sacrificed as the lamb—not *a* lamb, but *The* Lamb. Somehow it involved the manipulation of time, which he did not understand.

He had not seen or heard of such things in his temple worship of Isis, which he believed wholly scientific; indeed, science came from Egyptian culture, though he knew Isis was symbolic of more advanced, so-called off-world cultures. He had even heard— *Through the mist? The children at play? The World?*—about the moon being used for the harvesting of souls, which was later clarified to be human energy forms. His initiation into higher and higher degrees was also his psychological test to determine if he could handle the level of strangeness and knowledge about things, which were declared wholly mythological. Could he handle the truth?

He would have to wait until such truth was revealed, trickling in one step at a time, as trust was enhanced through the job he was doing. As a scientist he could handle it, but it was his wife, Jackson Kincaid, who wanted to delve further into the mystical realms of *inner sancta.*

He did not understand how in those primitive days the blood could have been manipulated. His job was to find those innocent, those privileged, who had given themselves to Christ, had become *born again,* and had displayed unusual behavior, changes that would typically alarm their friends, teachers and parents—for that was *the prophecy.* The idea was to study the conversion experience, as the higher-ups had a deep desire to use the same human notion to propagate their own new religion, which would sweep the globe, Kincaid was told. Dr. Kincaid had come across some unusual subjects, and he felt there was nothing notably wrong with them. They simply believed in Christ, and by all witness accounts they had changed for the better. They had rid themselves, in some cases, of the enveloping drug culture, of their need for angry punk music, death cults and antisocial activity and had cleaned up their appearances, had gotten jobs and ceased breaking the law, in one or two cases.

In one case, a young man labeled a sociopath converted to Christianity in a juvenile detention center, quit his newfound profession of breaking and entering, quit his gang, got a college degree, went to seminary and now wrote about Kincaid as some sort of demonic presence on earth! Clearly, this one should have been commended to the project coordinators, Kincaid felt, along with the ones who seemed full of the *Kool-Aid* that actually kills society and harms any chance for global peace.

It was Kincaid's goal to rid the world of barbarism, to truly bring civilization to a warring—if feeble—planet of human hosts. Manifest Destiny meant minds, not territories! To him, most territory would be better off in the hands of the elite than the uneducated, who squander resources and yet fail to recognize that they are polluting their very own lives. Education was the key, he often said. And education had come a long way. When he started, there were perhaps two or three promising research associates, now there were dozens.

When he began working alongside his wife, Jackson, his son Justin had been going through a sort of horrific verisimilitude to Kincaid's own patients at the Institute, displaying rebellious antisocial traits similar to Christians. This made sense, according to Geoff Junger, the prominent psychiatrist from Zurich and author of the *Primary Mind,* which had enlightened most of the scientific community, as well as influenced social policy. In his view, psychological disease had its origin in unaddressed trauma resulting from birth. Once a patient undergoes a reliving of his birth, and sees that it is good after all, he usually becomes a productive citizen.

Junger had a cogent explanation concerning Brand Kincaid's troubled son, Justin. He was suffering because his father was spending all his time, in those days, with his patients on the ward. His specialty was cult de-programming. Justin, then about thirteen and in puberty, which Junger said was the proof in the pudding, began displaying signs of personality disorder. He claimed to be the antichrist at one point, then he said he was born into the legion of antichrist, and his rebellion generalized to include his parents. Junger told Kincaid, in the words of this illustrious pioneer of the human psyche, that it was, "the absolutely normal presence of assimilation and normalcy—surely necessary for future sustenance." In other words, no need to worry about Justin, Kincaid told his wife, Jackson.

"It's just that...he's so convincing," she had said. "It's hard to believe he even came from me."

Being the astute scientist, she told Kincaid that the fact that they had worked together as a team in the past caused Justin to resent society even more. She didn't believe that it was just a passing phase, and Brand did not blame her for this. In researching her dissertation for her Ph.D. in developmental psychology, which included children like Justin, she had found a more pessimistic reality: that children who start off bad usually stay bad.

She would never let on to her most prestigious colleagues or her professors that this truth would be buried in exchange for stipends and perks, for parties and stature. Justin's rebellion was quelled, however, when Brand discovered a wonderful teacher who introduced Justin to the theater. From there, Justin began to act—he could really vent his frustrations and go through the hostility, alienation and separation from his mother. Kincaid introduced him to tennis and life at the club in Westchester. Connecticut was a breath of fresh air, rarefied air at that. Sometimes Brand Kincaid would get reports that his son looked like a homeless vagabond, that he was scaring some of the seniors who played bridge every Thursday. He'd get reports that Justin had dropped out of school and was singing in a rock and roll band. Brand slammed him into rehab and always knew the trouble was all because he, then a young psychiatrist just out of Harvard, wanted to make a name for himself, and he knew the only way was research, publishing, and presentation—this was, after all, where Justin got his notion to take to the stage.

Justin's history was on his mind, primarily because in his interview with seventeen-year-old Casey Smith, a wonderful candidate for the latest in deprogramming techniques, Casey had some peculiar similarities with his own son, who had escaped years before. He would not make the same mistake with Casey.

Today Casey was escorted into the *blank* room where all could be observed by several fiber optic cameras in the floor, in the walls and in the lights. He would not be given stimulus, such as colored lights, sound and loop recordings of his parents and siblings. He had claimed to be "of God," or "about the Lord's business," and that he had given himself to Jesus Christ, "who chose me before the foundation of the world," a statement which caused his parents to become alarmed. The official reason his parents brought him in was to save him from himself. They felt that it was one thing to go for the altar call at a local evangelical or so-called Bible-based church, but it was quite another to refuse to dine with father and mother or to speak with siblings. Casey quoted Scripture as a justification, speaking gibberish which he called Tongues, and prophesied great doom to New York City and especially to Los Angeles, or the "City of Angels" as he called it, and to all the unsealed wicked, of which his parents would most certainly qualify.

Elizabeth Allendale Smith, his mother, told of a wild biker pastor who wore long hair and tattoos and at one time put Casey on a fast for a month. When she instructed Casey not to go to the church again, he said, "Mom, you're persecuting me because I follow Jesus, who said: *I am the Way, the Truth and the Life.*"

His actions, of course, were horrifying to his parents.

What got the institute interested were the gradual changes in his beliefs that seemed clearly beyond the pale of the evangelical church. These appeared, at first, in the midst of fairly normal conversation. His beliefs were:

I'm not human. I have flesh, but I'm not one of you.

He's keeping me separate and pure for a task later. It will involve a warning to the inhabitants of the earth.

I do not need to study, as the Holy Spirit knows everything. (He had a 4.0 average.)

Most of the earth will perish, and they will wish they had never lived, and they will be as if they had never been. (This labeled him as dangerous.)

Every institution is satanic—every one. (This labeled him as antisocial.)

I do not need food, for I am filled with the Spirit.

God talks to me.

I talk to God.

God alone is sovereign.

Man is in a fallen state and cannot redeem himself.

All other religions are false; Jesus Christ is the only way to salvation.

I disdain the world; I love the ways of the Lord.

I serve the Christ, not man.

I am to honor my mother and father, unless they forsake me or ask me to commit sin. Then, though I forgive them, I am to accept God as my parental guide—He will not forsake me. This is the true meaning of honoring one's mother and father.

God is patient, not distant. If you seek Him, you will see Him.

I walk with God. God walks with me.

These evidentiary core beliefs in Casey could be multiplied now, as virtually all of his conversations contained variations on these and more. He believed that Jesus would come and destroy the world, that Jesus is God. He was told that this qualified him as a potential terrorist, but he cared little for what others thought.

The surveillance camera recorded that every night between the hours of 1:00 A.M. and 3:00 A.M. Casey would converse with whom they could only surmise was Jesus, or this God he spoke of. He would ask a question and then he would answer the question in a slightly different voice. Casey's father now had proof that his son was not just maladjusted, but possibly psychotic, a paranoid delusional, even schizophrenic.

Not to be trusted. Not ever.

There was nothing in their experience that could prepare the mother or Casey's father, Darwain Smith, for what course of action to take. They had been members of an Episcopal Church; he was a prominent lawyer in addition to being CEO of the appliance manufacturing company he inherited. They had couched all their sins (Casey reinvented the dreaded word) into a kind of reverence for the dead, believing God was a distant concept, not clear and sunny like serving a lawsuit on a supplier. God wasn't in the backroom with the girls and the money, and God had been removed from Harvard and Yale, where He is vilified and some say, for good reason. For them, Christianity was at the least unjustified and at the worst fostered hatred and intolerance.

Casey was saying: "I don't care what you do to me. My Father loves me, and He (he meant God all along) protects me. And I have another secret for you, Doctor Kincaid," he said calmly. "I'm not who you think I am. You must stop me because you hate me. And your hatred is unjustified."

"Let's just send him to the Maryland lab and be done with him," said Dr. Jeffries, the chief child psychologist. "All our work hasn't even made a dent. We're supposed to refer these kids on. You know that."

"But I don't know what happens then—there is no follow-through then," Brand Kincaid said, angry about this referral policy.

"Don't you get a kind of hollow feeling, that you weren't successful, that you did not reason with him?"

Jeffries said: "Look, this kid gives me the creeps. Bock should take him."

Of course Brand Kincaid knew Dr. Bock Wiley and dreaded the idea that a case would ever be "taken" away from him, for any reason.

They stood in the observation room with the closed circuit TV monitors and then Jeffries suggested Bock Wiley again, in earnest.

Just the name was shocking—a last resort.

"Look, sometimes physical stimulus is necessary to get through," Jeffries said.

Kincaid bristled: "But I don't believe all that—"

"You believed it with some—like the Brotherhood."

He paced around the conference room, which was filled with leather chairs around a long glass table, a bank of monitors embedded in the walls so seamlessly they seemed as if they were grown, aides dutifully bringing in coffee, papers and computer disks. Kincaid had finally arrived, working for the ultimate private global research facility, and his specialty, *minds*, was the commodity to be controlled and re-grown. Reality was to be homogenized for the first time in human history; fanatical religions were the perfect proving ground. He was going to prove that a person could be returned to society, with the right values, knowing and able to fulfill society's tasks and understanding the sorts of compromises those of us had to make in order to climb the social ladder. It was important to reduce Casey's anxiety over the notion of sexual immorality. For example, sexual stimulus could be utilized until a result was obtained: i.e. to eliminate Casey's obvious sexual guilt so that he would be able to communicate without hysteria or perversion or even neurosis at what might or might not be foisted upon him in various situations.

So far, results had never really been tested; his wife, Jackson, would say—it's all been experimental. Once a pervert or a hater, always a pervert or a hater, unless the mind could truly be taken away from the owner and rewired. Her research into implants and electronic stimulus, even when applied to the brain and the genitals at the same time, could produce Brand's desired results in an afternoon.

He would have to admit that his claimed results were never implemented. Misfits were the recruits, and he was paid more for delivering them to a place he did not know, an ultra secret research facility in Maryland, if the patients continued to hold fast to their belief systems. Dr. Bock Willey, the St. Louis geneticist turned behaviorist, would be a radical departure, an extreme measure, and Brand would not turn Casey over without a fight. He needed to prove that his methods were working, for one thing, and he needed to publish the results. Bock Wiley would not take that away from him.

He never understood how Jackson had such a taste for Bock Wiley's harsh methods of stimulus conditioning. If Brand failed with Casey, this would be the seventh child who had to be turned over in as many months. After all, the Serin Institute prided itself on results necessary to continue thriving in an increasingly competitive industry.

There had never been, in all seven young men who Brand turned over to Wiley's Maryland lab, any follow-up. Kincaid never knew what became of his own work, and he protested to the research council and even to the head of the charitable trust, the benefactor of the Serin Institute, Arthur Reddick.

"Look," he told his wife Jackson, "I'll work with him one more time before we turn him over. But under no circumstances are you to discuss with Arthur the boy's progress. It seems to me they can't wait to get their hands on these kids—and I have news for you, this one will be a success. His religious fantasies will be supplanted with a different world view."

"Well, that's what aberration is all about. It's finally come down to something I hate: God," said Jackson in the hall.

"Hello, Casey," Kincaid said earnestly. "How's it going?" He was sitting in his office with a panoramic view of the high desert, of cacti and mountains. Of weather and sunlight. Of darkening skies.

Casey was standing at the window. "I love my parents but it's in God's hands."

It wasn't just a case of religious conversion—Casey believed that he was...*different*, that there was an angelic realm from whom he derived his strength, his orders. He spoke of service, whereby he would walk "to and fro" over all the earth during its destruction, after he had been translated into a new body, a process, which was going on now. He could point to evidence, particularly in his corneas which were changing color from brown to hazel with the circumferences expanding.

Kincaid felt it wasn't just because Casey had become a Christian, as he had reported and had dropped out of so-called secular activities; he was suffering from a deep delusion. The fact was he was traumatized and hadn't gone along with his parents and the basic norms of social clubs, school and sports. Contrary to Jackson's simple solution, Casey wasn't swayed by sexual stimuli; he did not blend in with the normal boys. He *became* different—these things might not be changed.

His parents could understand if he had turned out gay, or if he had become overly aggressive towards girls, but to be celibate, to turn away from television, magazine articles, and all the logical activities good red-blooded boys are terminally involved in was alienating him from his parents and from their social group. His parents felt they may have had something to do with his unnatural development. To that Casey said, "My *real* father and my *real* mother are both the same person—*God Almighty*."

Casey was finally set up for betrayal, or so he claimed, and he was accused of spying in the girl's locker room and carrying a weapon to school. He had to be stopped before he could do any damage, like shooting up the school or raping girls (due to suppression of the natural sexual impulses). He must be watched very, very carefully.

His father, Darwain, who was proud of his own "Christianity," said one day in his Manhattan office, "He's unresponsive to me. I just can't relate to him—it's as if he came from a different father. I'm not trying to get out of my responsibility, but it's out of my hands now. God help him." Kincaid remembered Darwain's face was almost beet-red from his weekend of yachting off Long Island, and he wore a beret with his yachting insignia on it.

Kincaid knew Darwain was associated with the Covenant Association, an offshoot of the Brotherhood, which included the *intelligencia* of the world, with roasts and tutu parties as the prelude to a religion that Kincaid never really participated in, as he remained a skeptic regarding its supernatural claims. This was clearly a social situation, at his wife's direction, which led to more money and higher levels of responsibility. Even if there were people in space, and strange technologies out there, he worked *here,* "where the rubber meets the road."

"How are you today, Dr. Kincaid?" Casey asked with politeness and a self-possessed poise.

Kincaid was rattled. He somehow knew that this project was

the crux of his philosophy versus the high-technology mind control espoused by his wife and Bock Wiley. He *had* to make this work, had but a few days. He began: "I had a very good weekend, thank you for asking."

Casey looked at him with his hazel eyes and contradicted him, "You did *not* have a good weekend. *I* had a good weekend. Even in seclusion I had a better weekend than you, and I was not alone. You are alone, and you are full of sorrow, but I can help you."

This response was not promising, Kincaid felt. There had been several days of sensory deprivation, including no light, and before that weeks of violent videos involving Christians killing innocent people and some propaganda pieces showing Nazis going to church, intercut with death camps. Even his previous saturation with pornography with the hopes of transferring the patient's distaste for violence to the peaceful and pleasurable aspects of sexual play produced no response. There was no change, even when Casey was drugged with sexually stimulating agents such as Viagra, ephedrine and Ritalin.

"Look, Casey—"

"Yes, doctor." He did not mean to interrupt. He calmly looked into Kincaid's eyes with compassion and dignity and not a note of hostility.

"Don't you know what's going to happen to you if you don't change?"

"Change? Only the Holy Spirit can 'change' a man, and that's only if it's God's will. Change occurs in the heart first, and then the flesh follows."

"What is the Holy Spirit then?" Kincaid asked.

"The Spirit of God—don't you have a Bible?"

"I do."

"Well, He's listed throughout. For one thing, the Holy Spirit is God, I'm sure you've heard of the Triune God: Father, Son and Holy Ghost."

"Ghost?" said Kincaid, sure he got a morsel of meat for a change. "Do you believe in ghosts?"

"Or Spirit—look, you need Him and you don't even know it. He loves you even if you sin because He sent His Son to die for our sins. Understand? He's visiting with you now, and He will come to claim you if you're His. And he will hurt you until He gets your attention, understand?" Casey was smiling, the scars on his head no longer red from the constant electrodes and brain scans.

"Let me get this straight, Casey. You're threatening me from your *stronghold* here at the Institute? Don't you want to go home?"

Nothing from Casey.

"I'll make a deal with you—you act straight for a little while, do what we tell you to do, let us guide you in your development, and I'll personally let you take off anywhere you want for a week on me, okay? Please," Kincaid said, sorry that he used the word *please.*

Casey asked, "Have you ever been in trouble, in so much trouble that no one could save you—but then you felt at peace?"

"Like *you* now?" Kincaid said sarcastically, now completely amazed that months of psychological warfare had not at least done a bit more damage—to break him would take a *miracle* at this point.

"Yes, like me, *always.* You see, I'm not what you think. All your experiments won't have an effect. I'm not only *not* human, but I'm here to witness in a special way. Let me share my gift of prophecy."

"Don't you want to have a girlfriend? Go to school? Get a job at something you like?" Brand thought, even with the shaved head, Casey looked like a nice handsome kid—the *refugee product* of a wealthy family, or perhaps an artist of some sort, a socially acceptable misfit. He could not help thinking of Justin.

"This is my job, Doctor Kincaid—*you.* Your son is in trouble."

"You don't know that."

"I was given the gift of prophecy—and I have been tested. What do you think the *End Times* refers to? If you're here to deprogram Christians, that must tell you something about what's true, right? You're not here deprogramming Buddhists, right? Because what they believe, while it might be logical, isn't real. *This* is. God is in me and nothing can be done about it. I'm going to prepare the way—there are many of us—and then the Lord will come."

With that Casey seemed to be elevated off the floor! Brand shot out from behind his desk and looked at his feet. He was still on the ground—some sort of *mental glitch.* "Just sit down, Casey—let me tell you what's going to happen."

"I'm going to be sent to a place where they will kill me, and you don't want to hear that, do you?"

"Why would you say something like that?"

"They'll spend millions to accomplish my death, you know it and you won't admit it. Everyone else knows it."

It's true, Kincaid realized but could not admit this to himself.

"Only they won't just kill me—they'll torture me, more than you will, and they'll find out who I am, and they'll try to stop it—

God's warning, that is—which is the harbinger of truth. They're scared now, because I keep popping up everywhere."

Kincaid knew the treatments had formed these and possibly other delusions in Casey's mind. "Did your parents ever do anything worthwhile in your life?"

"Doctor Kincaid, sir. I'm sorry to disturb you. Would it be okay if we took a walk along that dirt road out there—it's my last walk. It might be good for both of us."

He doesn't even act like a child—he's fully developed, Kincaid thought. Perhaps it was the emotional aspect of life and growing up oddly different. In a distant conscience Kincaid might have thought him healthy...might have thought him fit for the world, as unconventional as he was. To the beat of a different drummer; he would have had a hard life, perhaps even, a heroic life, but Kincaid knew this thought must be banished. If allowed to fester, it might lead to a denial of all that was felt to be precious in this privileged and lovely world he had made. One might as well learn the way the world is and accept it, lest one become a fundamentalist, narrow-minded bigot. The way of the world, beautiful in its randomness, fashioned and fathomed by those far in advance of the social slave, and so we lay down in our finality, in our tethered and torn *psychogogic* cosmological ethos—the testament to the joke played upon the world by a 'cruel god.' So much better to do away with Casey than do away with the whole world! The world of man had rules, and if they were not followed, then bad things happen.

As they walked along the road, Casey showed Dr. Kincaid the early stars, "Those are angels," but as the sun set beyond the forsaken gorge beyond the institute, he looked worried. "So, will I be tortured now?" Casey asked.

"Why do you say that?"

"Because I'm different."

With every footstep in the magic hour of the sunset, there appeared to be the onslaught and seeping of a dread-like sickness, pervading all that was sacred for Kincaid. Something now seemed very wrong—something in memory, though Kincaid would say it was being foisted upon him by a petulant lad. "Why do you say that?" Dr. Kincaid asked.

"Because I'm not of the world. I'm of the Spirit. *Whoever shall save his own life shall lose it, but whosoever loses his life for My sake will gain everlasting life.*"

"I thought we took your Bible away," he said worriedly.

"You can't—it existed before the world was formed. Dr. Kincaid, you're dealing with the one who will kill you as sure as you walk with him who hates."

"Angry at me?"

"Of course not."

Kincaid responded, "Perhaps you should be."

"You haven't long to live—but you shall die serving God," Casey said with a loving and satisfied look in his eyes.

"I think we'd better get back," Dr. Kincaid said, cutting it short.

"Don't you know what they're looking for?" Casey asked. "Don't you know what they believe?"

"Who is 'they'?" asked Kincaid.

"Your tribe."

"I just don't understand," Kincaid said in a frustrated tone as he caught a glimpse of his wife's ruby red face reflected by the last rays of the sun against the bulletproof shaded glass of the research building.

"You like me, don't you?" asked Casey. "I don't wish you any harm."

"Don't you want to go home?"

"My home is not on this earth."

"Be honest! Do you want to be an island all your life, or a vital member of society?"

"I'm real, Dr. Kincaid. You've screened me now. I'm authentic." Casey paused and added, "Your son will die soon."

"You don't know that."

"I know you have a son, because he's like me."

"What do you mean, *like you?*"

"Your son and I, we're brothers, you might say. You can change, Dr. Kincaid. I'm not myself; I admit that. You won't kill me, I have perfect faith, not because of me, but because I'm born to do what I do now for the Kingdom of God."

Kincaid said: "When you came to me it was because you became a born-again believer, and your parents wanted to break the programming."

"Thank you for being frank," Casey said. "It's not too late. Remember *that* when you come looking for answers."

The fact that a seventeen-year-old could speak in this manner, and yet readily admit it's not him, but that he was born *different*, was interesting to Kincaid. He really didn't want to turn him over to Bock Wiley, the Nazi-styled hack, much less to a "doctor," lest he make him yet another assassin for one side or another.

"My name isn't Casey, but you'll find that out," he told Kincaid, who locked him behind the glass door near the day room. "You need to ask yourself why you're involved with me in a supernatural nightmare, because *something* is going to happen, *you* will be the cause, and God will judge, sir. All that you've seen, didn't it prove the opposite of what I'm saying? What did you learn about opposites in school, Dr. Kincaid?"

Kincaid stared at him through the glass door, then went to his office, gazed at the monitors of Casey—he was looking for something, a sign of truth. He watched while Casey spoke to himself and walked around his glassed-in cell with no apparent fear or anxiety.

Kincaid slurped a last minute scotch through the ice cubes and wondered what it would mean to toughen Casey up. If he did not know now that it was more than a reed bending in the wind, then when would he know? He did not want to lose Casey—he needed him. Casey would become his project, his *pet* project. He would show the world how someone so deluded, so utterly destructive, so lost, could be redeemed. He did not think this was some sort of neo-passé psychiatry thing; to prove the savage could be tamed was not the idea.

• • •

Dr. Bock Wiley walked in a crooked manner, as if one leg were longer than the other, Jackson Kincaid thought. He was always dutiful, and she admired him for that and other attributes, like having four Ph.D.'s (and numbers were what it was all about). Not only had he had garnered the National Science Foundation's prestigious Erin Grant for nearly a decade, but as far as she was concerned, the wonderful Wiley walked on water on a daily basis. It was unfortunate, she thought, that his face and physique did not match his achievements since she might be tempted—it would be an unmatched pleasure she was sure. But she would lose her grip on the undisputed leader of modern psychiatry, her husband. Yet Brand was only there because *she* put him there, and she had no compunction about doing what she needed to do to continue the *climb*.

"I don't want him to find out, but we really have no other choice," Jackson said to Bock Wiley in the lab.

Wiley knew he would get the call, either from her or someone else, perhaps back in Washington. But he knew he would get the call.

It wasn't that he was a team player, it was more that he was willing to go the extra mile. He had a team of government scientists and operatives who would see to it that the various experiments on inmates, for example, were profitable, even if damage occurred to the specimen, as he liked to call human beings.

"The boy is perfect, but Brand wants to keep him here—and he will fail. So I thought…" Jackson began.

"You thought right, young lady," Bock told Jackson Kincaid, exercising his sixty-three years like a man two decades younger. There was a twinkle in those cobalt eyes, and the disheveled lab coat and faded nametag were made more stylish by his tinted Bulgari glasses, which hung from a woven silver chain. He had a habit of continually sipping green tea in his office, which was filled with artifacts from China. Happy that he did not drink alcohol, Bock filled himself instead with a modest amount of caffeine. He was ecstatic to have the opportunity to work in secret in his own lab several levels below the surface of the earth. This comfortable situation was what he had always lobbied his CIA buddies for. The best they could do was either Los Alamos or some other site, such as the Nevada Test Site, even though he was conducting studies in the behavior of soldiers in battle.

"Jackson, Jackson, you have always been so loyal," Bock said. "I always told you your husband will go far. I would be delighted to assist with the boy."

"You know this Casey kid is one of them."

"We're still going to have a debate about that. If he is proven to be one of them, then of course he must be transferred to my lab in Maryland, and that would not hurt your husband's career, Jackson."

"So if he isn't one of them—"

"Then he can be brought into line, with the proper conditioning."

"Jennings and Marples will assist."

"I just might need someone to take out the garbage in case things don't go so well. You all right with that?"

Yes, she would have to be. She had heard of his distasteful techniques before. But had never seen them, or been responsible for them.

"You mean, if he—"

"No harm will come to that boy, unless he harms himself. And that's true of all my specimens."

twelve

Bauman had not been successful in locating Daniel, but he had made some headway investigating the kidnapping of Alice Garcia. Through his new network, which was incognito and inconsequential, low-key and forsaken, and located along the streets, in the alleys and near restaurant dumpsters, he was able to ascertain some very interesting information. For one thing, Ricky did not orchestrate the kidnapping. Though they were afraid of Ricky, Shep and John the Apostle knew all about the Pacoima 55's gang, and how they were used as runners of not only dope but weaponry. John the Apostle, the big, bristly bear of the homeless who knew the Bible, stated he recognized the boxes of stinger missiles. The kidnapping wasn't a case of being in the wrong place at the wrong time, what Bauman had originally thought—it was planned.

"I want you, John the Apostle, and you Shepherd, and all the rest of you to squeeze Ricky's territory and find out all you can. I'm going to see Pastor Ted," Bauman said with alacrity in front of the U-Store-It facility, his new headquarters. As quickly as they met, his network dispersed to the far reaches of his new beat.

Bauman's unique headquarters were all he could hope for. During daylight hours there was a convenient restroom, and he had found a hose he could use anytime for showering.

The wound on his face from his recent ricochet incident was resolved after Big Willy, the security guard, patched him up. Bauman's cheek wound was superficial; the piece of metal had taken a chunk of skin and kept going. It left a scar, but that was the least of Bauman's problems. Big Willy remembered how Bauman, who had been the local beat cop, had helped track down his car, which had been stolen in front of the Zippy Burger on Van Nuys Boulevard.

Willy was glad to have Bauman's company, but he did not understand what Bauman was talking about. To Willy, Bauman sounded like a lot of the cracked-up folks on the streets of Los Angeles. Willy felt he was doing his Christian duty to look out for him. A believer all his life, Willy's faith was his joy, and he wanted everyone to know Him as he did.

He blessed his mother every day of his life for making him learn God's word and His ways. He attended a Bible Study church not far from work; he liked the mix of skin colors and thought it proved something. Willy agreed with the pastor's message of obedience and especially his message about contentment, the lesson Paul teaches in Philippians that people don't need all that much to be sustained and joyous. One of the lessons of contentment, Willy remembered, is to be completely concerned about and to constantly submit to the needs of others. Bauman was simply his opportunity to put the teaching into action. Big Willy had allowed Bauman to call his wife from the office this past Wednesday. He felt sorry for Bauman, who believed, despite the fact she had hung up on him, that she still loved him. Bauman was using a mattress and a space heater that Big Willy provided. Although Big Willy wouldn't have allowed anyone else to live in the compound, he figured Bauman was an exception since he was providing a service, reporting anything suspicious. Big Willy, never a cop himself, understood that even if Bauman was cracked-up mentally (he reserved the idea that Bauman might not be, even with his strange behavior and new manner of speaking), that he was still quite valuable to the community.

"Willy, we're onto something big. I'm not just sayin' this—it's really true. Get ready for your new life to begin," Bauman told him.

"Hey, boss, got you some extra blankets—cold's comin' on. The mission had a bunch of extra food, so I thought I'd make that available too. Okay?"

"And another thing," Bauman said, taking the grocery bag as if it were owed. (As far as Willy was concerned, it was.) I want to make sure you find out why you've been held down so long. I'm not talking about skin color or anything like that, Big Willy, I'm talkin' about conspiracy—for millions of people! Now, how about helping with the stake out?"

"I told you, I can't do it."

"You told me that in the emergency room when I shot myself, but I always thought you'd see my point, that you'd—"

"Look, frankly Sergeant, I'm not sure what to think anymore. Okay? You scare me. I think you need help, man. Is it right for me to leave you here night after night—shouldn't I do something, call your wife?"

Bauman laughed himself silly. As the next private jet thundered overhead, blotting out the din and looking free like hope, landing a few blocks away, and as the sun set over the distant mountains that hemmed in the Valley, Bauman said: "That's a good one, chief. Look, you can't change anything unless you're willing to risk. This is big, and I can't tell you everything because I don't know all the answers. But there is one we have to find, and that's Daniel. Because he knows things. He knows where Alice is right now."

"And what happens if we find this place where they took Alice?" Big Willy asked as the phone in the office began ringing. "Just a second," he said.

Bauman, all of his police training still intact, was left on the street to observe the traffic—all six lanes, east and west. He heard a voice, which was becoming more familiar and helpful all the time, telling him to be especially watchful. He did not have to wait long. Right in front, attempting to enter the driveway, he spotted his wife, Sheila, and their fourteen-year-old daughter, Marta. From this distance, Marta, with her short, brunette bangs and blessedly thick hair, did not seem so rebellious, despite the piercings and tattoos, but she was smoking and looking like she hadn't a care. He wasn't ready for the escort, who was driving them in a new Ford 4-door pickup truck with all the fancy trimmings. The driver was not a stranger; he knew him, but he would not focus on that now, it could wait a couple of minutes. The pickup bed was filled with his own belongings: file cabinet, his dresser, and all his clothes were strewn about, including his crumpled unwashed uniforms. He was suddenly elated. He had thwarted the plan because she never suspected he would be there, of all places, hanging out at his wife's storage facility!

"I sure hope you're just helping out," he said to the man driving the truck.

The new driver looked guilty, and he was. Sure, he was tall, handsome, fortunate. Compared to Bauman, perhaps everyone was fortunate. When he spoke, he was polite, hesitantly so: "I'll... Will you please move; she wants to put some stuff in storage."

"Hi, sweetness," Bauman said to Marta. "Hi, Sheila—a little voice told me you might show up. Well, I got news for you. There's no room—it's a little cramped for you, know what I'm sayin', sweet? I missed you. But this mission's too dangerous. Buddy,"—the man with the pickup's name was Bud, he was sure—"please take her home and then you take off, 'kay, pal?"

She looked out at him through the window, horrified. His hair was matted, his face streaked with dirt, a fresh scar, red and scabbed, his shirt open and tearing into ribbons like the tail of a kite, creating holes under an armpit and along the shoulder line. The troubling thing was that he did not notice it. The dark hair and gray in his beard had started interlacing and his hair was now hanging about his neck like long, broken needles.

"What's wrong?" said Bauman. "I missed you guys, alright?"

Sheila got out of the car and approached her husband cautiously, as if he might be a donkey or an ostrich in a petting zoo. Not wanting to upset him. "I am so sorry, Phil. I am really sorry. Is there anything I can do?" she asked.

He looked at the sky and cried out gleefully, "Thank you, God! Thank you for that one piece of information! I have to tell Big Willy." He ran into the office.

• • •

He just wasn't the same, Sarah thought about her husband, Ted. He needed help. How could she continue to explain to the others that he wasn't himself, that something had changed in her too when he was shot? She felt that he should repent for the sermon he gave on the redemption of the few who are chosen and not redemption for all. It was one of the evil secrets he'd coveted, which he did not mean and for which he should repent. He needed the prayers now, in this time of recovery.

He'd always wanted an urban church, always wanted the six lanes of noisy traffic and the sprawl of Los Angeles. He especially liked it after divinity school in Texas, liked it more when the other pastor cautioned him about taking over. The crush of people of all stripes and colors and languages, those filled with superstition, those with religion, and those with temporal confusion didn't bother him. He welcomed the mission field of the electric valley, with all its people swimming in the unstable fishbowl. God is doing wondrous things here! God is vibrant here, he often told Sarah when she was pregnant with Carole and then with Beth. He'd always had a kind of bubbly positive attitude.

She noticed that his attitude wasn't so positive now. He seemed to have lost his touch, and she wondered if they should have let Alf Blicky continue being pastor. After all, he'd packed them in unexpectedly—he gave wonderful sermons, stories really, about conversions to Christ. One of them was a story about how an Indonesian girl's family was murdered in a church fire set by Muslim extremists. As a result there was a *jihad* or Holy War, which had continued unabated for years and years. He told how the young girl's picture was on the cover of *Time*, her body nearly half burned as she escaped the flames. He told how she prayed for her assailants, the very ones that killed her family, and how she forgave them through Christ—how she and the Muslim who started the conflagration met where he was incarcerated, and how he wept when she hugged him and said: "I forgive. I forgive you, brother."

The very next week the Faith Church was filled. Alf was tall and fit, a strappy fellow, very beachy, with stringy blond hair and a white mustache. He was married to Gwen, who was best friends with Ted's wife, Sarah, and a number of other women. It was Gwen, who had evangelized Sarah, and Sarah had met her husband, a young pastor named Ted Gunderson, in the church.

On the steps to the church, Sarah had asked in earnest: "Ted, don't you think you should let Alf do the sermons for awhile. I mean, you really haven't recovered from the wounds."

"Who is the head of the household, Sarah?" Ted asked while glancing at his open Bible.

"You're the head of the church as well."

"That's right—and it's my decision is to let elder Alf be an elder. If you want to become a deaconess, Sarah, then you could have a say—otherwise, I've heard nothing about my FITNESS TO PASTOR!" he declared angrily, as others turned away and pretended not to hear. "Sorry, Sarah."

"We need help, Ted. I'm scared."

He hugged her, then went to the bathroom and looked at himself in the mirror. He hoped no one would enter—somehow he knew that no one would.

The voice of the Holy Spirit told him that he was chosen. He had said that he, Pastor Ted, was to be one of the harbingers to serve the Lord by preparing the way for Jesus to return. He knew it was real. While on the toilet, he watched a line of ants carrying off a rather large carcass of a hornet. Some were out front, scouting and moving specks of dirt and other debris, so that the other ants could carry off the once threatening giant, the one-time Goliath. Those in front were alone, while the ants near the carcass were practically crawling over one another. Unity, Ted thought. Real purpose.

Yes, there are others, but I don't know them, he thought. There are many others—many! Perhaps hundreds or thousands.

"What is Christ?" asked his little girl at age four.

"What is Christ?" asked Carole at age six.

"What is Christ?" asked Sarah.

Who is Christ was the way it should have been asked, and he knew the Holy Spirit was telling him something, but he could never figure out what it was, until now.

What is Christ? It's a wave! It's every person. True, it is literally the Lord of Lords, Jesus Christ, who died on the cross at Calvary, who became sin, was punished by God the Father so that we could be reconciled to Him, thus ending the Fall through Adam's sin, and the one who will return to establish his millennium Kingdom and bring Heaven to earth.

But when one says "in Christ," then the term *Christ* becomes a what and not a who. So that means he did not answer their questions, because he did not know what he should have known. A wave, those in Christ are not stagnant but in a wave that transcends history—yes, that is what he would speak of today.

The beloved, a wave? he questioned himself.

We are chosen to be martyred and persecuted, and if we're not willing to accept persecution from the evil one, Satan, then we're not Christians. What they were was unclear to Ted. Perhaps they were even uninformed.

If they are not willing to *separate* themselves, or, indeed, if they are not separated presently, then they never were Christians. Now there was a message sure to end his career, he thought.

Perhaps, if they are not willing to pay the price, then they might not even know there is a price to pay!

Perhaps, if they are not willing to suffer, then they do not know the Lord at all. His Name is Jesus. That name is above any other. The Holy Spirit, which one receives upon truly accepting Jesus Christ as Lord and Savior, will teach all things to the brethren. Ted knew he could truly trust the Holy Spirit and not himself. The Holy Spirit delivers, not Ted Gunderson.

He would trust God for his words today.

He looked at himself in the mirror again as he brushed his teeth. Alf Blicky walked in and just stared at Ted.

What was he looking at, Ted wondered? My hair, my beard, my general appearance? Not the polished Christian of the burgeoning church? Not the gifted, clean-cut seminary student? So he's persecuting me because he wants my job; that was it, Ted knew. This is all pearls before swine. I forgive you, Alf. Go surfing. Kiss your pretty wife. You're young and strong and talented and God has blessed you well! Don't do this, Ted wanted to say, but did not.

"Ted," Alf started, "I'm...well..."

Look at him stammering—how he would love to take over, how he would love to stop the true message of Christ's return, the message that I have been holding for eternity. Ted's thoughts raged, though he continued to brush his teeth.

"How are you, Alf? Nice day today. Got one super sermon to give."

"Ted...pardon me for speaking up," Alf said.

"Why? You're going to do it anyway," Ted said with blatant hostility, throwing Alf off his strategy. In fact, silencing him for a moment as definite as a slammed door. Ted finished brushing, then rinsing. "Speak up, Alf, you knew I'd be in here, at least practicing in front of the mirror." Ted laughed hard. He looked in the mirror, messed up his growing, unkempt hair and continued: "I am the Way, the Truth and the Life, no man comes to the Father except through me—that's what got me through seminary. How 'bout you—oh, well, you're fortunate you never went to seminary. Or college for that matter."

"True," said Alf, "and that statement you just made refers to our Master, not you."

"I'm sorry, Alf. Forgive me. I tried to pull rank by saying it mattered whether you went to college or not. Please forgive me."

"Sure."

"Father, I want to repent—you convicted my snobbery, my sickness, and I am truly sorry. Please give me the strength to be gracious, let Your will reside in me—in fact, Father, I want to be more of You and less of me."

"Brother, listen to me. You wanted me to look out for the well-being of the church, right?" asked the tall, blond man.

Oh, caught him! Yes! Ted told himself. There it is—why should he even grace this man with a response? But one did come: "Judas, I suggest you go check yourself into another church, because this one doesn't suit you."

"Well, you give me no choice. We've had a meeting."

"You and the elders and the deacons and even the secretary? Without me, I might add—easier that way," Ted said, full of sarcasm.

"We think you need some time off. We're prepared to pay—"

"Oh, how generous of you, Alf."

"Listen to yourself!" Alf said worriedly. "Do you think you're fit to lead? Look, something changed in the hospital, or since your injury."

"You mean, Miraculous Recovery!"

"I can't talk to you about this now. I'm delivering the sermon today—you can either stay and worship with us, or..."

"Or what... This church was nothing but two sticks standing in fear of a stiff breeze, Blicky! I brought all these people here."

"The Lord did!"

"So the Lord works through the pastor!"

"Right!"

"Exactly!" said Ted. Ted checked his tie and coat—this evangelical church did not use robes or any ceremonious garb; it was simple, direct, and hopefully inspiring. Where the rubber meets the road, he used to say. All people of all walks of life are welcome, he said more than once.

When Ted exited into the hall where the offices were, the elders and deacons were lined up, staring. "Nothing to be alarmed about— I'm delivering the sermon. It's been decided."

"Wait a sec—" Alf tried to blurt out.

"No, they're waiting—let us pray," Ted said. "Dear Father, we thank you for our ministry. If any malice be in our hearts today, we let it go and forgive. We thank you for our church, for our fellowship, for our brethren. May we each do the Lord's work with a smile on our faces, with joy in our hearts, knowing that our Christ Jesus is returning soon. In Jesus' name we pray. Amen."

The echo of "Amen" went around the small contingent. Alf inspected all their eyes and found everyone leaning back to Pastor Ted.

"Okay," said Alf. "Praise God. He's working through you in a mighty way. I pray that this is the Spirit and not your own dementia."

"Will you listen to him? *Dementia*? Alf, you've been watching too many horror movies lately."

They all laughed. But Alf did not laugh.

They did not laugh when he took the pulpit as he did. Ted scanned the room, beneath the simple wood beams, the sturdy carpeted floor, the oak pews, the fullness of every face and every eye on him. The residue of last week's sermon, the waiting for the fall, the understanding and allowing God's love to creep in even where it was not wanted. Oh, the church is a hotbed of sin and disgrace, Pastor Ted thought upon looking—and he glanced away from their faces.

Sarah sat with Alf and his wife, Gwen, and another woman named Sheila Bauman, who Gwen had brought—one of her evangelical candidates. Someone she had known for a long time, who was in serious trouble in her marriage and in need of Christ.

It was Gwen who first cast doubt on Ted's ability to pastor. It was Gwen who was so proud of her husband, Alf, especially after his last blowout sermon that filled the pews and stuffed the coffers, and she had no doubt that they came to see Alf today, and *not* Pastor Ted. Indeed, Ted would ruin it. Like last week, and she noticed that this crowd had diminished slightly. Only her networking with the women's group and other phone calls explaining that Alf will be back and not to worry—to come this Sunday and they will see.

Besides, she was bringing another into the church. Truly this was glorious because it proved God's grace was evident in the church, and it proved, even with tremendous social pressure not to accept Jesus as Messiah, God was still calling in his own. Hallelujah is what she felt in her heart. *Hallelujah* is what she wanted to shout—but she could not if Pastor Ted caused them to flee.

This wasn't the first time the church had lost members, Gwen told herself. Before Ted was shot, they were losing congregation right and left. He was sad, and his heart was full of blame.

She wondered if she should take Sheila out of there right now. After all, she had been through so much, with her husband's breakdown and impending divorce. But when she sang the hymns, a smile perched itself on her face. She seemed riveted to Pastor Ted as he started to deliver his erratic sermon. Nothing was to be done about it now.

The more Sheila was drawn in, the more the words fell away.

Pastor Ted, imperious, spoke of another world in the midst of the current one.

"...And so, beloved, there will be no further sermons in this church," Pastor Ted preached, "because a sermon purports to teach God's word and God's will. You know, I am trying to show you God's ways, which are not our own. But you don't follow it. How many here know God's ways?"

No hands were raised.

Ted continued, tragically: "If even one of you were following His will, you wouldn't be here right now. You'd be out doing the Lord's work—you'd know you had a responsibility, heck you don't even own yourselves, don't you know that? You search around like a bunch of blind birds on a mission to rid the world of worms, those other than yourselves. You know not what you are."

They were leaving, one by one. Pastor Ted smiled as they did. Alf looked on at the other elders—strapped down, paralyzed.

But Sheila was intrigued.

He went on: "...You might as well cash out of the stock markets; you might as well sell your houses and cash in on your mortgages. This is prophecy. I am filled with the Spirit—and that frightens you, doesn't it! You should take your kids out of their schools, and you should not buy lottery tickets, never should have anyway. You are not good stewards, you are a fallen church, unworthy and probably not saved..."

At that point Alf went up to the stage, along with the other three elders and they turned off the mike. There was pandemonium.

Sheila Bauman stood at the stage, transfixed.

"Come on, honey, he's a sick man, it's nothing to watch," said Gwen.

Sarah ushered the children out. But Beth ran up to him, crying.

"You can't take me out of here! This is my church! Who will save you if not for Jesus! I am here to tell you that I have finally figured it out—all that seminary and all those sermons were fake! I've got it now—"

"Come on, come on! Look at your child!" cried Alf, almost in tears from seeing Beth sobbing at the stage.

"Now you listen to me, Alf, you can have the congregation. It's yours! But you don't know the way to Christ!"

He shook them off as the ushers emptied the Faith Chapel once and for all.

But Sheila stared at him. "Pastor! Pastor!"

"Leave me alone, Alf! Get your hands off me! It's alright! I quit, okay?"

"Leave then," cried Alf, with Gwen at his side.

"No problem."

Sheila followed him to the back. Gwen grabbed her, screamed at her to leave. "No, I will not leave!" Sheila belted right back and ran to the pastor's side.

"Pastor..."

Beth came running. "Daddy, Daddy! Please! Daddy, help me!"

That stopped him. He grabbed Beth, hoisted her up into his arms and made his way toward the back door.

"He's trying to kidnap your daughter!" Gwen screamed back at Sarah, who was already running down the hall.

An elder named Hap manned his cell phone and dialed 911.

Ted had not done anything wrong. He was simply caring for his daughter, they would say *after* he was arrested. He had been injured, and he had made a miraculous recovery, and his personality was changed.

He asked Sheila while holding Beth, "What do you want? Don't you see what they're doing now that I am real?"

Sheila took Beth from him and tried to soothe her—this was quickly interrupted by Sarah, who grabbed Beth and screamed back at him: "You're crazy—don't you come home again! Don't you come near us until you get some help!"

Alf and the others were praying in a circle by the door, while Pastor Ted stood staring off into the telephone wires in the back parking lot, the six lanes roaring by now, as two squad cars with lights whirling and sirens screaming entered the little lot with great force.

Gwen and Beth and even Sarah were in prayer behind Pastor Ted's back. Ted, whose eyes, flecked with tears, gazed aloft, his spirit soaring with the Holy Spirit. He knew.

It was a wave, and he had never experienced it, the peace that surpasses all understanding, the peace of God, the peace of the indwelling Holy Spirit. It wasn't supposed to be euphoric, which is what it was! It was euphoria, and waves of it. Ted knew this feeling was his first baptism, the baptism of the Holy Spirit. Tears flooded his face; he wailed in ecstasy. I'm not lost! You chose me too! I'll do your will, Father; I will do whatever you want me to do! It's euphoria above and beyond anything on this earth! That's why you can't understand it—this kind of peace is active. He was nudged aside in his body, and the Spirit looked out from the shield called eyes and said, "I will never leave you. I want to look through your eyes."

He turned so that the Spirit could look back at his congregation, as if not recognizing them. As the Spirit looked at the police and did not recognize them, as the blanket of love warmed and filled Ted to above his head, as he sunk to the ground on his face and wept for joy, he exclaimed: "Thank you, Lord! Thank you, Lord! Thank you, Jesus! Oh, I love you, Jesus, more than anything in this world!" Then he spoke in tongues—but in this case it was perfect Greek, then Arabic, or at least that's how it sounded—and then Hebrew! Sheila recognized it all, as she watched closely, so overpowered that she fell to the ground, face down, screaming. "Thank you, Lord. Thank you, Lord!"

She rolled over so she could see them pulling Ted Gunderson upright, the handcuffs on tight. "Praise God! Praise you, Jesus!" Ted screamed. "Thank you! At last! At last! I give myself to you, Lord—let me do Your will! Your will and not my own!"

"Sir, will you please get in the car—we don't want this to be any more difficult than it already is," one of the officers said.

"What?"

Sheila was still face down, screaming. She would be no problem for the second set of officers.

Gwen and the others watched with the scene with horror, but she recovered as soon as the cars were gone. She turned to her tanned and healthy husband (who was in shock): "Honey, you better get ready for the evening sermon." She smiled at him. "God's calling you now—this is *your church* now. And we'll keep praying for Ted, don't worry. I'm sorry I brought that Jezebel. She just didn't get it. I made God mad, didn't I?" she asked. "Alfie, didn't I make God angry by bringing Sheila, who was obviously unstable? What I mean is—"

Alf Blicky started walking away. His wife was incredulous—this was finally his chance and she was going to help him, just like it says in 1 Peter 3:1, "Wives, submit to your husbands." She was finally taking a subservient position. They'd gone to counseling; they'd been to pastors and prayer meetings. And he was not walking away from *her*, not now. She'd given up so much for him, she thought. She cried out: "Where are you going, Alf?"

Alf Jr., her sixteen-year-old son, looked lost. He was usually disheveled, almost resembled the drug addict she was afraid of. How it marked her, how it ruined her position for him to dress that way. "Alfie, go with your dad. Go on!"

Alfie pulled one earphone from his pierced ear. "What, mom?"

"Go on! Follow him! Bring him back!"

"Sure," he said, and his skinny frame followed in the direction his father had taken.

"Your wife is here, Mr. Gunderson," said Sergeant Jamison, a uniformed cop with a young face and a pleasing military resonance and civility. "Sir," he began, "we have no reason to hold you, or Mrs. Bauman. By the way, do you know how we can get in touch with Mr. Bauman, or...Sergeant Bauman? I understand you knew him."

"Sergeant Jamison, is it? You're not going to be able to set me back on the street, because I'm dangerous," said Ted, thumbing through an old *Church Today* magazine that one of the church members gave him. "Look at this—these will be the first to burn. Don't you understand, Sergeant, this stuff is real—it's all real!"

"Sir, we have no reason to hold you. You're free to go. I think your wife Sarah is in the waiting room."

"Well, I'm not going back."

"Sir, please."

"May I go to the restroom?"

"Sure. Right over there," said Jamison, pointing to a door in the back. "Well, you're on your own now—after you're finished you can see your wife in the waiting room."

"As you said. Son, do you believe in Jesus the Christ?"

"Sir, that's not for me to say right now."

"Not for *you* to say? Who is to say, sir?"

"I am a Christian. I just don't like to talk about it."

"Well, you better get on your knees and pray that you're really chosen. He gave me prophecy and I can see the church awash in blood. Why? Because you don't love him. You deny him! But it's not your fault. Let's pray right now," he said.

Jamison cringed, looked around. "Sir, if you don't leave now I'll have to remove you."

"Dear Heavenly Father, please help this one of your lost sons, he knows not what he does when he denies Your holy name. He knows not that I can see what you show me about the future, about this man's family—his son and daughter, and his wife—"

"That's it, sir! Is this some kind of trick—that crazy guy, Bauman, he put you up to this? Why, 'cause I took his job?" Jamison exploded, almost grabbing Ted, who sat in the chair next to the plain metal desk viewing the framed photograph of the officer's family.

Pastor Ted looked right down the pike at Jamison's baby blues, something awful came to his mind, now controlled, thankfully by God, and said: "You don't scare me, Sergeant—what good is prophecy if it doesn't strengthen the Body of Christ and edify the saints?"

"How do you know what you're saying! You spying on me? Who put you up to this?"

"I've been baptized, for the first time. I knew nothing before—I learned nothing at seminary, nothing from my ministry to the homeless, nothing from pastoring the church. The Word of God was lovely, and I needed it, but I never knew that it was not completely written yet, and yet it was, and yet it will be. I never knew how it communicated—what it was used for. I knew nothing! I've been purified now and no one can take it away. I can minister the truth—but no one will want that, will they, Sergeant Jamison?"

Jamison was already on the phone to his captain, suggesting psychiatric care.

Sarah waited alone, but she wouldn't have to wait long. Sergeant Jamison, the sprightly one, at least as long as Ted wasn't around, popped in. "Mrs. Gunderson?"

Sarah looked at him, almost through him, her eyes drained of tears. "Yes?"

"I'm afraid we've...well we've had a little complication. He's been sent to St. John's for psychiatric evaluation."

"You're kidding!"

"Well, we were going to let him go; apparently there was some sort of power struggle at the church."

"No, it was all a misunderstanding. I need him back, officer."

"Well, it's standard for those sent for evaluation to be observed for three days, and a staff doctor will be assigned. After that it's up to a judge to decide."

"What?"

"You can visit him at St. John's, ma'am."

She might have found more tears, but none came. She simply turned and walked out.

And kept going—out to the streets. Where she was observed.

Could it have been the trauma of being shot that changed his personality—was it the doctor's fault, she wondered? Was the pressure so great? Did she not see how he needed her to be more supportive and not so needy? She shouldn't worry so much about the kids—about everything. It was a sin to worry; it usually brought negative results. But that's what she did—worry.

thirteen

Cal was returned to Jupiter Beach, his plane returned to its harbor. Coates wasn't such a bad guy—he had arranged everything. He said they were in Florida, they had always been in Florida, and the plane had never left the Jupiter airstrip. Cal was warned that he should stop talking about what happened if he wanted to maintain his freedom.

Sally Anne, who lived a few doors down from him at the beach, wasn't dead. But she seemed different. She smiled a little too easily, he thought when he arrived. He walked along the beach barefoot, smiling at his strange trip. He knew that the black suits were messing with him—using him for some sort of psycho-warfare contingency, testing something, measuring—they were always testing, pretending, lots of mock reality stuff. He could take it—he'd done that.

He might even have been in St. Lucy—in some kind of laboratory. It was a wild assumption, but one that explained perfectly the lost time in the plane and being several hundred kilometers away from what he could clearly see with his eyes were the Florida Keys. Even his beloved Sam, still sitting on his shoulder, was decisively different. She just wasn't the same; she hardly talked anymore, for one thing, but she was dutiful as ever. No one could tame her to be like that, he thought.

She responded to her name. "So what do you think of goin' to see your mama, Sam?" he asked. She'd usually say something like, "Cornflakes taste stupid," or "Cocaine is illegal," or "The beer is too warm."

But today, nothing.

Nevertheless, the water felt good on his feet, and the bird could learn. Before he could get his favorite, "Tell me you love me, Sam," out of his mouth, Sam said, "Tell me you love me." He was satisfied now that everything was in order.

But still, he thought something was terribly different. Sally Anne's blonde hair was dull, tangled slightly in the back, her midday beer was usually hidden, her lines of coke usually in the bathroom, but today they were in front of him. A new boldness? Not caring? A maturing of her disease? Unaware?

She jumped up and down in front of that old gouged Dewey Weber surfboard, now a windscreen on the sand under a clump of dead palms. She ran out to him and kissed him—looking ten years younger. He noticed she was looking more and more beautiful. "Caleb, you dear man, I missed you. Thank you for visiting me, for making such a long hundred yard trip," she said, and her high today seemed quite fine. In fact, he might join her for a drink this afternoon.

"I feel like I haven't seen you in years," Cal said, kissing her, feeling the depth of his memories. He suddenly looked at the beach as if he hadn't been there in a terribly long time. It all seemed new.

He remembered ol' Bunny strutting around with his newfound bride, stumbling into the water just thirty paces from Sally Anne's shack—bought from his own exploits. He could see the ghost of Fred Fresco, the 1967 mayor of Jupiter Beach, and he remembered when Sally Anne needed help, and they took her up to Lauderdale with Frilly Martin and Baggs Ross and Sumner Phillips—all drunks and coke heads, just waiting for Cal to return with his marvelous candy. But she looked so much worse then.

"Darlin'," he talked sweetly, "you remember when we went up to Lauderdale, and you—"

"I don't remember yesterday, hon," she said while snorting up another line.

"Come to think of it," Cal said, "I don't remember so good either." He was smelling her—she'd always worn the same fragrance, a kind of L'eau du Temps, but not exactly—now it was perfume, high-class stuff. It was odd. And she had a dog. Didn't she have a dog? Yeah, his name was Dog. He was a mutt and she loved him, took him everywhere she went, even once to social services when she went for methadone.

"Where you been, hon?" she asked, pouring him a rum on the rocks in the one-bedroom cottage that seemed so new now, oddly—because it was a mess, but it still seemed new, even the papers and tools and dirty coffee mugs.

"Oh, on assignment," Cal answered.

"Yeah?"

"No, I'm not the candy man today."

"You don't need to be, Caleb," she said.

Always enigmatic, Sally Anne, who reminded him of a black and white Anne Bancroft movie, though Bancroft would certainly have to do some acting to capture Sally Anne. He kissed her, and suddenly he was flooded with fear. He took his drink, worriedly, then fled the house and wandered to the white-capped water's edge, far too beautiful a situation for the two of them, he thought. But in those days the beachfront was cheap. He'd had generous offers by big developers to build high rise buildings for the wealthy, but he didn't want to evict Sally Anne so no was his normal response. Thank you, no. Later.

What he meant was that it would be after she had passed on. Many friends thought she was dead and remembered a funeral—that was the reason he couldn't see Frilly Martin again.

"Say, Sally Anne, you ever see Frilly anymore?"

"I told you, there are no yesterdays for me." She snorted another line. Then popped a little pill and said, "Let's go swimming, like the old days."

They ran like a couple of kids into the 70-degree, soothing water. The air temperature was in the 90's and it felt good to grab onto her. He knew he'd been away now—because she had changed. "You working out—you seem fit," he said, puzzled.

"Sure. You thought I was dead, didn't you?"

"I never thought that, Sally Anne."

"Oh, Daddy, I can't leave you, you know that. I had to become immortal, you know what I'm talking about?"

She ran painlessly into the water—looking more like forty-five than fifty-five, and he knew he wanted her again. She was restored, not a fading and sickly junkie, but a new junkie with some life in her! He would have to get her some help, but this time it would work—he'd make sure of that. This time he would make love to her, no regrets, which was the way it used to be. This time would be different.

This time would be sacred. This time would restore them once and for all. He'd run another mission, just to shore up the finances, he thought, and this thought made him feel tired. He did not complete this mission. He did not know where his plane was, did not know if Sam was his parrot. He knew he had been *inside*. He knew it! A man named Coates was a shrink, he knew that much, but he could easily be pegged as covert. That's exactly what he must be.

He downed his drink but it did not stop the sky from turning a funny shade of purple, and he thought he was in the throes of a heart attack. He could see Sam (maybe it *was* Sam!) on the porch, just fine. Minding her own business, unwilling to fly away—that was Sam, no question.

When he turned back, Sally Anne was gone.

"Sally Anne! Hey, where'd you go, girl?" He looked around, came back to the house, spoke to Sam with a hint of worry. "Sam, this isn't the way it seems, is it?"

The bird sat there, as if not knowing a thing about Caleb Wilson.

"You're not Sam, are ya, girl?"

The bird stood convicted as promised.

"But that *is* Sally Anne, it has to be. She's so...perfect. She's so...casual. She's so...wonderful, don't you agree, stranger?" he now called the parrot. "Coates and the boys put you up to this, stranger?"

The trained bird sat happy and pretty as she could be.

He walked inside, and then it struck him—this was *not* her home. This was an abandoned, dilapidated building. No utilities, smudged and grime-caked sink, floors broken through to the sand below—it had been abandoned for years!

He looked around for artifacts, anything that could render him a sane man. He found a broken picture of Sally Anne, a torn photo album and some newspaper clippings.

He would not look again at the news—he would not look at the column in the *Jupiter Herald*. He would not look at the line that said that no one survived her. She had a survivor, himself. She had a place in this world—she belonged to Caleb Anthony Wilson! They might have had a divorce, but she hadn't been left with nothing, with no one! She had him, didn't she? He was there for her, wasn't he?

He was going to be. He had to fly a few more missions; he had to get the money, and then...

...so then they could be free.

He wondered why he got divorced. He thought he was in love.

It was silly—just infatuation. It didn't matter anymore what her name was; he thought he could not forgive a junkie, and when she...

When she went with....

No, he would not finish the thought. It was because of what she had been, because she needed a fix, and what she really needed was covering—no, she did not go with strangers, he told himself. Not ever.

He could not live with her betrayal once he found out and thought he was a fool among men. She did not understand, and he hurt her—and could never make that up. Everyone else was smart and he was castrated. Everyone else was high and he was submerged. Everyone else laughed and he took it, because he fell in love with a two-bit whore. He brought her drugs, and he couldn't be married and have children with her because she had had an abortion and the procedure caused *complications.*

"But look!" he said out loud to himself, "It doesn't say, Junkie, whore, call-girl, boat-wench, or anything like that. It says, *FOUND DEAD OF DRUG OVERDOSE, SALLY ANNE REYNOLDS. The one-time society heiress had fallen on hard times in Jupiter....married to Caleb Wilson in the 70's, lived alone on a beachfront property... developer Sid Sher had sued to force her into a sale...sisters Jennifer Reynolds and Stacy Benjamin have agreed to pay for the funeral services and cover the massive debts to credit card companies...thought to have committed suicide because of debt..."*

None of this was true! None of it!

He tore up the tattered news clippings. He shoved his hand through the kitchen cupboard and his knuckles bled. He twisted in the grimy, dusty, collapsing memory, and when he gazed out through the broken glass, he could see broken fences. The broken fence held a sign: SHER CONSTRUCTION COMPANY—14 NEW CONDOS.

He rushed out and ran down to where his house was but recognized nothing.

He looked back for Sam but the bird was gone. Like everything lately, nothing would last too long. He knew enough to think about it, but also knew if he did, he might not survive. He knew it all now, as he looked upon a row of beautiful beachfront condominiums, entitled aptly, The Sher Condominiums. He looked at the Sher Beach, and he looked at the sky—stars were twinkling in the daytime.

He studied the roster on the mailbox of the condos. Looking

for his house, for his nerve, for someone to kill?

He came upon one particular address that was very interesting. "Sherry Sher Coates."

Coates?

"Please help me remember! Help me remember!"

But no memory came. From the balcony overhead he could see Dr. Coates and his wife Sherry waving at him. Waving for him to come in!

No, way! He would not go. This was something terrifying. He'd been there before. Bad things happened there.

He started walking down the beach. Sherry, or he at least assumed it was Sherry (because she was arm in arm with Coates), laughed and sipped her drink, she and her husband both pointing at Caleb Wilson like he was some sort of circus animal! Confident overlords, perilous and beyond purview. Above the law.

Well, they would not have their way with him. He would get out. He kept walking and when he looked back, they were not on the balcony laughing.

He would not go back. He could not go back.

To what?

To things he did not want to know.

Down the beach, around the point, beyond the lifeguard tower, a man was walking toward Cal.

Cal recognized the ominous presence. There weren't many men Cal was afraid of, and to be afraid of this frail intellectual—a person Cal could not remember—simply did not fit. But there he was, bright as yesterday. The person Cal could not recognize, though he had to, was waving the way Coates and Sherry had waved; his diaphanous shirt, horn-rims and clipped-crisp balding head—this casual confidence was something to behold.

Cal thought he had gotten away from him, and he wanted to run the other way, back toward Coates, but he thought they might be coming after him from that direction. They were his bosses, he told himself.

If only he had access to his plane, which was all the way over in Miami being serviced, Coates had told him. That was a lie.

He was coming closer now. It was him: Dr. Wiley.

Dr. Gerald Bockwaite Wiley. Cal started to shrink into himself for the first time since the war. He remembered St. Lucy and all the carnage; Dr. Wiley made all time collapse; he made all things pervert to insanity.

That's how he knew that the opposite of sanity is perversion, because perversion is nothing more or less than insanity, but some folks would like to make it normal. The perverse is the inverse and, in their manner of thinking, its *opposite* is evil. The perverse is *preferred*, and its inverse, sanity, is scorned. Perversity and weakness were cousins, kissing cousins, no doubt. Dr. Wiley had once explained it pompously, guardedly, because no one knew what he had meant, not then.

But now...

As he turned around, he saw Coates and several armed military men, dressed in ski masks and sporting machine guns.

He sank onto his knees and kissed his mother's grave. She gave him the way, but he wouldn't heed. In Nam Syke gave him the key but Syke got shot. What kind of reward was that?

"Ah, but son, he had a smile on his face. He had the Spirit of God on him," Elizabeth Wilson, his mother, had said when he described it to her.

"But mother—"

"No buts," she said. "Come on, Caleb, your pride isn't going to get you out of this one."

He stayed on his knees and silently prayed: "Dear Father, this is your rebellious son. (Go on, son, go on—that's it!) I'm in some trouble with my life—it's at a close. I'm old enough that I shouldn't care, but I don't want to die with nothing—without you, if you still want me, Father. I...I'm sorry for everything I've done—I can't hold out, I give up, Father. I'm sorry, I got nothing left, and you know it—I know. If you don't help me, I....Oh, Father, help me, please. Oh, Jesus, I'm sorry. Please help me. Please help me, Lord God Almighty."

He could see Coates had Sally Anne. There was nothing he could do. "I'm sorry, Sally Anne, I'm sorry! I'm sorry I lost you, I love you! Don't you see, I love you and I left you to die." He rolled into his wailing of tears, sucking up the sand and sprawling helplessly onto what felt like the coarse sand of Jupiter Beach.

It did not matter what it was.

"Mr. Wilson, do you really think God can help someone like you? After what you've done?"

Yes, it was Dr. Wiley's voice. He could smell the sweat of those around him, and soon they would be picking him up. Instead he felt a sharp pang, and he spun about to see the hypodermic needle, and a smile on the nurse's face, the same woman with Coates.

"Mr. Wilson, you ready to renounce God now, or do you need more proof that He does not exist?"

"He *does* exist! My mother—"

"*Your mother* is the memory I gave you."

He looked up, and Bock Wiley's face was bearing down, leering lecherously, no leeway and no quarter. Full of optimism.

"Who am I?" Cal asked.

"Whatever we decide—and that can be changed whenever we want it changed. All your memories are mine, even your mysterious friend named, as only a psychiatrist could name a man…Syke."

"Holy God, please help me," Cal went on desperately. "Our Father, who art in heaven, hallowed be Thy name—"

Bock Wiley said: "Nurse, that did not do the trick."

Soon there was another prick, and he looked up and could see no one.

He could *not* see. Period.

Cal continued: "Thy Kingdom come, Thy will be done, on earth as it is in heaven, give us this day our daily bread, and forgive us our trespasses, as we forgive those who trespass against us, and lead us not to temptation, but deliver us from evil, for Thine is the kingdom, the power and the glory, forever and ever…Amen."

Cal remembered something just then—it welled up in him, a wave of warmth like a blanket on the inside, and it covered him outside too. Then it was all over him, and he could look up and look at them, and they could look at him and he could step aside when the Voice spoke to him, and him alone, and said, "I want to look through your eyes." And he said okay, and moved away, watching this unknown presence within him looking out at those who would harm him.

He knew this was the first time he had ever encountered what he could consider God.

The Voice said: "Caleb, you're my son. I love you and I will never leave you. Look, you can remember now."

He looked around, and he knew he wasn't in the same place. He knew now this was not Jupiter Beach, and he knew that this voice wasn't some programmed, implanted, false voice that had led him astray so many times.

They were smiling at him, sure they had him pegged.

Yes, I know that's not sand under my bones, he told himself, but would not let on to them.

Yes, I know you're Dr. Coates and you're Dr. Bock Wiley, and this is some sort of deep dark secret place in the middle of some-place I'll never know—and I flew missions for someone and wound up here—

"Look, you're doing fine, Mr. Wilson," said Dr. Bock. "The mission was successful—it's time to be debriefed."

He opened his eyes, finally. He wasn't in some shrink's office, and he wasn't at the place they took him after his wife died, he could admit that now.

The name of the place was clear now, though it had been hard to remember. It was called the Serin Institute.

The Voice said: "No matter what they show you, do not believe it. I love you, and I will not leave you again."

"Dear Lord, I'm glad you didn't leave after they... "

"Yes, my son."

"After they... they made me..."

"Don't believe what they show you," the Voice said.

More time passed, but he still couldn't open his eyes for some reason.

He finally woke at the sound of a Patois accent, and when his eyes were open he could see an open fire. There were shadowy people milling about—it was a camp.

He tried to sit up and felt a cold compress on his head.

Then he saw the bars before him—they were outside milling about; he was in some sort of prison cell, in a camp, and it looked like St. Lucy.

"Hello! Hey!" he tried to get someone's attention.

A few words in Patois, the sound of a woman, he could see her face against the candlelight glow. A few more words from the man named Gabriel, the leader it would seem.

A few more words from an American, and he heard: "Look, I can't take him right now."

Then a few words in Patois.

"I don't care."

Gabriel said: "He killed five thousand of our people."

That couldn't be...not about me, Cal said to himself.

"He did it with his own free will," said Gabriel.

"That doesn't make him one of them."

"He himself is one—did you enjoy your ceremony, Senator?" Gabriel asked.

From Cal's vantage point, the figures were shadowy, a glint of firelight, a glint of hopelessness, a glint of despair. There were two or three in white robes, which looked splotched in red, and they hurried into a helicopter. He knew it was a helicopter because he had heard the whir of the blades, and the wop-wop of what sounded like an old Huey, the sort they used in Nam.

Suddenly, Gabriel's face was framed in the door. "Hello, Mr. Wilson. I suppose you would like to see what you have wrought, eh?" He laughed and opened the gate.

By now Cal was beyond fear. He was prepared not to believe whatever they put in front of his eyes, but the Voice he had heard before and needed was gone.

The dawn crept over the mountain tops and over the banana plants. The helicopter door was opened—when he climbed in there was no one. Just a pilot.

And an envelope on the seat.

"Are you an American?" was the first thing he asked the pilot, who kept his eyes on his controls and said nothing.

Up they went, high into the new sunrise. Whatever they had done to him, whatever kind of cockamamie experimentation they had been conducting, mind control, torture ops, whatever—that was it! He was sick of it and he wouldn't do anything else, no matter how much money was involved.

The ride only lasted five minutes. When he arrived, all the bodies of all the victims were lined up in neat rows.

"Please get out," the pilot said and would not look at Cal.

"Why?"

The pilot turned and was holding a pistol. "Please get out now."

Cal obliged and left the helicopter.

He stood in the middle of at least a thousand corpses of young men. Neat rows, expertly arranged. All right, it was Intelligence, that's what it had to be.

He ran through the middle row and headed for the forest beyond. But he was met by a military commander named Jack Ritali, a two-star general who had something to do with germ warfare in the Gulf. He slowed and hoped for much-needed relief.

General Ritali looked right through him. He snorted a line of coke and smiled. "You killed all these men."

Cal looked at him—and knew not to believe. "No, sir. You killed them. Germ warfare?"

"It was broadcast to the temple. Look," said General Jack, pointing to an array of television cameras.

Cal knew the proper response: "Who do you think you're dealing with? I was on a snowball mission and you stole my dope. Why don't you explain it to Harrison and Bernstein; it was their deal—and they're waiting on it in F-L-A."

"You're in denial. You killed all of them."

Cal looked over at what now seemed like thousands of young black men dead in the field, with no visible scars. Dear Lord, You told me not to believe what they said, he told himself. You told me not to listen, and I'm not going to. Oh, my God, it's a slaughter of innocents. I have to...I have to stay sane, Lord. Please make me stay fit.

Watching Cal and the general on the TV monitor proved illuminating to Bock Wiley. He had gotten the call to come up to Serin in order to intervene and "break" a new adolescent who appeared to be the real thing. Perhaps he was just another sacrificial lamb—all that would have to wait until the St. Lucy situation was complete, he told himself.

The St. Lucy *sacrifice* was stupendously successful and coincided with the lunar eclipse. Something an idiot like Kincaid would never understand. He never had what it really took to enter the inner sanctum, and that's where the holographic universe comes to life. And the victims, as usual, are all the fools who follow Christ!

Bock laughed, toasted the others in the room. "Praise our lord."

One of them, a doctor named Raj Shupa, looked around. "We've pushed it back at least a few hundred years."

"To Jehovah. The Distant. The Impotent," said Bock, laughing. "Watch his reaction when he finds out that he really did fly the plane that dumped the poison!" Bock was enthusiastic.

They watched as one of the general's men arrived in a golf cart, and a TV truck followed from the side, shooting Cal Wilson's reaction to seeing his own plane sitting on a nearby runway.

Bock and company clinked their glasses when they saw the dumbfounded look on Cal's face as he inspected the pontoons on the seaplane and found two long canisters about ten meters long and three meters in diameter strapped to them. On the label was a skull and crossbones with a big smile on its face. Cal recognized it from his military days. It was poison, plain and simple—only these were high-tech, propulsion emission, and had to be activated and regulated by a ground crew. Two little canisters made carpet bombing obsolete, unless it was for show to the media.

It was *his plane*, and *he flew it*. He started to remember it in kaleidoscopic terms. They, the young men, were standing in the field in their white robes, cheering the plane as it approached. Then some tried to run as their friends and family members beside them fell dead the instant this toxin touched their skin or lungs.

Back in the media room, Bock and his colleagues laughed heartily when on the monitors they saw Cal fall to his knees and grab his head.

"I win!" said Raj.

A second shot revealed a silent Cal, a stone-cold zombified Cal. The men lifted him up for the camera—he stared beyond it.

"You might have won. I think he's about ready to fly for you, Senator," said Bock.

Senator Diane Mitchell and Dr. Jackson Kincaid were among the observers. Mitchell turned and smiled. "We're going to have a glorious crowning of the Pyramid. The elders will surely be impressed!"

"To Bock Wiley, ladies and gentlemen," said Jackson Kincaid.

"Welcome, Jackson, to the inner sanctum," Senator Diane Mitchell said. "Most do not understand ritual warfare and have no stomach for it. I know, I know—you haven't officially been initiated into the club yet. It's mostly a men's club—and that's why your initiation is so special."

"Well, my husband clearly doesn't belong. One of us had to...to do the right thing," she took a pause, then chuckled a bit.

"And your husband will remain a dutiful servant. Most of them are. Only a few can see what you've seen. We need and honor our servants, don't we gentlemen?"

All raised their glasses reflexively.

"I thank you for the opportunity to serve, Senator," said Jackson.

"Oh, let's stop with all the small talk and go out and party!" Bock said.

"I won," said Raj. "You said he'd last a few more rounds—I knew his God could not save him."

"What God?" said Bock, laughing. "*Science!*"

"And what is God, except for us?" added Diane Mitchell, the senator.

fourteen

To state that Arles Dubailles was more than a government agent would be understating the obvious. He was a skilled actor; he could appear as an angel of "light" for the St. Lucy male virgin sacrifice and promise them a great spiritual awakening at the same time—because he was, after all, the "Angel Gabriel." Voodoo ritual, which had roots in Haiti and Jamaica, owed its existence to the mix of African tribal religion and Catholicism and sometimes combined with traditional black magic. Arles had been a student of comparative religion at Columbia University, got his master's degree in African linguistics at Yale, and later studied all the manifestations of the Patois language and its evolution in the Caribbean at Harvard.

He loved playing his part, and his children loved watching him dress up in various costumes. Every day was like the dreaded "trick or treat." Even before the mansion, while still in the townhouse in Georgetown, Arles Dubailles and family were considered one of the premier African-oriented families to ever participate in what was perhaps euphemistically called the *inner sanctum.* Should secrets ever be divulged, of course that would mean death. Many, many initiates Arles had known simply did not make it. A slip of the tongue here, being at the wrong place there, a kind gesture or even attending the *wrong* church were all punishable by death, especially anyone involved in worship of "the Nazarene," he who is called Jesus.

Arles had transcended his culture. There is no racism when dealing with levels of reality so far beyond the warp and woof of every-day cognition that it would even boggle Arles Dubailles' mind if he dared to think about it. Fortunately, it was unthinkable, unspeak-able and undetermined—it had to be like this. He had become a millionaire many times over—all because he looked the other way a few times, all because he could orchestrate, all because he was a warrior who balked at nothing and therefore became indispensable. It was all because of finding, or being found, to serve a body of distinguished people of the world who were involved in ritual of the highest order, which continued the practice of human sacrifice, as it had been performed from time immemorial. To Arles, this was un-derstandable—his mother taught him: "Arles, learn the way people are and then fit in."

What better example to his own mother's advice than that which he became? His parents had been the product of poverty. His father, Alfonse Dubailles, was an immigrant from Jamaica who worked odd jobs in Harlem so that Arles could graduate Yale and move on to Harvard, where he was the only black man to participate in the Etruscan Society, an old pan-European mystery cult that had been rumored at the time to be connected with the drug and slave trades and had ties to Washington's elite.

He entered one degree and then a second. Each degree was an initiation into a deeper circle in a seemingly endless maelstrom of concentric circles, of which the *inner sanctum* would have to be at its center—or *axis mundi*, as the Etruscans and the elite called it.

When it came to defecating on the Bible, open at the beginning of Christ's ministry in the Book of Matthew, he graduated with honors. When it came to the orgies, the foul tête-à-têtes with digni-taries (as he became a Washington errand boy before he was moved up into the secret service), they were not only a snap, but enjoyable. Death was not so bad once he had sampled it. It wasn't as if the people who died deserved to live, usually they were only children, and hopefully good, God-loving children at that—this was the hoped for plan.

Arles was so gifted he did not mind being rejected by his father, who was ashamed of him as a "token Negro." Ashamed of him to the point of dying of pneumonia, a funeral which Arles seemed to forget about. He did send his mother a check for a hundred thou-sand dollars after that, and indicated through his secretary that he would send more if she needed. She sent the check back ripped up, and that was the end of it.

"To *be* heathen," he was saying to Senator Diane Mitchell before the St. Lucy operation, "is to be a caste below even animal life. This is why I take such pride and pleasure at my particular craft."

"I'm not sure I'd have the stomach for it," she commented.

"You don't have to, you're part of the circle." At that particular cocktail party, bits and pieces of truth were swirling about the room and in the evening air. Mitchell was stunning in Halston; Arles was a gem in a tux. The celebrants were magnificent as one perfectly ordered body.

The circle, as it was called, *was* the *inner sanctum*—where, Arles had heard, the so-called blood of Christ would be cultivated. He was not supposed to know this, and he did not ever mention it when his knowledge was tested. According to his superior, Dr. Prine of Greenwich, Connecticut, there were thousands of degrees, or levels of initiation, of which Arles knew nothing. Arles was a servant, and a darned good one at that, said Prine, "But keep your apron on, nigger—they'll never let you in."

Was he shocked at this statement? No. It was yet another test—they were always testing like that. No one, of any color, was to owe allegiance to their form, to their background, to their families—one's allegiance was only to the circle—to the brothers and sisters who were fellow initiates, period.

Arles' special gifts had helped him rise up and through so many times before, at Columbia, at Yale, at Harvard, in Harlem, in Kingston—he knew how to be all things to all people. He knew how to do things for people. He knew how to fix things. Build things, get rid of things. Things *they could not do*, either because of fear or lack of skill, or even...by conscience, because of birthright and the doctrine of "not getting one's hands dirty."

That left plenty of room for someone eager to learn the *true* way of the world.

The high-level training as a government operative combined with his Caribbean skills made him a good and ready candidate for the ongoing operations of the slave trade and the ritual trade, both of which paid vastly better than the Secret Service, which was, in Arles' own words, "filled with stupid jocks who wouldn't understand illumination if it burned their retinas and creased their backsides."

Arles was, if anything, an astute climber into the stratosphere of inner circles and higher realms of initiation. Even some presidents have had more than a bow before the great power and pontiff, whom

Arles happily served.

He wanted to know more. He knew that this power superceded all the world governments; it was truly its own godhead, not to mention the off-world entities (Arles could only imagine) it served. But for now, the Frères Rouge, the Brotherhood of the Blood, the Brotherhood of Light, or simply *The Brotherhood*, which to him was the true *holy grail*, would be his next conquest. He had done more for them than most of the *members*, who were obsessed with only one thing.

He was not supposed to know what that one thing was. He was not supposed to know how it all connected, and he was not supposed to figure out the wild rumors that there were others. The mysterious out-of-this-world others had conquered the physical realm and were immortal, or skip-jumpers—who took on the bodies of others to continue the work of the Super-Intelligence, the creators of Enlightenment. The Brotherhood was in charge of all of it, and worship always belonged to their ascended masters, which stemmed from Greek mystery schools with their hermaphrodite priests, all the way to the Washington Monument and beyond. History had simply been changed to reflect the Egyptian culture as a race of super-human slaves capable of finding, then lifting the stones to build the sacred pyramids—all to a perfected degree beyond the skill of the most notable architects and builders today.

The universe, large as it is, had been conquered for some time by beings that had been referred to as *angels*. Not that he knew, but he guessed that Lucifer was the being referred to as the head of the fallen angels, and he was an immortal being. He would come as ruler of the earth, an angel of light, gate-keeper of total potentiality (How could anyone deny that this was what life was all about, he often thought.). Lucifer was in charge of the earth for a time.

And that time could be expanded by the Brotherhood.

Arles knew full well that he worked for him, or the people, at least, who claimed to serve him, though he had never had contact with a being named Lucifer. He would, however, privately believe that all the supernatural stuff was more scientific principle than Luciferian hoodoo-voodoo. Arles knew he loved himself, served himself, worshipped himself, and sacrificed his early principles so that he could elevate himself.

Innocence is what they wanted—and he prided himself on providing the complete opposite from a term he hated: *holiness*. Children, virgins, good-hearted people, adults who were pillars of the community, these were the ones they wanted, especially Christians.

For Arles to progress any higher in the organization, the ones sacrificed had to be true Christians, with perfect faith.

When he returned to his Washington, D.C. home, he was greeted with an urgent message and a surprise from his wife, Mary Sue, and children, Samuel and Rachel. Their surprise scared him to the bone because he had eliminated surprises from his life.

The limousine dropped him at 7:15. The snow was glistening as he stepped out and pulled his cashmere coat around his shoulders. He marveled at how beautiful and pristine the neighborhood was. His turn-of-the century Italian revival house was an acquisition he had never imagined having and was something to behold with its seven bedrooms and ten baths. He was greeted by his manservant, Baupàz, a dutiful immigrant who was pliable and amiable, an unlikely mixture of Turkish and Basque.

"It's a cold one, isn't it, sir?" Baupàz asked strangely.

"Baupàz, do we have any Russian Vodka—I'd like that."

"Of course, sir," he answered, admiring his tall, handsome and successful employer. The manservant was convinced Dubailles would be a prince someday.

"And I'd like some caviar and champagne for later. Also, please call Michel and order some of his salmon tartare and that faux crème desert, will you?"

"Celebrating, sir?" asked Baupàz.

"Not particularly. And get yourself a single-malt from the spirits room."

"Thank you, sir," said Baupàz.

In the den, Arles was served his caviar and hi-grade Vodka, ice-cold, as he liked it. The beluga was a special treat sent over by *friends* in Moscow, the still-functioning *old boys*.

"Say, Baupàz, where is everybody tonight?"

"Oh, they're getting ready."

"Ready for what?" Arles asked, snuggling into his leather chair with the *Wall Street Journal.*

"I think it's your birthday, sir. And by the way, I got you something interesting." Baupàz produced a jar of tea from Sri Lanka, in a candy wrapper the likes of which Arles had never seen. He knew Mr. Dubailles would love this, since every morning he insisted on Ceylon tea and lemon, which would not be complete without Damascus dates.

The phone rang. Baupàz handed him the portable and left the

room.

"Hello," said Arles Dubailles, looking forward to an invitation to the secret temple, a long awaited privilege.

The voice said: "You're a marked man," and hung up. Arles leapt up quickly.

He turned around in the library/den, festooned with a museum-grade tapestry that one might well expect in a "quality" European home, to see a rather unimposing, unobtrusive man with a long gray beard and hair.

"Ah, yes, Mr. Dubailles. Still believe that the supernatural *does not* exist?" the stranger asked.

"How did you get in here?" Dubailles demanded as he quickly grabbed the phone and dialed his control at the office.

"Yeah," came the gruff voice.

"Alan, was this your idea or the senator's?"

"You're not supposed to find out about that yet."

"Look, I am *blue*, right?"

"Blue as blood, and ignorant of truth."

"So what do you want?" he asked, fear increasing with every breath. Dubailles had never been afraid in all his life. He had never let them down, after all.

"Happy birthday, Mr. Dubailles!" said the voice on the phone.

Dubailles bristled. "Listen, there's a man in the house—he's threatening me." He spun around to find...

Nothing. The man with the long hair and beard was gone. Or he never came.

"N-never mind. Not a funny prank, Alan, my house is always secure, you got that?"

He walked across the polished teak floor and over the Huriz rug to look out the bay window; he could hear someone hacking, or trimming the leafless hedge!

Opening the window, the cold was threatening like a block of ice, he peered through the sticks that would one day be green again. Standing in what would be a lovely garden in spring was a man with a long gray beard and gray hair; he was wearing a white linen robe and clipping the bare hedge!

"Hey! You! What's up, man!" he yelled from his perch.

Nothing, no response.

"Hey idiot, I asked you a question!"

The man just continued to clip the hedge. Dubailles drew a pistol from the Louis XIV desk drawer and aimed it out the window. "You want me to blow your jerk head off or what?"

The man looked at him with ancient eyes, completely immune to the cold, then went back to his hedge trimming.

Dubailles turned and ran for the door just as his wife Mary Sue came to the door. "Hon, hi." She kissed him. "Happy birthday." She clearly wasn't dressed yet, and he anticipated at least a bit more fanfare. "What do you want to do?" she asked.

"Like I told Baupàz—settle back, enjoy some catered goodies. Where's Sammy and Rach?" he asked.

"Oh, I almost forgot—I need you to fix the DVD in the theater. Could you come now, please?" she said.

"Did you hire a gardener?" Arles asked.

"What are you talking about?" she asked worriedly.

"Well, look!" He grabbed her and went over to the window.

"No wonder our heating bill is through the roof—you leave the windows open," she said, while looking outside and seeing no one. "What am I supposed to see?"

"He's right there!"

Arles gazed out the window and saw nothing. "I am really, really upset."

"Why?" she asked, stroking his head.

"Did Baupàz bring someone here—I mean, there was someone in this room who threatened me! Was that supposed to be a birthday surprise or something? I thought it was the boys at the office—but—"

"There is no one here," she said in a worried tone, and he caught that worry.

He grabbed her, spun her around. "Don't lie to me."

"I'm not lying," she said. "I've got to get ready for dinner. Please fix the kids' DVD. They're freaking out." She brushed her dark hair back, had already covered her mouth with deep red, which he liked. She was getting ready for *something*, but he didn't know what, and that just didn't happen in Arles Dubailles' life. Not ever.

She scurried out—he could see that she was worried, which made him feel better; he was pleased with her. He had learned to wait and see what developed. It wasn't beyond the office to play tricks. Or to test!

He thought it had to be some sort of test, a pre-initiation trial. He wasn't going to give them the benefit of the doubt. He finished the drink, poured another one, and calmed down. He opened the office drawer, poured out two lines of premium cocaine, took his snort, and got himself in a kind of floaty-light party mood.

Once again, he heard the hacking of shears outside. He looked out and saw the man. "Say, my friends at the company put you up to this—you don't scare me—your gag's over, alright?"

The old man in white linen replied: "You are an enemy of God. And you will be slain. This is a judgment."

"You guys just don't get it, you dumb geezer." Arles was laughing now, enjoying his one-upmanship. "Go back and tell Alan that whatever he's paying you, I'll double it if you scare Senator Di and I'll double that if you'll threaten the President."

He slammed the windows shut and laughed to himself.

He quickly left the den and went to the media room, a theater replete with row seating.

The man with the gray beard and hair sat in the captain's chair behind the video control panel.

"Welcome," he said.

"I'll kill you if you don't get out right now—"

The ornate movie screen lifted up and suddenly, huge letters leapt out in gold and red: HAPPY BIRTHDAY, ARLES!

When Arles turned around, there were two hundred guests thronging the room. His sponsor, Senator Diane Mitchell, and Josh and the boys from the agency. A cake was wheeled in and out popped a nude woman with pasties. She started dancing around the room.

The kids, Samuel, sixteen, and Rachel, thirteen, stood and watched—almost with bored contention. As a Pee-Wee Herman film came on the theater screen, Rachel danced around with the buxom girl, who was making sexual advances to Arles.

With the film as background, disco music began and the crowd, elegantly dressed in Karan silks and adorned with Tiffany rings, twirled and swayed. Waiters scurried among them serving the most expensive liquor and wine. Amid the party buzz, Arles thought about his mother. What kind of life would he have wanted if it could have been given to him, as it was to nearly everyone else in the room? He had chosen this one, but he had had to work very hard to get the recognition he felt he so richly deserved.

There was more to consider, more to take stock of. Would there be the usual ceremony, the usual orgy, the usual sacrificial victim somewhere late at night? Would the victim wind up in the smoky haze of yesterday's buried news, neatly wrapped with cords after having been dismembered by chain saws and disposed of in the Potomac? The large noose going down, never to pop back up again, tethered for all eternity, while the bacchanal went on despite all efforts to stop it by those who would be reformed. Was that to happen this night, he wondered?

This event was to be a triumphal entry, a reward for the thousands of male virgins on St. Lucy. It was to be an *epiphany*—the *coup de coup*, the ultimate excellence—all the difficult duty that no one else, not even the generals of the "family" would or could do, except, of course, for their initial inner sanctum initiation, which involved gutting innocents right up the esophagus.

It wasn't going to be a straight shot; it was no pleasure vehicle on a destination to the inner limits of sanity, of handling the thing opposite of what he knew was good, or what would be good for *his* children, or what he had to forget. A lot of them had had a head start, from their parents, from *their* parents' parents and from *their* ancestors and all the way back—not bloodlines, not exactly. They had the gift of guiltless sin, but they dare not call it that, lest they be deceived and lose their place in carnal immortality, forever and ever.

Arles was drunk and high on drugs and sexuality. His children had been dismissed for now. One day *they*, like all privileged children, would have to be initiated, which would be another test. Should either one of them show promise—and of course they would, he thought—they could slide into this class without problem. He would then be elevated further, buoyed by what might be called Tradition. All was fair in love, and loving the world was the key. Arles loved the world; he loved it very much.

•   •   •

They'd been watching him for some time. He'd been in and out of sleep, and each time he nodded off to sleep, the plan was to blast him with loud music, voices, and static—this went on for days. Casey Burns Smith seemed undaunted. But he would have no further contact with Kincaid, not directly. Instead, Kincaid sent in one of his trained psychologists, a woman named Cynda Demarker, who had received her Ph.D. from Stanford but had studied under Kincaid at NYU during the fall of '93. She had liked the behaviorist approach, was a devout atheist, espoused through essay and article that the world should be rid of religions for the benefit of mankind. What good does superstition and ignorance do for mankind's evolutionary advancement in the new millennium? Man should, according to Nietzsche, give way to man's ascent, now that he does not have to kowtow to God and any sense of absolute moral value. Hegel helped tremendously, providing the basis for pragmatism, progressivism, and relativism, and Goethe provided the ultimate truth when he said: "It is quite beyond me how anyone can believe God speaks to us in books and stories."

Cynda's passion was the hands-on training of soldiers-to-be, to make them, in the words of General Archer, *tougher*. She received the Kramer Award for her paper on stimulus response and worked in the intelligence *industry* for a time, but found that she did not think they had the stomachs or the will to do what was necessary to really find out what it takes to permanently change attitudes of human beings. To turn evil into good and good into evil were concepts which had more to do with the appropriation of feelings, than with absolute doctrine. Such research, she felt, was key to understanding socio-pathology, and how the fruits of such research might rebound to the benefit of society.

All this research and especially all her results on human guinea pigs served to underscore her faith in the *brotherhood of man* concept as the only approach to planet earth that made any sense. To that end man would do well to take care of the earth, limit population and spread education—especially humanistic education based on compassion and the greater good—to the far corners of the earth.

The number one enemy of this thinking, of course, was fundamentalism, especially in religion, and by that she meant Christianity, although extremist Islam and Orthodox Judaism were certainly high on her list, but nowhere near as dangerous. Terrorism and *jihad*, so often associated with Islam, was more of a class struggle, she believed, and legitimate. The war for the Muslim state was exciting because with every terrorist attack there were new levels of social control possible, implemented by Washington. She loved using brain microchips to radically change the behavior of any organism, especially the human. The idea that the human population would be implanted with microchips for *identification purposes* was a fantastic ruse, and she understood the true meaning of *security in the modern world!*

Evangelical Christianity had simply gotten beyond the pale, because it took what was supposed to be a tool to control society and made it internal, or "spirit-filled," as she had read in *Church Today*. By being Bible-based, this type of Christianity was the most dangerous; believers would take what amounted to science fiction, the Bible, and make its literal interpretation their belief system. They would let God make all decisions for them and engaged in a heinous practice which they called *convicting* others, as if those convicted were guilty of a crime and needed sentencing!

They would divine what to do and where to go by listening to this inner voice called the Holy Spirit. More disturbing, they would make predictions about the end of the world and live as if this was about to occur at any moment.

Evangelical Christians called it *evangelizing* others, and hoped to expand their beliefs, or what amounted to legal insanity, from border to border, coast to coast, and spread their ideas to the entire population of the globe. Intolerance, disunity and a fundamental belief that the Messiah was returning to destroy the world, was horrific to Cynda. She had differentiated between the evangelicals and those she knew to be tepid believers—churchgoers who perhaps even read the Bible, who worked in charities and foundations that aided the sick and the poor, but were participating more as a public service than with a conviction to do so by a preposterous being called the Holy Spirit. These people fit into society and lived by certain ethical standards. They were also quite tolerant of life as it is found at the water cooler, in the locker rooms, in gay and lesbian communities, or in the peculiarities of other cultures and ideologies. Multi-culturalism, religious pluralism and a term called ecumenicalism were just fine for them, and Cynda understood this aspect of the Church as a good thing—to provide a social dimension for people. A sense of belonging and doing good works was beneficial for society. This was the whole point of the churches, she believed.

Dr. Cynda knew that evolution would take care of the Christians—indeed, all religions and superstitions eventually. Someday these stunted people would not have their artistic impulses muted by the human creation of angelic beings, heavenly hosts or outrageous prophecy based on destruction and hatred.

For Cynda Demarker, the denominational churches, especially the ones that were seeker-friendly and tolerant, were to be commended for their true spirit of humanity—their *community spirit.*

Cynda did not desire to paint them all—the lukewarm or *cultural* believers—with a broad brush; she was completely gratified that they would not exploit such an extreme and frightening work of fiction as the Book of Revelation to their congregations and especially not to unwitting children. She knew of churches that believed Revelation was simply a totally symbolic dream dealing with Biblical times, that the Bible itself had no prophetic value, and that it was no more sophisticated than a children's book, an unbelievable one at that, with hate-filled intolerance of sex, unbridled anger, and unprovoked judgments.

Being in accord with all her teachers since high school, Cynda had a single-minded purpose to discover why hatred, intolerance and violence persisted, despite all the evidence and all the benefits of peaceful living, and why people would allow their children and themselves to be brainwashed to do evil. Bible-based Christianity was akin to hatred, she felt, believing that it enflamed the animal nature of man instead of subduing, supplanting and evolving that nature into the higher dimensions of compassion, kindness and generosity; open mindedness, sensitivity and good values based on human regard, charity, education and the recognition of the need to share resources for the purpose of creating a better, more peaceful—even joyous world, which would understand rather than condemn the emerging trends in human sexuality, spirituality and cultural diversity.

She believed it was incredible that anyone who had attended a non-sectarian university in the United States of America or Europe could feel any differently.

Those who would expound the Bible as gospel, evangelizing by force, brainwashing, falsely educating, promoting separatism—which seemed to always be the case—was tantamount to child abuse. There should be laws preventing children from being exposed to right-wing Christians until they were at least educated and could make up their own minds. The sheer amount of abuse on Western culture by Christians was breathtaking, and government had begun to fight back, but it was painfully slow. A few courageous judges got the ball rolling by taking the Ten Commandments off a few buildings but forgot about the rest of the country. Each case had to be fought one state at a time, and this was excruciating.

There was absolutely nothing to the claims of healing, social reform and especially *regeneration*, a term which meant that after one accepts Jesus Christ as his or her personal Lord and Savior, the Holy Spirit would *regenerate* the subject into an upstanding citizen. This was nothing short of denial and personality fragmentation, which should be labeled as a crime, not a solution! The doctrine of Christianity was nothing more than promises broken, a mass delusion to make life more tolerable for the miserable uneducated rabble, and if not kept in check, akin to fascism, Nazism or other extreme systems, Cynda believed. Her passion was to undo the damage, to help the world become the brotherhood, which was possible only through re-education.

． ． ．

After Casey had been deprived of sleep for almost five days in solitary confinement, Cynda Demarker, bright-eyed and concealing a nasty cough, entered Casey Smith's life for the first time as The Mother Figure, full of smiles and touching and compassion for the seventeen-year-old.

In the meantime Brand Kincaid had been observing Casey's progress on his computer screen. He knew he had only a short time to get the results; Janeway had sent him a fax indicating that Bock Wiley was to take charge of the "peculiar" boy if no substantial results were achieved.

The walls were light green and fading in spots; sweat poured down from a little ground level window. Sometimes the window was open and sometimes it was shut. Sometimes the toilet worked and sometimes it did not. Sometimes they would medicate him, telling him it was for sleep when actually it was Ritalin, which made him alert—all of it confounding to them because Casey would simply kneel and pray or sing praise songs about Jesus.

After many days, both Cynda and Kincaid thought there was progress when they observed Casey yelling and banging his head against the wall. They rejoiced while observing his behavior on Kincaid's monitor screen.

"This is so exciting!" Cynda exclaimed, proud of Dr. Kincaid. "It's a breakthrough."

"Listen," said Kincaid, "I'm sorry about the time, but this is an emergency, you might say; you have to reach him within forty-eight hours, or we lose him."

She closed her notebook and prepared to enter the realm of Casey Burns Smith. She was wearing her best cardigan and knee-high wool skirt, her long hair was styled instead of pulled back into a ponytail—everything she had learned from the photograph of Casey's mother, Elizabeth Smith. She had even matched Elizabeth's lipstick, which was a deep rouge color, and she wore pearl earrings and a diamond crucifix around her neck. It was fun shopping for the darling necklace—the diamonds were two carats and the chain was eighteen-carat white gold. She had had an enjoyable drive to Scottsdale, Arizona, just two hours from the Serin Institute's laboratory. One of their exclusive malls had a Tiffany store, and she felt like Mrs. Smith shopping on Fifth Avenue. She believed she had found the perfect match to the photo necklace; Kincaid disagreed but felt the match was good enough for their purposes.

She had never played the part of a mom; she had been girlfriends, wives, prostitutes, and her favorite, a fellow inmate. Her least favorite was her role as Cynda Demarker. At thirty years of age, she was sure that she would have her own laboratory soon, her own house, and her very own grant, or perhaps a chair in her honor at her alma mater. These accomplishments were important because society was paramount to her.

Today the walls looked a bit blue instead of green; it must have been the outside light. Casey had stopped screaming and had regressed. He was on his knees, in constant prayer. Kincaid saw the behavior as a reversal of the breakthrough head-banging and screaming; he preferred the screaming.

Cynda, as Mother Smith, knocked and politely entered as a woman who had been suffering. She wore a blue silk scarf over her head and a formal coat. She brought ammo—cigarettes, chocolate, a thermos of Coca-Cola, some Twinkies and a bag of Doritos. "Hello, Casey," she said, thrilled to make his acquaintance for the first time.

He looked up, his thin beard and shaved head were nothing compared to his piercing eyes—searing, yet alluring. Daunting. Full of promise, she thought. "I'm going to be working with you," she announced.

He said nothing. He didn't need to. He simply stared at her, then went back to his prayer.

"You know you scared a lot of people the way you were screaming and banging your head. You all right?"

He looked at her again and smiled confidently. But said nothing.

She poured out some Coca-Cola, ignoring the stench from the open, prison-like toilet, designed to provoke. "Want some coke? Kinda hot in here, don't you think?"

"Sure," he said. She handed the cup to him and he slurped it down fast and she poured another and he gulped it up as well. He looked at her and smiled and gave her a big hug. "Thank you. I forgive you. I love you."

She wasn't ready. She hadn't been informed of the exact problem. She had been told it was cult programming, her favorite social ill: Christianity. In this case, to the alarm of the parents, the literal belief in it as well as his talking about the supernatural—a challenge and something she needed to write about. Casey's was a particularly difficult case. The family was prominent, but he seemed to have the grace of someone unspoiled, educated and genteel, qualities she admired in children, though he was fast encroaching on manhood.

"Would you like to take a walk? I'll bet you would?"

"Sure," he said, picking up a warm sweater to go with his blue jeans and simple white T-shirt.

"Late afternoon, it starts to get a little chilly," she said in a motherly tone.

fifteen

Kincaid received the call from Justin. Since he had no idea where Jackson had gone, he was now feeling that Bock Wiley might be the best, last resort for his own son. He had begun to realize that he had failed because he had done what he had always promised himself he would never do—try to win the prize all by himself. To be the hero. To be the one who could succeed when everyone else could not. To be the savior, prove once and for all to his son that he was worthy of respect, though he could never let on what he was all about, lest the kid run him through with the samurai sword that hung over the fireplace in Manhattan.

He felt it had been good for Justin to go away, drop out of college and disappear and then become a famous, or at least semi-famous rock star no less. No casualty here—not his Justin!

The call sounded alarming, and made him forget how much happiness the sold-out notice in the New York Times for the Madison Square Garden performance secretly thrilled him.

Jackson had thrown the ad into the fire and laughed, "He's just a spoiled brat. I'm not bailing him out when he fails—he'll be sorry for how he embarrassed me."

Kincaid's response to Justin's call was more or less rote: "What do you want? What kind of drugs are you doing these days? Do you need to dry out? How's the band?"

He received the kind of disturbing dialogue that was inappropriate for a child to ever utter to a parent. The telephone lines were supposedly secure, but how did he know for sure?

The call was too much about Kincaid's work. Someone had to have put him up to it. Justin was always a jokester; he was always the one for drama, huge drama.

"Look, Dad, I just want to tell you that I know the truth, and it's all right. I learned about orgies and throwing up on myself and staying up for weeks on end partying and all that, and I just figured that you and Mom would occasionally sow some wild oats with your strange friends and that was it. But you're really at the center of it all. At the very heart and soul of the universe, as it tilts your way, Dad. So congratulations," Justin said.

"Look, do you want to come in?" Kincaid asked.

"Oh, yeah, like last time, when Dr. Mom got her hooks into me—I'm still lucky I never got a lobotomy."

"Son—Justin, listen—"

"Too late, Dad, I'm not your son anymore. You gave that right up, remember? I know about the *Inner Sanctum*."

A heart attack might have been a better choice. A gunshot to the head might have been better, a knife in the back, the tragic car accident, but not those words: *inner sanctum.*

He couldn't mean that, could he?

No, he couldn't have said what he said, Kincaid reasoned. Did not even say what he intimated that he said. Did not say *those words*. He, of course, meant something else, as in the collective *inner sancta*, as in the collective of all sin, as in the collective experiments for the good of humanity, of which Justin was never a part.

"I resent you always being coy with me—the Holy Spirit told me that Mom wanted to kill me."

"Justin...are you with your band now?"

"No, I'm in a hotel room in LA."

"Good, just tell me where—"

"Oh, no. Not so fast. I called to warn you. Okay? I know who you are, Satan! For I am one of *THEM* now. A traitor, your very own son," Justin said.

"Look, could you call back when you're making more sense, when you've had a chance to sleep it off?" asked Kincaid, sweat pouring down his face and dripping onto his hi-profile metal and glass desk. He popped a Xanax when he felt his heart start palpitating, and before he could say anymore, Justin spoke again.

"So, Dad, I love these long silent periods on the phone, it's very special. I'm just calling you to let you know that you and Mom have about two slammin' seconds to get to Christ, or you will be toast,"

Justin said, panting hard, as if he were constantly walking.

"Justin, you say you're in a hotel room?"

"Didn't you ever question what you were involved in?" Justin asked.

"What do you mean? I'm a scientist."

"You're an abomination."

"Okay, I don't think I have to put up with this too much longer."

"I love you, my father, and I forgive you. I am trying to help you," Justin pointed out.

The next silence ensued like crushed ice over a warm meal. There was reticence; there were equal amounts of anxiety to *do something*.

"I love you...Justin. You know my door is always open," Kincaid said.

"You know *my* door is always open to salvation. Dad, you *can* change, you can repent for your sins."

"So how long has it been since you've been awake?"

"I don't know how I'm saying this. He wants to look through your eyes. He, God, sees you. Some will walk around on the earth and witness for Him and prepare the way so that He can return and when He comes, He will destroy everything, Father."

"Call me Dad again," Kincaid said, listening intently.

"Here is truth: I was born into this family, but I didn't belong. God had me all along. He put me here, Father. Look, I never knew about God, I never had any training, I never went to Sunday school, I never read the Bible, and I still haven't read the Bible, but if you check me out, you'll find everything I'm saying IS the Word of God. They don't understand me; they don't know, and it's got nothing to do with drugs. I use drugs, I use them to keep a few steps ahead of them," Justin said.

"You sound psychotic—it's an amphetamine psychosis. Remember, I told you to watch out, I told you, but you went back again."

"What does it matter—the Lord is my mind. Everything I do and say is Him. Everything I think is Him. I have no will of my own—He is talking to you right now, and you're holding onto your legacies like a dragon chasing his tail. You will be made dust, and all those around you will be tossed from their towers and ripped from their limousines. Here is wisdom: Judgment is always going on, wrath is always poured out, not just at the End Times—even though this is THE END of something, for sure! You and all those like you are The End. Society, the one you built, is now at The End. Today is The End. Yesterday you were nothing. Today you have nothing.

Tomorrow you are as if you have never been, and that would be truth."

"I don't understand. Tell me where you are and I'll fly out and help you."

"You can't help me. I belong to Him. It's like a seesaw; I must rise so you will die, Father."

"Just call me Dad," Kincaid insisted.

"Thee are my father, and I will speak to thee with the respect you deserve. However, I will not defile myself or thyself. What I learned in school, what I learned about fornication, what I learned about child pornography, and what I know now about the thing you're practicing—it's Death. En masse. You know what I'm talking about, don't you...dad?"

"No."

"I mean," and now he yelled: "THE INNER SANCTUM!"

Kincaid hung up the phone. He ate more Xanax—it did no good. He was prepared to medicate himself out of the situation. He could see Justin in the room, floating around and exclaiming, "Sorcerer! Sorcerer!"

"What did it mean, what did he mean? Was the call real?" he said to Jackson, who had entered and was saying: "I think we've made a breakthrough."

The phone rang again. It was Justin. He picked up and looked at his wife: "It's Justin."

"Well, hang up on him," she said, shook her head and left.

"Father, I will tell thee the truth of truth: I will only live a short time. Whatever monies I have made, I want them given to all the poor people on the streets, all the homeless, all the naked and the sick, the widows and orphans...understand? And I want Bibles distributed to every one of them until the money runs out—and if they can't see, then give them glasses, and if they can't read, then give them tapes or CDs or a radio. Okay? They need to be armed to take on people like you."

"What are you talking about—you sound like that crazy guy from Waco—"

"Oh, that. Human sacrifice. You remember your mind control experiments. You did not understand why the cameras were there—the broadcast went out to the honor of Lucifer, the angel who was cast out of heaven, who deceives, who lies, who appears as an angel of light."

When Kincaid turned around, he saw Bock Wiley standing before him, his head shielded the shaft of light from the setting sun, and Kincaid was blinded.

Not just his vision, but his soul.

Justin continued, "He appears and promises peace, but peace doesn't come. He promises power, but power leads to betrayal; he promises sex, but disease follows, and he loves it when you die."

"See here, Kincaid," said Bock. "I just flew in and Jackson tells me you're still working with the Smith kid. I would like to interview him."

"Hold on, Doctor," said Kincaid. "Look, Justin...Hello? Justin! Justin!" He hung up and looked at Dr. Wiley. "I thought they told you. I haven't finished our program."

"Well, I'll just assist."

"You will *not*," said Kincaid.

"I'm afraid I will," Dr. Wiley said, smiling through his perfect tinted glasses, as he produced a document, which Kincaid could barely read.

It was a letter, and some of the pertinent parts spoke about "colleagues" and "results" and "if the candidate qualifies for the program, then Dr. Wiley will make that determination and arrange for the child and his effects to be brought to Maryland."

"Not trying to rock the boat, Dr. Kincaid. Why don't we go out and get a drink and get better acquainted."

Kincaid was covering when he answered: "Sure...Sure, Bock, may I call you Bock?"

"Bock is fine. Just don't shut me out."

"No."

"Your wife said something about your son, that he...that you've been having...problems?"

"Oh, Justin, he's—he's...I'm not sure what he's up to."

"What does he know?" Bock asked.

"What does *he know*?" questioned Kincaid, unsure.

"I mean, you know—what we all know but no one says."

"Oh...he knows nothing. Absolutely nothing."

"That's not true," said Bock. "You know the rules. How did he get away?"

"He dropped out of school and joined a band—and he left. You want a drink?"

Bock nodded, and Kincaid strode, almost proudly, to his built-in bar on remote control. "Is that beautiful?" he asked. "What'll you have?"

"A bubbly water," Bock replied. "And there was no follow-up?"

"Follow-up?" Kincaid asked, while stirring his Scotch and soda.

"We need to know what he knows," said Bock, the scientist.

"I told you, he knows nothing. He was babbling on about some...he's just very confused about me and he thinks I'm in some inner sanctum or some cult."

"He used the words *inner sanctum*?" Bock asked, stunning Kincaid.

"Look, maybe he read a book on Freemasonry, but that doesn't mean—"

"He used the words *inner sanctum*? It's a simple question," Dr. Wiley insisted.

"No, maybe it was *inside track* or *inner realm* or something like that." When Kincaid turned around with the drinks, Bock Wiley had left the office.

sixteen

The sun shone wide and flat on the desert horizon as Cynda walked with Casey Smith on the grounds. It was magical, it was real, and she felt she was actually getting somewhere, not just biding her time. He wore the coat his mother bought him in Phoenix just a few weeks ago, when it was thought, at least Dr. Kincaid said so, that Casey would only be there a short time.

"Suppose I tell you, Cynda, the story of your life."

"*My* life?" she questioned, bemused and undaunted.

"Do you understand systems?" he asked.

"Systems, what do you mean, 'systems,' you mean like modeling systems, such as in science?"

"Precisely," he said, sure of himself. "I mean systems of thought, of behavior, of money, of love, of education—"

"—I think I get what you mean. Oh, it's so beautiful, isn't it—look at that sunset."

"Of course you won't understand what I mean, because you haven't experienced the real world, because you do not live in it. You live in a *system*, a world designed by someone and sustained by others so that you may live, think and write, learn, love and experiment, eat and sleep, and so forth."

"Are you sure you're only seventeen?" she asked, leading him along the Serin Institute's walking path.

An eagle soared overhead and screeched at no one. "Tell me about your mother," said Cynda, watching the sun set in Casey's alert eyes.

"My mother is God. He is also my father. He is also my foundation, my peace and my serenity."

"So you believe in Jesus Christ?"

"He is coming soon and this is wisdom: The Lamb of God claims the earth for Himself and His own—and that could be you, Cynda."

"Tell me about your earth mother," she said, about the only way she could say it. She picked up a rock and threw it at a Joshua Tree as the distant mesas grew colder in color, less orange as the sun evaporated on the flat and increasing distance.

"Your mother was a generous woman. She worked hard as a waitress so that you could move away for your education, which you did and fulfilled her dream. She was a fallen, though Godly, woman. She was a frugal woman; your parents were alcoholics and forced you to go to their Pentecostal church. Your father, when drunk, would beat your face with his Bible, which caused you to make a vow that you would never, *ever* give yourself to such hatred. And when they were ecstatic and speaking in Tongues, you were embarrassed. And when they died, you were relieved."

"*Stop*! You don't know *that*. You don't know what you say you know! You can't! *Who* told you *that*?" She noticed she had grabbed hold of his arms and had actually been shaking him.

He felt her face with his hand just as a helicopter roared to the heliport at the three-story curved glass structure that rose, contemptuously, in the distance.

"Who told me *what*?" he asked sternly. "Why am I not fatigued? Why am I not famished, why am I not upset with my captors? Why do I forgive them—why do I forgive you for the ridiculous charade of imitating my mother? Don't you know? All the ideas in your 'system' don't amount to much compared to the mind of God."

"I suppose you're right," she said, and by now she knew she was out of her element, that she would have to recommend him back to the team, particularly Dr. Kincaid, and wash her hands of the whole thing.

"I want to tell you, Cynda, that you are a lovely person, and that God loves you, and that *I* love you."

"Do you love everyone here, including your parents, who put you under Dr. Kincaid's care?"

"Most especially, and I weep for them, and I pray for them to my Father in Heaven, and my Lord Jesus Christ who sends the Holy Spirit to comfort me and lets me sleep with my eyes open. You don't know that you're not hurting me."

Casey stunned her, yet he walked so easily and steadily, his bald head covered by the ski cap. Cynda started coughing, uncontrollably. "Sorry..." she said, but her cough continued, and she started to spit blood in small globules. She was not surprised, and Casey was not surprised either. "Sorry, Casey, I'm...just trying to get over the cough."

"Come here," Casey said tenderly. "Come on, come here."

She looked over to the building, knew they were observing her and knew this would be mistaken as either progress or regression (as they liked to call it in the psychiatric world), but Casey Burns Smith was reaching out. She saw something in his eyes, which made her feel deeply for him as he blamed not his parents or the Institute. He did not say he wanted to leave or stay, or be moved back to his room, or stop being tested with electrodes, and he never complained about not having clothes or having his head shaved. It was all there in his eyes, lit by the falling sun.

"Come here," he said again, and she came closer. "Sit down," he said and she sat on a small boulder. "Now I'm talking to the *real* you, the one who was searching for answers and settled on science and arcane philosophy."

She coughed again and it was painful—she started crying but stopped. "I didn't settle on science, it just seemed like the most...(she coughed again)...the most...reasonable thing."

"And now you know better, don't you?" he asked.

She looked at him and started weeping. "Yes, I don't know—I think so. They told me I only had a few months to live, and I was afraid to tell anyone, and I didn't want to lose my job, and I really didn't think it would be so wrong for me to just, you know, hope it went away. And here you are, basically an inmate because they can't break you, because you believe in God, which I made a career of hating."

He hugged her, stroked her hair. "Everything you touch, everything you see, everything you think is governed by Him, Cynda. Everything you are, or everything you shall ever be, He gave you. And all He ever wanted was for you to know the truth, and to love Him in return, and to let Him give you the things you can't give to yourself, but you so desperately need."

She looked at him again in his cell.

The next day she woke up in her apartment in Phoenix, ready

for the drive up to the Institute. She arose clumsily, feeling cozy in her old boyfriend's sweatshirt as she made her way to the kitchenette. She put on the electric tea pot, a necessity wherever she went since tea had been the elixir of life since her college days. The Russell Hobbs was the only machine that made a perfect cup of tea the way she remembered it from that summer at Cambridge, the way she remembered it when everybody else went to Starbuck's. She cut a half lemon, to clear the phlegm that she usually developed at night. She was afraid to cough, as she did not want to exacerbate her wounds. The previous night had been fine, and she felt better than usual. At this point she only hoped for time, not the lack of pain and certainly not remission, perhaps a gentle remission, and that was always thought of as more time.

Her faithful yellow lemon press had served her well, and she wondered to whom she might bequeath such gifts. She knew that she was only as good as her last paper, but the computer had since grown weary, and she never liked the little apple with the bite out of it, for it reminded her of her own weakness. She always thought of the apple as illness and not knowledge.

She pressed the half lemon into the bottom of the plastic glass, filled it with Evian, poured a little sugar in and prepared for a bit of pain, maybe.

She drank it and there was *no* pain in her throat. This was certainly unusual for her first gulp—but she would prepare herself for the second hurdle. Ready to clear her throat, she braced herself against the counter and noticed that she could use a manicure and even a pedicure. She took her breath and then gave coughing up the phlegm a try. All she got was a little mucus, and *no pain*! Excited, she went to the mirror, looked around—perhaps all those teas and especially the supplements that Dr. Yo-Yin Woo gave her, which she could never read the names of, were finally working. *Something* was working!

She cleared her throat again—now *no* mucus, the lemon water took care of that, and no pain *again*!

Something was working. She thought of her dead mother and father, both of them smokers and alcoholics. Casey had been correct—both so-called born-again Christians of the Pentecostal bent. The embarrassment continued even after their deaths, the apologies, even faking her own background so that she would not have to explain; it haunted her more after their passing. Her only victory was a cremation in the Pacific Ocean, as their Oakland lifestyle of poverty would only allow for cremation. When she found the Neptune Society of San Francisco, her prayers, or as she called them, her *intentions*, were honored. It was no wonder, she thought, that she had spent all her time on the East Coast, attempting to fit into an upper class of intellectual elites that would provision no place for her.

She had decided to wear a simple, conservative dress, blue with gold buttons, no scarf this time, and she allowed her hair to be down, long and straight, and instead of wearing her pumps, she opted for sandals. She posed in the mirror—looked undecided, cleared her throat, and again, *no pain*.

She did not want to get her hopes up in fear of what had happened during other so-called remissions. She did not want to go to a doctor because, though she never liked to think of herself as superstitious, she did not want to *jinx* it. She had always noticed a correlation between doctor's visits and a worsening condition. Why, she did not know. With only a few months to live, she could afford to *never* see a medical doctor again.

She changed her mind and put on her jeans and a light sweater; her sandals were fine. Her age seemed more like twenty-two than thirty, and she bounced down the stairs and out to her rental sedan.

She felt *good*.

What if it really is remission, she wondered? She had known it to happen before; she had heard about it with others. She had gotten her hopes up about herself numerous times, read about remission in journal after journal, and practiced visualization. Lately the use of Ayurvedic herbs were just the thing she needed. She knew that she had come to the conclusion that she was an agnostic, not knowing if there were a God or not, but she wondered why she could not get Casey's words or his eyes out of her mind. Was it something transmitted through him perhaps or was it superstition again? Perhaps God was a distant force, but in her case and perhaps through Casey, He came closer. She still rejected Jesus and all that hate in the Bible; it was not for her.

When she arrived at Serin, Kincaid didn't recognize her at first, and she could see that he looked troubled. She urgently needed to see Casey, at least to tell him her good news, to see if he had anything to say about it. She wanted to relate to him not as a subject, or an experiment, but as a human being.

Compelled to set things straight and to assert herself, and having only a few hours left to work with the boy, she knew that precision was a must. She would have to behave as if she were still on the same case—though Casey had proven to her beyond a shadow of a doubt that they had lost the battle to win his mind, which fascinated her.

She just had to see him and she would insist upon it. Her assertiveness was the only way she had ever acquired anything in her life, and it was the only way to deal with powerful people such as Dr. Kincaid.

"Look, I want him out of seclusion. Seclusion wasn't clearly indicated, nor is it working. I want to take charge," she demanded in Kincaid's office. "It is very important that we bond, that he sees me as someone who can make his life better. I need more time alone with him, at least another few days, then you may have him."

She was too intent on her purposes to notice that Kincaid was disheveled, he hadn't shaved and his rather drawn face was pale.

"Fine, Cynda—I'll grant you five days," Kincaid said without protest. He didn't request a report, ask about other options or ask how yesterday's session went. Too excited about her upcoming session with Casey, Cynda was oblivious to Kincaid's mood.

The new room was luxurious, just what Cynda wanted. Casey had a private bathroom on a floor with other "patients" who were all there undergoing various treatments, from psychological testing to military application. The floor was filled with basically sane people, and there was a view of the desert and the parking lot. It all seemed quite fine. With no present concept of real evil, she wouldn't discover until later that everything being done there was evil.

Casey, however, knew that on the next level, the fourth floor, true atrocities were occurring. "God will liberate this place and you, Cynda," he said while looking out his window. "Even though many will die," he added in an odd tone.

She turned to him, saw his face in the light of morning. His new quarters did not seem to make any difference to him. He had already been at the Serin Institute about three months, living on the other wing in his own private room where he'd had no contact with others. Dr. Kincaid had ordered him moved to seclusion, in the now vain attempt to break him and get him to re-accept his parents, his school, and his social world. To accept the facts of life.

"To accept those things, which are from Satan," Casey told her.

"You know, Casey, you have the most beautiful blue eyes," she said, wondering if her new super-youthful appearance made any difference.

"They were different before He started changing me," he said.

"*Who* started changing you?" Cynda asked.

Casey pointed upward, and she nodded, remaining humble in the face of her seemingly healed condition. Then Casey blurted out in excitement what was obvious to him: "You're healed, aren't you? *God* did that!"

She suddenly felt full of sadness, as she looked out over the desert, the sea of cars belonging to hidden researchers, the genetics and drug teams streaming in, the behaviorist/mind controllers streaming out. The influx and outflow of stupidity, she thought, when she considered her new hero, Casey Smith.

"Let me tell you what goes on here, Cynda. The doctor wants to make breakthroughs in science, in medicine and in psychological shaping of citizens. He is earnest in his approach, and I will never be able to lodge a complaint about the fact that I am not here of my own free will, but because of a bogus court order that says I am a paranoid schizophrenic. Did you know that?"

"No, Casey, I—"

"My name is *not* Casey."

"Oh. Well, what is it?" she asked.

He yelled at her in a manner so otherworldly that the sound seemed to be emanating from the walls: "YOU THINK YOU KNOW EVERYTHING AND YOU KNOW NOTHING— DON'T YOU REALIZE WHAT YOU'RE GIVING UP?"

Two aides immediately burst into the room, always two steps behind any live rat. "It's all right, gentleman," said Cynda. She hugged him, and he cried in her arms.

The aides left.

"It's okay, Casey...it's okay—just cry. Go on, cry," she said. "It's okay—let it out. I'm here."

Mission accomplished. Bonding had taken place, and he had begun the process of reintegration, she liked to call it. She would try and heal his psyche, not destroy it as Bock Wiley might, not let him be recruited as some sort of mindless assassin. Only later would she realize that what she had been involved in most of her professional life was evil.

"I love you, Cynda," Casey said. "I'm sorry, this is so strange to find a friend after all these generations."

"Tell me about your parents," she said defensively.

"God made no mistake with you. Heaven loves you more than all the rest," he said and then he sat on his bed, kicked his feet up and stared at the ceiling.

"Casey," she said. "Casey, hey..." She sat down on the bed and stroked his head full of stubble. He was so cute, she could not deny that—a word she had never used since her old boyfriend left. "Casey, can you hear me?" she asked. "Can you hear me?"

Nothing from Casey, he simply stared. She admired his sinewy arms and his face, which was angelic. He was beauty personified—and she hadn't seen it at all until just now! Had she said the wrong thing? Had she applied the wrong approach? She got him to break and now it's pushed him into the place psychiatry is terrified of—true sanity.

"Please, Casey. Please talk to me again," she asked, ashamed at her unprofessional demeanor.

But she could hear his voice in her mind: "Cynda, He chose you from the beginning. He chose you before the foundation of the world. You were healed by the stripes of Jesus Christ—his scourging became your healing. Be at peace. He loves you."

She burst into tears, a well that had never been tapped in all her life. She wept over him.

Bock Wiley watched the monitor screen with keen interest. He told Jackson, "She is very, very good. Amazing. I'd like to train her, I'd like her to assist me from here."

"He broke," said Brand Kincaid in the conference room. "And so *we* will take it from here."

Bock chimed in: "She lost him. If I don't step in, I fear even his...*cognizance* may be lost."

Jackson Kincaid asked after Cynda's session ended: "Well, Cynda—*is* he lost? You give up?"

Cynda sat mesmerized, drawing interweaving circles on her legal pad. "He loves me," she said in a soft, girlish voice.

Jackson was horrified. She looked at her weakened husband, Brand, who said nothing. Bock motioned for her to meet him in the hall and the meeting was adjourned. Half a dozen psychologists also left the conference room.

The only ones left were Cynda and Brand Kincaid, each looking beyond the other.

"He loves me, He has forever," Cynda repeated.

Kincaid quickly snapped to attention. "Cynda! Listen to me. What happened in there, it's just reverse-transference; you were supposed to get him to love you, and now you love him, is that right?"

"He loves me," she said, drawing concentric circles, one after the other on her legal pad.

"It's not your fault," Kincaid said, "but you can't afford to make even *one* slip around Wiley, or he'll take Casey away from both of us."

"I can breathe again. Maybe I can live. *That's* what I know," she said.

"I'm not sure we're on the same page, Cynda. I need you right now—you have no idea what kind of...situation this is. I need you to, you know...snap out of it and get with the team—that's why I hired you, Cynda. Don't do this to me now," he said, knowing that look, that rebellious emotion swirling on her legal pad in concentric circles. "Cynda?" he asked, trying to get her attention, but she did not answer him.

"Have you ever stopped to consider, Brand, that *we're* wrong?" she asked, and she would later think of him as sad.

seventeen

*T*he Los Angeles Forum, no less. Warming up for Bluefish, the number one band with a bullet for their latest release, "Sex Kitten," mattered not in the least to Justin. He was just as happy in bed in his hotel room, continuing his vigil of staying awake and staying out of the midst of the controversy involving Anton's untimely death. He thought about the death and did manage to write the widow in England, a letter he gave to his record producer, Rick Lowie. Rick was not as concerned with the death as with warning Justin about his behavior and about how the label did not want to give the band any more money because it all went up too easily in drugs and parties.

Rick was ready to hear a sarcastic comment from Justin and was surprised when he said, "Rick, even though you're a Jew, you can still come to Christ, He loves you."

"Does Christ approve of your meth habit?"

Justin rolled out of bed, looked out the window at the afternoon sun sinking below the Sunset Strip, below the sea. He was sure Rick was a prophet.

"I'm sorry—please forgive me," he said, on his knees before Rick.

Rick laughed, believing in band shenanigans and replied: "Okay, I'm sorry I criticized your drug habit. Will you forgive me?"

"God is giving me the drugs because he wants me to see when he's ready for me to stop, He will stop me. And in me He says it's time to pour out wrath on the whole world. I have to be given up so that He can come."

"Sounds like great lyrics—why don't you write 'em down," said Rick.

Katarina burst out of the bathroom, full of smiles, and leapt back in bed with Justin.

"Oh, yeah. Rick, meet Katarina, Katarina, meet Rick."

"My pleasure," she said, shoving her tattooed hand out to shake Rick's hand. She was beautiful, no denying it, and Rick wondered if Justin and Kat, as he would later call her, were an item.

"Do you sing or play an instrument?" he asked.

"I'm an actress," she answered. "I sing, I dance, but right now I'm doing Justin."

Rick smiled. Well, this was nothing compared to Led Zeppelin, after all—and it was strange he was remembering that time when he was fifteen and already working with his brother as a gofer at World Records. "Looks like you landed your perfect role," he said.

That little thing—one comment—made the difference between success or, as in his brother's case, dereliction, Rick knew. If you could take it, it's yours—no one owes his brother. If you can take his girl, do that. If you can take his job, it never was his in the first place. This is the only code viable in a town so specific about what it rewards and punishes.

Katarina frowned as Justin gazed through hotel glass to the sea and asked, "About the next record..."

"Oh, yeah, that's why I came up here from the lobby. I wanted to tell you that's been pushed back. You won't be in the studio until we can get Bobby to work the dials, that cool?"

"Work the dials—I can work the dials. Look, there's just one last thing I have to say, and then...it won't matter."

"Don't you love this guy?" Rick said, openly lusting at Katarina, who was returning his gaze with the innocence of a naughty child. "Look, Just, it's important that you guys blow Bluefish off the freakin' stage, you got it? How do you feel, energy wise?"

"You going to get me some—"

"Already brought it. Here."

He handed Justin a little bag of white powder. "But after this I want you to dry out, then we'll talk about the next album."

"I told you I have a few things to say, and I think I'll say them on stage tonight," he said, loading up his glass pipe with the crystal and taking a hit. He offered some to Katarina, who took a puff, and Rick took a puff as well.

"Why don't you check your suit and tie in, Rick. You're no better than us," she said.

"I'm not better than you, Kat. I'm a sinner."

Justin and Katarina laughed.

"You're cute," she said to Justin with cool derision.

"Thank you," Justin said.

The phone rang. Justin did not hear; he was now pacing back and forth talking to himself.

Rick, producer of record and authority, picked up the phone. "Yeah," he answered. "No, it's not Justin. Who's this? Yes, he's here. Who may I say is calling? Dr. Kincaid?..." He looked at Justin who had placed himself against the glass as if he wanted to fall to the pavement below. "He's uh...can he call you back? Oh, Dr. Jackson Kincaid, oh, hold on." He looked at Justin pathetically: "Hey, buddy it's your mama. Come on, you don't reject your mother. I thought the commandments talked about honoring your mother and father.

"It's...my mother hates me," he said.

"Well, she really wants to talk. Here." Rick handed Justin the portable phone; Justin looked at it for a moment and then he responded.

"Hello?" he said. "Hi. Sure. I'm glad you called because I'm putting you on notice. Tonight you will be exposed for the devil worshiper you are. God is great—my Lord is Jesus Christ! And He will come back—he's not a lamb anymore."

She answered: "Justin, we just want to know if you're all right. You'll be at the hotel for a couple of days?"

"Yeah, and thank God it is far away."

"I love you, that's all I wanted you to know. You're my son. I want the best for you. You've changed. Did you really convert to Christ, Justin? You don't sound like yourself. Your father says you're on drugs again; is that true? You just don't sound like the Justin we care about and love. I'm worried, dear."

Against his better judgment, he decided to respond: "First of all, Mother, I *am* myself. I *do* sound like myself. God lives in me and He can do anything."

Rick and Katarina weren't paying attention to the call because Rick was on the bed serving her coffee, feeding her room service sausage and helping her wash it down with orange juice. She pecked him on the cheek and indicated that the Justin thing "isn't exactly like, forever..."

She winked at him, which made him laugh because it was so manly—and so he asked her: "Do you like to be strong or weak?"

"Depends on the man."

"Good answer."

Justin paced to and fro in front of the window, and then yelled as loudly as he could, "I *am* myself! I *am* the Way, the Truth and the Life. Here is wisdom...let him who has an ear listen to what He says! *Holy, Holy, Holy, Lord God Almighty, who was, and is, and will be forevermore!*"

Katarina and Rick were spellbound at Justin, silhouetted in the window of the setting sun. Rick found the Gideon Bible open at page 1659 and the passage from Revelation 3, verse 8. "Hey, bro, get your own lyrics man!" Rick said, laughing. "I was beginning to think you were possessed."

"I am possessed—even though I'm fallen, even though I am an abomination. But He puts the words in me, don't you understand? Both of you, hear me. I only have a short time. I'm the harbinger— a lamb with broken legs, and when they take me, someone else will follow. Do you understand? Do you? There are others, you know, not just me. It's a baton passing in a race, know what I mean, Rick?" He did not seem to care about the developing situation between Rick and Katarina, not in the least.

Rick and Katarina now looked like the concerned parents. "Should I take away Justy's drugs now? Naughty naughty, getting scary on me two hours before the gig?"

"Be at the show, Rick," Justin said, not feeling high anymore. "Dear Heavenly Father, please help me to be spotless before you. Use me, Father, to do Your Will. In Jesus' name. Amen."

"What about me?" asked Katarina, demurring plaintively.

Justin turned and gazed out the window, dismissing them.

eighteen

waiting trial, Stephen J. Petchick had heard the news of his mother's passing. It could not have been more of a failure, and he was devastated. So much more time, so much more he wanted to do for her, so many things he wanted to say. He wanted to read God's Word to her and pray with her and share being together in Christ...

All was lost now. She was gone, and certainly to heaven. He had called the pastor for a visit, and he did get a visit. They spoke about things that were superficial, and there was a prayer.

"Dear Heavenly Father, please watch over your son, Stephen J. Petchick," the pastor said, "and help him to walk in Your grace, to live by Your Word, and help him to stand strong, to be a good witness for You and all those with whom You deal. Most of all, please send your Holy Spirit to comfort him in his time of the loss of his beloved mother, Anna. In Jesus' name we pray...Amen."

Stephen's problems were all about the fact that he was awaiting arraignment on circumstantial evidence from a fallen woman who had no identity and could not be located.

It was so familiar to him—jail. Prison. The whole world was a prison and in some ways prison provided a much fairer playing field. The truth was the truth and the lie could not hide, at least now that he knew the difference. All agree on what is, lest he be a fool, and then he sees what he wants to see.

But sometimes the fool was the wiser, especially a fool for Christ. Who exposed the world as a lie. Who exposed the individual as incomplete and false. Who reduced humanity to a mere gaggle of liars, intent on foisting their ways by might if necessary, even if the children screamed. Especially if they screamed.

He would pray and ask, "Lord, please protect those little ones. Help me to help rather than remain selfish. Help me to know your ways, to live for you and not me."

When he met with the public defender, Henry Klotzke, he was heartened by the fact that Henry was over thirty, and he was amazed that Henry knew something of the Bible. So he did not prejudge, he simply stated the DA's situation—a dead body, stab wounds, a man by the name of Anton Blodgett Duffield, forty-two, with a family in London. The coroner was explicit, the bruises indicated a struggle; Duffield was violently stabbed with what he surmised was a steak knife, then held underwater until he succumbed. Stephen was strong enough, and he had motive: taking over the band management since Justin took a liking to him. Stephen's girlfriend, Kathleen Kenroby—aka Katarina—had said she saw him do it.

"She's not my girlfriend," he told the public defender. "Maybe *she* did it."

But why would she lie?

The answer was found when the Los Angeles County Sheriff served a subpoena to Justin at the hotel; they also served Katarina, which angered her greatly. Did she think she'd just skip off with the band after lying about a murder and then they would not want to hear from her again?

"Look, Stephen, I've gotta be honest with you—I don't know why he hasn't thrown the case out. They have no right to hold you. All Kennedy said was that it's got something to do with the FBI. Did you, you know, deal in contraband—or were you a mercenary or something? The problem is that you've got a criminal record. And the M.O. fits. Know what I'm saying?"

Stephen walked around the cell week after week. He would usually share it with drunks or junkies, which he hated because of the vomit smell. No matter how big, no matter how tough—Stephen had done the time. He had all the necessary attitude he needed, and it helped tremendously now.

"My mother...she was buried without me even being there—her house, her things..."

"Stephen, we've been over all this. Look, you don't owe anybody anything."

"I owe *her*, Henry!"

"If you could just post bail..."

"You know I can't."

"Don't you have any friends?"

"Sure, but not on this earth."

Thankfully, Stephen had been able to read from his New King James. He knew the world was changing and God was putting something special on his heart. He read out loud to the new inmate, who looked like an old gray-haired homeless guy—with a sackcloth he might have been Ezekiel or a prophet of old.

"I would like to hear it," the man with the searing eyes said.

"Honor the Lord with your possessions," he read. "And with the first-fruits of all your increase; so your barns will be filled with plenty, and your vats will overflow with new wine. My son, do not despise the chastening of the Lord, nor detest His correction; for whom the Lord loves He corrects, just as a father and the son in whom he delights." Stephen finished reading and looked up at his new cellmate. "Proverbs 3:9-12."

"Yes, and how about this one, my son?" the mysterious old man said. "And all the trees of the field shall know that I, the Lord, have brought down the high tree and exalted the low tree, dried up the green tree and made the dry tree flourish; I, the Lord, have spoken and have done it. Ezekiel 17:24."

"I'm...how did you—have you been studying a long time?" Stephen asked, confused, amazed, gratified and encouraged.

"Yes," he replied mysteriously. He got off his bunk and looked squarely into Stephen's eyes. "I'm here to tell you that you are one of God's warriors. No matter what you see, know that you shall be blessed. This is the precursor. This is the harbinger." Then he threw himself on the floor face down and started shaking.

Stephen leapt up, thinking it might be DT's, that he was some sort of drunk, who for the first time had sobered up and was now in possession of his faculties. Perhaps he had studied the Bible and here was a chance to help one of Christ's get back on his feet. It made the entire incarceration experience make sense. God needed this man restored.

He dropped out of the bunk and put his hand on the man's shoulder. "Hey...hey...you okay?"

The old man was still as death, as still as a sponge thick with water. Then he calmly turned over and looked up at the young man. He smiled. "Selah....selah. Holy, Holy, Holy, Lord God almighty,

Who is, and was, and will be again."

He did not know how he got back in the bed, or how the old man got off the floor; he only knew it was the next morning and the mystery man was gone. He wanted to help him. He felt a bond with him, a closeness he hadn't known since before his father left—something he needed was *in* that man, but he was gone. "Lord, I want to help him—I pray that he is safe, and that his journey leads him to live Your way, for Your purpose. And Lord, I'd like to see him again. In Jesus' name I pray. Amen."

Ketch, the guard he'd gotten to know over the past two weeks, brought breakfast. "So, how's it with you this mornin' Stephen?"

"Pretty good, Ketch," he answered while finishing his pull-ups on the bunk and then started sit-ups on the same floor on which that the old man had been prostrate.

"Any idea why you're still in the hold—no idea when you'll be arraigned?" Ketch asked sympathetically.

"Nope—don't know what's going on."

"How come you're so calm? I'd be screaming my head off."

"God wants me here."

"Son, let me tell you something," Ketch said, fumbling with his skewed badge and messing with his slick shock of black hair. "God does not want people in jail, or doing bad things. Now I'm not saying you done anything wrong, but I don't see God wanting those things."

"Hey, guard," said someone in another cell. "Can I go home now—I'll even let you live?"

"Strathern, you mouth off one more time, your new digs is a rubber cell, got it, homes?" he replied to the tough inmate.

"Paul did his best work in prison, and then he was put to death—he was God's greatest leader," Stephen said. "I mean, besides the Master, God's son."

"Who's Paul?" asked Ketch.

"Paul, who killed Christians when he was Saul. He was converted by the Holy Spirit; he became the greatest evangelist of all time and established the church of Lord Jesus and sojourned all over Italy and the Middle East and Greece and Turkey. You know, Saint Paul," Stephen replied.

"You seem like such a good kid," said Ketch. "But you got a pretty bad-news record. You did what, a nickel for grand theft, resisting arrest. We put you in here because they said you were dangerous. Something about a knife fight?"

"I was forgiven. I still am forgiven, by my Lord. And I repented, and I keep a short list, because I sin every day my mind wanders from the Truth," said Stephen, starting on his pushups. "And God loves you," Stephen told Ketch.

"So God made you a considerate, seemingly good egg now?"

"Only God can put Humpty Dumpty back together again. He can, Ketch. Think about it."

"You're a good egg. Well, if I don't see you again, take care of yourself."

Ketch liked him because he reminded him of his son, who was still serving time for murder. His son was nice like this kid, he thought. They're all nice until something goes off. He was locked up in a semi-private cell to protect the other inmates in the holding tank. Ketch could not fathom Stephen Petchick as violent, but usually if they're in for murder, they go up for murder, he knew that. But something did not add up, and it bugged him endlessly.

When it was time for lunch, his attorney came. "Look, Stephen, you ever been in special ops—you ever work for the CIA?"

"CIA now, huh? That's sweet," he said.

"Tell me what's going on," Klotzke responded, standing in the middle of the cell and staring at Stephen sitting on his bunk. "Because they're transferring you this afternoon. No judge will hear the case, your constitutional rights are being violated and no one will explain it—only that they have orders. I mean, *who are you, man?*"

"I'm no one, you know my record. I'm a car thief accused of murdering Anton Duffield, accused by Kathleen...Kenroby, is it? She goes by Katarina."

Klotzke nodded worriedly

"Look, Stephen—how can I tell you this? Look, you're not being held for murder, because your witness was subpoenaed and she disappeared. I mean, the DA says it's out of his hands, and technically you're free to go, but they won't let you out of here. I do not understand, but I am really upset right now."

Stephen J. Petchick sat back and smiled. He visualized hugging and kissing his mother as he might have done when she was alive, and he suddenly a thousand prayers later, and God was filling up his marvelous cell with the smell of incense and the taste of the food was sweet like honey and filled him with warmth. "Men cannot understand God's ways. They are different than ours," Stephen told Klotzke, hoping to comfort him.

• • •

Bauman did go to the station, did help Sheila get out of jail. He did warn her—as Daniel had warned him. But she wasn't interested in warnings. "The Kingdom is at hand," she said as they sat at Sergeant Cates' desk.

Bauman said, "Wait a second—you're an orthodox Jew, and we—"

"He's real, Phil—you and I should *never* have been together."

"I'm *not* real, He *is* real—I understand. And I need to know— I'm taking lots of notes," Bauman said angrily.

She said: "I have to follow him—he's our pastor."

"You're not a Christian!" Bauman shouted.

"I have always been with the Lord, and his name is Jesus. And His pastor is Ted. I'm not well," she said.

At that moment Marta, who would not look at her father, came for her mother. Bauman noticed the contractor guy but refused to look at him. As they quickly left, Marta stared at her father with a look that screamed: stay away!

Cates watched it all, seated at Bauman's former desk.

Bauman, who was wearing dirty clothes with holes in them, had looked at himself in a bathroom mirror at the station and realized he looked no different than the homeless people he had once shuttled along the endless road.

"Sheila's pretty warped, Bauman—maybe it's better this way," Cates said, trying to console him.

"Don't you see, Cates? You and me, we should work together on this thing. I wonder if a ransom play would work?"

"Oh, man," Cates said. "Listen, get some help, Bauman. Now, for the *last time: Alice Garcia is dead.* The case is still open—but we have no suspects. Okay?"

"Why won't you look me in the eye?" Bauman asked. "What, I'm embarrassing? You don't think I know what I'm talking about?"

Cates fidgeted about in his seat, unwound several paper clips. The guilt was piled around the department like garbage bags, blocking everything from view and letting loose ten thousand elephants as one of their brothers had taken a fall and not one, not one of them, stretched for so much as a five-spot.

"What are you all looking at! Don't you want to get Alice back?

Why won't you help me?"

The desk sergeant, as well as some of the other officers, started shoving Bauman out, "You don't care about Alice?"

Cates shoved Bauman up against the bulletin board and said very loudly: "We found Alice face down in the LA river last week, and we told you that! It was in the paper, and we questioned you several times about what happened, about what you remember, but you act as if you never heard this news. You can't stay here, man. Come on, out!"

He was deposited nicely on Van Nuys Boulevard. He started crying like a kid who found out there was no tooth fairy. There was only God, and he had just played havoc with Bauman's mind. He knew now that even if they offered him medication he would not take it—he no longer needed it.

Sheila had been converted, he muttered to himself, as he walked along. *She only thought she was in love with Pastor Ted*, Bauman discovered from a new voice that made him feel warm inside. The fervor of her conversion filled her and it was not something supernatural. Alice was not dead, that wasn't the story; she was not at the bottom of the LA River facedown, naked, raped and discarded like garbage. She was not drained of blood from four mysterious wounds on her feet and wrists; she was not in pieces, but in one piece. In addition, Daniel had said she was alive.

Then again he called many people "dead" and they were still walking around. Weren't they? Bauman never really understood what Daniel meant—but he would investigate.

"If they are dead to God, they die in their sacks of sagging flesh, and they are proud of themselves," Daniel said.

Bauman walked with Daniel. He had a new notebook, had a new face after the rain, and after his tears, and after a shave, which he got thanks to Big Fred and Big Willy. Bauman was much more amenable to the voice (The Voice, which resided in his head or maybe in his mind and in his lungs too). The Voice sometimes wanted to look through his eyes, which he didn't mind at all—he was grateful for the company. He knew it was not his own voice, which was usually confused, confounded and desultory; or accusing, angry and guilt-ridden; ashamed, embarrassed and frightened; sorrowful, anguished and full of futility; or full of fury with no outlet; disturbed, quiet or muttering. His new voice (Friend), which announced nothing of its origin, was truly a *new friend* and made living at the warehouse incredibly tolerable, sometimes joyous, especially since it knew a lot of secret things like Daniel knew. Sometimes he would think that Daniel put it there. Oh, was he happy to have found Daniel again, the one true key to the riddle of Alice and perhaps many other things.

They warmed themselves around the fire at the back of the closed Ward's store. John the Apostle was talking nonsense again, but everyone listened because he was a storyteller.

He told them Jesus Christ was God before he came to the earth, and he had appointed beings on earth to walk to and fro, preparing the way for the day of the Lord. Big Fred, an ordained minister who was a missionary at the Rescue Mission, said Brother John was correct. (He would not, under any circumstances, call him John the Apostle—this was the source of constant frustration and much handwringing.)

Big Fred wondered how John knew that. John had also said that John the Baptist was the greatest man on earth, and that the present time is like the old times, except now the lamb is the lion—and "woe be to the inhabitants of the earth."

Bauman understood none of this. He had a case to solve.

There was a network and Bauman was excited that he was finally making progress toward understanding, though perhaps not with Sheila, who could not stop talking about one thing: the anointed Ted Gunderson, who had been transferred out.

When Sheila got out of the little pickup, she walked away from Bauman, but before she did, she told him that he must find God; only God could help him. Bauman said he was on the verge of finding the truth—and she laughed. "I love *you*, Bauman. You don't believe that—you're full of all kinds of weird ideas. Right now, I'm lost. And I'm not responsible for what happened to you."

He wondered what God she was speaking of.

What he knew was that Alice had not turned up. The precinct would only tolerate a visit from Bauman as the Christian thing to do, and he wondered if the police chief was a Christian. When some caring people gave Bauman loose change, it gave Daniel a laugh.

He had found Daniel, and boy, was Daniel connected! He knew all about Pastor Ted, knew all about the coup d'état at the Faith Church, and all about his wife filing for divorce—he had answers. Very important answers. The problem was, when he needed Daniel, Daniel was always disappearing.

"I have many to attend to," Daniel said, scorching him with his intense blue eyes. He was such a striking figure, Bauman thought. Tall, long gray beard and those eyes—no one could escape. He would talk to Bauman on Bauman terms, about Bauman things, in a Bauman way and indeed, he became Bauman at times, and that was a little scary.

"Where are you from?" he asked Daniel, and the response was always either nothing or something like, "East."

"Why Los Angeles?" Bauman asked him once.

Daniel replied, "It's the city of angels."

"You like angels?"

"Sometimes," Daniel answered.

One day, when Bauman was out on patrol with Brother J (who only liked to be called John the Apostle) and Shep, who was young—probably only sixteen, Bauman thought—they found Daniel clipping the hedge at a place he was not wanted, the Faith Church. On this day, the new pastor, whom Daniel called "an antichrist," arrived in a brand new truck and had a new haircut and a new suit.

Daniel spoke of Alf's wife, Gwen, as Jezebel. And Bauman knew what he was talking about. When he was on beat, he remembered this Alf Blicky, a surfer behemoth with shaggy blond hair and a blond mustache. He remembered him as an usher, though Bauman had never attended services.

It was anti-climactic to find Daniel clipping the hedge at a church where he wasn't wanted, not more than a few blocks from headquarters. Could it be that Daniel wasn't whom he thought in the beginning, that is, a man of answers? Could it be that Daniel was only working for himself, and pretended to have answers? Could it be that the answers were wrong? As for the reliability test: Daniel failed. Daniel was nothing more than a dumpster jockey with a huge attitude, bigger than the rest. Bauman could not get on top of the situation—mysteries remained.

Regardless, this Daniel had one gift, and that was the gift of knowing what was what and who was who and who was doing what to whom. He knew. He knew the name of John the Apostle, but John the Apostle said that he *had known him before*. What in the world did he mean by *before*?

What did he mean by *after*?

That didn't matter now, he fingered Pastor Alf as Lucifer, and that was good enough for Bauman. About people, Daniel was genius. Accurate information was the key to good police work, Bauman told himself while staking out the Faith Church.

Lanky Shep had run for microwave hot dogs from the food bank over on Saticoy. The missionaries kept asking Shep when he was going to bring in his friends, and what about Shep's relationship with Jesus? Shep would tell the program director, Big Fred, that he loved Jesus as his personal Lord and Savior. No one could dispute it, and they would pray for him as a condition of his getting and then running away with the food. Shep said something interesting: that the Son of Man had no place to lay his head, quoting Scripture no less. When they asked Shep where he had heard that particular line of Scripture, he said: "From that guy, Daniel."

"Who is this Daniel that you guys are always talking about?"

"He's...," Shep was clearly confused. "He called me the Shepherd. Because I feed the flocks."

Louis, the other co-director, choked up a bit, then stuffed it back down. Come on, this was only Speedy Shep, whom Daniel called *the Shepherd*. It's not prison, the other ministry of the Rescue Mission; it's not Santa Barbara, the boxcar crowd. This is the San Fernando Valley, and Louis closed his eyes as Shep left. Fred looked at him and they both nodded. "Something's going on, we better check it out," Fred said and asked, "What do you think of Daniel?"

Louis looked around and shook his head. "We're taught, I mean the Bible teaches two things: God's ways are not our ways and miracles happen. Look at us, no money, no prospects, yet we have enough food and money to feed all ten thousand of our brothers and sisters on the street. We didn't even advertise, it just came."

"Praise God," Big Fred, the ordained minister, said, wiping his glasses on his T-shirt.

nineteen

"Why can't you get it right?" Justin demanded.

"What's wrong with the line-up we have?" asked Rope, the guitarist with the new tattoo of Satan curling his tongue around a nude and helpless girl on his wrist. So much for Sibyl, Rope thought. Got the best tattoo queen now.

"We're not the headliners, that's what's wrong," said Justin in front of everybody at the warehouse in Santa Monica. "And this IS the new video, right Rick?"

"It's not decided yet," said Rick Lowie with Katarina not at his side.

"I want to start today, or no show in Long Beach."

"Look, you got by the Forum, barely."

Justin fell on the hard cold floor and laughed. "Right, and they hated us."

But Lowie was no slouch when it came to prospects. Yes, the revues were spectacular. With only three-quarters of the PA that Bluefish had—they literally had blown them off the stage. In fact, Justin had been so spectacular, and the band so tight, that Bluefish did not want to go on at all.

Rick Lowie gave them more P.A. toward the end; the crowd booed Bluefish and wanted Strange Muumuu back.

Lowie's handpicked manager was a round guy named Chip. He was dressed in a dapper style, fresh from Big and Tall, and his crew was superb; his computer skills were as good as his organizing abilities. He was able to rehire lighting, sound and tech; he was able to garner new guitar sponsorships, new drums, new mikes, new clothes—for essentially no money, just promo. Lowie had built bands with Barrow, and now he'd landed him a primo position and of course the best part of it would be that Chip would keep a very good eye on Justin and call in with information when necessary.

There were shadowy figures Justin could see through the lights of his rehearsal space, dwarfed in the airplane hangar at the Santa Monica airport. "Look, I told you I work in privacy."

"Justin, there's no one here," Chip cheerfully pointed out as he looked at Rick.

"There's no one here, Just," added Rick, craning his neck and looking for Katarina.

"Oh, no? Well, what's that?—I SAID, WHAT IS *THAT*?"

Before Chip could lunge into battle, Justin had thrown the mike, kicked his monitor, knocked over the digital Betacam, approached the edge of the room, and started screaming at what looked like air to Rick.

"I told you to leave me alone! You'll get what you want! Okay? You can be points of light but I can't concentrate, and it's not time yet, so blow outta here or I'll make you wish you never were."

Even Katarina, who arrived with the bag of Chinese, which Rick always ordered when he was stressed, was shocked.

"Points of light?" asked Chip, wishing he hadn't said anything.

The band members were complacent or just tired. They lit cigarettes and wandered around silently.

When Rick gauged Katarina's reaction, fear set in, then he knew there was only one thing to do: appease. "Okay, Just! Hey!" he yelled across the five-story tall, wide as a football-field hangar. "Okay! We'll do your video—I'll have Ross direct, cool?"

Justin looked at Rick with total suspicion. "Don't you people understand what's happening here? This is the beginning and the end. The Way is being paved. I have to fall so He can rise."

Chip got busy walking toward the other side of the hangar to talk to the drummer, Jeremy Styles, who told him that Justin "scares the hell out of me, man."

"Me too, bro," Chip admitted.

"And you, Jezebel—you will fall when I fall," Justin blurted toward Katarina, with an unsaved and unrepentant Magdalene on his mind.

"Was he religious as a kid?" Rick asked Katarina, who was looking stunning after her splurge on Main Street in Santa Monica. "Did you know that the initials of Santa Monica are S and M?" she asked.

"Honey, can you do anything?" Rick was insistent.

She expertly grabbed a Kung Pao shrimp with her chopsticks and delivered it to Rick's stressed mouth.

"*Can* you?!" Lowie demanded.

She laughed. "I can do anything."

"You look great by the way," said Rick, calming and in need of her, or a tranquilizer.

She did not know what he meant.

twenty

*S*erin will not be used as a holding tank for problem children, who will just be shipped off when things don't go right, Kincaid told himself. His wife, Jackson, was smart, and now that she was gone, northern Arizona was just big enough for him, but not big enough for Bock Wiley *and* him. Yet Bock knew things, knew people, and he seemed to be pulling the strings, and now Brand was thinking that Bock had been overseeing the operation all along. Any illusion about owning his own research center now hung in the balance, and any notion that he controlled the funding was false. It had been a sham from the beginning, he realized; he didn't have the real authority, autonomy or an autocracy of science, with the best scientific results winning.

He wasn't cold-hearted; he cared about his son, Justin. He planned to leave for Los Angeles to try and help him. Jackson was in Los Angeles at a conference with Bock Wiley and cross-discipline luminaries like Spence Colfax, the father of laser brain surgery, and Benchley Westing, the father of electronic stimulus therapy—or brain implant technology. Bock and Jackson were probably discussing the future of the Serin Institute, and those plans might also include the Casey Smith case, a project which Kincaid well knew was being viewed as the test of Kincaid's resolve as well as the Institute's.

He slurped another vodka and tonic, popped another Xanax and laughed about how often he'd criticized his son's drug use, how he did not recognize himself as a doctor, a man or a father—no, today it is obvious. Failure. Justin was the abomination, the opposite of everything Kincaid stood for. Society was not something to be condemned, society was to be shaped; the future was bright, the angels had spread their wings, *gestalt* applied to the ersatz random or factionalized structures loosely organized and deemed "society." But for those who backed Kincaid, society was to be transformed, transfigured as *deity,* was to be a *stitchless whole* thanks to research, experimentation and constant media homogenization. From the *axis*— the Serin Institute itself—societal norms were to be formulated and instituted. Conformity was king. Conformity was the rule.

He just had one last thing to do, one last cog in the wheel.

Brand Kincaid, though only fifty-one-years-old, would be the one to fashion the cornerstone and lay it in the foundation and thus finish the creation of the world *ex nihilo*, like the *exhale* of God Himself! *Couldn't they see that?* Couldn't they see how far he had gone, what bold new vistas he was seeing and thus appropriating? What new possibilities now existed precisely because of his research and steadfast focus? How phenomenally close they now were to perfect societal control?

Even beyond homogenization?

Of course they could. That's what they wanted of him—goals aligned perfectly in a seemingly random universe. They wanted the Serin Institute for themselves, and they wanted authority and dominion over everything they might survey.

And they had it all along, Brand was finding out.

How could he *not* know that he had played into their hands? Just in choosing him and commissioning research, presentations, press releases and proclamations of new breakthroughs, it was clear that he was definitely guided.

How could they disguise their intentions? Did they regard him as stupid? They must have.

Or was it something else he feared? *Magic? Spirituality?*

Was there something spiritual about being controlled?

He popped a Quaalude. It was amazing he never lost his demeanor and that no one knew about the drug use. He could function brilliantly, and he would insist, to himself and others, that of course there was no drug problem. The drugs were all prescription, and after all he was a medical doctor, a pharmacologist as well as a trained psychiatrist. He had never completely understood the gift of his intellect until he was warmed by booze or Demerol or pharmaceutical cocaine or something else he would not divulge. Now, he believed, someone was probably using this information to damage his credibility, compromise his power and test his authority.

He was a hypocrite and he *knew* it—so were all of *them*! Surely it was even more hypocritical to pick one hypocrite out of a fulsome field of hypocrites!

He had no right to judge his son, not as Jackson had—she'd written him off and practically burned every miniscule article about him or the band. She hated him, and she hated me, he told himself.

Justin was no Christian. Was not into strange irrational cult activity. Was, if anything, a victim of an evil world, hosted by men whose sole intention was to destroy everything they could not possess. No, not Brand—*others*.

And Brand was not guilty, he felt. No, there was no blood on his hands; there would be no curse or judgment on his son's life *because* of him. It would *not* be discussed over cocktails anywhere, not entertained in casual discourse, and avoided at all costs if ever asked formally by higher-ups.

That's why he would go now to Los Angeles and straighten out more than his son. He would show up and gain entry; it was long overdue. He knew about their *convention*, as they called it, at one of their many country clubs, their political rally—all the important things that Brand now understood he was not part of.

And he never had been.

And he should be from now on.

• • •

There would be payment for St. Lucy, and tonight was the night. Arles had already played eighteen holes of golf at what was referred to as a "restricted" club—but nothing was restricted to him. He had been to parties with celebrities, had his pick of the most gorgeous women on earth. Was filled with caviar and conversation with judges and diplomats. Danced in tutus and wore funny masks and could have his pick of any "controlled" child, if he had so desired. Dubailles' secretary had to book him into certain events in Los Angeles. All leading up to the high time of the year—Easter. This was when things would happen. This is when he would *see*. It would be his initiation—Palm Sunday, when the sun was high, and he could only guess how they would translate the blood, to propitiate the god of earth. Of wealth, of power, of immortality *in the* flesh, commanding the very material world themselves.

The City of Angels wasn't the same as D.C., yet at the hotel he saw their shadows—a senator here, secretary there, a committee member down at the café, and out at certain restaurants, he saw them too. They knew him, and they were courteous. He was one of a handful of dark-skinned men, but the only one at his particularly rarefied level, and that made him feel proud. So long since the Harlem days and so far from his own mother who tore his money up and turned her back. So far from Yale and Harvard—far up the ladder from the grunts in the secret agencies, from the spies. Soon he would find out who was who and what was what. He would be one of those who *ruled in secret.*

How would it go, he wondered with anticipation? Would he be called into a secret ceremony? Would it be like a roast, a bunch of nasty jokes at his expense, then welcomed into "du monde" or *axis-mundi* at last?

He had not paid for anything, not the private jet, not the hotel, and certainly not every restaurant he went to, especially with Senator Diane, his sponsor and partner in many a global adventure.

He recalled the avalanche in Switzerland that took the tram as well as killing every skier on the mountain, mostly children, and he had used such a small detonation device. There was the World Air 770 flight, which he made sure was blamed on Iranian terrorists. Or the space shuttle, one of his first real victories. Countless train wrecks, collapsing buildings and war baiting, which was a major part of his business. He was given hearty congratulations for starting the current Middle East conflict in Israel. He was awarded badges of honor, big paychecks and secret titles that he was told would mean something later. September 11 would always be his proudest moment, not to mention the evacuation of his friends from Building 7 of the WTC complex just before the collapse. Such timing! Although the coming biological and nuclear attack profile for Europe and the Americas was utterly exciting. How much power could he bestow on the brethren from his shenanigans—nothing sort of total dictatorship. Dubailles' reward would be tall indeed.

Was he alone in the war? Of course not. There were very strong competitors in total opposition—five to be exact. But none were *grail*-based. None had turned Jesus into a weapon of mass destruction! So they were superstitious, especially those who based their entire supernatural base on a skull or a sword. The Holy Grail was king, and Senator Mitchell would deliver such a skilled warrior into the family with open arms.

But he did not know for sure. This was the first time in his life that he did not know *exactly* what was going to happen. This time was the crux of the whole matter—where and what, exactly, was going to happen? He didn't like it. Everything had always been pre-planned, including the deaths of his...adversaries. Which was why he never got anything coming back from any intelligence agency. In Washington they would leave Arles Dubailles alone. He had never, never had anything to fear from any man on earth.

There would be a call, and it would be later. Downstairs in the Beach Bar he continued his version of excitement; his breather filled with cocaine, sipping champagne cocktails and ogling girls.

The bartender looked at him in a funny manner—yes, he was familiar...and after a little sniff from his helper, it suddenly became clear: *This was the bartender from his birthday party—from his house so far away!*

A plant! Exactly, Arles thought. They are observing—they have to be careful. This time his long dark hair was braided, but that dark brown beard and that white Hindu style shirt were strikingly familiar. Here he was bartending and acting like he knew nothing, especially about Arles. Of course this was a cover. Of course he looked different. Was it was the idea that Arles was too stupid to not know, or was it supposed to be entertaining, a practical joke? *The joke* didn't sit well with Arles, especially since he had never seen him at the party. Josh had told him the man wasn't one of his, and he had passed it off as some sort of glitch.

Glitch? This plant? This interloper? This adrenaline flight now underway?

There could be no glitch!

It was no accident; the bartender did not behave in any manner of strangeness, or most importantly any manner of recognition. He didn't even look at him except to ask him what he would like to drink. Did not look at him except to smile and be serving, as if looking for a nice tip!

Of course it was a setup, and there would not only have to be evasive measures, but something stronger to send an implacable message.

That feeling of raw power coursed through Arles' veins. He was tired of looking at all the lowlifes around the bar, pretending to have position or place—the uninitiated, *unilluminated* people with a lack of something combined with nothing—no tradition, no knowledge, just a tentative half-life; actors without a script, never playing a cherished part, no director or makeup artist, just raw and awkward.

Arles was looking at a man about to die, he thought. "You don't remember me, do you?" asked Arles.

The strange man with the braid and dark beard continued pouring drinks for various customers.

"Seems I remember my birthday party, where you attempted to tell me in vain, mind you, that I was, how did you put it, *a marked man*?'" Arles said, swilling his champagne drink and breathing a snort for his "stuffy" nose. "Seems I remember you being in my house and Josh said you weren't one of his, and I'm the only one I know of at this hotel, so...."

"Would you like some oysters?" asked the stranger, who did not seem to fit the Beach Bar.

"Of course."

A young woman sitting next to Arles chimed in, "I just love oysters."

"Do you love the beach as well?" he asked her as the bartender disappeared.

She pleased him visually: waif-like, tall and pouty, but ancient in her daddy-may-care opulence, and he liked the nihilism too. "You seem like someone I'd like to talk to," Arles said. "Champagne?"

"I might like that," she replied coolly.

"Well," he said. "There's more where that came from."

"You a producer or something?" she asked, blowing her cover.

Arles lit her cigarette. *Another bartender* asked her to leave if she wanted to smoke. Arles told the *new bartender* that it was okay, in fact it was quite fine—and if there was a problem to call the manager and tell him that she was with him.

"Oh ye of little faith," he said, quoting his favorite verse from the Bible he defiled.

"Are you a Christian?" she asked. "I think Christ is cool. In fact, I love Jesus."

"You?" Arles questioned, caught now in the lurch of his own misperception. "I would have figured you for a Buddhist, or possibly an atheist.

"What's the difference?"

"Good point, you're not educated but you're smart. I like that."

She frowned at his intimation. He searched the room, even

though the glare of the sun setting over the Pacific Ocean made it nearly impossible to see, silhouetting all who stood between. They seemed for a moment to be staring at him and seemed to be looking toward the bar, at the very least. She took one of the oysters, swilled some champagne and placed her hand on his leg, while he was straining his neck to see better. Then he turned and saw the blond bartender with a Hussong's shirt on and wondered where the *counterfeit* bartender was.

"What bartender? I'm the bartender till ten tonight—and I'm already tired."

"No," said Arles, "I meant the bartender with the beard and the Indian-like long shirt who brought me the—"

He would have continued, but the new arrivals crushed in quickly to see why the young woman had fallen to the floor, out cold.

When Arles checked her pulse, he knew she was dead.

"Call somebody!" Arles urged.

The *true* bartender had already called security. They wanted to talk with Arles, and they cleared the room.

"I...she ate an oyster..." was all he could say.

He withdrew quickly—told the police what room he was in, and he was told that she was a hooker, not by the bartender, who claimed to not know any details, but by the officer present. "She's a pro. She's from Vegas."

"Really—do you know anything about that bartender, the one I mentioned?"

Officer Backs said he knew nothing about it, that the other bartender seemed to think that Mr. Dubailles was involved simply because of his bizarre claim that there was *another* bartender.

When he left the bar and entered the waterfall atrium which housed all the inside rooms eight levels up, he saw the man with the long gray hair and beard clipping one of the plants on level three, just as he had at Arles' house!

His training kicked in. He dropped his cell phone into the trash can, ripped his way to the elevator, then approached the planter where he had seen the guy with the gray hair and beard. But only a woman with plant spray was tending to the waxy tropical leaves of potted palms and lilies.

"Have you seen an old man, or do you have a guy on staff, an old guy with gray hair and a beard—blue-eyed gentleman, I believe," Arles asked the woman, who would not turn to face him.

"No," she said, refusing to turn around.

"Well, I just saw him up here. Look, I'd like to see the maintenance manager, or your boss, if I may. Who is that?"

"Mr. Jenkins, he not here right now," she said in a Hispanic accent.

"Well..." Arles strained his neck, looking over the balcony, searching for something, anything to put his mind at ease. Initiation, he thought. This stuff doesn't come easily. You don't just get into the Brotherhood because of service, no matter how dastardly the deeds had been, no matter how loyal you were perceived to be, no matter how knowledgeable you were or how far ahead of your colleagues you were or your contacts or whom you slept with or what you've fixed. You had to be indispensable—they had to, under protest, let you in. You had to be self-corrupted, and he had already done that. The elders must try up until the last moment at the blindfolded initiation (he was guessing here) to thwart any candidate, preferring entrance by birth and connection to royalty.

Since his was not a royal birth, and since he was dark, from the wrong continent, with the wrong heritage, he knew that *here*—like anyplace—he might be considered a token, or worse, it was a set-up. That he would be the house nigger for a short time, which he overcame in Washington to such an extent that he frolicked at tutu parties and oversaw the initiations of all the blue-blood boys, and he was proud to call himself "blue" as well. Diane Mitchell was a sex buddy, and he'd seen presidents naked and had of course looked the other way. He had been in the bedroom and up the noses of so many dignitaries; he had far more on them than they had on him, and they trembled when he walked. No other man of his heritage had been this high. Instead of fighting the pan-Europeans, he would join them; instead of fighting their rituals, he would learn them.

Upon returning to his suite he saw the red blinking light on the phone. He also had received a fax from his wife, slipped under the door. He checked the messages.

"This is Diane. How is Los Angeles treating you? There is a...a banquet tonight at eight-thirty. I'll send a driver, say around eight, if that's all right. Call me if you have any questions. Looking forward to you tonight, Arles. Take care."

Good, he thought, that settles it, it would either be tonight, or it would be in a couple of days, and it would consummate on Easter Sunday *somewhere* on the planet, but either way, he had to go through it by *not knowing* exactly what would happen.

Those men were mysteriously annoying—did they actually think that he wouldn't remember? It was strange they should continue testing him—he'd passed every test, the final one being the island. That was the finest performance and the best ritual sacrifice ever; he just needed to know where the satellites were pointed, where they were beaming, who the players were, what kind of money they were talking about. He wasn't worried about money—just what kind of situation he would be entering into.

The fax:

Hi, hon. Hope your business trip is going well. Rachel's come down with a severe flu bug, we think. Dr. Light said if her fever didn't break, she'd have to go to the hospital. Please call when you get this. Love, Mary Sue

He was on the phone, and he could see from his window the man with the long dark beard and Nehru shirt walking on the Santa Monica boardwalk, talking with a bunch of people that seemed homeless. The gray-haired man—the false gardener—was there also.

"Hello?" came the plaintive voice of Mary Sue.

"Hi, honey," Arles said in a concerned manner.

"She's...I think you'd better come home. Dr. Light wants to put her in the hospital tonight—you know, for observation and to break the fever," she said worriedly.

Of course Arles was torn. On the one hand he had retrieved his 32 cal. Beretta and strapped it to his ankle, ready to tear down to the boardwalk to find out who and what these people were who were in his house and somehow were following him across the continent. On the other hand he wanted to find out from Rachel or from the doctor just what was going on with this sudden illness. He did not want his daughter to suffer; that's why he had done all this; he needed his family to lift up into the light. Rachel, always the healthy one, never got ill, he reiterated to himself. He didn't quite trust the situation—what if Mary Sue was put up to something? What if it's a factional thing, a warring one at that? What if his house were under attack while he was away? He had his share of enemies, the worst disguised as friends or colleagues. He had killed mightily and many. Assassinations, moving past senior intelligence agents, ratting on colleagues, he'd done it all to get where he had gotten, yet the sponsorship and affiliations to the most prominent organizations were supposed to protect him endlessly, omnisciently, and all his assets besides his person.

He could feel secure.

"Look, can I call you back in a few minutes?" he plaintively asked Mary Sue.

She stammered and paced around the library, he could tell. "Arles, your daughter is sick and she's going to the hospital—I'm driving her. She can't eat, her fever is 103 to 104, and—"

"This is a big deal for me. You want me to drop it and come home or what, Mary Sue?" he asked, angrily. Then: "I'm sorry. It's a big deal and I...well, you know, the senator's here, as well as many...well what are we going to do about Rachel?"

She was crying—that was the silence now. He could hear her whimpering between breaths. He could hear her fear, and he quickly dismissed any foul play on Mary Sue's part. She could not lie and he knew it, she could not know, did not want to know, and that was that. It was clear that she did not know what to do, and it was equally clear that he should do something. He felt the guilt and anger dance in his stomach as he watched them below: the gray-haired guy with the blue eyes and his buddy, that dark- haired bartender with the Nehru shirt who said he was a marked man—didn't he say that? Or something like it? He saw some homeless men who wore what looked like discarded bean sacks for shirts and dirty pants several sizes too big held by twine. One was a fairly large man, the other more compact and he didn't look like he was homeless, but not by much.

"Look, honey...what good would it be for me to return now?" he asked calmly.

"Because she needs us both! How can you be so selfish? I knew you'd put your...whatever you call it, *business* above us! Don't you have enough money, don't we have enough status? Rachel is...she might be dying and no one knows why!"

"Give me the doctor's phone number, right now! RIGHT NOW, you stupid..."

"What?"

"I just...I'm sorry. It's just, well lately whenever I get something going you shove the kids in my face."

"*Stupid?*"

"I said I was sorry, honey, come on," he said.

"Fine, Arles, fine—whatever you say...You're the boss, and you're a lousy father!"

"I am a business leader, I am—"

"Here's the number, alright? Alright? 202-455-4556. Will you call me back after you talk to him—on my cell, because I'm driving to St. Mary's now."

"Why not Washington General?" Arles asked.

"Bye." She clicked off and Arles threw the phone and the receiver into the wall and ran to the window. He opened his briefcase and found his favorite serrated knife, Spyderco Special Forces *Light*—all plastic, great at airports and in all high-security areas. Actually, it was titanium with a Teflon coating that could not be seen by metal detectors, and when he whipped the handle, it flew to stealth attention—the silent one. It's no problem at all, whoever you are. Won't take but a second, he said to himself, watching them from the eighth-floor window.

He donned his sweatshirt, the blue one with the hood right next to his Armani suit, which was meticulously hanging in the closet. He pulled on the Champion gray sweats and laced up the Nikes. "Just get me to the church on time..." he started humming, "...just get me to the church, get me to the church, get me to the church on time!" Excited, he was. He always loved the adrenalin surge of battle.

This is fun. It's not a test. I am having a tremendous time, backyard at the beach, he mused. A few minutes and somebody's going to be very surprised. These situations had always helped him before—eliminate the competition or scare the competition and you became that much more indispensable.

Humble them, they exalt you.

twenty-one

Alf Blicky, all because of the deft workings of his beloved wife, Gwen, was now the pastor of the Faith Church on Sherman Way in the San Fernando Valley. Even Wednesday evening service was packed from entrance to exit.

When Alf stood before them, he requested a *double* offering, one for the church and one for the new prison ministry that he wanted to launch. Gwen had organized weekly women's groups and couples' parties at the church. Money poured in, and they became the couple of the hour. Daniel had observed Alf (an antichrist) but Daniel was now banned permanently by Gwen and the police.

Ted's wife, Sarah, and her two children, Beth and Carole, had been the subject of much prayer, mainly because they never attended again. Gwen would tell new members Alf was changing rapidly, thanks to the Holy Spirit. She told her friends at one of her organized luncheons: "He is simply anointed. God wanted a real pastor for the church—and it was clear that Ted was possessed by demons. We feel so sorry for his wife and especially his daughters. We really must reach out to them."

The congregation agreed. Megan, Honaria and Suzy all told Gwen that Alf was almost magical in his ability to attract people. "Praise God," Gwen would answer, and her style improved with her status. The Elders and deacons agreed. Alf was in; he was hired. He was salaried and that salary would increase as the congregation increased. The church could hold up to a thousand, if crammed, and many of the tithes were increasing.

Alf read line and verse from the gospels—his themes were primarily centered around prosperity through tithing. "You cannot *outgive* God. You can't. If you could understand this, instead of ten percent of your first fruits of your paycheck, you would give twenty or thirty percent. One of our members gives fifty percent of everything he earns. God has done more with that fifty percent than he could have done. And his fifty percent has made more than his eighty percent just the year before. Look at Philippians 4:19." Alf did not need to read the Scripture; he knew it. "*My God shall supply all your need according to His riches in glory by Christ Jesus.* What that means, beloved, is that God in his fullness and abounding love will supply MORE than you could ever give to God. How many here have found that giving produces results?" He waited while a few hands went up. "Powerful, isn't it?"

A few nods of acknowledgement.

"There is no reason why we cannot transform this city, this nation and indeed the world into an abounding, loving and joyous place, with plenty for all, with more than enough. It begins with the tithe to the church. When Gwen and I gave more of our income to the church, we were blessed with promotions, new opportunities and salary increases. We prayed on it and told God that we would like to give more next year, and indeed, more came in, so we had more to give. That is a prayer you can give today. This is how to bring God right into the heart of the world. Now will the ushers prepare for this morning's offering?"

The ushers all went forward to the stage, where they picked up the offering plates. The praise band played their own music, written by one of the members who was also a composer for television. Gwen had brought him in and changed the music program to feel-good contemporary pop. "Music is the heart and soul of giving. Who wants that old-fashioned organ music anymore? We need to get into the spirit!" she said joyously after auditioning the new praise band, actually wooing them from a much larger church up in Topanga.

The elders added it up after Wednesday night. They did not see the man with the slicked back hair wearing a black jacket with a red silk vest and sitting in a chair in the back. Gwen noticed him during the service because he looked like a mannequin. She was concerned; it had only been a few months since Ted Gunderson had been shot by a stranger. Strangers were scrutinized. This stranger wore some kind of mask, making him appear inhuman.

"Honey, you'd better go talk to the man—he's been hanging around. I don't think he's trouble. Deirdre said he put two hundred-dollar bills into the offering plate. He didn't use an envelope or anything."

"Maybe he's rich. We've been getting more and more new people, and boy do they have disposable income. One of them drives a…I don't even know, but it looked real expensive," he said.

"Praise the Lord," she said. "We are truly blessed. But could you—"

"Yeah, I'll check him out. Is he still there?"

Ben, the treasurer, gave a big thumbs up from the "counting table" in Alf's office. He smiled.

"Well?" Alf asked.

"Try thirty G's."

"I knew it! If we hit that, we get a raise, honey! Thank you, Lord," said Alf, slipping into his jacket and giving his wife a very embarrassing kiss from Ben's point of view. He walked into the hall to find the mysterious and generous gentleman. He leaned back in and added: "Maybe he's looking for a wife. We've got plenty of single women."

"Two to one," Gwen said, smiling.

"They give more," said Alf. "The Lord's work will go forward now."

"You can forget about bankruptcy," said Ben. "That is now out of the question."

"Okay, give me a couple minutes, hon," Alf said to his wife.

"Sure," she said, openly submitting.

When they returned to the worship hall, the man was sitting calmly reading. He was thin, appeared in his mid-forties; his gentlemanly demeanor gave him the look of a politician, or a well-to-do banker. Alf could see the vest that had appeared red was a fine silk vest with a faint red diamond pattern stitched up and down. The buttons were fabric and the jacket was a fine gabardine. His hair was meticulous, and Alf wondered if he should start using a little hair ointment too.

The stranger wore what looked like Italian loafers, and sported a solid gold—obviously Swiss—watch; the same brand watch had been the only inheritance from Alf's grandfather. The watch had essentially paid the down payment on their West Hills condo, in the days when Alf was working as a movie grip and Gwen was a secretary for a toy manufacturer. Gwen had gone on to selling real estate, which paid very well if houses were selling. His movie job had led to his becoming an expert lighting technician.

It was a great time to become a pastor, Alf thought. He had worked film production in the City of Angels for twenty years; he was a member of the union and had a nice pension already built in. But this, the Faith Church, was his true passion. He had arrived. He could still work production, if he wanted; it might even win souls to Christ, he told himself. He was beginning to think of himself as nearly holy.

"Hello," he said politely, offering his hand to the gentleman, who sat reading the Bible.

The dapper man looked up to meet Alf's gaze. Now that the crowd had left, the room was a bit chilly, and it seemed bigger than before. "Enjoy the service?" Alf asked.

"Yes," he replied, standing politely and extending his hand, which bore a large ring with a dark stone that almost looked like glass.

"I'm the pastor—Alf Blicky."

"A pleasure, Mr. Blicky. My name is Jordan Star."

"Oh, you just visiting or..."

Star was enthusiastic as his pale eyes bore into Alf, silencing him. His smile was captivating as he commented, "I thought your sermon was wonderful. I especially liked the part about giving. It is so true. He blesses us when we give to Him. I never thought of it that way before. I had always thought you made the money, and then you gave. But giving *before* you make the money...this is extraordinary. Let's not tell too many people about it. By the way, please allow me to live up to your sermon by adding a tithe based on...well, a hunch."

"As a guest, you've already done too much. If you come back a few times, then—"

"—No, no," Star said, pulling his checkbook from the jacket pocket. "I insist."

Alf learned never to turn away money. Never to argue with a man about to give. "Thank you very much, Mr. Star."

"Please, call me Jordan," he said, handing Alf a check for $5,000.

When Alf saw the check, he trembled, but he would not let Jordan see his excitement. No way. Grace under strangeness.

"A tragedy, what happened a few months ago. One of the members was telling me," Jordan began. "Your church was failing financially, or so she said, and there was a shooting?"

Alf nodded. "Unfortunately, the devil sometimes attacks when you least expect it."

"But your congregation thrives," said Jordan eagerly. "Are they all new people?"

"Many of them," Alf answered. "Those loyal to Dr. Gunderson felt conflicted when I replaced him. With the trauma of a shooting, it's no wonder."

Jordan, the newcomer, smiled. "I like it here. I like it very much."

Alf smiled beautifully. Jordan liked him, Alf could tell. "Well, Jordan, we would love to have you here, and you don't have to make such large donations in the future. Unless, of course, you're really..."

"I am. And I need to," said Jordan Star. "I have been blessed by wealth, and I want to make sure that it keeps increasing. According to your sermon, giving is the only way to do just that."

"Sir, do you believe in Jesus Christ, that He died on the cross and shed his blood so that you could be delivered from sin?"

"I'm learning," Jordan said. "I'm not sure what the word 'believe' actually means."

"Faith," Alf said. "We're justified and saved by faith. That's the main thing."

"Nothing else?" Jordan looked puzzled.

"Let's put it this way: do you love the Lord Jesus Christ?"

"Absolutely," said Jordan. "I am intimately connected with him. I *love everyone*." He politely smiled. "It was very nice meeting you. I have a feeling this place will be a bonanza for God," he added and started to withdraw. "I look forward to Sunday's service."

"Same here," Alf said.

When the door closed behind him, Alf let out a howl of delight. "Praise You, Lord! Now I know that I am truly on the right track. Now I know that you are blessing this place."

"What's all the shouting about?" Gwen asked worriedly, running out from the back hall.

"He just gave us a huge donation and he wants to give more from now on."

"Does he love God?"

"Yes, I think he's on his way."

He showed her the check and she started dancing around. Ben had gone home and so it was just the two of them, minus their son. "Hallelujah! Hallelujah!" they both shouted gleefully.

"We praise You, Lord! We praise You!" Gwen shouted, confirmed in her thoughts that pushing Ted out to save God's church was the least she could do. Relieving Alf of his unemployment as a lighting tech was also a benefit. Oh, sure, he thinks he made money and he thinks he laid up a nice retirement IRA through the Credit Union, but she knew that he had been finished for some time. He'd been living in the past. Truth be told, most of the light techs, the grips, the electricians and the construction guys were ten years younger. If you didn't get that cushy union job working the generator for $500 a day, then you got pushed out. But she—or God— fixed it, praise the Lord. He became employed, salaried, and she knew that she would be able to draw a nice salary also as the executive director of the church. The board had unanimously voted them in. Look what God has done, she told herself. He saved my husband and He saved His own church! The cloud of a shooting and the outing of a false teacher occurred with such alacrity and efficiency that she knew it had to be the Hand of God.

Or else she had learned very, very well from her Ventura Real Estate office about maneuvering, especially in tight markets. The success seminars helped tremendously. It's what Christians needed, they needed to learn to be more assertive, to be more aggressive. To be more practical. God intended us to be good stewards, not failing sheep, she mused.

"I am so proud of you, honey!" she said again and kissed him.

He wondered if there would be more to it now that he had pleased her.

"We have to get you some new clothes," she said. "I have to make you look...you know, successful."

"Hon, the donation goes to the church—it's not ours."

He did not know how the check went from his hands to her hands, but it did. All his checks went that way. She held it right in his face so he could see it. "Pay to the Order of *Alfred Blicky*. He wanted *you* to have it. God has blessed us, Alf."

He stared at the check with incredulity. "I...I guess I didn't really look at it too closely, or I would have—"

"God is blessing us and this place, which was cursed and overrun by demons," she said.

He nodded. "I mean, I never went to seminary."

"But thanks to your mother, God rest her soul, you know the Bible."

"We need to be honest here. We need to call Mr. Star, explain to him that this is a personal gift and not to the church, and may not be deductible."

She frowned. "I know it's for us," she said and started for the door at the side of the stage that led to the hall and out to the back parking lot. "Come on, honey. Let's talk about it."

Alf ignored himself and followed her. "I guess all things are truly possible," he said, feeling guilty with the sudden realization that he had been blocking miracles all his life, until now. God wanted so much more for him than he even knew was possible—it was truly the teaching of God, and for the first time, Alf Blicky felt truly blessed.

twenty-two

*H*e was still living on the beach in Jupiter, Florida, still filled up, busy and tired—still innocent. He now knew she was dead after all. What were his *handlers* thinking? Once he'd gotten into the shrinks and sub-worlds beyond anyone's evil imagination, he realized they could have their way with him.

As he watched the helicopters of darkness landing, the palms seemed rubbery and he knew the airstrip in the Glades was invisible. The hangar door was open; he remembered it was Hanger 9. His De Havilland Otter had undergone a few upgrades he was not privy to. He was told it was being used in service to the country. He wanted to find out about it, but he couldn't get to the hangar; he had a *mental* block. Flying to California to bring some big VIP dignitary back from Los Angeles would be his last mission. General Ritali thought Cal would be perfect, for a variety of reasons.

The chosen jet was not his trusty plane, which now seemed to belong to a world *underneath*. Or whatever the weird world was called with the guys with sideburns who worked in their gym outfits and drank Bud Light. The world with a commander named General Jason Q. Ritali and some kind of jet Cal was to fly.

He had flown jets, mainly private flights—his first was the DC-10. Now it was the Boeing 767 with no markings. He liked it, blue and white. It used to matter, lots of things had. But every time he thought of the past, his head hurt. He couldn't really remember. Every time.

Even if it were a news item or someone's name—an excruciating headache would ensue. This time he was excited by a new mission. They told him he would be retiring to the Keys; they had already showed him pictures of his house and some friends they said he had, but he did not remember them. An area right out front of the house was for the plane to sit docked and covered by the shade of some aged palms; there was good fishing over the reefs and a disposable income—they had showed him all this and it was pleasing.

General Ritali approached him cautiously. "So how are you feeling now?"

"Now, sir?" Cal asked, feeling reinstated despite what was happening, and psychologically well. "Never felt better, General. Glad to be in the service of my country, sir."

The general smiled and shook his head. "Ever wonder, Wilson, why we're going with you on this one, so soon after your...*mission fatigue*?

"No, sir. I just know that I am one hundred percent behind the program."

Outstanding, General Ritali thought. Really amazing what can be done. Stupid jerk doesn't even question the mission anymore—he'll do whatever we tell him. "Cal, did you know that we're very proud of you?" he asked. "For all your years of service, of courage."

"Sir, that's not for me to know," Cal said in the most formal manner imaginable. He was wearing jeans and a T-shirt, but his demeanor was perfect.

"At ease, Captain Wilson. Let me tell you a prophecy," General Ritali began. "I'll bet you don't understand our missions, do you? At least the ones that you have participated in."

"No, sir. It's not for me to ask why—just to...." And then he fell to his knees.

"Truly amazing. You may rise, Captain."

Cal rose up just as sure as he was ordered. Ritali called Dr. Wiley later, informing him that the treatments and conditioning process had worked, and that Cal was ready to fly.

"Splendid, General. I told you that you could rely on him," said Bock. "Just remember, if he gets in trouble, just ask if he understands the mission. From that point he should—"

"Already did it, Doc. He fell right on his knees. He's looking over the plane now." The general swept back his hair and looked over at Cal. What an absolute fool—all those years, and he still doesn't know.

"He's worth fifty million bucks, cowboy," said Bock.

"I understand, sir. What about his age?"

"He checked out—fit as a fiddle and ready for war. This mission is worth the risk, from what I understand, but then again I don't understand much," Bock said. "I have my profession and you have yours."

"True, it's eyes only," the general said confidently.

"Good-bye, General."

The clouds had been gathering; the humidity was rising, and the deadline was coming more quickly than previously thought. General Ritali would retire now; he had been a noble soldier—and he prided himself on it, which is why he didn't wind up like Nance and Avery and why he did his service and understood nothing—just kill or be killed.

Cal watched as the plane was backed out and turned, ready to taxi out to the tarmac, which was steaming with spring and Florida heat.

• • •

Stephen had never had a trial; he had never had anything resembling American justice. There had been no arraignment, just a cell, then moving to another cell in the middle of the night, then to another location, and finally to a place that he could only describe as anomalous: a room, not a cell, with two beds, a contemporary lamp, closets, and a bathroom. By now Stephen surmised that he wasn't even in the American justice system anymore. It must be more serious or even worse, he thought, and they did not have anything on him so they had to make it up as they went along. How he missed the old man from the first couple of nights in jail. That man knew the Word of God; he seemed to Stephen a holy man, a man without sin—but there he was in jail. How he would love to see him again.

They must have taken him a long distance two nights ago because he remembered the drive, though he was sleeping most of the time. The beds and furniture and closets and bathroom gave him the creeps, and he quickly bent his knees to the floor, bracing himself against the bed. "Dear Heavenly Father, thank You for watching over me, thank you for all your blessings. Whatever this is, please pave the way to Your truth, that I may glorify You in how I handle the situation. I know You're with me, Father, however Your Will be done, I am here to make it so. In Jesus' name I pray. Amen."

He slept on top of the bed and kept the fear away by imagining himself in a real hotel with a view of the ocean out the window, the very same experience he'd had with his girlfriend once, up near the Oregon border. The blue motel on the beach. The Marlin Inn, or was it the Del Mar Inn? He dreamt about her every so often, and he had prayed for forgiveness for separating from her after living in sin. He learned about sin slowly, first in prison, then when he got out, and especially while working on Harleys in Scottsdale.

He had only stayed in Los Angeles a couple of times, but he remembered it as dangerous, as a sort of amplified Phoenix, as a modern day Sodom and Gomorrah, as a place where Jesus is present, and as a place, like all places with people, that could be saved.

He dreamed of it and wondered how they were drugging him. He did not remember eating, yet he was not hungry, did not remember changing, yet he now wore clothing he did not recognize. There were lapses, clearly, and he knew he was in the grip of something so much larger than his rights as a citizen. As he continued to pray, his courage increased and gave him the strength to trust God and sleep.

When he slept, he saw the tidal wave rolling over Los Angeles—it wasn't just a wave. How could he call it a wave if it reached the tops of the downtown buildings and then continued: a five-thousand-foot wall of water surging wildly toward the first range of mountains? It was horrifying and he woke up screaming.

"Help! Hello! Guard! Someone!" He leaped out of bed, banged on the door and slammed his fist against the wall. An hour later he found himself waking up and wondered if he had woken up at all. He thought that what he had seen was a vision. He remembered Daniel 7:23, which he had recently read in the now lost Bible his mother had given him. "*The fourth beast shall be a fourth kingdom on earth, which shall be different from all other kingdoms, and shall devour the whole earth, trample it and break it to pieces.*"

The lights were on, and it looked like daylight.

He realized that where there had been a ceiling, now there was nothing but an open opaque area and there was nothing but space above him.

He was afraid. He had been in the shadows of reality before, and it was always a time of prayer and confidence that he would be delivered, somehow.

He then saw something else, even more disturbing. Someone in the bed next to his, a roommate! It wasn't a cell, it wasn't prison, someone had taken him, kidnapped him and he was involved in some sort of deception. He remembered a Suburban with blacked-out windows and men wearing conservative attire, yet they were not law enforcement.

Was it persecution? Was this the face of the thing that had been rumored and talked about and promised for those who followed Christ?

He dismissed it—he would not say what it was, he told himself as he shook the man next to him, who slowly woke out of what seemed like an endless sleep.

Seconds later the man was sitting on the other side of the room, awake.

Stephen recoiled, afraid, alarmed. Said nothing. Could say nothing anyway, nothing that would or could or even should make sense.

"Don't be afraid," the man said.

Stephen knew this was a dream, there could be no denying it.

The man had long dark hair and a beard, and he called himself Michael. He wore a white T-shirt with a broken bridge on it, what looked like drawstring surgeon's pants, and was barefoot. It reminded him of his last Bible reading in Daniel 7, and he was willing to entertain this visitor as real and therefore part of his family. "How can I help you?" Stephen asked and felt foolish.

"Nothing can hold you, if you don't want it to," Michael answered calmly. A man of regal stature, he had dark eyes and bushy black brows. A God-inspired vision told Stephen this princely, sovereign being was divine.

Michael stood in the center of the room, as if not in Stephen's presence at all, but looking beyond the walls. "This is the beginning. There is one among you whom God has made the key to the Last. He is the innocent one. If ye hath an ear, listen..."

Michael floated upside down in the room, and Stephen trembled with great fear.

"God's Will be done. Amen. Even so, Amen. You shall protect the Key and he shall be your guide. You shall have help; you shall know why you were chosen for this task, which is not beyond you. You have always been with us. We have always loved you, Stephen."

Stephen was weeping uncontrollably.

"You shall love the Lord Your God with your whole heart, with all your soul, with all your mind, with all your might, and you will trust Him in all things, for He is Lord Jesus, who will return again soon. But first the earth is to be prepared, the way cleared. Go, and tell the peoples of the world what awaits them if they do not repent and seek forgiveness through our Lord Jesus Christ, Son of God. This is mankind's only hope. There is none like Him. He will come for His own, but not until great woes come upon this earth. The earth will be in a state of deprivation, war and disease. This is not to be confused with what the Bible calls *Tribulation*. You live in your own time and shall not know the hour of His return. You shall know that the earth will be plunged into darkness, and they will blame one of the lambs, who is protected by Him who made the earth. Who will be the earthly helper of the innocent ones. And ye shall know them by their fall. This lamb, who prepares the way, is one of us—that is, an angel, cloaked temporarily in flesh. There is a mystery to it, as he was translated away, but then he is here. He is not who he was, as his soul is that of an angel. Like Enoch."

Stephen became calm, his eyes opened wide, and he was in love with God for the first time, and Michael was His Angel. He felt the peace that surpassed all reason, and he loved Michael, who was now a cloud in the room, floating up at the ceiling, which seemed to be very high.

Michael's voice emanated from the cloud, and he gave Stephen his final instructions. "You shall know a woman who is with the boy."

Stephen asked: "This boy, who is he, what is his name?"

"His name is Innocence, yet he is wise. His name is Wrath, yet he is gentle. His name is Light, and he illuminates the Lord God. God's Hand is with him. His gift is that God speaks through him. His persecution begins God's return to vanquish all enemies of God. He will protect His children. The boy is one of us, an angel who will make war, as he executes God's judgment on your cities, filled with those who would harm God's children, and now He is provoked to wrath against your people," the angel replied.

Stephen turned in his bed, and when he awoke the lights were on, shining brightly. He was alone. It was a dream, but it seemed more real than anything he could remember before. It was more real than when he had had a molar pulled, and they had put him to sleep with nitrous oxide and he dreamed vividly. But this was real. On the other hand, *what* had he dreamed? Who would save him from a cell in the middle of a void called a structure?

The other bed was made; he couldn't have had a real visitor. The ceiling was real, the light of the lamp shone on a painting of a bouquet of flowers, he was in his clothes, and had not slept under the covers. Was this a hotel room? A holding tank? A protective cell?

He pounded on the door. "Hello! Hey! You're violating my rights, man!"

He laughed at himself. He was not hungry, his three-day beard wasn't scraggly yet, and he wasn't angry.

He wasn't worried.

He wasn't tired, but he felt like sleeping.

twenty-three

Brand had left the Institute; he needed to see his son. He had realized a couple of things that had seemed blocked before. He had yet to think that what was happening was due to something hidden. He was thinking it was *shadow*, a conspiracy, and that he was losing his grip. He had had a powerful *dream*, while passed out in his office chair, that the Institute was using him, and that their degrees and initiations, which he had always doubted, were indeed *real*. Everything he had attained, all the deprogramming of Christians, all the studies he had conducted about faith being the most violent and intolerable scourge on humanity the world had ever known were commissioned by someone invisible, someone more powerful than humanity itself.

He checked into the Regal Suites Hotel near the airport. Low-key. He rented a standard car and paid cash for everything. He was worried, more so because his wife had not called. Cynda was making progress with Casey Smith, whom they had tried to transfer out to that place which does not exist. The Institute had suggested that Brand return to Manhattan and teach another course. There had been a memo suggesting that he turn over the reins of the Institute to Dr. Wiley. He thought it was merely a suggestion. After all, the Serin Institute didn't exist either; there were no patients in northern Arizona being held against their will, or transfers from prison; all the criteria was unknown anyway. It never was under his control and he now knew what he had suspected all along—*he had been used.*

Apparently Bock Wiley had organized some sort of screening criteria for prisons that sent their prisoners to the Serin Institute before officially signing on as the chief psychiatrist. The bulk of Serin's patients had been coming from these prisons. Brand knew these prisoners had been suspected of cult activity. Most of them were treated or interviewed and then sent back to prison, with the possibility of parole for good behavior. Donating their minds to the government for a brief period of time would be seen in a favorable light. That's all he had to know.

He did not have to know that they were never returned to their cells. He did not have to know that when they disappeared, no one ever inquired about them. Did not know that his Institute was in fact some sort of front for Wiley to acquire plenty of fresh meat on which to experiment.

He had heard about military applications and implantation, the re-ordering and manipulation of young men into some sort of fighting force. He had heard of it in relation to Bock Wiley, but like every rumor that floats around in the dark world of black ops, he had to filter out most of it because a rumor could be, and most of the time was, false information.

Serin was military—its funding came from military. Kincaid belonged to a group that practiced a strange religion which had more in common with what was considered *science*. To him it just seemed like some lame excuse for hedonism. He was beginning to realize that the money came from their strange institution of worship. Did it work? Of course—look at where he was now—the facilities, the power, the *almighty funding*.

A strange truth was closing in. At this point he had to consider his entire role as that of a puppet. The fruit of his labor was the fruit of their religion. The world was a theocracy and he was a slave.

His wife Jackson was "liberated," or *libertine*, and she urged Brand to change his ideas and join in. It was an "open" marriage—or no marriage at all, Brand was now realizing.

He had never had the preposterous thought that all these people who would let their hair down at various locations around the world were involved in actually running the world. They were senators, doctors and lawyers, judges and rich housewives, country club mavens, foreign dictators and dignitaries, but he had always given it about the same credence as all the other secret societies and orders. It was all overblown, all an excuse for unbridled partying and networking, or so he had naively thought. Frankly, he had told himself, it didn't interest him.

What did interest him was shaping society to be kinder, gentler, and more educated. To end drug abuse, to cure cancer. To end psychological trauma by eliminating or changing our collective mythology so children would not grow up to become disappointed with the world. The world was the way it was. The way of the world is what needed to be taught. Certain groups stood in the way of peace, prosperity and love, and he believed it was his job to at least diffuse them.

He had thought that Christianity was the single most hate-fostering concept and culture to grip the planet since cannibalism. How and why people would come to believe it, he could not fathom and he had firmly believed it was a sickness. He rose fast because of his research and experimentation into cults.

Some things he did were wrong; some things led to the deaths of people who had no idea they had been the subject of experimentation.

He found it difficult to think that he, Brand Kincaid, with all his history and all his credentials, had found something under the surface, which, unbeknownst to him for years, had in fact ordered his entire existence from the start. Everything in which he had been involved was some sort of sham; he had been working for those who believed wholeheartedly in the Bible and Christ, which was precisely why they had to eradicate it.

And they chose *him* to do it!

Because it was a spiritual threat and nothing else. It had been right in front of him and he had missed it every time. There really was something to all the ritual, to all the meetings and events. There really was a world more real than his own, and he was not part of it.

"Silly," he said to Jackson over the cell phone, while reading the *New York Times* entertainment section at a Denny's restaurant.

"So how's it going with the James boy, is your girl making any progress?"

He would not let on just where he was, since he was waiting on the call back from his son. "Why does Bock want him so badly?" he asked.

"Who said anything about Bock? It's the child's well-being I'm thinking about," she said and hung up.

Jackson Kincaid glanced at the clock on the wall. She laughed and looked at her assistant, who had just gotten out of the shower and was half her age. He was also a bodyguard and had once been a model. "Is everything ready for Mr. Dubailles?" she asked.

The "assistant" looked worried. "The plane arrived an hour ago."

"Splendid," she said.

The phone rang. It was her husband, Brand. "What now?"

"I just want to tell you," he said, "that you're not fooling any-body."

She wasn't really worried; she was excited about tonight. She was excited about doing it again. About her love for her deity and her knowledge that he was real, he took care of her and was well pleased with her offerings.

"Should I drive Mr. Dubailles?" her assistant asked dutifully.

She smiled and waved him off, then returned to her husband on the phone. "So what are you getting your panties in a knot for?"

The line was dead. She laughed. You would think that no sex in five years would at least make him intrigued as to what she was up to. She thrived on jealousy, anger and deceit—things she had mastered. But he did not give her a challenge. Yet she would not rock the boat. No one divorced in her group anyway.

You are so beautiful, Brand, she had once said to herself. At one time he was. But she had no respect for those who don't quite get with the program.

She looked out the window of her suite, gazing down upon the well-to-do as they shopped the local boutiques. She wondered if they knew why they were so wealthy, if they knew who had paid the price for *them*. If they knew that their wealth could be taken away just as easily as it was given, but if they were ungrateful, or if they did not produce fruit, if they had not sacrificed one of their own to the cause, then they might be erased. They were peasants, and laughable, she thought. They should pay more respect, she told herself. They should be forced, if necessary, to comply with the rules—that way, those who inherit the wealth could be tested to see if they deserve it, and if not, then the tactic would be con-fiscation and humiliation. No one should eat from the trough unless they have been successfully initiated, self-corrupted and witnessed.

No one should be able to ascend unless they were blessed by the one who rules the world, the flesh, and the mind.

She would look forward to tonight. She would look forward with great anticipation. The sun would not set for a few hours, but the moon would be in the perfect place.

She was just that confident.

Katarina was not there, and Rick Lowie wondered where she had gone. If there were ever a time Justin needed calming down, it was now. She could talk to him gently. She could kiss him and make him think that she preferred him over Rick. Rick, who she knew was more appropriate—at least that had worked a couple of days ago.

"We can't perform it tonight!" said Rick, employing the royal "we."

"We *can*," insisted Justin. "*We can.*"

Katarina just wasn't there. Where she was, or why she was missing puzzled Rick. He had done everything he promised himself he would not do: credit cards, driver, his bed for sure. Then it was her own bedroom in his hilltop estate—and a promise for her own condo over the Strip, where she liked to play with strangers. He wouldn't tell her it was all debt. And she couldn't use her south-side savvy to figure out anything more about him because all his real information was under another name.

Nothing was left to chance. He'd had the pleasure of women at his pad before. They would come and go, and sometimes he'd have more than one and more than one of his buddies and sometimes...

But it had always ended badly, an empty, apologetic nightmare. By thirty-five a millionaire, but he still hadn't learned.

When she arrived, she wore gray spring wool and a red scarf, was well made-up, stylishly coifed and at the ready.

She was worth waiting for. The mystery and self-reliance were admirable. She would make it in Los Angeles, he told himself. Everybody would know that right away.

Justin finally got back to the stage and bowed to the ever-beautiful and mysterious Katarina. "A cat with more than nine lives is a demon," he said.

That was just the sort of thing that Rick had been noticing. The poetry changed, despite the fact that Justin had suddenly quit taking drugs or drink. He spoke strangely, and he spoke in another language, something with Hebrew-sounding words, but it had been too long since Rick had studied Hebrew. He even forgot the sound of his own name.

"Shalom, Louis," Justin said, as Rope strutted across the stage, showering from his guitar a shattering wall of controlled feedback from his '64 Les Paul. Justin remained fixed in the darkness as the lighting techs tried to do everything Chip was telling them. Then Justin stopped it: "We need Stephen, man—Chip, you are not anointed."

Chip looked at Rick. "I think it's an improvement."

"Justin knows what he wants," Rick said, slamming Chip. He looked at Justin with incredulity. "Hey, Just, you need drugs, dude. Your memory is gone. Stephen's in jail because he murdered your manager."

"Not for long," Justin said, laughing hysterically.

"You are so awesome," said Katarina. "You're not afraid anymore, *are you?*"

"Queen of the damned. I am God's prophet. And He is coming back to judge the whole world!"

"Aren't you going to save me?" she puckered.

"You put Stephen away, and when he returns—"

"There is no return; he's gone, okay? He was dangerous. Don't you have any feelings for Anton?" Rick asked, indignant.

"*Shhhhhh,*" Justin nodded to Rope, and Chip told the tech to cut the lights.

"Okay," said Rick... "Okay, he's going again. I personally think this whole angry prophet religious song thing is a mistake."

The feedback from Rope's cosmic, shatter-every-mind chords silenced the room, and Justin came out of the smoke, and Katarina's red lipstick looked like blood in the refraction of the lights. The airplane hangar, dark now, had no exit.

"I am you, a lamb, and I am the key to unlock, and I am here to say...." Justin spoke, while the wall of bass, drums and chording guitar swelled into a deliberate and steady beat. It was poetry, spoken with the full force of cosmic destruction of the universe.

Then he screamed: "And the key will unlock the door—and He is coming back. One greater than all. One with a name above any other—do not back away from the door, for you have *nuh-thing.* Without Glory, you are Death, you are desolation, you are thirst and forever...love, oh, love, oh, love, oh...my...loved ones. Oh....my...little ones...."

Katarina started crying, floating the mascara into the lights, as Rick sucked down a Marlborough light and Chip stared at Justin as he rose from the floor to suspend himself in front of what in a few hours would be an audience. "He is the King of Kings and Lord of Lords. He is the Way, the Truth and the Life. He won't be a little lamb next time...all knees will bow, whether dead or alive, whether in hate or in love—all will know the truth. Give it up, give in, little ones. Don't hide, don't run—it only gets worse. Because He loves you. Because He loves you. Take me, take me....take me now... I die but He lives, forever and ever. I die for Him to live....I fall so He will rise, oh my God," Justin sang as if on a mission of death, of judgment, suspended and beseeching the imaginary crowd, as it will be again, in vain.

He was lowered back down to the stage and released from the suspension by one of the technical crew. Chip was glad it was over.

Katarina's phone was ringing. No one was speaking.

When she answered it, she was pleased that it wasn't for her. Because she could not talk after that. Her hands shook, and she shivered. "Justin...it's for you. Please take your phone back—I don't want it anymore," she said, hoping that rudeness might cover.

Justin stepped away from the rigging and took the phone. "Hello?"

"Probably his drug dealer, yes!" said Rick, hoping to stop Justin before he ruined the band.

He had not received a call from Kincaid in at least three and a half years, yet he answered as if he expected it. "Hello, Father."

twenty-four

He was awakened when the building started to shake and the lamp shattered on the floor. "Help! Hey!" Stephen yelled again, thinking they might be doing this on purpose, perhaps to break him into a confession for the murder of Anton Duffield, the manager of Strange Muumuu.

The walls crumbled, and he was thrown back and knocked out.

When he awoke, the real sun shone on his face, hot and bright. There were no sirens.

"Hello! Anybody in there? Anybody!" a woman's voice was calling out.

He opened his eyes and looked around—he had been in a locked building. As he struggled to sit up, he realized that he had originally been higher up in the building, and it had descended below the earth's surface. As he looked down, he saw them, the dead bodies of what looked like lab technicians. He brushed off the dust and attempted to stand. He didn't have a scratch!

The blood all over him wasn't his, it was a woman in a lab coat, her head gashed badly by a chunk of concrete.

There were also limbs, a leg in strips of flesh with the bone caught in a penny loafer, a jagged arm buoying a severed head, and there were various other horrors of greater or lesser degree. There was nothing but carnage, but the greater mystery for Stephen was discovering where he was and why. Interpreting Michael, whether he were dream or archangel, mattered not at all. The devastation Stephen noticed seemed truly apocalyptic, but he knew it was foretold.

"Hey! Hello! Anybody down there?" he yelled into an elevator shaft that went down into the darkness many floors below the ground. He caught a glimpse of himself in the desert sun on a jagged piece of mirror glass. He looked at his eyes—they were not the same. He felt his face—it was lighter, softer; it seemed different.

He was at peace. Had he been delivered into some other place and time, some other plane of reality, as Michael had seemed to indicate...or were his perceptions simply different now that he was traumatized?

"Hello?" came the woman's voice, and in the sea of rubble without a living soul except her voice, he wondered if it was Anna Petchick, his mother.

"Hello?" came the woman's voice again. She was clearly farther away, as it was a large building. Now it was a compound of concrete, an amalgam of metal and waste and girders twisted and tied together like lazy shoelaces, as if rubber and not steel.

"Hey! Over here!" he yelled and wondered if she was alone, or if she was going to arrest him—but mainly he was concerned that she might need help. "You all right?!"

She was distant. She was alone. There was an awesome silence, and he could hear the hearts of all the dead beating like they might have done just a few minutes before. He climbed down what he estimated to be about three stories of above-ground structure. Through windows he saw men with ties and no legs, women facing each other as torsos on a girder that shot through the room, not surprised, simply staring at each other. Whatever had happened, and he felt it was simply an earthquake, had done away with the place, as Paul's prison in Philippi was shaken to the ground, but here there were no guards to be convicted or to run away.

"Hello!" she screamed from the desert ground.

He looked down from his jagged glass sheaf. He stared at her, and he stared at the young man next to her, and he did more than stare, he did more than look, he did more than know. It was *that* boy, *that young man*, whom Michael had spoken of. He looked right through Stephen and smiled *as if having lived through all ages past, present and future*—as if having done all before, *many times*. Stephen could not understand his thoughts, and yet he knew that it was the end of something, the end of himself, to be sure.

"Are you all right?" she asked in quiet shock, wide-eyed and beautiful.

Stephen nodded his head. Oh, yes. I am very much all right, he thought.

"Is anyone alive?" she, the woman with spirit-filled eyes, asked.

He continued to look at the young man, and "wheels" of information were exchanged, back and forth like throwing a basketball, only these wheels went *through him,* and he knew that a wheel was like the Word of God. This young man *sent a wheel into Stephen,* and he was edified, and Stephen sent a wheel that looked like a disk full of eyes back to the one who would be Casey. The Holy Spirit would later call him something else. Casey smiled, satisfied.

"You saw him," Casey said.

Stephen slid down the glass, around the jagged edges, over a broken girder like a child's slide, and he yelled as he slid into freedom; he rejoiced and was met with laughter.

She, who would be Cynda and then something else later, started to weep.

They could all see into the building.

"I'm Cynda, and...and they're all, I mean there's no one, except us?"

"What are you, a doctor or something?" asked Stephen.

Casey looked at him and said: "He lives."

"Who?" asked Stephen.

"Please stop it!" she yelled.

"Did you see him?" Casey asked Stephen.

"You mean Michael?" Casey nodded. "Yes. I did," Stephen said.

"All glory to God," said Casey, falling to his face.

Stephen joined him. "Praise you, Lord. Thank you, Lord. I am beyond myself, thank you Lord!"

"Thank you, Lord! We hear you!" Casey said.

Cynda fell onto her back and stared at the sky.

"Don't you know who you worked for, Doctor?" asked Casey. "Didn't you hear anything I ever said? Didn't you hear what he was saying to you?"

Pools of tears were Cynda's answers as she stared at the sky and could not listen to Casey.

There were no survivors, and there was nothing but desert on all sides and vehicles, twisted and mangled in the collapsed parking lot. A few on the road were in perfect condition. But no survivors in the building, no one else but them anywhere near.

Casey took silent authority, knowing himself and possessing himself, which Stephen recognized as the Holy Spirit. Stephen wrapped an arm around Cynda, who was shivering, the layers and conditioning peeled away like eels off dry glass, her mind slid like sand from a broken hourglass; there was not a scratch on her. Stephen was about to speak, but Casey cautioned him, nodding no, no, then smiled and said to him, "This is all of us."

"God bless you," Stephen said, holding onto Cynda as the sun set over the sea of jagged mountains and a fading sky.

When Casey was silent again, she took care of him, and he knew that she did not know why.

She took a torn piece of coat from her arm and she damped Casey's brow. Stephen hugged them both.

"He's coming back," young Casey said. "He's coming back. And not as a lamb."

Tears rolled from his eyes, and Stephen wondered if, when he hot-wired the Suburban with government plates and blacked out windows, it really was an act of God. He felt the miracle of his vision fleeing him, and he began to understand what had happened as he now saw the broken telephone poles, like twigs, as they were illuminated by the emergency vehicles passing him. Then he could see the wrecked cars, some sticking up out of the desert sand, half-sunk.

There were broken overpasses in the distance and people wandering, dazed.

The rescuers had heard all about it on the radio, which reported an earthquake of a 10.1 magnitude, a mega-quake, the epicenter of which was northern Arizona, but was felt as far west as Catalina Island and as far east as the Mississippi!

The aftershocks destroyed Tucson and Phoenix, with constant magnitude 5-plus aftershocks, which silenced the commuting and relegated business transactions on the Internet.

Some services were open despite the calamities. When they stopped at the local 7-11, they understood why the shopkeeper was armed and at the ready, as the radio had reported looting. Seismologists had no earthly idea why this quake would occur. It put Casey back into perspective for Stephen.

The vision must have been because they had given him drugs and kept him in seclusion. He wondered what his status was since he had had no trial for the murder of Anton Duffield, since he had been kidnapped from the Phoenix jail and taken to a place that apparently didn't exist, a government operation, according to Cynda.

But they were fugitive just the same.

They stayed the night in two rooms at a Motel 6 outside Tucson, and Cynda said: "It's not real. The world."

Casey was convincing when he told Stephen: "The veil remains for a little while, and then it will be lifted. Because what you've seen does not find favor in your mind, you will try to reject it. But you will be unsuccessful."

Stephen saw Anna in a dream, when she said to look, he looked and saw Casey standing in the air, wearing white. He was barefoot, his hair longer, and perhaps even a bit older but of no specific age, a beautiful glowing being. "Do you know him, mother?" Stephen asked, and when he turned to find her again, he could not.

• • •

The earthquake had not affected the Los Angeles area, though residents were now cautioned to be earthquake-ready. The news coverage was around-the-clock, and it was amazing that the only real casualties were in the north, at a "government research facility. The amount of casualties, however, is unknown."

It was early, and FEMA had kicked into high gear—it was miraculous that the damage did not extend beyond to cities like Flagstaff or Sedona, since they were so close to the epicenter. The aftershocks had had a rolling quality, which even the brick and concrete buildings managed to weather.

• • •

Cal waited. He wore a blue suit, had had his hair cut, and he knew he was not out of place. He had his wings; he had had them for a long time. He was still taking care of Sally Anne; he had taken care of her for a long time. He made love to her, and he had damped down her fever. He painted the shack, despite the condo developers. He ate with her, and he was ministered to by most of the preachers across the Glades, across the dampness, but the tents and the darkness were no comfort.

He was told to do as the Romans do, and he was shown a relative world, shelter from the randomness and the mistake of Creation, the accident of unhappy consequences and the suicidal impulse subdued with alcohol.

He *really was* taking care of Sally Anne.

Wasn't he?

He was Meaning. He was Truth. But he was also Flaw and thus he could not do it—being a provider of nothing. He did not help her, he knew that now. But now he had the job to do—transportation, work, payment, and retirement, which he must provide for Sally Anne, despite all the rumors about her death and burial.

What was there besides Sally Anne? What was there besides retirement? Besides being debt free? What was there? Anywhere?

My country. My government. My social and temporal security. My wife. My missing children. My missing God, no. That was not part of the world he was born into. No one could understand what a man facing old age, facing responsibilities to be secure, to be prudent, to be reasonable, to be wise, would *really* experience. Not the way it came down, not the way it was, devoid of Pentecostal musings under a tent where somebody faked speaking in tongues and healed somebody perfectly well.

Not at all. So it was power. And glory. Mothball, back out now. This was Caleb Charles Wilson, officer, once a gentleman, full of secrets, classified and on the hook. Without honor. After the Caribbean, sir, there is no way back, that is what he said, before he was put back in the program.

So they would see it as mission fatigue; he would see it as sour. He wanted to find death, but they would not let it come, particularly Bock Wiley, whom he did see after the *five thousand deaths*, and especially the man to be picked up tonight, Arles Dubailles. He knew of him but Sally Anne filled his thoughts, and he did not remember so well after thinking of her.

Someone said wake up, and when he looked around he knew he hadn't given anything away. In the lounge at LAX Arles arrived with one bag, looking like an inside salesman making 30K a year, divorced and alcoholic.

"Hey, you, Cal?" Arles asked upon arriving in the Fortune Bar.

"Sure, got your ride ready. You want me to get the bags?" asked Cal.

"This is all I have. I'm—excuse me," Arles said, distracted.

"You hear about the quake?" asked Cal in an easy manner.

"Oh...just a second," Arles said, calling on his cell. There was no answer, no destination. Diane did not answer the so-called "hot" line, her second cell, actually a satellite that could be called from anywhere. He did not know about the *other* way of communication. She might have thought him an idiot—at least he was beginning to believe that.

"We felt nothing here," said Cal, happily sipping his *illegal* Bud Light (at least before flying). "I was almost afraid to land—at least they revised it down from a 10 in some outlying areas to about a 6.5 in Phoenix. But it seemed—"

"Will you please shut up?"

Cal obeyed instantly.

"Sorry," said Arles, worried.

Finally, his cell rang. "Hello?" He was relieved, and relief was what he exuded.

Cal smiled at his relief and thought about walking around the plane; he thought about the lights and the memories that surrounded the night. How many flights of fancy during the nights, 35,000 feet up and nothing but a holographic screen of loved ones and things he might do, especially when a little drunk, which he would only do as a passenger. Even in the trusty De Havilland, he might let things drift in a cloud and remember all the milestones and all the faces that meant something and touched his heart.

Alone and under the tinted glasses, he started to cry because of Sally Anne, because of false starts and a failed heart. Because of a need to gain and a lamentation on futility—suicide was in a glass and there was nothing in his life other than the unsolvable puzzle, defeated and appropriated to the bubbles and the shattering of fate.

He laughed because he'd had more than one Bud Light—no one ever said he couldn't have six. Somehow, he'd fly drunk. He'd have to, because he was ordered to.

It was God, he thought, watching Arles, a nervous, little wiry man who he forgot was Gabriel...until the haze of beer cleared his mind.

"He's...oh...he's—"

He could know now, he could remember, five thousand male virgins, no more than sixteen or seventeen, cut down and televised to the temple where they sustained the whole of creation! That's what the beer told him! He was waking up!

"I'll have another," he said, watching Arles across the bar, now filled with Russian soccer players, a few Tibetan monks and not one prostitute. Which also helped to clear up the confusion. They were real! The people were not fake. They were not plants. They were not the people he had had placed in front of him for months now and for years before that as his mind was owned, but now busted by the Bud Light!

"Don't you see! Don't you know? Caleb Charles Wilson, arise, my son. The truth will reign—you will remember," the Voice said, and he felt a surge of warmth all over his body. Arles, surrounded by people who didn't see him, was angry and still trying his cell phone.

Cal was filled with rippling waves of love for everyone in the airport bar, with its windows that looked out on ticket counters, benches and payphones with computer hookups, and the to and fro of crumpled suits—the uniformity of reality. The remembrance was warmer than Caribbean sunshine and New York steaks, but nothing was warmer than Sally Anne Martin's smile.

Oh, the calamity! He had killed and the Voice was telling him it was all right. Five thousand or one, it made no difference. A fool's paradise, the Voice said—numbers—worse sin than the last one, worse with ten than one, better with less than more.

He could see them walking about for the first time. "Hi, there," he said to the salesman next to him at the bar. The beleaguered saint, who knew warfare and had not killed, but had to have vanquished in order to eat. Something from nothing was the game, and he was tired. "Buy you another?" Cal asked.

He looked at the old man, Caleb. "What?" he asked.

"Buy you another? You look like you could use it," Cal said.

"Yeah, sure," the young, dapper, shorthaired, ex-jock, and maybe even ex-military, replied.

"You got kids?" Cal asked.

The beer was arriving and it was the least the salesman named Joe or John or Larry could do. "Yeah," he said with a smile. He opened a wallet and there were pictures of reality.

There were things Caleb Wilson remembered.

"You in the service?" Cal asked.

"Yeah, couple years. Put me through college."

"Ever get a bad hair day?"

He knew the question, which was why he never mentioned serving in the U.S. military. "No, sir—never saw action."

"You knew what I was going to say, but let me say this," Cal said. "Had you seen service, I would have been proud to serve with you, because you saved my life. Oh, you don't know it now, and I look and sound like some eccentric, over-the-hill, out-to-lunch, drunk, disorderly, bordering on *and* exceeding in insanity old man."

"That was awesome!" said the salesman. "You're really tweaked. You're not too drunk to drive?" asked the salesman. "Can I offer a ride home?"

Cal slurped his eighth beer and smiled. "I feel really good. Because I know who I am."

"Wow," said the salesman.

"I know who *you* are."

"Here's to you, man," said the salesman, wondering how his daughter might have done at the swim meet.

"You'll be glad to know that you are not going to be flying with me this evening."

"Get outta here," said the salesman, disbelieving, at first. He didn't believe that this longhaired, extra-bearded, lost in the bushes sort of guy could drive a golf cart, even on his best day. He likened him to the homeless on Sherman Way in the Valley.

"Yep, private jet. I'm in my uniform, buddy," Cal said.

Yeah, the salesman thought, standing back a foot or two and donning his glasses—yeah, you're wearing quite a uniform. "So you're...so you're like flying this big jet tonight and you're sauced?"

"More than that," said Cal, elated. "I'm flying that gentleman over there."

The salesman, by now, became genuinely concerned for Cal, though he still thought Cal was joking, so he remained a bit aloof: "Sounds like fun."

"I'm going to crash, then it'll be fun," Cal said, bursting into laughter. "Oh, I feel good now that I know I'm not nuts."

The salesman looked over at Arles Dubailles, who seemed diminutive next to the crew of what looked like college basketball players crowding around the video game next to Arles, who spoke on his cell phone.

"Yeah," said Arles, "I'm...well is it a big deal?"

Diane Mitchell said: "Of course not. We understand. Your family is far more important. There's another window in Brussels on the 28th. Why don't you—"

"—You brushing me off, Diane?" Arles asked, watching Cal over the heads of eager beer sloshers.

There was pause, and he could hear her breathing, and he knew somehow that the true test of initiation was to put everything second after the Order.

He had made up his mind—he would not go.

"Diane, I've—well, I've...changed my mind. Send the driver, I want to fulfill the promise, I want to buy the package," he said, and flipped through his phone book, scanning the bar for Cal again, who was laughing and singing with his arm around an unknown person.

"Well...it's called off," she said abruptly.

"Look, I want you to know that I put *it* first."

"It's called off—just forget it now. Look, we'll talk at Sherry's party after the White House thing. Okay?"

"Don't push me out."

"Arles, this is your buddy—don't you remember?"

He mainly remembered mainly taking care of her needs from time to time plus doing other things she needed that seemed so perverse he could not bring himself to associate it with her at all. Death was easier to associate with her, such as the five thousand male virgins on St. Lucy.

He remembered why he had gotten the opportunity.

"The order has arrived, ma'am," he had said to Diane Mitchell from the island that day. Even the cameramen were wearing gas masks. He spoke to her on the monitor of the satellite hook-up truck. She wanted one wide shot, one panning shot and she wanted the cameraman to film the execution of the witnesses in close-up.

Arles followed Benoir, the cameraman, up and down the aisles of the dead. All wearing white, all sixteen or seventeen, no older. All purported to be virgins. All Christians. All black. All innocent.

He could hear the moans and groans, and he could hear her breathing heavily—and then silence.

As "Gabriel," Arles was the angel who would save the island by having all the young men line up in the field for a prayer vigil to save the island's failing banana industry. Costa Rica and other producing islands nearby provided too much competition and the only place they could sell the smaller bananas was in England and France.

Oddly, England and France had traded this island several times, and Arles knew the blacks here were still slaves. He was proud to associate with white Europeans and fashioned himself a warrior-king, like Charlemagne or Alexander the Great.

He fashioned himself as above five thousand virgins or ten thousand babies or even a city, for that matter, and could even see himself detonating a nuke in Paris or London or New York or even D.C., if necessary. Death was his friend, and as Gabriel, he could blow the horn, call upon his personal savior and climb the power ladder.

Then that thing about the blood, the grail, Christ—about appropriating His blood for personal purpose through a magical rite called *inversion*—this, the most significant of all secrets, would be made manifest tonight. It's what all the killing had been about, he thought. They would not reschedule, and for the first time it wasn't working. She said ritual worked; she said candles worked, and that visualization and fantasizing with a familiar spirit and various objects of power worked. He learned all that from his grandmother, who went to church and cooked up quite a spell or two, including zombie dust, she claimed, for that rare individual who would try to cross her or her husband. She had every root, every sacred doll, all the carved images of saints, of Jesus on the cross, and much hair and clothing, collected from the local populace. Her name was Cleesa and she played a trick on a man who she said was once her boyfriend. Even though Arles was just a small boy in Kingston, she did show him how she liked to have her way with little tricks. She took a discarded male doll and set it on her altar in her room. Then she disfigured the doll and made it into a woman. And sure enough, over the next few weeks, he saw the man slowly pervert into a feminine creature. Gone was his popularity, and he now had to fend off the advances of what used to be his friends; he became a slave to his wife, who was proud of her elevated status. "You see," she told Arles, "this is what he deserves for cheating on his wife. Now she's the one who has dates with men, and he do the housework. The Lord works in mysterious ways, little one."

Of course, this *lord* was most certainly not *The* Lord God Almighty! That he knew. But this lord works powerfully and produces results; the One in church would only do His Will. Arles would never accept anything except what worked for Grandmamma.

She had it down to a science. You simply think it, visualize it, focus on an object, a key chain, a mirror, or any familiar and well-used thing, and it would happen.

For Arles, the main thing was self-image. He had made his vow to the *lord* of the earth and had had it easy ever since. He simply had to help people out, do things for them, help those in need, little things, like drugs, sex of every variety *except* that sanctioned in the Bible—prostitutes, child slavery and murder, a specialty. And he was rewarded every time.

He had moved up.

When the police arrived and viewed the horrific rows of dead on the windward side of St. Lucy, he told them that all had been made zombies by the local witch, and that they could be revived, and he, Gabriel, would do it.

Then those who investigated were murdered on camera. One camera was up on the tower, two on the ground and one roving, back and forth between the coconut palms.

Diane returned to the monitor.

"There are more," he said.

"Good. Good," she said. And she disappeared.

He ordered Benoir, the roving cameraman, to follow as he machine-gunned the police and the military drivers in the style of the Jim Jones footage from Guyana in the '70's.

"Now hand me the camera," said Arles to Benoir. "I want to shoot something."

Benoir acquiesced. Handed him the camera. "Sir, I feel sick— I..." and he vomited right on the spot, relieved not to be filming anything.

Arles mounted the camera on his shoulder, raised his Glock .45 acp pistol and shot the close-up while firing point blank into Benoir's head. He filmed the stream of blood shooting in the air and then turned to close in on the man in the tower, who started scrambling down the scaffolding.

Arles beat him to the bottom of the scaffolding, trapping the man near the top. "Please, don't. Come on, man! Hey, I served under you in Kuwait, come on!"

Arles quietly set the camera on a wide shot of the small tower, which resembled a lifeguard tower with a larger flat area on top. He stood at the bottom and aimed the pistol up underneath, so that a bullet might pierce the wood and pierce him, perhaps making him suffer instead of killing him so quickly. He fired a few shots, then heard a scream.

"My leg! My leg! Captain! I'll give you money—I'll, look, I'll do your killing for you, if you want, just don't kill me."

Arles said nothing. He reloaded, smiled at the camera while aiming behind his back, without looking he fired, keeping his eyes on the camera.

He was struck in the knee, in the foot, in the chest, and the neck. But he was not dead yet.

Arles gave him a chance to run, and he fell from the tower and pulled his bloody body over the first of five lines of dead boys, who had been poisoned and were not bloody.

"Don't mess up their shirts, Jake!" was all Arles said, hoping the blood didn't ruin the Brotherhood's sacrificial ritual. These boys, after all, had to be in white linen. Had to be surprised, confused and submissive as they fell in neat rows in the field of freshly mowed country grass.

He knew that everything somehow depended on worshipping Isis and sacrificing at the pyramid. He knew the Masonic symbols were traced back to Egypt and the obelisk was a phallus, a thing that seeds and kills by piercing, is dualistic in nature—the heart and soul of a religion he practiced but never really knew. It all had to do with the earth and her cycles. He understood something about Osiris and the Egyptian resurrection, which wasn't just for divine kings but applied to the here and now. The power, left by secret doctrines held in the Vatican but burned at Alexandria, told of the mystery halls of power and initiation, whereby one could ascend into immorality and dominion over not just the earth, but the known and unknown universe as well.

He knew that there were advanced beings. Someone had told him the term *nephilim*, which he knew meant the beings created when angels had intercourse with humans. These new beings created a race that eventually took to space, and apparently were cast out of heaven like the angels. God made the shining one, Lucifer, the lowest creature, which would have to slither on its belly and eat of the dead. Though reptilian, he would rule the earth until Jesus' return. Those who were beautiful and not reptilian, the nephilim, would nevertheless be cast out of Heaven forever and would work with the reptiles.

Arles knew they existed in other dimensions, and that they too had sex with humans; their story became myth and legend, exemplified in abduction literature.

He knew about the serpent; the *Order of the Dragon* was one of his first initiations. He worshiped the dragon and that's when he saw his bank account soar.

He had never seen these hidden things that were rumored in the halls of power. He had never seen other beings from other places. He understood that the power to ascend came from *them,* and that they expected his worship. He gave it, constantly saying: "Praise to the beast, or all glory to the dragon," or "I love you, serpent, I worship you, and I serve you, oh, Goddess of the earth, tell me what you want me to do."

This worship was usually in conjunction with a phone call to his control, who would give him an assignment—*intelligence* belonged to the serpent, as everyone knew but no one would say.

The senator had said that although the Bible is an abomination, if people understood it and followed it, they would ruin it for all beings of light, as she mistakenly referred to herself. "Which is why we can never let people know that it's real. We're not going to awaken the giant who will kill us all," she said laughing, one day last Spring when the orgy around the maypole was bedded with ripped pages from Bibles. She enjoyed the onionskin very much, and watching the elite sometimes eat the pages. "Take the power, take it!" she said, laughing because her poll ratings were assured of shooting up ten points the next few days, as the efficacy of the ritual took hold.

There was protection and reward for all those who knew what life was like and didn't mind looking the other way, or growing up and smelling the coffee, doing what was asked with a glad heart and a smile, satisfied at their self-corrupted release, which was currency while protecting their wives and children at home. But to talk about it outside, to utter anything about the truth, would mean execution, usually by accident, made a fall guy for one of the many cover-ups in process. Even if a young initiate slips his tongue, the family is scourged. Any innocent who turns away from the truth is to be killed before he can tell what he has seen—that is the only way high success, domination of industry, in scholastic endeavors, and in politics is achieved. Everyone knew about this but no one spoke because there had been so many examples made of those who had. Like presidents in the past. That shut people up. That's why no one would ever figure out what UFOs were, because it would lead to the truth, and the public is never to know who really rules the earth, who or what *the beast* really is, what the fallen angels really are, where technology really came from, that the Bible is completely true in every aspect. It would spell the end of life on earth, as the fallen ones knew. After all, the earth was their only consolation, and their fall was really their ascent, and they would not give up one inch of territory.

Ultimately, in the inner sanctum, the most abominable acts were beautiful and sustaining, and would be Arles' foundation in immortality. Arles had always known of its existence, but this fact was never spoken of. The top rulers of the known world had come to the inner sanctum in eons past to supplicate their gods and strike fear into the brethren; this was where a man could not falter, lest he be killed; and this was what the world—*in its entirety*—was based upon. This is what could never be spoken of, or so he thought with great anticipation. Arles felt confident; there could be nothing foisted upon him that he could not handle.

He asked her again from the bar: "Please, Diane, I want to do my part. I want to prove myself to them. To you. You know I belong. You know I have proved myself already."

"Yes, you have. That's why our committee was so puzzled this evening when you called," she said and grew silent.

The silence was piercing, and suddenly Arles Dubailles realized that there was no one in the bar except Cal and the young man he was commiserating with.

"There are always obstacles when you ascend in power," she finally said.

"I understand, and I have dealt with that obstacle, and I want to come in. I have to...I need to come home, Diane. Please."

"Very well. You have passed the test. Manny is in front of the terminal waiting for you. Your daughter is not in the hospital, and your wife will be waiting submissively for you in your suite tonight for your victorious arrival. Congratulations on the first test, but I warn you, be ready to complete your task, or you will wish not to exist." With that little threat, she hung up.

It was incredible—such a gift! Most people were better off as slaves, not knowing whom they served when they were used to propagate the dragon's power. It was key to burn innocence to propel the internal combustion engine power, through politics, education and world peace, through criminality and pornography, through every channel without end.

This way there would be no nuclear holocaust; there would be advanced technology; there would be wealth created for most people on the planet—they would learn the ways of the serpent and embrace knowledge and self-power rather than looking for something that cannot touch or see. Though he would have to admit he had never seen a serpent-being, or reptile-humanoid creature, he knew the dragon gave him the power to stomach anything. He knew the long-honored traditions of kingdoms, tribes and principalities. The uninitiated did not understand, and should *never* understand; let them be as they are: commodities, cattle to be grown, then souls harvested for trade somewhere "out there." He did not need to know the details to see what kinds of businesses these people were running—it was supernatural and hard to comprehend, but he could at least see that much.

The *New York Times* would not state that terrorism in America or genocide in Africa or Bosnia was some sort of ritual sacrifice. They were told to present an ongoing, never-ending story to the public, one which they could understand, and one that would curb their curiosity while they were distracted by the need to make money and solve complex social problems, of which there was no solution.

Bottom line, he learned, was to keep two things from happening: 1) people believing the Bible or the truth that Jesus Christ was and is the Messiah, and 2) keeping the End Time prophecy from ever occurring. Sustaining the universe simply took innocent blood, which through ritual became the grail of Jesus. High technology stopped the prophecy clock of the Bible, or something like that. He wasn't sure of all the details, but he had seen that the world continued to flourish with no end in sight, and he now believed it was the substitution and *trans-substantiation* of lamb (innocence) for Lamb (Christ) that provided some sort of universal key.

Whether this was true or just an excuse for ritual killing and sex didn't matter. It was all about appropriating this technology ("god") and its power for himself, as others had done. It wasn't occult, it was not hidden; it was blatantly obvious. Even *he* knew that a true master simply thinks it and it happens. He thought up his wealth and position, and the means to achieve it arrived at his doorstep. The secret of immortality was next, and he had heard stories of those who faked their own deaths and funerals and were able to design a new body that could access other worlds and realities far beyond this one. He would do anything a serpent or a senator would ask for a little more.

Tonight would be the start of the truly exotic inflow of knowledge, the truly esoteric meaning of being god himself, of the awesome responsibility to create that which is in harmony with the universe and all that is in it. Nothing evil about that. Harmony was a good thing, he thought.

He would know more after tonight, and he prided himself on always being ahead of the curve on any initiation they might throw at him. He would behave politely when bestowed with the next scroll, as he had done with every scroll. He would have the fortitude to look and not turn away, ascending to ever deepening inner circles, which at some point would be critical mass—immortality, the god-man translation.

He realized that eventually it's all ritual and worship, and it's all obedience and faith...to the Order first, and the hierarchy as he ascended, but always to the Brotherhood of Light. There is no such thing as killing when it is a duty, and he had never killed for vanity, or because someone had angered him. He had not lost the Biblical morality of his youth, which his mother attempted to teach. He had simply reconstituted it for higher purposes. He always understood that slaves do not understand freedom, certainly not those tied to ghettos and governments and corporations and country clubs—after all no one would worship the dragon if he weren't real.

He looked at Cal across the room and at the new arrivals coming in for their daily dose. The crush of a crowd made it easy to leave without an explanation. This setup would not take him down; he was just that good, he told himself, chuckling, while slipping out the door unnoticed, leaving Cal with a new friend and now the relief that he would not be expected to fly while drunk.

"You ever hear about Christ?" the salesman asked Cal.

"Where'd my client go?" Cal asked, looking around.

twenty-five

*E*x-pastor Ted Gunderson, who knew he was certainly no danger to himself or others, had just spent the best three days of his life incarcerated in a lock-up mental ward. He had gotten to know some very fine people and had three days of witnessing for the Lord, the God he had just come to know personally in his own heart. A life of preaching, which turned out to be something he really had known nothing about, had ended very badly in human terms.

His stay in a psychiatric ward was a gift and he did not want to leave.

Bob Orly, Darnelle and Apple were three people the Lord had told him to disciple. He would keep in touch with them, and they would comprise his first real church. Orly was a paraplegic, the victim of a diving accident, who had used pain medication and had finally come in to dry out. Darnelle, a dancer and ex-prostitute who had bitten a politician's arm and had threatened to kill the President in a public place, was always willing to listen and said she knew Jesus personally. Apple, whom they said was schizophrenic, was a young man who was being prepared for drop-shipment over to the state hospital as an interim step until the staff could figure out on what alley or street corner to dump him.

Apple's way of speaking, his so-called *schizophrenic dialect,* was not intelligible to regular folk, as Ted had found out; yet with a little patience on the part of the listener, Apple made perfect sense and had a metaphoric and speedy method of communication. God had separated him from the mainstream. Usually, Ted reasoned, God did things like that for great purposes. "He works all things for good for those who believe in Him," he told Apple. This angelic being had no sin in his heart that Ted could discern.

With his small new church, Ted wasn't just getting out on his own. Even though he had no money, he knew he would be getting a place to take care of them all. "The Lord provides," he told Orly.

"Will the Lord make me walk again?" Orly asked, struggling to stand in the hallway without his crutches.

"You will run a race and win," said the pastor, no longer supplying his own words, his own responses or even his own impulses.

"Thank you, Lord," said Orly. "I know what *that* means!" He broke down and wept and laughed and kicked his legs up in the air. Two staff members, alarmed by the noise, ran out from the nurses' station.

"It's okay, guys," Ted said. "He's in better shape than you."

The staff did not like Pastor Ted. They were glad to kick him out the door of the hospital after the court-ordered three-day hold. They did not ask if he had a ride home or even if he had a home. There had been no answer at the residence for some time, and Ted wondered about his wife and his girls.

Apple, his roommate, said he saw angels in the room, and Ted said that he had seen them too. Apple said that the angels were "scared because they know someone's going to start the clock."

Ted asked him to elaborate.

Apple, the twenty-three-year-old extraordinary child of God hidden in a pudgy body with an awkward pair of thick rims, was flying low and always under the radar. He came forth with his extraordinary gift—prophecy: "There is one they can't kill. God hides him right under their noses. The one they will kill next is the one they wouldn't kill if they knew he would start the clock instead of stopping it. He was innocent but born into the devil's womb." His prophecy continued, "They thought he was human, but he wasn't. He was taken by God because he was something else—but the blood from his body starts the clock. Even their angels will drown in the flood."

Ted looked toward the door leading into the well-lit hall, just up from the nurses' station. He felt like he was in some spy ring and spies were listening to their every word. They probably were—except they had written this "schizophrenic" kid off long ago. Nothing he had to say would be talked about; they felt he was always speaking nonsense.

"Apple," Ted insisted, "what else? There's something else." Ted turned in bed to face him. He thought he had seen it in a dream the night before, or it was something he thought he knew but could not remember.

Apple looked up at the ceiling, the most confident young man Ted had ever heard. "You're there, and so am I. And others. They're killing every one of them but they missed the one who brings judgment, the harbinger. God hides him. But the one they shouldn't kill, and do kill, he starts the clock."

"You mean because they kill him he starts the clock?" Ted was fixing on the mind-screen of the ceiling, seeing a movie of Apple's prophecy.

"Yeah, and then there will be earthquakes. There's truck drivers blocking people who are saying, 'Does anybody have the fare?' There were others up on the off ramp, and they were broken and screaming. But then the dollars fell into the hole, and nobody had money to buy things that don't exist anymore. Then the one they kill to stop it all will live and he will make God's wrath come onto the earth. And many of God's believers who die will go to heaven without pain—families happy to all be together. They will be happy, and they will not remember what happened. But those who aren't God's will suffer."

"Whoa, slow down, Apple. You mean—"

"No, I'm not going to slow down for any reason. We're going to ship things to other places, and there are people underground getting fat. I don't know why they don't understand we need love."

Ted knew he spoke truth, even if he did not understand. Many times he did not understand God, not until later. It was God telling him all this, because when he prayed he always got the same answer: "Apple is the eyes and ears," and so he knew Apple spoke *the language,* knew because he felt that confirming *warmth,* despite seeing falling overpasses and food lines, high-rises underwater. He didn't know what it all meant, not exactly, but he would wait on the truth, as waiting was something he hadn't done before.

"So why does this happen?" Ted finally asked after a long silence, wondering whether Apple had fallen asleep.

"You're *not* the pastor, and we're not truck drivers, and there's someone on a windowpane in underwear screaming for social workers, but there were none—"

"Stop," the Pastor said. "I can't understand. I'm *not* the pastor any more?"

Apple screamed as if attacked.

"Hey!" Ted leapt up and held his arms down, "Shhhhh..." He knew what they would do, and he did not want to see Apple mistreated again. This was an epileptic seizure—it had happened before in the hall. Ted knew to just hold him in place and prevent him from swallowing his tongue.

Then the seizure stopped.

Apple spoke in *tongues*, and this fact was equipping Ted for his ministry. Apple was prophesying, and that was preparing Ted for what to expect. Apple had a line to God; he was a sweet, spirit-filled prophet with no bitterness or personal bias in his word—a gift beyond measure—and no one, except Ted, had ever heard him speak.

Speaking in Tongues does mean it's another earthly language, Ted reasoned, which separated those faking strange sounds that no one understood from those speaking in *another tongue*, the Voice of the Spirit. Another language could mean symbols, or even signs when it came right down to it, could mean using a variety of words to convey something entirely of God. Ted knew the gift of Tongues could be a mix of Aramaic, French, Italian and arithmetic, but it meant nothing unless understood—and understanding could only happen if Ted were in the Spirit. God's ways were so far beyond comprehension that he knew now to be, or at least try to be, as innocent as a child, and allow Him to whisper in his ear, as Apple was doing. How encouraging to hear the Spirit speak!

Because it is always Truth.

Apple was so much the innocent, so completely untainted and quite nearly holy, so utterly pure that God chose to speak through him. Ted would never divulge this secret; he knew that God had secrets when He said: "This is all to be sealed up, my son."

"Apple, I'm going to get you out of here, because even though you don't know the Lord Jesus Christ yet, he—"

"I *do* know him—I've always known him, from the beginning."

Tears streamed down the Pastor's face. It was the only answer possible: Apple was a prophet of God, and he had proved it. The Word of God had been sown in his heart from the beginning, and now was finally bearing fruit! "Yes," said Ted, "listen to this." Ted flipped his Bible to Paul's letter to the church at Ephesus and read aloud: "*According as he hath chosen us in Him before the foundation of the world, that we should be holy and without blame before Him in love.* Apple, you are so right! He *did* choose you. You have been with

Him—and He wants me to tell you about Christ Jesus."

"Preacher Ted," Apple said.

"Yeah." Ted felt foolish, reading the Scripture, knowing his record on evangelizing away from the pulpit was somewhere between slim and minus zero. He set his Bible on the floor, atop a newspaper article on homelessness in the Valley.

"Do you believe in Hell?" Apple asked.

He looked around, not sure if he wanted to answer; there was so much he *believed* in, so many wondrous things in Christ, which was where belief had to start, only then could a believer understand the notion of hell stemming from a loving God. He wanted to answer this bright beacon of hope called Apple, and so he asked: "Apple, who gave you that name?"

"My brother."

"Why?"

"Because I liked apples. I ate so many apples that they called me The Apple. And then they shortened it to just 'Apple,' which I liked a lot better," he answered. "But all the strawberries and the under-lings who eat with big forks and spit out cigarettes, and all the messy people screaming MOMMY, MOMMY! Can I go to bed now?"

Ted responded to the first part, and he'd pray about the second. "Well, then I'll call you Apple, but I'd like to call you Zechariah, which means 'The Lord Remembers.' He speaks through you, Apple, did you know you have the gift of prophecy and that the Holy Spirit dwells in you? And yes, there is a hell."

"Do you think I should be a truck driver?" Apple asked and awaited an answer.

"You could be a wonderful truck driver; you'd be awesome," Ted said, fighting back the tears. Not sure his wife and daughters were safe, he thought of them and the church. They must have counseled them that ex-Pastor Ted was possessed by demons, and after he got help and was cleansed, there could be a reuniting. The man to do just that would be Pastor Alf Blicky, the head of the Faith Church, the spiritual leader of Sarah and Carole and Beth. The man who rehabilitated *ex*-pastor Ted Gunderson, had so kindly had him held for seventy-two hours so that the wife and child abuse ministry of the church could secure Sarah and children new, safe living conditions. "Will you pray with me, Apple, for my wife and children?"

Apple stared up at the ceiling, motionless and silent.

"Dear Father, please watch over my wife, Sarah, and my girls,

Beth and Carole, send your best angels to protect those in your church, the Faith Church, and purge the church of its false teachers. Dear Father, I know none of this can happen unless we forgive. I forgive the man who shot me, because it was a gift from you, you opened my eyes and I could see, yet I blamed the devil and that man for my fall. I even harbored suspicion of my brother in Christ, the new pastor, Alf Blicky, for setting me up so that he could take over as pastor. Oh, Father, how wrong I have been. I forgive him and his wife, Gwen, and You. I forgive all those who hurt Your innocent lambs, the flock of Lord Jesus, and I beseech You to help me protect them from now on, without a bitter heart. Oh, Father, thank You for raising me up so I could finally see You and the truth. Thank You for your messenger, Apple, who is an anointed prophet from You, who is above me always. I will protect him. I will make a place for Your innocent ones, Father. In Jesus' name I pray...Amen."

"Amen," Apple said, and turned to look at Ted. "Amen, preacher, tall man, large job. Amen and Amen—Jesus is Lord."

"Thank you, Lord," Pastor Ted said, his silent prayer about Apple's faith answered in full.

"Jesus is King."

"Thank you, Lord," Pastor said, "and Amen and Amen!"

"Jesus is my shepherd, I shall never need anything else."

"Oh, hallelujah, praise God!" the ex-pastor said, now joyous, now blessed. He jumped up, like his first day in church. Apple was already standing on his bed, for which one night they locked him up, and he started jumping up and down.

So Pastor Ted started jumping up and down and screaming: "Hallelujah! Hallelujah! Praise God, Your prophet speaks again! Praise You, Lord!"

The staff ran in and took Apple away to the sealed seclusion room. He was strapped down so long he soiled himself so badly no nurse would get within ten feet of the room; the smell was foul and no one wanted such blatant guilt. Robin, the frail, elderly night nurse, said out loud, "He should live in his own stink until he gets the message. Under no circumstances are we to clean him up, is that clear?"

Ted knew he had no place to sleep. He only knew of one place to go after being released. He would plan to receive Apple and possibly Darnelle and Bob Orly into his care and plan the foundation of a new church, based on truth and not error. For now, he would wait on the Lord's answer, and he would walk toward his former church.

• • •

By the time Cal and his new friend left, he was so drunk that he remembered what they did to him. He wept in the salesman's car. Joe Spruug, who had two kids, a wife, and a little townhouse in Chatsworth, told him Jesus was the only way to save Cal's soul.

Spruug had figured out that Cal was in trouble and needed to be hidden from view. He knew Cal had to be physically taken from the airport, especially when he saw the man Cal was hired to fly sneak away like a thief.

"They took my mind, and they made me do things—military. But then...they made me kill innocent people and they were happy," Cal explained to Spruug, before he wept and wailed.

Spruug wasn't sure what to do with him at this point. He did not make sense. "Do you want to go to a hotel or a—"

Cal was unresponsive; he only cried and screamed as they got off the freeway at Topanga Canyon Boulevard.

"This is...this is the way it is—they kill innocent people so they can...they execute, they have military people doing this and they film it and it's....there are angels involved," he told Spruug in a disjointed way.

Dear Lord, Spruug said silently, I need a miracle. Is this a demon? Can I handle this? Am I putting my family at risk?

To which he got an answer: "You, my son, are a servant of God, and this man hungers for Christ, and you knew this in the beginning."

Spruug said to Cal: "All right, listen—you're sort of putting me to the test. You want to sleep it off at our home and then I'll drive you back to the plane tomorrow? You don't want to be arrested for drunk driving a jet, right?"

"They made it look like a football game—a parade, and I was dropping candy and confetti...but it was *poison*," he cried and wailed.

Spruug pushed his youthful shock of blond hair out of his eyes, he wanted a cigarette, and he wondered how Isabella would react. He knew the boys wouldn't mind. "We have a Christian home," he said to Cal, who was still into his confession.

"And it was *poison*," Cal said incredulously.

"I want to pray with you right now, okay?"

"And they all died. They were just kids."

"My wife's name is Isabella."

"I'll tell you! I'll tell you! I'm not the person they think I am. I...I can't live with myself," he said.

"Dear Lord, please help my friend Cal here. You tell me he hungers for the Word of God, that he needs Christ, that he's a brother. Help him now Lord, please..."

Cal had already opened the door and before Spruug could say anything, he rolled out onto the street, right into the traffic. Spruug swerved fast over to the curb, then ran back for Cal, who was standing in the middle of the street, running at the swerving cars in a sad attempt to get himself rammed.

"Kill me! Kill me, you cowards! Take me! Take me—you worthless sheep! You stupid cattle. Even the traffic lights know what you did! No more! Kill me!"

"Cal!" Spruug yelled, grabbing him and shoving him, grateful he was 6'2" and had been a college tight end and a gymnast. If he were not physically fit, he could not have forced Cal to the side of the road and onto his knees, head down in the gutter with Spruug's knee on his neck while he slapped Cal's face. "You're not going to die! Jesus can save you! Nothing you've done is too much for Him— give it to Him, take forgiveness! It's yours. Even Paul killed innocents before he was the greatest human in Christ! *Take the forgiveness!*"

No one had ever told Spruug that evangelism would and could be done by force, but this situation warranted it.

No one had ever told Spruug he could evangelize a ham sandwich, and he had never been a soul-winner for his church. The elders pointed this out constantly.

No one had ever told Spruug he could see without his glasses, but somehow he would now.

No one had ever told Joe Spruug that his wife Isabella would now come to the Lord *in her heart.*

No one had ever told Spruug that it was all real.

No one would ever tell him otherwise again.

• • •

In the middle of the first set there was an earthquake. A radio station had proclaimed it was a 4.0, Chip told Rick Lowie. Katarina smiled as she had yet another whirl with the new tattoo artist named Bullseye. She told him in the dressing room, with the door locked, that she would need an ally, and he obliged. "Look, I really love you," she said. "I feel as if I've known you. Do you believe in destiny?"

He smoked something in a pipe bowl and swigged the band's brew. "Sure."

"Rick is a piece of garbage," she said.

"But he's the man, you know," said the purple-haired, pierced and scarred tattoo man.

"Look, put the drugs away," she said. "I want you to say that you saw him do it."

"Who? Do what?"

She left the room, sealing their fate with a kiss. He was relieved to have gotten the sort of sex he never had before. It made him feel special and he told himself that his luck was back, and it wasn't going to go away so easily again. That woman had taste, she knew the secret, she was the way into this gig, and soon they'll want my songs too, Bullseye told himself, with nothing to do but sit there for a few bucks an hour in case Rope needed something tweaked.

Some people tried to rush out of the auditorium when the little earthquake occurred, but most lit matches, flashed love signs and cheered, chasing this fright with plenty of marijuana and smuggled-in brew. Later they would find out that it was only a 3.3 on the Richter scale, which was what Rick was saying backstage.

All cheered when the band started playing again, as Strange Muumuu cooked with their hit, "Man-o-War." Justin pranced and stared and leaned out, then leapt into the moshpit, and *led* them with command and superiority, star-quality and self-effacing looseness—taking the bold caress of each listener, yet respecting no one and nothing.

Leather-jacketed Brand Kincaid wept, but under the dark glasses, with a Tommy Hilfiger ski-cap assuring that no one could see him and know who he really was. He did not look like any age; he actually blended in, like he had in the late '60s or early '70s. Like he had when he listened to rock and roll and dated Jackson. Like when he had been blessed with Justin.

Now, seeing his son's immense talent, his total poise and artistry, his power, Brand burst with pride and sorrow, but he quickly collapsed into self-pity and paranoia.

The mobile phone rang. It was an emergency. He was to board a plane in two hours; there would be a high-level meeting of a classified nature. "I thought there was no damage in the quake—that's what my wife told me."

"You will be briefed at oh-twelve-hundred hours, sir," was the response.

"Where is the briefing?"

No further communication, dead.

He went out to the hall and listened, and he could hear his son, no longer singing but speaking to the audience. The band had stopped playing. Justin actually sounded like a preacher.

Brand had received a backstage pass, courtesy of Justin. Justin had offered his father a ride in a limousine to the auditorium in Long Beach. Brand arranged to pick up the tickets at will-call and said he might want to watch the show from the regular seats. He called Jackson and by her silence knew *she was shocked to hear his voice.*

He could never truly comprehend the depth and scope of his wife's talent for evil.

He lied when he told her he was in his office when she mentioned the quake. He said that the office shook a little and that was it.

He could never lie to her with success—no one could.

When he tried to call Serin, there was no answer because the power lines were down. The news reports reported casualties only in Phoenix and Tucson; both cities were pretty much destroyed.

He had not heard about the destruction of his vaunted Serin Institute.

He had tried Cynda's cell and got her voice mail.

This was to be *his* trip—he was going to bury the hatchet with Justin, who had to have been sane or he could not have conducted himself with such prowess and purpose.

Brand went back to his seat, but now Justin wasn't performing, he was...*talking.*

Everything had stopped. Rick Lowie had a full crash and burn psychosis on his hands and a sea of agitated fans. He had to pull him in—he had to reset the idiot's crank-head delusion of God or whatever he was going on about. Rock and roll fans don't want *that.*

Never did, never will.

Lowie was screaming, "Just get psycho-boy off the stage! I do not need this—I built a rep no burnout Jesus freak is going to—end up ruining my life right now! I told him no preaching—somebody give him some dope, man."

Brand watched Rick, who watched helplessly as the band members left the stage, *on Justin's dismissive command*!

Brand knew that this was *his* moment—*his son* needed him. He felt the love he knew was there but feared he had lost forever.

He was threatened that if he ever talked about what he had seen with respect to the Brotherhood or the Order, or if he ever inquired what had happened to any of the adolescent boys or girls he turned over to what he only knew as The Foundation, he would be executed on the spot. If he ever so much as breathed a word about any public official, he and his family would be killed. If he ever carried himself in any manner that might indicate something was wrong, or if he ever became infirm to the point that it disrupted the Institute or were to cast it in a negative light, he would be dealt with in the harshest possible manner, whether it was his fault or not. His children were never to say *anything*, never to resist being educated properly, never to complain or be too sensitive about any of the things they were asked to do or not do in order to fit into the modern world, sustained and created by the elite and foisted upon the worker-bee middle class as a Mystery They Would Never Understand.

Anything, any word, any thought, any action that would disrespect the *beauteous, limitless world* created by men and gods of great intelligence and compassion would be seen as a crime against humanity itself. Therefore, for the greatest good, the swiftest possible solution, especially those of an elite status, would be automatically implemented. All would toe the line, all would see green when told it was green, and red when told it was red. This had never before bothered Brand Kincaid.

He was never one to "go it alone."

Justin got away, but he knew too much.

Justin was discredited. His music made him visible, and therefore untouchable. His lyrics were always about how evil the "payola corporations" (the name of one of his songs) were. The lyrics were rebellious and undermining—a popular outlet for kids, not unlike other nihilistic, politically motivated rock groups, or "hypocrites in training," as Justin Kincaid had so often called them. He wrote that the overthrow of the government would be the only way in the future. He meant the overthrow of the elites, the corporations, the guilds on the left and right, and especially the Christian Church that subscribed to society's favorite pastime marketed fervently as *God's provision.* They even called it Charity. Even Grace. Accomplishment. Gifts of the Spirit, no less.

Yes, the churches wanted money, honey. And to get it they'd offer up their children. And they would tell them it's God—God provides! Isn't He wonderful? Now conform or we'll kill you! Amen?

Yes, *Someone* had to provide—not God. Someone had to be trusted, not Jesus. Someone had to live in the real world—God doesn't really understand.

All this was simply *The Lie for the Stupid, Gutless Pigs—also referred to as the Idiot Brigade.*

Whose salvation is assured because they say they love Jesus. They even have that label on the outside of the church buildings.

The lyrics were coming along:

The gutless, defending what they do not know, fire of hatred, evening glow.

How rich the man loses the world yet gains his own soul.

While pigs, pretenders and fairy tale queens suck at the trough of Death.

Stick your thumb in a pie, pull out a plum and cry, Oh, what a smart boy am I! Jesus is the Light, Jesus is the Love, and Jesus is not the World...

It felt good...he wouldn't try it tonight. But it was getting there. His newest song was an invitation of the slaves to leave the churches—probably get him killed. Airplanes are always good for sacrificing rock stars. Overdose—too nebulous. Angry fan? Interesting. The piglets and drones would carry it out—He had the prophecy. He was going home!

Brand Kincaid was now ashamed. A lackey, that's about all any intelligent person could say about him. Oh, he thought he had a big job, and he thought he had a big life—he had the answers. He was a shaper of destiny. Oh, he was brilliant!

How could a delusion grip him so completely, and for so long? Was it denial? Stupidity?

He was an idiot, he thought to himself. No question. Oh, how he could hear the laughter and scorn. Yes, pointing and laughing—an idiot, an idiot, an idiot.

Kincaid knew his wife paid the best sorcerers in the world plenty of large stipends to simply stop her son's ability to make money—after all, he was a total embarrassment. He could jeopardize her hard won *position*. Brand would hear it over and over again.

She intended for him to hit the ground and hit hard. The fact that nothing they did could make a dent made her increasingly angry to the point, Brand thought, of obsession. After all, her methods had always worked before, on others more prominent and capable. She knew that the hurdle must be her husband, so she continued to pay the best sorcerers to *cleanse* him and do away with her son—which meant *death*. She had already picked out the coffin and the cemetery; she had composed the guest list and even the liturgy. Justin's best friends would be there, prominent people and government officials, and they would all feel sorry she had had to endure such a terrible ordeal for so long, only to end in a tragedy for *her*, Jackson—The Saint—Kincaid.

And now a father was watching a son's *deliberate* meltdown, truly at the end of himself. "Son! Justin!" he yelled, the look of madness not escaping all who wondered about this interloper in the wings.

Justin did not flinch, not a bit, not even if he heard his father's call. Brand quieted down on the threat of being subdued by a security guard. "That's my son," Kincaid said. There was a pierced eyebrow cast his way; and he glared back at the man without backing down.

All the attention was on Justin, who paced back and forth across the stage with the borrowed Gideon's Bible. He continued to speak: "It's not enough to understand the levels of reality you people were robbed of. You need to see it on the ground, where the rubber meets the road. I am only a key, and when the lock is turned..."

The crowd grew eerily silent, as the lights started to flicker and Justin rose up into the air slightly, where he *stood*. Brand could not see the wires, neither could anyone else, but Rick Lowie assured everyone that there was a wire, that they had rehearsed it, and added: "I'll be thrilled when he gets back to the set, and then I'm going to send him a bill for my shrink."

Justin went on speaking to the congregation: "Truth is depth." He was shrouded in a bright, electric blue swash of light. "Truth is memory of future past. God is too big to wrap your mind around, but He lifts up, He gives it all, He protects, He cleans, He restores—He invites you to Eternity and never casts you down. He never leaves you or forsakes you. He makes you live not just a day—FOR-

EVER! WHO CARES ABOUT THIS WORLD WHEN WE LIVE FOREVER IN HIM!"

Cheers and candles and more marijuana went up as a bizarre propitiation. They weren't booing anymore! Katarina looked angry as she watched from the side. Rick had dropped her, had changed altogether, and she wanted to bring down the show, no matter if the audience wanted Justin's oratory or not. This was a music show, and that's all it was. But Katarina never wanted them to martyr Justin— it might harm her future, she was thinking, reflecting on her contract and the promise she just made to be delivered into luxury.

"And He's coming back," Justin went on, the lights turning to a glorious magenta and white hue. He read Revelation 5:12, while *standing* in mid-air: "*Worthy is the Lamb that was slain to receive power, and riches, and wisdom, and strength, and honor, and glory and blessing*!"

The crowd let out a tremendous cheer.

"Glory to Him, beloved, I'm His own, and when I knew that, a few days ago, He showed me that I lived in eternity. *And so can all of you*!"

More cheers and more protests. Katarina started crying—he was ruining it for her, she knew. Tears fell like lost raindrops, hitting her leather jacket, staining her clogs.

"We are the little lambs, the flock—those who resisted, those who resisted the norms of rock & roll as well as our parents and teachers when they sought to make us do what we knew was wrong and made us cover it up in secret. They did not have the guts to say what it was: a prison, a life not your own; old age, sickness, and death are your rewards, just look at your parents! Sold their souls for the mortgage, the shopping club and the almighty approval and all those smiling friends who make their lives a real treat here on planet earth. The drone husbands and the frivolous housewives— sold it to play house for a year or two before somebody packs them off to the rest home, with money for diapers and a dirt plot that nobody will visit, ever. Sold it for thirty pieces of silver and a noose called Death. Defend it to death from behind the bushes. Called themselves Big and Brave—Cowards and Thieves! Wanted the money, honey! Needed the money, you spoiled brats! Who are you to criticize? Who are you to speak? Who are you to live? Who are you to think—who are YOU? You're GOD'S CHILDREN! If you can admit you made a mistake—and that's harder to find these days than a heart of gold—then you can live. If you can drop that mean pride, He'll give you everything that instant! Jesus will take all who turn to Him—no matter how far down the ladder you climbed. No matter how many people you lied to, stole from or killed. Even you, Dad...He'll take you home and never leave you. Because He loves you.

Brand Kincaid was cheering, "Thank you, son, thank you, Justin, how I love you. Thank you, thank you! Oh, thank you, God. *You exist. You exist!*" He fell to his knees, as general confused fretting and frittering occurred all around him. No matter, his son was his gift, after all. Only God, he knew, could help him now. He surrendered, weeping so loudly that only the confusion around the stage prevented him from being thrown out of the hall.

Security had lost track of the comings and goings of those on the guest list, not that there were so many coming in from behind the auditorium. But one came in who looked like a musician, and he brought a guitar case with him. Chip had thought he was a rep from one of the guitar companies, perhaps an attempt to get Rope to use one of his guitars. They didn't know Rope.

Katarina let her guests in, those with whom she spoke and did not know, only that they were the Powers That Be. The Powers That Be had contacted her, on Justin's cell phone no less—and they wanted to...how did they put it to her? Observe?

She would look the other way when she heard that word. She always felt justified anyway, a personal victory against those who would even think they were able to beat the real power of the world—they deserved what they got.

She did not need a formal announcement to understand that these guests, in very stylish clothes, chic eyeglasses and perfect makeup were the Powers That Be. They said a couple of words like "light" and "initiation," and even "covenant," and she knew who they were. Because she had served in their temples as a sex object, she knew who they were. She had served them when she was underage and they needed to make her do things in front of a dark congregation. She knew them as senators and business executives, preachers and social workers, experts all, and she knew them when they murdered. She had become their witness, and she would do anything for them, because they would not turn their backs on her now, this favor was the biggest and one of the last she would have to provide. Now she was going to get to know them, they would *let her in* now, because she would do anything.

Justin continued: "They will use your flesh, your senses, and they will make you think it's beautiful, make you think you're blessed...make you think you're holy. Oh, brothers and sisters! My, my, my..."

Brand was cheering: "Yes, son...tell the truth—tell it, I don't care anymore! Tell them what I am, tell them what we did!"

"Don't let them fool you when they kill me—they think I'm a traitor because I'm telling you this. But my God knows everything, and He prophesies through us, and He keeps you safe, and He lets you know who is around you. They cannot do that, not on TV or by telephone or with lots of surveillance wires. Friends, the answer is always Jesus Christ. That name above any other. That name above Satan's rather...ahem...jolly old kingdom. You speak that name: Jesus, Jesus, Jesus..."

The crowd broke into it: *Jesus, Jesus, Jesus, Jesus...*

That name above any other.

That name above any other!

That Name beyond all flesh!

That Name beyond all flesh!

"Keep your little world, Satan—me and my brothers and sisters, we're going to see our King and live with Him forever!

"Let the Holy Spirit come into your heart, your soul, your body—He'll move in and kick out the devil, right now—Listen to Him...He wants to live in you and look through your eyes and be your best friend. See Him now? Hear Him?"

Cheers of adulation went up as Justin, suspended, angled upside down. Chip ran around the stage, grabbing Rick Lowie and screaming: "No one's operating the line. I tried to drop him like you said, but it didn't happen—he's suspended in midair! Nothing is holding him! It's...oh...what is happening! This is not happening! I can't handle this—it's...I'm outta here, man!" he yelled and then ran from the auditorium, very much afraid.

Justin moved out over the crowd; he was suspended above them in a prone position in the air, facing straight down. His audience adjusted their necks and looked up, as light hit him from every direction. "If you don't think God is in the business of signs and wonders, look again!"

Cheers went up all around, but no one thought he was without support and suspended in midair.

The gunman did not think so either. He simply adjusted his sights accordingly, placing Justin neatly in the crosshairs. A perfect "X" right on the mark's chest. For the .223 Remington rifle, from the gunman's angle atop the scaffolding behind the stage, Justin's height actually made target acquisition that much better. It was an easy hit. All he would have to do was wait until they turned him a bit so he faced the stage. And he had already started turning.

Katarina was smiling, filled with visions of power and wealth to come. No one would call her "whore" again. She would never again be somebody's throwaway, certainly not some record grunt like Lowie.

Brand was weeping on his knees. "Please forgive me. Please, Lord God Almighty, forgive me."

The Lord spoke to Brand in the form of the Holy Spirit, who lifted him up and made him feel warm inside. "My son, I am with you—I will never leave you now. I forgive you."

Brand wept like a baby. The band members looked on, paralyzed. Rope was afraid and ran out the back; the others huddled in the dressing room snorting coke and swilling whisky—but nothing could stop the collision of opposites. Nothing but surrender.

Some of the women in the audience were crying, and some of the men were looking up, caught up in a sudden shaft of clarity and spiritual birth.

"I love you. I love you all—love is the answer. His Love. Not the cheap counterfeit the World offers. You can't love without Jesus. He is the answer—He became your sin, your failure, your hatred, your rock & roll, your shallow flesh, your fear and your hope. He took what you deserved, and God paid for you so you could be forgiven, so you could be made perfect, so that even though you still sin, God can see you and love you and lift you up and call you His own—because Jesus was, and is, and always will be, God. Jesus *is* God!"

Cheers of conviction went up on the words.

"You were made clean by the Blood of the Lamb, who is coming back again." He had finally given them what he had practiced for, what was on that pamphlet tucked in the Gideon Bible in his hotel room in Hollywood—those exact words.

His voice amplified, though they tried to cut off the PA. Everyone in the auditorium heard Justin's words louder than any music; it flooded their senses. Many were weeping uncontrollably, and many were holding their hands up in the air screaming, "Jesus, Jesus! Lord, I love you! Jesus, I'm sorry for being so weak—I let you down, and you helped me! You loved me! I believe in You, forever! Lord, You! Lord, praise you! Lord, You, not me. Lord, You, not me. Lord it's all about you..."

Justin let the Bible fall, and many raised their hands to receive it. But it just dangled, descending slowly, and some thought it was on a wire.

The gunman in the T-shirt, jeans and ponytail aimed, and started to squeeze the trigger. He hadn't seen or heard anything unusual. Just a stage act that was now turning into the right angle for a head shot.

"*Beloved*, that's what God calls us. He loves you—don't be fooled. Mark my words, as He gives them to me now, because I am ignorant without Him. I am one of the keys because I'm one of His. Here is the prophecy: they kill me and they celebrate by mistake, because I am one of His. They try to make it His blood and they think it prevents Him from returning. Now hear me! This is the beginning of God's judgment on the earth, and on the wicked. They are correct; I am a traitor to Satan and all he stands for! But I'm not the one they are looking for...I gave myself to the Lord and I live in eternity, and they can't kill me. You can come with me, please come." He paused and smiled with beaming eyes at those who were weeping, some so much that they lost themselves and fell to the floor or between the seats.

He continued, prophesying what Brand knew now was the truth: "So when this lock is opened, woe unto them. There is another who loves Jesus and who is not exactly human—*who is the harbinger, who makes the way for the Lord's return*. He will bring many to Christ. The Lord says this, beloved, and hear me now: *You shall know them by their fall.* Even so, Jesus, come back! Come soon!"

The crowd cheered, never having heard anything like this before. But many were afraid and ran away from the auditorium. Far more fell backwards, passing out or weeping.

Though no one was operating the light board, Justin was suddenly lit in blazing white light—and the shot rang out.

All saw it with perfect clarity.

They were showered in his blood.

His body fell out of its harness and he was broken on the concrete floor of the 27th aisle. They tried to revive him, but the crush and noise of panic prevented it.

How they screamed and stomped each other as they pushed for every exit. Four or five were trampled underfoot by the stage, their rib cages, stomachs or heads crushed. Two of them, witnesses would say, had been convinced by Justin and accepted Christ in their hearts, proclaiming He was their Lord and Savior, and they were weeping with joy just prior to their deaths. The others were not convinced or even knew there was a decision to be made that very moment.

Brand Kincaid's eyes were wide open, and he wept no more. But he could not understand.

twenty-six

*T*he Faith Church had finally turned around. Not only had the tithing nearly doubled on Wednesday, Friday and Sunday morning services, there were generous donations from two members who had gone to be with the Lord, who left their entire estates to the church rather than passing it on to the next generation. These members were so stirred by Alf Blicky's sermons they felt they had no choice. They knew the End Times were upon the world, and it was far better that their children come to the Lord than die without salvation.

Because of Pastor Alf's background in film lighting, the church would benefit from a generous fee from Sable Studios. When he had finally contacted the studio, they made plans to use the church for the first time one night after the service, offering ten thousand dollars, which was more than he had originally bargained for.

Pastor Alf had not seen Jordan Star since their first meeting after church, but he had received a gift pledge of $5,000 per month from Mr. Star's office, enclosed in a personal letter:

Dear Pastor Alfred Blicky:

Thank you for your continued service to our community. Please accept my donation of $5,000 per month for any purpose you choose, whether personal or church-related.

I look forward to seeing you and your lovely wife again.

Best of luck,

Jordan Star

Gwen, who was delighted with Jordan Star's generosity, had used the money to update their personal wardrobes, and she had gotten her son Alfie into a prestigious art college at the suggestion of Star himself. Since she handled all the public relations for the church, she couldn't resist networking with Mr. Star's office, getting him to call Sable Studios as a reference, which resulted in the church's facilities being booked to be used in a film entitled: "The Brotherhood."

Hollywood had always excited Gwen; she had grown up close to what she felt was the most electrifying industry in the world. She had auditioned for various acting jobs, finally landed a job as an extra and then got a speaking part on a toothpaste commercial. She had met Alf during the commercial, and they discovered that they were both Christians.

She and Alf attended Faith Church, and they both thought the world of Pastor Ted Gunderson, his wife, Sarah, and their two baby girls. "Sometimes God uses tragedy to teach us things. Obviously, Ted was wrong for Faith Church, and my husband was chosen to take his place," she had said over the phone to Jordan Star.

Star said he would attend the service the night of the movie shoot if he could get away, and added, "Alf's ascent to pastoring the church is blessed by God himself. It's evident in every single face in the church. Tell him he has the power to heal. Tell him he can feed the poor just by thinking it. And tell him to talk to his angels—I can see they are all around him."

But it was *Gwen* who had the visions of beautiful angelic beings, both male and female, not with wings, but with faces and physiques more beautiful and sensual than humans. "I'm the one that sees the angels," Gwen told Star.

"Oh," he said, somewhat surprised, "*you're* the one. Somehow I knew it was one of you. Beautiful aren't they?"

"Oh, I'm glad I'm not in their world—I'd be tempted."

"I don't think it's adultery if it's not human...but you'll have to check," he said in the most serious yet charming voice she had ever heard.

"I'm sorry," Gwen said, standing in her office, a sudden feeling of heat in her stomach and shoulders. "What is it that you do, Mr. Star?"

"Charity work—healing Mother Earth, feeding the poor. We work with the United Nations and have our headquarters in London. Our outreach office is here in Los Angeles," he replied.

She did not hear his exact words, she heard: "Just let yourself go, do what you feel. Be the woman you need to be, and confess only to your angels—let them be your *guides*."

"Okay, Mr. Star. I also want to thank you for your gift."

"So much more for you if you follow your new inner voice," Jordan Star, the benefactor, answered. "I'm trusting you to keep your husband on track. Why don't you come watch the shoot to-night?" Then he added, smooth and clear so she understood: "Better you come *without* your husband. You know how movie shoots are—not a place for a pastor."

She heard: "You will come to the movie shoot and you will do whatever is asked of you."

"Yes, sir. Thank you for all your help," she replied.

"It's my pleasure," he said.

Alf had been concerned, because of the sudden rain, that there might not be a full congregation. He wasn't worried about money since the check had already come from Mr. Star's office as well as the ten thousand-dollar check from Sable Studios.

All his fears had been unfounded; the congregation was full—the parishioners, the elders, the deacons and the choir were all there. The new praise band brought a contemporary element into the church, and there were many more young people, who looked like actors or entertainment people of some sort. He recognized them from his work. They were the other side of the tracks; he had been a grip and lighting tech, and they had been talent.

Some of them held hands, which gave Gwen the idea of having a dance in the chapel. "Alf, we need to get with what's going on in Christianity today. No alcohol—a place for young believers to meet and dance. You know."

He had said: "Don't you think things are going too well with all the money coming in? People we don't know filling the seats. I don't even have a theology degree...I—"

"Mr. Star is behind you all the way—he is a very important international figure. He's made sure you will go very far, television's next."

"You're kidding! You've done so much for me, Gwen—I love you."

"You can overlook my being so aggressive and wanting to work out in the world," she told him.

"Yes, I've always preferred it that way myself," Alf said, thanking God for all his blessings. "I think all that submissive stuff can be interpreted to mean fearing God, and things are different today—we have to apply the Scriptures to the fact that women *are* in the workplace."

"We have to be more tolerant of various lifestyles too. There are many...well, who are...you know, they have different ways—not evil at all, just...what they had to do to have love—and *they* want to come to Jesus. He's the Lord of love, not of hate."

"Amen, Gwen."

Soon there was a whole congregation of young people—not the straight-laced Christians Alf had known his whole life, not the conservative, Bible-based believers that Pastor Ted had revered and loved and disciplined, seemingly his whole life. This whole new crop of believers with orange and purple streaks in their hair, tattoos and many piercings came within a couple days of Star's visit, just as soon as the check cashed. They raised their hands in the air and screamed *Hallelujah* and *Amen* and clapped whenever the new praise band ratcheted the sound up loud.

Even the older people were enthralled by the glitz of the band. Soon there were painters painting the church blue and white, stonemasons building up the walls and using stucco, and then came the new landscaping. Alf did not ask Gwen how it all happened so suddenly, for fear mainly, that it might not continue if he questioned it. It had to be in the category of miracle, he thought, and this thought was supported with a stout defense from Gwen and her new staff.

"And next are these hideous offices. Ted had such bad taste, you know, honey," Gwen pointed out.

"It just seems so fast. What if Pastor Ted launches a bid to get back in?"

"*You're* in. Voted by the majority of our members. That's in our bylaws."

For those couple of weeks of sudden prosperity and change, Alf was feeling like God had lifted him up for a very large purpose. God was making sure that he had not only what he needed, but that he was groomed for participation on the world stage where, he was convinced, he could win many to Christ.

The sermons had been mainly about performance. He liberally quoted passages that supported the popular prosperity doctrines—that it is indeed our right and heritage in Christ to receive whatever we should ask, to receive wealth beyond measure if we so desire it, and if we pray in Jesus' name.

He spoke boldly of tithing as a method to *get increase*. The sermon tonight was no exception. He was handsome with his blond hair and his trimmer cut of clothes. He wore an Italian blazer, which came—*mysteriously*—from "a secret admirer." He told them, "If you want to increase your finances, give as if you already have that level of income. For example, if you want to make five thousand a week, then give $500 to the church right now. If you want to double your income, double your tithe *before* you double your income. You cannot out-give God!"

"That's good preaching, Pastor," a rock and roller shouted.

"Amen, and Amen," shouted a young woman.

Some of the old timers chimed in: *Hallelujah. Praise God. Good word,* etc., all of them approving the new prosperity doctrine.

"Turn in your Bibles to Philippians 4:19," Alf said, shoving his hair back, checking his watch, sure to end it so the film crew could enter the church at the close of service.

The congregation turned to the appropriate passages in their Bibles and Alf continued, fortified.

Gwen was gratified that Sarah, of all people, had been so cooperative. It had been a traumatic time, but it was wonderful that one of the church outreaches had found a house for Sarah, Beth and Carole to move into, a place where Ted would not be able to find them upon his release from the hospital. She had told her: "He's so unstable, and until we can all pray together, and until his condition is assessed by the elders..."

"I know," Sarah said. "I've never seen him like that. But what if I'm wrong?"

"You're not wrong. He's a very sick man right now—and he may even need an exorcism."

Sarah had been a simple, happy and submissive wife to Ted, and she had never complained when he was a very poor pastor with two suits and a one-bedroom apartment to call home in Kansas City. She had met him at the university, and she was the only woman he knew who would not even kiss until marriage. That was exactly what Ted was looking for. Total obedience to God.

Gwen and the other women always knew there was something wrong with Sarah. They of course knew her story, but they had not been fans of the kinds of goody-two-shoes, holier-than-thou crowd of kids who were in Christ since birth anyway. The newer Christians had much more fire for the Lord and were much more obedient to elders and attentive to the directions the church wanted to go. But Sarah seemed lost, as she attended services without joy, a lost sheep, too dumb to find its way back to the pasture. The other women in the church struggled with real sin, and lately, they had been gratified that the direction of the church had started to become more liberal, with women playing a much more significant role in management, and two more of Gwen's good friends slated to join the board. She had plans for Heidi Corning to speak on tolerance, especially for women who wanted to become pastors.

How glorious all the plans were! Sarah just didn't fit in. But she was in a place now that was holy ground, receiving visits from Sharon, Heidi and others, reasoning with her that she and her husband might not be able to be together. They told her he was a terrible influence on Christianity because he was filled with hate, and she should view herself as a psychologically abused wife.

As pastor Alf continued his series on prosperity, Gwen held Sarah's hand, remembering to listen more to her own feelings as she looked around at all the handsome people, all looking like magazine covers. She envisioned a Christianity that was glamorous, worldly, vital, loving and multi-faceted, and especially not hateful and violent!

Alf said again, "You cannot out-give God! Now listen: You all have Philippians 4:19?" Everyone looked at the Scripture as Alf read, "*And my God shall supply all your need according to His riches in glory by Christ Jesus.* In other words, beloved, you *cannot* out-give God. It took me a long time to recognize that fact. I see there are a lot of new people here tonight. Raise your hand if this is your first time at Faith Church. Let's welcome 'em." He was trying a new style, a more rah-rah, cool-rap kind of approach.

"Anybody here in the film business?" Alf asked, smiling.

Sarah sat motionless, holding Gwen's hand.

The "Young Ones" were cool, sitting and smiling, looking through tinted glasses and grooving to the new band playing songs by rock and roll praise bands and a few of their own. There was no lyric screen yet, that was next, Alf thought, as he was blown away by seeing the filled offering plates, some overflowing with hundred dollar bills. It was something he had never seen, and he praised his wife silently.

"Let's pray," he said as the ushers delivered the offering plates to the front. "Dear Heavenly Father, we thank you for all the blessings you've bestowed upon us. If any one of you has heard our Lord stirring your hearts (the organ sounded especially sweet as he said it)—keep your heads bowed, now—just raise your hand. If you've made a decision to come to the Lord today, just keep your hands in the air. No altar call, nobody will see you—every head is bowed. If you heard something deep in your heart tonight, raise your hands. Yes, many of you. Oh, hallelujah."

Every head was bowed, but Alf saw *all* the young people's hands going up and staying up. "Come up here afterwards and we'd be glad to give you some material to read, and a New King James Bible. If you need to pray, elders will be standing by outside the prayer room. Thank you, Lord, for all the blessings and all your wonders and signs and miracles at the end of this age. In Jesus' name we pray...Amen."

With that the service ended. There were trucks outside and new security guards, but Alf did not feel like the leader when Gwen asked him to leave.

"Alf, you go home and take care of Alfie. I'm going to stay here. I used to be an extra—there's a chance they'll use me tonight!" she said excitedly.

"I love you—Spencer said the plates were stuffed tonight."

"I love you too," she said as she watched him get into his new Silverado and quickly pull away as the production trucks circled the church. A bus with blacked-out windows arrived, and prop people (Gwen supervised) were bringing in all sorts of knives and robes and other strange objects. She guessed it: Satanic ritual. Yeah. That was it. A horror movie. She'd been in dozens and knew that she could handle it, even if her counterparts could not.

Arriving by Mercedes limousine was Jordan Star, the new benefactor of the Faith Church—Gwen practically kissed his ring. She melted at the sight of him, and when he spoke—she felt submissive for the first time in her life.

"Okay, I'll...I'll wait in the dressing room."

"My dear, you are so beautiful," he said to Gwen. "But it's a closed set. I hope it's not too...inconvenient."

"Not at all," she replied.

She went to the dressing room and would have chained herself to the closet door if she had to. It was deep within her to obey *him*, Mr. Star; for some reason he was the first one who had the power to *make* her obey. It wasn't necessarily that he was handsome and commanding. Nor that he was ageless, timeless, not his appearance in tailored suits and polished demeanor, not that he was new and like nothing she'd seen before. He was anointed, she would say—God had His hand on him, she would think. His accent that did not seem to be from anywhere in particular, it just seemed European, added to his allure, his mystery, his majesty.

"Unfortunately, angel," he called her, "we'll be closing the Los Angeles outreach office soon. Our headquarters are in London, and I'd be personally honored if you would visit me there."

She shook her head and took another look, and then she said: "Not sure if my husband likes traveling that far—or if he could even get off."

"I meant you. You'll be perfectly safe. My assistant, Chloe, will take care of all the arrangements. I assure you, you have nothing to fear from me."

"I know I don't, sir," she said, smiling.

The people she saw going into the church were all wearing dark glasses. They were all working quickly, rigging wires and altering the appearance of things.

Suddenly, there was another earthquake. "Oh, my God!" Gwen said as Jordan Star reached out and held her, preventing her from hitting the ground.

"Just an aftershock," Star said, and he was right. A little shake, the aftermath of the 3.3 the night before.

"I'm just so...nervous. I...I want—"

"Is everything satisfactory at the church now?" Star asked, inhaling a very thin cigar and smiling, tipping his hat at a man in a suit, who walked by the trailer and looked like his eyes were glowing from the inside of his skull.

Makeup, Gwen thought, and she said: "Yes sir, Mr. Star."

"Call me Jordan," he said.

Gwen pushed her brunette perm back, wondering if she had any number six on her lips. She knew she was completely in love with this man: the only man who could ever make her do anything.

"I want you to wait in your office. Bridget will be there with something for you to wear. Smile, my dear, you're going to be in the movies."

"You are so wonder...ful," she said, and he kissed her on the nose and walked away.

Bridget brought her back to the room. She sat on Alf's desk while Bridget slipped her into a sheer gown, revealing her nakedness, revealing what her training had told her was a sin, but his voice appeared in her ears, as if implanted: "You're in the house of God, Gwen. I love you. They cannot understand you. Not like I can. They will see a chaste and beautiful woman...do what you feel you must...come on. I love you."

"Sure," she told Bridget. "No problem."

Bridget laughed and left.

She deserved it—yes, she did. Woodland Hills, right-wing parents, Baptist schools—who needs it? She was going to be...*needed.* Not just by anyone. Her father would have liked Jordan Star, much more than Alf.

Whatever Jordan Star would ask of her, it would be an honor to oblige. Jesus Christ would understand. God must have his hand on Jordan; he was the gentlest, the sweetest, the most lovely man she had ever known. You see, Alf, you idiot, her mind raged. I was made to serve. *But you couldn't make me do it!*

Yes, she would make love to him right away—because he could wash away her sins.

Alf *could not* do that.

Jesus would understand, she thought she heard Jordan say.

twenty-seven

*B*auman was briefed by Daniel. He went to the Apollo Coffee House and saw them all sitting there with their laptops, staring at the same screen, and that was most interesting. There was a bright glowing pattern and they seemed hypnotized by it. The message was clear, and Daniel had said there would be an earthquake.

The real break in the case came when Shep returned with the coffee and they made their way toward the Faith Church. "We're making tremendous progress," he told Brother J (who desired only to be called *John the Apostle*). "Look," he said enthusiastically, seeing all the cars lined up in the parking lot, "this does not look normal, does it?"

They all witnessed the production trucks and saw that the church was cordoned off by armed guards.

They had just seen Daniel holding a lantern at the corner of Victory and Van Nuys. When the small earthquake hit, he held it up, directing all the pedestrians to the east. But Bauman was sure he was not pointing in any particular direction. John the Apostle was simply wrong.

Bauman pointed them toward the church—that's what the new Voice had said to him. So they came to the church.

John the Apostle said: "Let us pray. Dear Lord, on this dark and evil night, let us not shrink from our duty—give us Your blessing to stand firm, to not back down, no matter what we see."

The Voice had told him that everybody in the Apollo Coffee

House was hypnotized by their computers. Though Bauman did not know anything about the Bible or Jesus, he did know evil. He remembered Alice and the luxury SUV and how they had taken her. They returned a cheap imitation, a mannequin they called human. Alice had been drained of blood, raped, and marked with a diamond-star shape on her stomach. He saw the very same pattern on the computer screens, and he warned the others about drinking fancy coffee drinks, which might somehow taint them. While they were walking toward the church, Bauman reminded them again about the coffee house, "Just get regular black coffee and don't put anything in it, 'kay, Shep?"

"Look, boss, I'm not—"

"Are you the leader now, Shep?" Bauman was glaring.

"I'm not the leader, but I'm not stupid—they're filming a movie. That's all," he said.

"You don't think we should call for backup? You don't know these people. The Voice says it's evil, and I've tried calling Sheila several times—nothing."

"You think she's in there?" asked John the Apostle.

"Why is it so dark inside?" Bauman asked. There were lights on *outside* the church, but not inside—which was strange.

"Just a movie, no big deal," Shep told Bauman.

Bauman saw Daniel standing on the roof, but only for a moment. When Bauman pointed him out, the others looked away, an act of patronage and politeness Bauman did not need right now. "What, you don't think I'm telling you the truth?" he asked.

"The guards have it pretty well sealed," said John the Apostle.

"Daniel says we can get in the back. At a certain time," Bauman said.

"They got food," John the Apostle said. "Always food on movie sets."

• • •

Stephen knew the old man in his prison cell wasn't a natural person. He knew he had been with the angel Michael, and he knew everything pointed to Los Angeles. Knowledge wasn't soft; it pierced.

The news came on and he heard the news that Justin Kincaid had fallen from some wires and died. That's about all he knew—but he would find Katarina, as he believed she was the false witness who accused him of murder.

Casey rode beside Stephen, while Cynda was lying on the back seat, traumatized or in shock. "Lord, please help Cynda and Stephen to know that you have chosen them for this task; help Cynda accept your forgiveness, and thank you, Lord for showing her the truth. We need her back, Lord."

"Yes," said Stephen, fully trusting.

Casey went on: "We need you to show Stephen where to go. We rely completely on you, Heavenly Father, as we have nothing of our own anymore. In Jesus' name I pray. Amen."

"Amen," Stephen said. "So *who* are you?" he asked pointedly.

"I'm God's. Like you."

"No, you're not like me. But you're no devil either, because everything you say points to Lord Jesus."

"Praise Him," said Casey.

"Who are you!" Stephen asked as he pulled the car over near Victorville.

"I don't know. I'm not like you."

Stephen got out of the car, frustrated. He sunk to his knees and beat his hands on his head. He could not understand—how could it have such symmetry? How could this be of God?

"There will be another earthquake; He's going to pour the wrath out now," said Casey. "He saved us for something, and He will reveal it."

"No! Shut up! No!" Stephen said.

There was a hand on his shoulder. "Brother," Casey said. When Stephen looked up, he saw a glowing being. He was no longer a child, a boy of seventeen, but a fully mature man. Yet he was Casey. "Some of us will walk to and fro, preparing the way for the Lord."

"This isn't Revelation, is it?" Stephen asked.

Casey said: "No man knows the time. Go to Cynda, call her Rebecca from now on. God will bless it."

Casey got behind the wheel and Stephen knelt down beside Cynda, and he said: "Rebecca, that's what Casey said to call you. What do you think?"

She kept saying: "I'm sorry. I'm sorry. I..."

He hugged her and she wept. "Shouldn't we go to the police?" she asked. He pushed her hair back across her face, and he saw the future in her eyes. He saw in her eyes the moment of truth. "It's real, it's all real," she said, alarming Stephen.

He held her tight. It's alright, I'll take care of you, he wished he could say.

Casey turned around, a mere adolescent boy, and said: "There will be earthquakes in diverse places. They're all going to die. Those in Christ will be in heaven. But the angels weep. It's a judgment. And not only here—but everywhere man has built his cities on the blood of innocence. It only starts here. It's *judgment*. Understand?"

"But this isn't the Tribulation?" Stephen asked, frustrated, pounding on the seat.

Cynda answered: "Don't you see? Kincaid's experimenting on us. You're not real. This isn't happening—they can make it look real. It's...it's something no one really understands, another world...it comes out, right on top of this one and it has its own rules—you can't fight it!"

"It's *not* real—"

"It's *more* real!"

"Rebecca—"

"Stop calling me that," she insisted, but *Cynda* could not be found.

"It's Satan's kingdom," Casey said, matter-of-factly. "It's real—like an amusement park is real. You see, Rebecca—it was always what you thought, but then it wasn't there, and then it was."

"Yes," she said. "Yes, all right—yes," said the atheist. "Yes," said the scientist. "Yes," said the *realist*. "But how could I...how could—"

"You didn't understand—you were taught that you didn't see anything. You were brainwashed by the world."

"We have to come in—we have to tell the truth—we have to find safety," she said.

"You've never been *safe*," said Casey, and Stephen saw in his face the angel he had seen before.

"Oh, Father, praise God, thank you Lord," Stephen said.

"Shut up! Quit all this craziness—it's all an experiment!" Rebecca blurted out. "It's not real! It's mind—for the...for the CIA or the army or—"

"No, it's not," Stephen said, interrupting her, forcing her to look him in the eye. "It is not an experiment."

"Yes," said Casey fervently. "This is not the amusement park, but the real thing."

"You were working there as Cynda—but you were innocent, figuring science was science," Stephen said.

"That is exactly what she was doing, Stephen—you're even impressing God now."

Stephen continued: "You're *Rebecca* now because Casey is the angel you saw, and the miracles you've seen are real." He turned quickly to Casey, looking at his eyes in the mirror. "Right, Casey?"

"I'm not Casey—I'm *no one*," he said. Casey looked ahead and added, "He wants those who are His. I'm one of the lambs who isn't slaughtered. The last one before the judgment. All roads point to Christ, every knee will bow—the seal is broken. And you're both to be with me."

"Jesus warned about those saying they are the Christ," said Stephen with alarm.

"I'm *not* the Christ. I was born into the womb of Satan, a church-going family who looked the other way but knew wealth, secrets, not repentant, but proud. Who I am I cannot say now. They had a certain amount of time to change me, and when they did not complete their task, the path was cleared for our glorious Lord; they killed all the others and made the blood an imitation—but you don't understand. It's in God's hands; His are true signs and wonders, not false ones. No man knows the time of the end. First the earth will be plunged into darkness, but we don't know when the dragon will rise again." He turned on the news, while driving the speed limit in the Ford Explorer.

It was a news bulletin that got Rebecca's attention. She reached over Casey's shoulder to turn it up. It continued: "A bombing of the Russian Embassy in New York City has left hundreds dead, and perhaps thousands near the blast are missing. The city is once again panicked. The President told reporters that a response is expected, but there would be no comment until further notice. New York City is under curfew until further notice. Russia has blamed the United States and has filed a protest at the UN. The Russian ambassador has stated that his country will not hesitate in using nuclear weapons if the United States does. Meanwhile, in Tel Aviv, a suicide bomber entered Israeli police headquarters and detonated the device, killing dozens of officers and prisoners. U.S. forces are on high alert, as the peace negotiations have come to a standstill. In other news, the currency crisis of the U.S. dollar has been joined by the Euro and other currencies, and markets are expected to be closed until further notice...."

Casey turned it off. He shouted with glee! "The key was turned! That martyr means we will succeed! Their world falls now, Rebecca."

"Don't call me Rebecca!" She started crying again.

"It's a judgment," said Casey. "God works like this: for one to rise, another falls. Satan tries to imitate it, but can't. If I live, they die—and so we must save as many of God's as possible."

"Insanity," said Stephen. "You...I don't understand," he said, in awe of the being called Casey who had no name and was driving and knew things that were going to happen and was what he said he was. So Michael had proclaimed. Stephen knew he was not crazy, somehow, deep in his heart, he knew these things to be real, despite *Cynda's* pleading to put Humpty back together again.

"Please stop it," she said. Please, let's just go to the cops and turn ourselves in," she said faintly—and was falling asleep from shock.

Casey said: "Soon there will be a solution, and that will be evil. I will be with you, and they will take my blood, but they will fail. Because I won't be in a human body."

"What are you?"

"Don't know," Casey said. "Let us wait on the Lord."

Stephen did not know whether Casey knew the darkness that he harbored in his own heart. Katarina. Yes, he would kill her if he saw her. Indeed, they were headed to Los Angeles, and Stephen's task was to find Katarina and put her out of her miserable existence before she could contaminate any other soul. He had to get away from Cynda and Casey; he had to determine his own reality, and he still reserved the idea that it all might be some supreme mind control spook sort of thing. Casey didn't know he was thinking this—if he was so smart or so anointed or so enlightened, wouldn't he know that? Couldn't he know what Stephen was thinking?

Stephen was going to desert them, flee the ship, but Casey seemed calm and happy. He wasn't well, that had to be the only reason—after all, they were driving in a Ford Explorer going a little faster than the speed limit. Never mind the cover-up of the earthquake on a sensitive government installation, disguised as some private foundation—he could wrap the noggin around that, no problem.

But he had to get away from Casey and Cynda, as sure as he needed to breathe.

"Rebecca," Casey said. "The Lord loves you."

She bit her knuckles and hid her face in her arms, not wanting to hear another word.

twenty-eight

He arrived at 12:01 a.m. and marveled at the little "holy" church. No big cathedral, no Cardinal in flames, no dumpster babies, no Hollywood celebrants, no DC power-mongers, what in the world were they thinking?

Arles Dubailles knew this was no inner sanctum.

They were all in black business suits, every suit the same. Women with over-the-knee skirts and the same jacket. Diane Mitchell nodded as Arles was brought out before the altar.

They were few in number, but now Arles could see they were players after all—intelligence, business, government, entertainment—they were all there, famous, but no one would regard their status here. Here they could finally be their true selves—in the light of truth—which they felt was an eternal flame.

Jordan Star held the funeral proceedings. He was bathed in red light; if he did not wish to frighten anyone, he did so despite himself. The Faith Church crucifix, which was behind the pulpit, hung upside down, with a mannequin representing Jesus fastened to it. A vat—*to capture His precious blood*—was placed underneath the *head* of the upended "Christ."

The congregation acted without fanfare, as if it were a funeral, some so practiced and desultory in demeanor they would yawn and check their watches. Afflicted with apathy, but dutiful nonetheless.

"We are gathered here to celebrate unholy matrimony—our church of the one true god, to initiate a long-suffering disciple, who has earned our respect and trust," said Star, in a low-key, business-like manner, covered by no less than four broadcast cameras.

Two naked women stripped Arles of his clothing and blind-folded him. He was then instructed to lie down on a wooden slab. It was nothing like he had imagined. There was no fanfare, no hoopla, no *symbology*, which he had learned over the years was vitally im-portant to all their rituals—the position of the sun, a certain lamp stand, a certain dagger, the precise geographic location, nothing like this in evidence. This little church, under the guise of some entertainment project, did not make sense to *Arles Dubailles*.

He had not been briefed, but after all the ritual killings, orgies and charity banquets he'd attended, this seemed cheap, like a Vegas theme club too late even for a summer's eve. The atmosphere was usually rarified, sanctified to the dragon, *unholy holiness*, as it were. Nothing like this.

He had seen the cameramen—two on tripods and two roving, had even seen the satellite truck outside broadcasting to someone somewhere. Wasn't he in the *axis*, referred to in their terminology as *axis mundi*, the center of the world?

Of course he wasn't shy about removing his clothing and lying there with a dagger in his hand.

Arles had no idea what was going on. He could hear squelched whimpering right next to him. He could smell the blood as they sponged it on him.

Finally, he heard the moans and groans of those in the audi-ence—the sexual trigger was stimulated, but by what? What was he *not* seeing? Defiling God's temple was the usual fare anyway.

They sat him up, stripped off the blindfold, and then he saw what he could not understand. Something beyond him.

A true test, nothing anonymous.

"Come, let us celebrate our race!" Jordan Star said formally. When they all stood, they began to move around among the con-gregation. Arles knew it as random sex, incited by watching a hu-man sacrifice in front of the crucifix.

There were three sheets atop three standard hospital gurneys. Three victims for Arles to kill, and three large urns beside each table for the capturing of the blood, which, as Arles understood it, was to be drunk in order to stave off the return of the Christ. Always the same motive, always the same ritual. He wondered whether he would see the true ritual, using alchemy to turn the blood into the Holy Grail, the *Blood of the Lamb*, they called it. The elixir of Satanic power on earth, rule forever and ever—the loophole that no one had ever known before. The secret of every secret society, the thing that could never be uttered lest the spell be broken—and that was why the ritual had been held tightly by so few, for so long. The culmination of knights, King Arthur, John the Baptist's skull and bones, the secrets of Pythagoras, the holy knowledge at Alexandria, later taken to the Vatican; the instructions, the *satanic matrix*, a holograph, or even the blueprint of the mind of God! The very thing that could stop the Bible from coming true, to prevent Daniel's seventieth week, as they feared and disdained the return of Christ above all. The Bible prophecies would have already destroyed their wondrous world. That is, if it truly existed *in time*. If a key ever turned, a seal ever broke, if a clock began to tick again...the return of these meant only one thing, one terrifying end to the reality they had built, their glorious Way: *the human being exalted above all.*

Not in time, but *in cycle*—the same cycle, over and over again. Eternity for those who understood, who had elevated their consciousness, death was for those whose duty was service, not self-glorification. For in the real world, one would never see what powered the mechanism of mercy—utopia was now, *forever now*. A place where children did not weep, where *the good* did not die, a place where pleasure was love, and love was all that was required to buy or sell. Love, yes of the flesh—but a mystery never to be revealed. Love was synonymous with *desire*, because it was evil to separate the two.

And sacrificial love was the highest love—a gift to all.

They believed they had put an end to God's prophecy clock when they appropriated Christ's blood long ago. That blood was the physical universe, so long as they repeated the cosmogony, or *self-creation* of the world by *inverting* Jesus' atoning sacrifice, thereby covering themselves and foisting sin in the *Holy of Holies*. He had studied all the esoteric knowledge, and he now understood the silent teaching of *the one in a turban* behind him. All the supplicants were now at various stages of sexual dominance and submission, and the *Turban* told him of the world to come, that this particular sacrifice would sustain until they found the last key, which the visionaries claimed would be soon.

"What do you mean...*the last key?*"

The Turban walked away, *straight through the wall, gone.* Arles sat up, very much afraid.

Jordan Star, standing at the head of the stage, was orchestrating some sort of orgy in the darkness, waving benedictions approvingly. It looked and sounded like cannibalism, which was *not* what Arles had understood.

Arles was led, dagger in hand, to the larger adult human, whom he knew was compressed under the sheet, strapped down, gagged and pierced in the feet and hands.

He was not ready for what he would see when the sheet was pulled back.

"My dear friends, Mr. Dubailles is about to test his mettle and will prove worthy."

An armed guard pulled the sheet back but Arles was not ready to see his wife, Mary Sue Dubailles. The other two strapped, sheeted figures were his children, Rachel and Samuel.

He paused and wondered if *they* thought he was afraid.

He wondered if *they* understood his *desire* for truth.

Could *they* see his burning desire to *want*?

To want *this*. Yes, to want this very badly!

Jordan Star was confidently encouraging Arles to do what he had been groomed for. "You thought it would be more difficult, I know," he said easily. "I assure you, everyone here will call you brother, as you will step into godhood with us." Then he turned to the dark melding crowd: "For such is immortality!"

Arles caught a glimpse of Diane Mitchell sitting right next to Jackson Kincaid; they were holding hands and watching intently. Their eyes were wide and they looked like children, as the feeding torrent carried on, and as what looked like blood sloshed around the floor.

The cameras were all trained on the ritual, on Arles' dilemma.

Did they think it was a dilemma?

"Why *them*?" Arles said. "Why my children?"

Star seemed alarmed. "Is it not acceptable in the eyes of our lord—Lucifer, the almighty angel of mercy and love?"

Had Arles finally stumbled? Had he finally found the secret and it wasn't to be? This was a test, not a ritual to reverse the Bible prophecy or anything of the sort. It was just plain blood lust—pain lust.

"Your *devotion* is the single best insurance and justice for us and against the God who has scourged our people from time immemorial. Mr. Dubailles, make us live, sir!"

He could not.

This made no sense. He dropped the dagger as he looked with horror at his wife's face. Several guards then subdued him.

Bauman was watching the "film shoot" at the Faith Church from the distance. As the movie crew was loading the trucks, as vans with blacked-out windows and limousines pulled away, he suddenly saw it—Ricky and his drug-dealing pals. And the Cadillac SUV that took Alice.

Daniel was holding the lamp and now pointing to the abundantly lit Faith Church. He was pointing as the answer came: these were the people *who kidnapped Alice Garcia*, and these were the people who killed her and left her body in pieces in the Los Angeles River, a concrete sewer to be sure.

He approached with caution. He still had his .45 acp Glock, and he was ready to do whatever was necessary to bring them in—or kill them with extreme prejudice, if necessary. John the Apostle grabbed Bauman, holding him back. "No!"

Daniel turned back, looked at them—shook his head no. His feet *were not* touching the ground.

Alf Blicky suddenly arrived, angry. He stepped out of his new truck and stormed up to Jordan Star, who was exiting in a self-satisfied manner. "Where's my wife!" he demanded.

Alf was arrested by the guards and stuffed into a police squad car, as if anticipated. Star did not so much as glance back at him when he passed.

"What do we do...what do we do?" Bauman asked, wondering where his daughter was at this very moment.

"Pray," said John the Apostle.

"I'm...I have to know what's going on!" Bauman screamed.

Then the secret service agents trained their eyes on the rabble, including Shepherd, John the Apostle, Big Willy (who was now a believer in Bauman, if nothing else), the gray-haired stranger named Daniel and the others. The agents all had earpieces and spoke into their lapels and also on cell phones.

"Scatter!" Bauman yelled.

As they started to run, another earthquake shook them all to the ground. Cars ran off the three-lane boulevard, which now resembled ribbons in a chaotic wind.

The security team, sure to be rogue federal agents, and the guards finished loading their vehicles and sped away.

Bauman and the others were hugging the ground. "Oh, my Lord! It's God! It's God!" exclaimed Bauman, a new believer.

Daniel was nowhere to be found.

Suddenly, flames erupted from the roof. Bauman and the others wondered if Daniel had started the fire with his lantern. All they knew was that the growing conflagration spread to other houses, as power lines had fallen, openly showering the street with sparks. Was it the earthquake?

Sirens pierced the distance and seemed to come from farther and farther away, and the forever night was not likely to end.

Shep had a small transistor radio. The only thing they could hear was the Emergency Broadcast System: "The Los Angeles area has been struck with a 7.2 quake. Emergency shelters are at the following locations—Anselm Church in Los Angeles, Harvest Chapel in Santa Monica. Taft High School in Reseda...."

They watched the fire as it burned brightly—soon the building collapsed and burned itself to the ground.

Bauman had headed for his home—he used his gun to coerce a driver out of a Dodge truck, and he took John the Apostle and Shep with him.

Big Willy went home, and Daniel was seen walking along the street carrying two bags of groceries or supplies.

"We're finally going to get to the bottom of this case. We really are!" Bauman screamed. "I don't care if this whole world shakes to the ground—"

"Dear Heavenly Father," said John the Apostle, "Please help Sergeant Bauman accept You in his heart. Jesus is true—Jesus is returning—and if they do not heed his call, they will go to Hell. Please help Bauman come to You Lord. In Jesus' Holy Name I beg of you—"

"Okay! Okay! I admit, it's...it's true, and Daniel's not one of us, I mean... Daniel proves it. So what? I have to find my wife and daughter."

That was all John the Apostle had to hear. He smiled, as the aftershock nearly pushed the Dodge off the road.

twenty-nine

*A*ll Cal knew was that he had to take care of Spruug's family and get Spruug to the hospital. The beam that had hit his leg snapped it like a twig, but the local hospital's emergency wing had collapsed, killing several who had been in for treatment.

TV transmission was up, and there were Red Cross facilities in the area that could attend to Spruug. "I'm alright. My Lord's coming back. I think it's a judgment," Spruug said enthusiastically.

Cal was weeping because he finally saw now that Sally Anne was indeed deceased, and without her, life made no sense. He had really used his prized plane for killing children, and he would have killed himself now, except that Spruug's wife and children needed help. But after that he would die as quickly as possible, by any means possible—and this gave him a modicum of joy.

"Can't you see them, Cal?" Isabella asked, watching the television after the electrical power came back on.

"That's our church, Mom!" said Preston, Spruug's delightful bushy-haired ten-year-old boy.

Isabella Spruug was referring to something on the screen that he could not see.

"Mom sees angels," said Preston, matter-of-factly. He looked at Cal, who was keeping Spruug's leg on ice. He knew how to attend to the wound, but Isabella was shaken as she held Jesse, her little one, on her lap.

Spruug was shivering, and Cal kept him in a blanket. He had already made a makeshift splint out of Preston's snowboard. "Look,

I'm alright, honey! I'm alright!"

"I can see them—they're hovering there, over the church!" she said.

"It's our church—or it was," said Preston, looking at his father. "They got this cool new pastor, and now—"

Cal was in combat mode, in survival mode, and in defense mode—nothing would, under any circumstances, penetrate the perimeter.

Spruug said, "Cal, listen, we need to pray. The Lord will help us."

"Preston, keep that ice coming."

They were all amazed that the lights were still on. They were gratified at Spruug's prayer, and as he went on, smiling while lying on his back in the living room of their townhouse on the hill, they all were focused on his lips. "May the Lord bless us and keep us; the Lord make His face to shine upon us and be gracious to us; the Lord lift up His countenance upon us, and give us peace. Yea, though I walk through the valley of the shadow of death, I shall fear no evil, for You are with me, Your rod and Your staff, they comfort me. Thank you, Lord, for watching over my family. Thank You for all your blessings. In Jesus' name I pray. Amen."

Cal had never seen nor heard such a commanding presence under a wound before, and Isabella seemed suddenly *changed* as well. Preston came in with more cold compresses.

"Listen, the beam in the garage, it's ready to cave, man, this whole place could go in one more aftershock—why don't we book out of here," said Cal.

"Then we go to the shelter?" Isabella asked, sighing.

The child Jesse wanted to show Cal his dinosaur and Cal very much liked it. "That's a fine looking T-Rex—"

"That's a raptor," Jesse said confidently.

Cal asked: "Are you a dinosaur hunter?"

Spruug was clearly passing out from the pain but did not complain.

Jesse smiled and nodded, a cute six-year-old.

They were after him, Cal realized, and Spruug and family had opened their home to him. Cal suddenly felt the truth and a sense of purpose come over him like a warm blanket.

"I know who I am. I know who I am!" Cal exclaimed.

Spruug smiled. "Oh, good. The Lord is here."

"Something's here. I...I understand what to do now," Cal said.

Suddenly, Isabella's eyes were affixed, as she had been before, to the television. "Oh, look, they're hovering over the church—they're on the rooftops of the burning buildings. They're in the air with the helicopters! God is truly saving the day!"

They would not know who the stranger was who knocked on the door, but neither Cal, nor Spruug himself, was completely convinced that Isabella was seeing angels, or whether it was just wishful thinking, or worse, Cal thought—delusion based on trauma.

But the doorbell did ring, and it rang again.

When Isabella opened it, she found a man with long dark hair, a long dark beard, and burning, happy blue eyes, and a youth who defied his obvious age. He carried a child into the house, a little Latin girl of eight-years-old, who had been burned. Her arm dangled, severed and hanging by a ribbon of flesh.

Cal could see that she was unconscious, and quite possibly dead.

"I thank you for your hospitality," the stranger said. "Her building collapsed, and she was lost in the rubble."

Even Spruug, when he leaned over, could see that this little girl was very close to death, if not dead already.

"Do you have some lemons?" asked the stranger. "Oh, by the way, my name is Michael."

"Hello, Michael," said Cal. "Sure. Isabella, you sit down. Chief (he was referring to Preston), you make sure your daddy has everything he needs." Cal tried to take the child away, as he felt that this man was in a state of denial. He'd seen shellshock before, and it could happen with just one trauma, or sometimes it took several, but this was clearly that. "Michael, give her to me."

He would not. "Please do as I ask," Cal insisted. "Michael, man—she's probably dead."

"Are you saying that you will not give me a lemon and some water and a towel?" Michael asked, calmly.

Cal did not want to upset an already topsy-turvy situation, and did not want to return to himself; he wanted to help, he *needed* to help. It was as if the emergency had cured—somewhat—his suicidal condition, or maybe it was Spruug's prayer. Either way, he was not hurting, he was converging; his faculties were not fragmented, they were uniform and with one purpose: to help these people.

When Cal gave Michael a dishtowel, a half-lemon, which was in the fruit bowl, and a bottle of water, Michael looked at him, and held his hand. "God bless you, *Caleb*," he said.

Cal turned deathly pale. It all flooded back, the paranoia, the brainwashing—once lost, fragmented, tortured, and then, some-how, now elated and sustained. It was too much for Cal to process, to fathom or to rationalize. He was simply frozen on the spot and could not move.

Isabella kept watching TV out in the living room, and Michael said: "You're with us, Caleb, don't you understand?"

Cal trembled and sank to his knees to worship the numinous creature. "No, Caleb—don't do that!" With just his finger Michael waved Cal to his feet. "Help me," Michael said, his long dark hair and beard occasionally masking his luminous quality as Cal saw flashes of a glowing face, hair and white linen. A tear in the fabric of an illusory world—*this world*.

This world was fragmented, not him.

Cal held the girl's dead arms as Michael did something strange with the lemon, as if he breathed it in. He looked at Cal and said, "This is for me. My Lord does not want her yet. She's not dead, as you see."

Cal noticed that the little girl was indeed breathing, but barely.

"She has too much to do, she has too much love to give. She will live on."

Cal trembled nonetheless, looking down at the precious face of a little girl with burn wounds and a disconnected arm, pale from loss of blood. Passed out? In a coma? Worse? Yes, it was undeni-able—she *was* breathing.

She was still alive! Was she dead before? He just couldn't re-member.

"You are forgiven, Caleb," Michael said. "Don't kill yourself."

Cal could not look at him. He kept thinking about Isabella watching something on the TV screen. He started crying but he knew he deserved nothing.

"You *are* loved, Caleb Wilson," Michael, whose knees were above the carpet, said! He acted as if floating were quite normal. "This little one is not dead; she is very much alive. Do you agree?" asked Michael, staring through Cal's eyes and into his heart.

Cal kept looking and there were no burn marks, her arm was not dangling as it had been before, her face was not smudged and bloody, and perhaps it had never been. Cal had seen reality shift like this before, and unfortunately, had become accustomed to it. This strange man could not be some operative, some spook shrink, or part of some military operation.

They would kill him now if they saw him. You do not desert

your post, if on duty, as he had done at the airport. This sort of anomaly is not permitted because it is an indication that the programming had failed. And failure is not in their vocabulary.

She was breathing, and Cal wept openly. Michael used the lemon skin to wash the dirt from the little girl's eyes, and she coughed.

When she sat up, Michael was gone—departed. Or so Cal thought.

He hugged the little girl, and she told him that her name was Soledad. Her eyes were big and precious and Cal held her close.

Then he heard Isabella screaming. When he looked, Spruug was standing! Cal could not speak, he could not move as a foggy mist covered the living room. When he was able to enter, he saw Michael as he was before, wearing the humble clothing of a laborer, work boots and blue shirt.

"You will be witnesses," said Michael. "Look now," he pointed, and they saw a man with a long gray beard and gray hair on the television. He was on a street paved with gold, and there was no difference between the television and the vision.

They saw men and women clothed in white linen, congregating. The man with the gray hair changed and became youthful, perhaps in his thirties, and he opened a book for the others. Light shone from no known source.

The face of a youth filled the screen. Michael told them: "This is the one who executes God's judgment. He who holds the book is Daniel."

Spruug suddenly became aware of himself, and realized he had forgotten all about his wound.

Jesse was smiling; he knew the television was off, and they were standing in a transparent room, which was made of gold but transparent as glass. He knew he'd seen this before, but the others did not understand.

"Our Lord is glorious," said Michael, who stood in the air. Daniel held a lamp before a shining figure clothed in an ankle-length garment, girded about his chest with a golden band. His face and hair were white as snow, and his eyes were a flame of fire. His feet were like fine brass, as if refined in a furnace, and He spoke the Word in a language they all understood but had never heard before.

Michael, now invisible, said with a voice of authority, "This is the Son of Man. The young lamb survived, his blood was not spilled. The Adversary did not know, nor does he now know. Look!"

Isabelle stood transfixed as the seal of the book was broken. The book was a scroll now, and became a road, which the Son of Man walked, and none could look upon him, as He shone like the sun.

"Lord have mercy on me," said Isabella, and she took Jesse and fell to her face. Preston, Jesse and Spruug imitated her, and fell to their faces, as the heat from the glowing path that was a book opened up and rolled into space and into the room where they all were.

On the screen they saw the face of the one Michael said had been mortal, but was translated because his soul was not of this earth.

"Now, beloved," said Michael, "the seal of Daniel is broken," and on the television there were glowing clouds hovering over the city of Los Angeles, and Isabella was not the only one who could see.

Spruug walked around, feeling no pain, and he looked at the television set, which was a transmission of Michael's face, as he spoke directly to them.

Soledad held Cal's hand and would not let it go. "My parents have gone to the Lord," she said. "But God is here!"

Michael said, "You shall see death, but His love surpasses, and you shall not feel pain. *One lamb lived*, my loved ones. Our Lord and Savior, whom we all worship in Heaven, will come again. But not now; first there will be a terrible warning, a warning unlike anything you have ever seen, and you all shall be the remnant."

"What if it's blasphemy?" asked Spruug. "The devil can trick us. Daniel is a book of prophecy, and it is sealed up. We're not to know."

"The Devil cannot heal, he can only destroy," replied Michael. "You know the Word, Joseph. Here is wisdom. The truth of Daniel, that is sealed up until the end of all things. Here is a key: *Daniel is a clock*."

"But no man shall know the time!" said Spruug, who had been called Joseph.

"Correct, Joseph, time belongs to God, to do with as He so pleases, and that time has begun; it was *always* going to begin. How foolish are they who *think* that they can change even one of God's holy plans," Michael said in what seemed like several voices speaking in unison.

Suddenly he was not in the room, on the television, nowhere to be seen. Spruug was suspicious, and Cal kneeled before the girl named Soledad. "Joseph," Cal now called Spruug, "please lead us in a prayer."

• • •

It was daylight, and Kincaid had wandered for hours. He did not return to his hotel room, nor did he go with the body of his son. A man in a black suit had appeared next to him and told him he was to walk away; he would be met by others who would know him, and they would give him instructions.

When he left, it was as if no one could see him. A faceless man in a dark suit gave him a ride in a limousine from Long Beach to downtown Los Angeles, where a shelter was open in Little Tokyo. It was a modest Japanese evangelical church where the men remained on their knees and prayed, and the women sat in the back and read Scripture, and prayed while sitting. The pastor said he knew something had changed, "But I am only a man, and I cannot understand God's ways, but He tells me to help you."

Kincaid said nothing. The concerned pastor knew Kincaid needed help, and he told him it would have to be the Holy Spirit that would do this work. It would have to be supernatural. There were signs and wonders, and the pastor was worried that he had seen angels at work. He knew to turn to the passage in Hebrews 13, verse 2: *Do not forget to entertain strangers, for by so doing some have unwittingly entertained angels.*

thirty

How many angels were there, wondered Stephen Jenkins Petchick? Was God still making them? Their number was incalculable and this was comforting to know. It was good to think about.

He was driving a person—perhaps two people—he did not know, but he would manage to get out in Pasadena. He would not go all the way into Los Angeles. He was determined to make his inquiries.

Cynda, *now* Rebecca, rubbed his shoulders as Casey slept soundly. "Thank you, Stephen."

"You're awake," Stephen said, casting his mind to a more personal aspiration.

"I feel different. I believe in God," Rebecca, said.

"Well, I'm going to just pull over here—let's get some breakfast. What do ya think?" Stephen asked reflexively. No, she did not just say she believed in God—no need for concern.

"I feel at peace," Rebecca said, brushing her hair back, then adjusting Casey's cap.

"It was just an earthquake. You were a government researcher. I was detained illegally; Casey was your patient, and we escaped. You can go back and tell them you were kidnapped," Stephen said worriedly. "You can go back and tell them that you're still traumatized. You're in trouble—you need help. And you would be justified, Cynda."

"Rebecca," she insisted.

Rebecca—he wanted to call her that. He wanted to say: I love you more than you could ever know, because we were chosen to be together. God told me through His Spirit. But he would ignore what must be patent fantasy based on fear! The traumas that came in waves were traumas nonetheless.

Today the radio spoke of the embassy situation being under control; the Russians were blaming Afghani terrorists now. The earthquakes in Southern California were nothing unusual. Casey stirred and said: "It's a wave."

"*Rebecca*, you like that name now?" Stephen asked.

Casey turned and looked at them. "He is King of Kings and Lord of Lords, and He is not a priest in the order of Melchizedek, but One who changes not, who reigns forever and ever. To answer the question that is on your mind, Stephen, there are countless angels, and they are gathered here now, and the fallen ones are here. It is the City of Angels, is it not?"

Stephen was unconvinced, as ever.

"They hid me—I'm one of them," Casey said.

"Yes," Rebecca added. "Oh, Father, forgive me." She cried again, and Casey laid his hands on her head, and he spoke softly in her ear.

Stephen was wrenched in thought. It just couldn't be! And if it is, *what is it*? Stephen wanted to scream.

"They will try to stop Him here, and they will try to stop Him there, and they will try in Egypt, and they will try elsewhere. I was 'Casey' only as a disguise. Many of us wear disguises. You know this by now—you've seen us, Stephen."

"Will you shut up with that kind of talk! I was dreaming or something when...in my room—they drugged me, that's all. This is crazy! So please shut up, okay?"

"He is a righteous God, and He killed them all so that we could do His will, but we take no gratification in their calamity," Stephen heard Casey's voice say, but Casey did not speak. Casey's voice was clear, it was loud, and it was real. Stephen slammed the car over to a burger stand, leapt from the Ford, disappearing quickly into the restroom.

"My name isn't Casey," the voice said in Stephen's ear while Stephen washed his face. "My name is *Harbinger*, it's *Make-The-Path-Straight*. I come because a lamb returned. God will judge now, and though many will perish, it is only a warning. After God's warning will be the end. And Christ, whom we all live to worship and praise, will return—and I will serve you then."

"Please shut up! Shut up! Get out of my mind!" screamed Stephen, alarming a boy and his father, who scurried out as soon as they were done. "God, please help me," Stephen said out loud. "I'm weak in my mind. I'm failing. I'm not okay—none of this is real, but I'm cracking up, Father. Help me. In Jesus' name I pray."

The mirror reflected Casey, who had called himself Harbinger. Stephen was dizzy, and felt sick to his stomach and weak in the knees.

"You will marry Rebecca, as this is chosen. The remnant will bear children, so you glorify the living God," Casey said from behind him and then continued, "A remnant is always God's work, when He could always destroy the world if He so chose...He will destroy because they blasphemed the Holy Spirit by translating the blood. But God is not thwarted by any act of sorcery. I told them this when they asked me to petition God to allow those angels back into heaven. God refused. So they gave women the power to divide the root and cast the spell, to divine and to supplicate with the blood and make it Christ's. They believed that ended *time*. But the last lamb came home, and even by their rules, Daniel's clock began. There is no way to stop it now. God bless you, Stephen."

"What are you talking about?" Stephen asked, as he saw the mirror reflect the reams of sweat pouring down his face. "I don't understand you! And I don't want to!"

"*Warfare*. You were chosen," said Casey, but all Stephen could see was his own distraught face.

"Oh? By whom? And says who?" Stephen asked fearfully.

"By our Lord God. His Word goes out from my tongue," Casey answered. He hugged Stephen, which alarmed a truck driver, who quickly left the restroom. "You believe, you know it's true. Stephen, the judgment to come, as I prophesy, is true. I was His, born into the womb of the adversary. But I was hidden, you see? I was not *them*."

Afterwards, as they ate their breakfast specials, Stephen marveled at how normal everything was, despite a 7.2 earthquake, now revised down to 6.5. It had killed a hundred or so but was much worse in Arizona, where thousands were dead. Both cities were at a standstill and it would be a long time before things righted themselves.

"I can't talk in here," Casey said. "Prophecy is for the Body, it's not fortune telling. But one thing I can say—"

"Rebecca, feel free to chime in at any time," Stephen interrupted, hoping for a distraction.

"We have to warn them—we have to bring them to Christ, even if I leave you."

"Do you think you're God or something? What's all this about supernatural powers, and angels and all that stuff? I read the Bible and I study God's Word, and try to live by it. It's mainly invisible."

"Not anymore—never again for you, Stephen. He chose you for this, son."

"Son? You're seventeen-freakin'-years-old for—" Stephen caught himself before the flurry of expletives left him.

Rebecca laughed and looked up at the neon lights above her and said, "Thank you, Father. Thank you, Lord, oh, how I love you."

"And she's *ruined*. I hope you're happy," Stephen said.

"Rejoice! All of you here, rejoice, the Lord is in this place!" Casey yelled, addressing the nosy ones with apparent magnanimity, and some cheered, and others turned away, embarrassed. The manager came over but Rebecca would not quit her praising of God.

Stu, the manager and originally from Albuquerque, was only a manager in training who had acclimated himself to honest work after dealing in drugs. Stephen recognized Stu's prison tattoo just before Casey touched Stu's hand and the tattoo *changed*. Only Stu noticed the transformation, but his eyes lit up and he walked out of the Burger Palace and kept walking.

"He won't be back."

"Okay, you give me the creeps, kid. You're of the devil—"

"I didn't come from here."

"You're a...what, a wizard, a warlock, a sorcerer?"

"Thank you, Lord," Rebecca, who was in her own world, was saying. "Thank you, Jesus, how I love you. Oh, Lord keep me with you."

"It's called the Holy Spirit. In Genesis 5 we learn what happened to Enoch—he wasn't one of you, either. Some say he owes a death, because he's human—but I can tell you the truth now...he did not possess a human soul. His soul kept him separated, directed by God—who walked with him every day. Why? Because He was a Son of God...as in *angel*."

"I'm leaving," Stephen announced, very much afraid.

"Because you never had the baptism of the Spirit. She's having it today, and you're insensitive," Casey pointed out.

"Oh, that's a good one. *I'M* INSENSITIVE? ARE YOU OUT

OF YOUR MADCAP MIND, MAN?"

"Stephen, I can help you," Casey said.

"No! Get out of my head, man! I'll walk, I promise you that!"

"Let me—" Casey reached across the food for Stephen's head.

By now the impromptu congregation were all crying and scream-ing for no apparent reason. "They are all receiving it, Stephen. I'm sorry, but our God is supernatural. Jesus our Christ is supernatural. Some of us are walking to and fro. Countless angels intervene every minute of every hour all over the world, unseen by humans, but not now, because many will die if we don't help."

"What's...what's wrong with you people!" Stephen screamed as he got up. "You're of Satan!" he screamed at Casey.

Rebecca leapt up and grabbed him: "Stephen! No! You belong here! Many depend on you," she said, then started speaking in Tongues.

Stephen could understand her, though her voice sounded like some ancient Hebrew or Arab dialect. She told him: "God is going to warn, and many will die. Casey is His angel."

He did not remember hitting his head, or if it was his head that he hit, or his shoulder, or the top of his neck. He had fallen, yet he did not feel it. He was not equipped, period. He'd have to check the Scriptures—wasn't this an attack? Wasn't it some demonic scourge? It was magic! It was totally overwhelming and he hurt himself. No-body can claim to be something other than human, but Casey did not say he was an angel.

"But that's what I am," Casey said, correcting Stephen's thought.

All was black anyway—comforting black. The lack of responsi-bility and suspension of time were soothing beyond measure. The rumble of the motor and the nightmare of the past were both com-forting, in that the past was past and the rumble was hypnotic.

You aren't crazy—you need rest, came another voice, a voice that was comforting.

Right, well, I'll take care of that.

I love you, Stephen. May I look through your eyes? the Voice asked.

Who are you? Will you please go away—if anybody found out about this, they'd...Who are you? The thoughts raced around in Stephen's mind and he was afraid, though he could not wake up.

I want to live here; I am Peace. I will never leave you, loved one. Let me look through your eyes; let me see how you see.

It was not Casey's voice, but something of His own, familiar, heartwarming.

Will you give everything up now—and let me live in you? the Voice asked.

"Please help me," Stephen finally said, opening his eyes. He was not looking through his own eyes anymore. Stephen touched Rebecca and she touched him. They were his family and he somehow knew that now more than he had ever known anything. "Please help me," Stephen asked again, and lay back against the back seat, feeling what he just felt before, but this time he knew it wasn't some survival mechanism in his body.

It's the Holy Spirit, Casey said in Stephen's mind, once again. "He's here to indwell and never leave."

"Stay," Stephen said, while Rebecca drove and was still crying joyously for everything that had happened.

"I was wrong," Rebecca said, "and if the Holy Spirit didn't show up and correct me, I would have had a nervous breakdown and I would have been dead. I'm sure of it and now I don't care."

Stephen could not fight back anymore. "I never was a Christian."

"You were always God's," Casey laughed. "Hallelujah!" he screamed out of the car, as an aftershock forced them off to the side of the 134 Freeway.

"Wait till you see what's going to happen to I-95," Casey said with an authority no longer checked.

Rebecca got out and looked at the beauty of life everywhere across the broken freeway and beyond to endlessness. "You know," she said, "if we were up in the clouds, all this would seem so far away."

They surveyed the freeway, cordoned off up ahead. An overpass had collapsed. They looked back toward Pasadena, and they knew to proceed further.

"He will pour His judgment on the fallen ones here," Casey declared. "It will be water."

thirty-one

*T*hey had been searching everywhere. Intelligence operatives were combing every piece of e-mail, every letter, every telephone call, all with the aid of their top-secret computer, which was not called *Echelon*. Jackson Kincaid knew there was literally nowhere to hide on the entire surface of the earth, or elsewhere. She had been in Intelligence all along. She ordered the hit on her son Justin, which had earned her a higher ranking, though not off-world.

There was just one messy detail, besides a spiritual problem that she would take care of later. Brand Kincaid was supposed to have died. The destruction of Serin was indeed planned, that was the word at the briefing. It had become too hot, too confined, and the experiments were never to be discovered.

What was he thinking, she mused, as she and Senator Diane Mitchell boarded the private jet for Washington, D.C. "Thigpenny will have to know, so will Barcher," the senator said, while perusing the President's proposed budget.

"We cleaned it up, it all went according to plan."

"Except one got away, and there was no body at Serin of the intended recipient, *Casey Burns Smith*."

Jackson was wondering about her status now as a high-profile operative. "Do you think the brass—"

"Yes, the brass especially."

"So I screwed it up," she said, worried. Now she felt the hatred for her husband that she had known but had not let herself really enjoy. "I'd like to do it myself."

"You can't. That is, unless you want to be delivered."

"I'm... Why is this all about *that?*"

Diane lit a cigarette and scanned her perfect nails and five-carat ring. "Is it really like that for you?" Diane asked.

The jet climbed high into the hazy sky. "What about the quakes?"

"Just honest to goodness quakes, honey. The cattle are in a state of hysteria, it's so cute," the senator said, writing in WE NEED MORE SCHOOL LUNCH PROGRAMS on the budget. Then: HOMELESS. Then: WORKING POOR? WHO BENEFITS FROM THE TAX CUTS? Her whole life she had been fighting for the monies to be distributed evenly amongst the people, and the thugs from another world had the audacity to slow things down, to muddy the waters with God and religion.

There was only one religion, and she knew that her friend, Jackson Kincaid, was not long for this world—she just didn't believe.

• • •

Heading up the City of Angels operation was none other than Cal's control, mentor and chief handler, General Jack Ritali. It would have been a cause for concern if Cal were still under the control of Ritali's army, which was not operating under the laws of any particular region or principality. "We speak the same language everywhere," the General said into his Iridium phone, while Arthur Reddick paced nervously in his office, high above the fray. "Good, thank goodness for radioactive socks. We'll take out the city if we have to. Johnny, if you don't see him, it doesn't matter, get Forgy and Stone together and rev up Atwater's boys. They haven't had so much fun since downing that Taiwanese airliner for the Chinaman."

Reddick bristled. He was an elderly man with the look of a dignified banker. Conservatively dressed in an off-the-rack suit, he appeared modest yet had the wisdom of serpents and sorcerers. His knowledge began with Balthasar Gracián's *The Art of Worldly Wisdom* and Sun-zu's *The Art of War* and continued to include the philosophy of Freemasonry, where reality was grail-laden, blood-lusting, yet covered by charitable works.

But all was wrong now and he knew it.

The nuclear bomb was designed to hurt non-combatants, a pleasing aroma unto the lord of the world—which resulted in bucks, big

LAMB

bucks. Now, unless they are innocent, the sacrifice would always be wasteful, without efficacy in the physical realm. Reddick was pleased with the angle involving terrorist attacks on American cities, which provided on the spot footage for live broadcast into any number of worship centers. He thought they were further ahead. He thought the kingdom he hoped to bring in was only a few steps away, namely, cutting the population by eighty percent and implementing all the science both public and secret to bring about the Brotherhood of Man.

But things had come unglued again. He was a man surrounded by fools—never once could they think, speak, or be in the realm of truth. For they did not understand—yet they thought they knew everything. For such is the way with fools.

And yet Ritali, still on the phone, prattled on: "The quake has been cordoned off. They have a curfew, so do your duty, soldier. I want this matter resolved by 1600 hours. Roger that." The General sucked on his cigar and sat back on the sofa in Reddick's office. Arthur's face was no consolation. "What the devil is wrong now?"

"General, this will end badly."

"What are you talking about?" asked the General.

"Spirits."

"I'll believe it when I see it."

"I thought we had more time," Reddick said, and exhaled as if he would never breathe again.

"Time, sir? As I understand it, we make time. We also make opportunities."

"You, sir, do not know what you're talking about," Reddick declared.

"Look, the way the world is and has always been is just the same now, you told me that," the General replied.

"I told you that there are rules, and the wise man learns what they are and learns to adapt."

"You sound worried."

"I am, General. I made a mistake, like you. And I won't be getting out of this one with anything of value, and neither will my children or grandchildren."

He sounded like a man who lost his Prozac, the General thought. How he hated the lamentations of guilt—the world was the way it was, and men like him were in the driver's seat. True, Ritali didn't understand why they needed so much blood, but they did. A disaster here, an accident there, a dirty nuke, anthrax—all blamed on oil-rich countries which would soon be enslaved. No one was talk-ing *nuclear war*. No one was throwing the baby out with the bath water. It was government, and what it needed to grease the wheels, right? Isn't that what the *summa cum laude* stature of his knowledge accorded him? So what about the reptiles? They had a funny way of getting people to show loyalty, the General mused, chuckling about Arles Dubailles

"There are threats now," said Reddick. "My concerns are about the sevens, not the sixes."

The General knew what he meant, and he asked, "Since when has God interfered with our little world and the galactic?"

"The galactic, as you say, is spiritual—and negative."

"We worship them, sir."

"You worship their technology. You worship their pyramids, you worship their weapons."

"I do, you bet I do, and if I had just one tenth of their goodies I could surgically take care of the Brotherhood's business without any problem. We could lose the press corps, the politicians—which translates to efficiency for the Temple."

Arthur Reddick suddenly threw everything off his desk, incensed by this shallow thinking, this ignorant fool. "And where is the Temple, General?" Arthur asked.

The General sipped his scotch and water purposefully and slowly. "I don't know."

"That's right—you do not know where the transmissions go."

A call came in on the satellite-phone—the General's aides had located Cal Wilson after all, the exact spot where his socks were still walking around. It would take but a few minutes to secure him to the afterlife and then there would only be one piece of business left, and he hoped that Reddick would not bring it up now.

"God's boy lives!" the General exclaimed without a build-up. As if this piece of information explained everything.

The General had never understood the importance of doing things on certain days and under certain conditions; he did under-stand the surveillance of the whole world looking for certain kinds of innocents to slaughter—*lambs*. And he did understand the buzz words programmed into the system: "God," "Jesus," "Holy Spirit," "End Times," "Prophecy," "Virgin Birth," "Adam and Eve," "Corinthians," "Ephesians," "Daniel," "Isaiah," "Revelation," and all the books in the Bible. There were many important related words: *saint, sinner, sin, elder, prophet, priest, lamb, baptism, forgiveness, re-*

mission, before the foundation of the world, until the end of the age, and numerous other phrases which would track anybody and everybody who came to Christ, some of which could be fed to those who needed to know in the intelligence trade. But there were specific ones, and they fell under the category of Project Innocent, as they had been so brutal that even the General began to feel there was a lack of discernment from the higher-ups. Killing virgin boys on Caribbean islands might even lead to massive killing in cities and blaming it on God.

Reddick started laughing, "He is alive, and I think I'll root for him. I hope he brings us to an end."

"Arthur, we've been friends for twenty-six years. Talk like that will get you killed." General Ritali chewed on one of his Cohibas, then rolled it around in his mouth, preoccupied and gladly so.

"Do you know why you were called in? To take out the garbage. This would not be a problem without the quake. This would not have been a problem if you had just done your duty with your marksman. I had verification," Arthur told him, "that the Kincaid boy was martyred for Christ. And that he was one of God's, and got away at an early age. So we botched it; killing him only caused harm to us."

"Hey, Dubailles did his job, so it balances out."

"Serin was televised, and the only survivors were the only intended victims, did you know that?"

"Luck," said the General.

"*They* don't do luck, General, luck is *our* business."

"Stupidity then."

"Sir, you have stirred forces you do not understand. I'm sorry. You *were* a good man," Arthur said.

Arles Dubailles entered, smiling. Within seconds he was next to the General with a 9 mm Beretta equipped with a silencer and had fired two rounds point blank into the General's head.

General Ritali had not moved when Dubailles walked into the room. He seemed to know what was happening and offered his head willingly. He smiled at Arthur, as if confident that he would see him soon where he was going.

Arthur had children and grandchildren to think about, an important charity function that evening. He looked over Dubailles at the body, as several maintenance men in uniforms entered and cleaned up the "mess," severing off limbs over a tarp and rolling them into individual garbage bags. They stuffed the body parts into a container labeled: *contaminated, radioactive.*

Arthur put his hand on Dubailles' shoulder. "You know what you have to do now?"

"Yes, sir."

"You know what I'm talking about?"

"I'd like to know more, sir. I truly would."

"You are the best agent who's come up in this organization in a long time," he said. "I want you to know that if you fail—"

"Sir, that is not an option," Dubailles said, straightening his India silk tie.

"Don't they know that there is no guarantee?"

"Who, sir?"

"In power. If our lord leaves you, he leaves you."

"You mean—"

"You don't know him? Oh, he is magnificent, he appears in the flesh, and you met him at the inner sanctum."

"Oh..." and Arles suddenly pulled up the file, 'Jordan Star'— The guy who—"

"Yes, he has many faces, many forms, but ultimately, he is not human."

"I only know what you need me to know, sir."

"No one can truly come to power unless they pass this test. I warn you, there are more tests to come. Fail a test, and we do not know you. There is no loyalty from our high god. But there are riches and pleasures unimaginable to those who win."

"Win, yeah, I *always* win," Arles said.

"But you still have to care about life, and then do your duty, or you will fail."

"What do you mean?" Arles asked.

By now the body was gone, the blood was gone, the phones were ringing, and secretaries were bringing in everything from lunch to faxes, to pictures from outer space.

"Did you care about your family?"

Arles did not answer. "I thought I did. But then...it just—"

"The only criticism I have is that it was perhaps a little too easy. You need to maintain civility. You come to the Children's Hospital with me this evening; I'll be speaking. See to it that you care for the kids, perhaps adopt one. You can do that when you meet your new wife."

"Thank you," Arles said, joyous at the beautiful sunset over the Pacific Ocean.

"I've been around a long time, and if you don't care for your family, all the riches in the world won't matter."

"I will care about my next family, sir," Arles said, looking Arthur straight in the eye.

"You've not seen the *inner sanctum*. You're in a very rare place for someone like you, but there are further dimensions to it."

"I'm willing to learn," Arles said eagerly.

"When you're notified about your wife and children in the accident, do mourn for a long time in your house."

"I will."

"And mean it. You *do* mean it, don't you, Mr. Dubailles?" Arthur knew the answer.

Arthur sounded sure, exactly like the father Arles never knew, nor ever had. And he could be looked upon as pious in the community; this was a very attractive thing. Charity was always something in which he wanted to be involved.

"Mr. Dubailles, good works and charity mark all our men's lives. This is what we have in common. See to it you learn."

Of course he would learn. He knew when he delivered Kincaid's head and Casey's warm innocent body to the altar, the kingdom would be his, the keys to immortality in the flesh, and a world that would then not ever end.

thirty-two

The Gulfstream V-SP suddenly lost cabin pressure and dropped 5,000 feet. The flight attendant's head went through the plastic sconce of an overhead lamp, but when she fell hard to the deck, her shoulder became dislocated.

Jackson Kincaid knew it was a setup when the oxygen masks dropped. She knew better. She shouldn't have taken the plane. She knew she would have been scourged for her husband having slipped away from the auditorium. She knew also that she blew it when Brand was missing from the Institute when it was detonated...or *earthquaked.*

This was clearly beyond *luck*, this was an *opposing* force—invisible and unfair—the enemy, she thought.

"Diane!" Jackson yelled. "Is it because of *me?*"

Mitchell calmly took her mask and started to breathe as the plane evened out.

The concerned co-pilot came back to check on the passengers. When he heard the flight attendant trying to stifle her moans, he helped her into a chair and strapped her in. "Wendy, we'll be down in a couple of hours, can you wait?" he asked

She nodded, biting her lip and smiling gamely.

"Good. Don't know what happened," the co-pilot said. "We hit some...I don't know, a pocket with no friggin' air, a monster vacuum, man. Unbelievable."

The mood was tense. Jackson wouldn't take the mask, so the lanky co-pilot gently yet firmly forced her to strap it on. "Sorry, we've got regulations."

Jackson ripped it off. "No. Go play airplane, or whatever you do to occupy yourself."

He did not grace her with the standard double take; instead, he nodded, tipped his hat, shot her his pearly whites, a winsome smile, and Jackson got her way.

She had heard the co-pilot tell Wendy they were over Omaha. Jackson pondered her situation, analyzing what they might think. Everything was *mind*, she knew, and the culprit, now, was Diane Mitchell.

Jackson instinctively knew the senator would turn her over in a heartbeat. Although Jackson had done more for the cause, gone to greater lengths than Diane Mitchell, it wouldn't matter in the long run.

If circumstances or a bad turn of luck jeopardized a position in the Brotherhood, which meant *Sisterhood* as well, even though it wasn't her fault, Jackson could not expect support anywhere—she would be history. She knew that was the risk, which meant a mission needed to be performed perfectly, every time. If someone from the Brotherhood ever wronged another, it was up to the wronged person to exact justice; there would be a fight, and to the victor went the spoils. She had seen it her whole life, even in childhood.

While working as an aid for senator Klindous in New York, Jackson had seen her involved in extortion, blackmail, theft, breaking and entering, and of course, in sexual exploits. She had learned from her. She had accompanied Klindous to meetings ironically called the "department of education," which later became "sex education." Klindous had explained: "Every institution in the world is satanic—it's how the world works. When in Rome, you know, Jackson, get with it."

And she *got with it*.

Jackson had proved herself; her lack of an Ivy League background that usually provided automatic entry was somewhat balanced with the advantage of blood ties to French royalty on her mother's side of the family. Jackson worked for government officials and cut her teeth on providing favors and smoothing out difficulties ranging from altering murder investigations to covering up suicides, sex scandals and the like. Sex and murder were very much an inside business. In America, she understood, the only ones who went to jail for murder were the heathen—the uneducated, the poor, the stupid, the laughable, the meek, the pathetic, the weak. It was so easy to plant evidence then watch the public servant—the average Joe, Mary or John—meltdown. It was enjoyable to see their shock and dismay from being accused of some heinous crime; investigations and confessions provided great video entertainment. The confessions were blatant, the snare brilliant. Those in power very much enjoyed it, the source of perfect pleasure, in the perfect way, as any false witnessing, causing calamity or a fall from grace and especially loss of innocence, were all deemed worthy of higher status.

She had always known Innocence was the key. Later she had heard how Innocence might fight back. This was problematic. This was more than just a curse, it was outright unjust. She could *pretend* to be a Christian if needed. She found many innocent ones in the churches, and how the higher ups delighted in defiling that temple then blaming it on the hypocritical membership and launching an investigation. Defiling the temple, the so-called "abomination of desolation" as in the Bible, was paramount in achieving status in the Brotherhood.

The idea of Innocence or Righteousness fighting back seemed impossible to Jackson, but the rumors persisted. They said if a person came in righteousness, or innocence, or purity, or separation— truly accepting Jesus Christ as Lord, or some poppycock notion like it—then God's judgment of the wicked might occur.

Jackson thought Christians looked foolish trying to live and work in society, even when they were derided mightily, mocked, demoted, received unfair wages, or were fired outright. They always seemed to accept their fate with a glad heart, smiling dumbly as if they *smiled* their whole life away. Christ was a ploy to keep the masses down—it was Satan's best ploy, in her opinion.

She worried that Christians would wake up one day. She hoped she would not see the day they did unless they followed their Christ who admonished them to return good for bad, turn the other cheek, to extend charity and service in return for nothing of value. These principles were brilliant, and she felt Jesus must have been Satan in disguise.

Those who believed in Jesus were the innocent ones, and worthy to be slain (what profit was there in slaying the defiled?), she believed and practiced. Let them think they are covered in the blood, while I, Jackson Monsoret Kincaid, appropriate for myself the untold riches of God's power *without* His blessing!

Sitting next to her, Diane Mitchell was behaving far too calmly, as if she had fearlessly accomplished something. Jackson thought she could detect a feeling of gloating, which was inexorable proof that something was going on beneath her cool exterior.

"So, it's that time, right?" Jackson asked, trying to look distracted.

"What are you babbling about, Kincaid?" Diane put down her magazine. "Just be happy you're still around to serve."

Jackson knew she would not live longer than the hour it took to land.

The stewardess continued to moan. The senator moved over to ease her discomfort, leaving Jackson alone.

• • •

Bauman was sure he had seen him, the man in the black SUV, or was it a dream from the night before, aided by the aftershocks? Bauman figured he could catch him. He seemed to walk through dreams and appear as a well-dressed, wealthy man of stature and power, not to be associated with drugs and especially not dealing with the likes of Ricky the dope peddler.

When Bauman arrived at the condo, he found Sheila was alone with their daughter, Marta. The new boyfriend had gone. "Look," Bauman said, "you guys have to come with me. We have a safe place."

Refusing to look at her husband, she said: "I see him, Phil. He's been here—he asked me if I wanted to *improve* our lives. He's an angel."

Bauman could not overlook this interesting development. "What's he look like?"

Sheila continued to drink the last of her six-pack of beer as Marta sat quietly, worried. "He looks like an angel," she said. "He'll help us. Alf Blicky knows him—I was there, I saw him at church."

"Honey," Bauman said, "the church is gone. In fact, the church was overrun by criminals. You felt that Pastor Ted was the answer, and now it's this man, and I can tell you, he's probably a criminal. Daniel said—"

"Daniel?" she asked. "He's that... Look, Gwen told me that the gardener was evil, possessed. He was asked to leave, and he has an ax to grind."

"Do you believe Gwen?"

"I believed Pastor Ted, but then they told me he was possessed too. And this man, this angel—he's real. I mean, he's a real blessing."

"The church burned to the ground—we saw it."

That silenced her. He had to take care of her needs, that was most important now, especially since Sheila and Marta were out of food. The garages attached to the building had collapsed. She had no transportation—the local store was out of supplies, and the phones were down. People were roving the streets in search of food—looting stores, and hiding in alleys. He impressed upon her that she would get an answer, but only if she came to the shelter. They would have church; there would be a pastor.

"I've been listening to our friend, Daniel. Pastor Ted's not possessed, he's the real thing—and Jesus Christ is real," Bauman declared. "I have accepted Him as my Lord and Savior. He *is* God, Sheila."

"I know," Sheila said. "Come on, Marta. Time to go with your father."

Marta smiled a bit, but was still unsure whether to trust her father after all that Sheila had said about him.

The Rescue Mission was full of displaced persons, young and old, but mainly poor. Under the auspices of Big Fred, Louis and the other missionaries, a shelter and a makeshift church had been set up in what used to be an insurance office, a few blocks from the food storage warehouse and the offices of the Mission.

When the Baumans arrived, there were several missionaries sharing the Gospel and praying with the beleaguered victims of the quake. Hot food had been prepared and Bauman made sure his wife and daughter were taken care of as Big Fred and Big Willy led the congregation in prayer.

Sheila no longer had any doubts about the truth of Jesus. Bauman had also become a believer. Not only had Daniel shown him in his dreams that Jesus was the Messiah, but Big Fred had explained how Jesus fulfilled every Old Testament prophecy. The odds were trillions to one he could have done that unless he were truly the Messiah; there was far more evidence than would be necessary in a court of law for a full conviction, say, on a murder rap. Big Fred told him Jesus' disciples preached the gospel and would lay down their lives for their belief that Jesus is the Christ, the risen

Lord. There were several hundred eyewitnesses who saw Jesus resurrected after his death, far more than necessary to convince Bauman Jesus was Who He said He was: God, the Messiah. Jesus had stated it accurately when He said: *Before Abraham was, I Am.*

What really convinced Bauman was The Voice, which was inside him. The Voice was a warm blanket, telling Bauman it would never leave him, but wanted to look through Bauman's eyes, wanted to use Bauman's limbs. The Voice told Bauman he was loved and God had a divine plan for his life. The Voice was leading Bauman to Christ, as it said: "He is the Son of God, prophesied in the Old Testament, of the Tribe of Judah, of the Branch of David. He is the One. He is the only One." Big Fred explained to him that The Voice was the Holy Spirit because that *still small* voice would always lead to Christ.

"Who is Daniel?" Sheila asked her husband after settling Marta on a cot so she could sleep.

"He's...I don't know," Bauman said, while scanning the room.

Cots lined the walls, food was served in an adjacent "shop," and medical services were being administered in the building that used to house the dry cleaners. After removing the equipment and boarding up the windows, the building served as a place for first aid, vaccinations and ministry.

"Dear Heavenly Father," Fred prayed in front of the weakened beings he would call saints, "thank You for Your blessings on Your flock today, thank You for shepherding us, calling us home and calling us firmly to Your protection. Bless us, Father, and help us, every one of us."

"Yes, Father," "Thank you, Lord," "Praise God," and "Thank You, Jesus," went up around the room, and Big Fred, his friend Bernie, and Leslie Adams sang inspirational songs about the glory of the Kingdom and the mercy of Christ.

Bauman hugged his child and wife, and all of them wept openly. "Thank you, Lord," Bauman declared. "I'm home! I'm home!"

He told Fred later that he had gotten to the bottom of the case—the Holy Spirit had anointed him; he had been given the gift of prophecy. "I got this voice, Fred, and it tells me who's who and what's what—I mean, I always had it as a cop. But now I know—I know much more. For example, Alice Garcia was not murdered, she was sacrificed to Baal, a pagan god."

"The Voice told you the word 'Baal'?" Fred asked, astonished, reflecting on his research at the seminary.

"Ask Daniel."

"Who?" Fred asked.

"He knows everything about what's going on. He knew that Alf, the second pastor at the church, was fallen to Satan long before the church burned down."

"Who is this Daniel guy I keep hearing about?" Fred asked, not only alarmed, but prepared to do spiritual warfare in the form of fast and furious exorcisms, if necessary.

Meanwhile, Shep and John the Apostle tended to the needs of the sad ones. Shep was always running back in with more food, more first aid, and a blessing that went well beyond a missionary's calling.

"We're a family again, we're a family again!" Bauman said to his wife at her cot. "I know I can't solve the case without you and without God."

"Dad, please...you're upsetting her."

Sheila was despondent and not speaking, perhaps not able to speak. He noticed her ripped sweater and bruises on her face. How had he missed that! How could he be so casual?

He hesitated, looked around at the miraculous ministry, truly hundreds coming to Christ, virtually every single one who crossed through the broken door.

"Did *he* do that to her, the boyfriend?" he asked Marta, his maturing and beloved daughter.

She started crying, and she threw her face into her father's jacket. "Oh, honey—God will protect us. Do you love Jesus?" he asked.

She nodded, her tears spilling down his jacket and onto his hands.

Daniel stood over them, in the midst of all the confusion. Bauman nodded to Fred, as if to say "There he is! It's Daniel! He's the—"

Fred didn't see anything or anyone but walked over to Bauman. "Everything all right?" he asked, distracted with all the needy strangers.

"He's right there. Daniel, this is Fred, the head of the mission."

Bauman finally understood: *Fred could not see him*, though Daniel stood right next to him.

Bauman finally knew what Daniel was, and that he wasn't human. "You don't see him, do you?" he asked Fred.

Fred looked at Bauman, concerned. "I heard you were on medication," he said.

"Look at me, Fred—do I look like I'm crazy?"

Fred looked again but couldn't see Daniel tending to one of the babies, holding her in his arms, comforting her.

"He's got a baby in his arms—you can't see that?"

Fred shook his head and walked away, too many needy folks. He would return later.

So many needing help. "Oh, Lord, we haven't the capacity to help everyone tonight. Help us. If you don't help us, we will fail," Fred prayed silently and unheard, except by Daniel, who looked at Fred and tapped him on the shoulder.

When Fred turned around, he saw the gray-haired man with the long beard, with the bright blue eyes. Next to him stood a dark-haired man in simple clothes, his eyes were not of any color, there was too much light in them.

"They will all be saved," said Daniel. "Tonight, not one will go without."

Fred said nothing because he had known this day would come and now he knew more. The ordained minister looked around at the others, and clearly he was the only one who could see. Bauman, Shep, John the Apostle, Big Willy, Sylvia, no one except Fred Mercurio, the missionary, could see him. "Are you of God, of Jehovah God?" asked Fred, knowing that if he wasn't, he could not lie, at least if his reading of the Scriptures was accurate.

"Some are of war, and some are of peace, and we all worship Jesus Christ," Daniel answered.

Very much afraid, Fred sank to his knees. Daniel pulled him back to his feet.

Big Fred was yanked to his feet, not by the gray-haired man, but by something he did not understand.

When he looked to see who had lifted him up, he saw that everyone had food, that all were praying, reading the Word, singing and rejoicing. There were no more moving through the door. They were in neat rows of thirty-five or so, each seeming to be coping with the displacement of the quake.

Bauman leapt up to see Pastor Ted Gunderson enter the room and make his way to the microphone. "It's...look, Sheila! It's Pastor Ted!"

Sheila looked up and smiled through her tears.

Fred and Louis and the other missionaries and their wives all knew Pastor Ted. They had attended the Faith Church occasionally, though they were not members.

thirty-three

*J*ordan Star wanted desperately to apprehend the beings who had broken through the *wall of separation*. He could see they were clearly visible in the air—to all those who cared to look up. Hundreds of disc-shaped objects, usually mistaken as being occupied by beings from outer space, zipped about over the city for at least an hour.

These objects were supposed to be interdimensional—they would appear and disappear as a function of mind...*Star's mind!* It was to be an interaction with those who were called, those who were to be brought in. Those who were to be culled. Those whose minds were linked to the *hidden matrix*. The dimension Star liked to call the *Magick Kingdom*—it would simply surface out of thin air, corrupt and defile all those in certain social circles, then disappear before anyone would know or understand what had happened. Such was the case with the so-called UFOs. How silly people looked running around after the truth, when it was simply hidden out of sight!

Star later told Gwen she was to bring her teenager to the temple, which was in a downtown warehouse. "You will do this, in memory of your husband," he said. "And then I will tell you about the things in the air. You shall be with them, as it has always been your birthright. Our brotherhood is one of light, and we are everywhere."

"I need to know where my husband is," she insisted.

"Still?" Star asked. They were in his penthouse apartment overlooking the City of Angels, as he called it.

"I don't feel anything," she said.

His acute sharp eyes bore into her, piercing her mind. He had no need to move his lips. *You belong to me now, child. I will take good care of you. If you obey me, I will unlock the entire universe for you.*

She asked, without moving her lips, "Who are you? Where are you from?"

He answered silently: "I'm no one, and I'm from everywhere. Understand?"

He soothed her, took her to the bedroom, and she gave in willingly. "You will bear a child," he told her telepathically; they had been silent for many hours. He made her inhale smoke and soothed her with a green drink, and she felt warm and tingly. "You love me, don't you Gwendolyn? You love me, do you not? You worship me, don't you?"

"Oh, yes. I worship you," she felt herself saying. Her body had changed, it was no longer her own. She found she was not alone with him, but she could not feel ashamed anymore. "Thank you, lord," she said. "Thank you."

When she looked again, the earth was spinning below her, the beautiful bright blue orb so full of beauty and light. Gwen who was Gwendolyn knew now she would single-handedly find the ex-pastor and her son, but she wept not when she saw Alf Blicky's body suspended in a vat of liquid in a room full of blinking lights.

He showed her beyond the Wall of Separation. "I am not allowed to show this to anyone, unless, of course, you are one of us. Do you desire it?" he asked alluringly, his voice smooth like a little brook along a gentle stream.

"Yes, yes, yes," she felt herself saying.

She had no other answer within her. It was too late; she was made for him.

"Alas, my child, you were chosen," he said.

She saw him as an angel of light.

thirty-four

*I*t was not difficult.

It happened as soon as Rebecca called her mother and told her about the Kingdom of God, about the glory of Jesus Christ.

It came up on one monitor screen in an installation in Europe, on a computer known as the *living one*.

Casey knew about it. He told Stephen and Rebecca he was transitional and that *they would now take him*, but neither Stephen nor Rebecca knew what he was saying.

The three of them approached a police barricade on the off-ramp leading to what had once been a busy boulevard, now a gauntlet of fallen street lamps and lifeless wires. Stephen was frightened and said: "So what do we do, turn around?"

"No," Casey replied, referring to himself as protected. "You have each other, and you will go your way. As for me, I am with the Lord now—He honored the agreement."

"What agreement?!" Stephen demanded.

"Get out of the car. You will know them by their fall and the judgment to come, which is a warning to the rest of the world," Casey said.

Rebecca looked at him, and pleaded, "Stay with us, Casey. You don't have to do this. We need your help."

"All will be revealed, and you will see me again," Casey replied.

"We want to serve our Lord, and we hope you are of our Lord and not a deception."

"You know," Casey said. "I was in disguise. My name is something like *Omega*, but I can't say it. I am not human, and you know this by now. Look at this." He pushed his hand through the dashboard, and then withdrew it.

"Blasphemy! The Bible says we're all equal, at least in spirit! And *you are* human!"

"He's not!" said Rebecca, already exiting the car. "You have to have faith. He serves Lord Jesus."

"Don't you know that I came into the womb of Lucifer, and God *hid* me. I was blindfolded all my life, and they attacked me because I wasn't one of them—not human, not of the same mind, not the same species. I could not serve them. That's what they want, after all—for their children to serve them. They sent me away to be trained, to be forced to conform to their social order, so that they would not suffer embarrassment. They thought others could force me into what they needed, and then when they saw that I was truly different, they thought *lame horse, sitting duck, wrecked, ruined, useless*, so they wanted to make a blood sacrifice of me, which is their way for those who have seen but cannot comply. But God intervened. You encountered angels along the way, and they are angels of war, but there are millions of us. Let me quote, 'Do not forget to entertain strangers, for by so doing some have unwittingly entertained angels.'"

"Hebrews 13," said Stephen, who then cried out: "Please help me, Lord. I don't understand. I don't understand anything."

The tears were palpable, and Rebecca dried his eyes and held him.

"It's true, Stephen. It's true."

"So what is your name—it's like Omega, you said?"

"It can't be uttered here. I am an angel of the Lord and I worship Christ Jesus. There have been many of us here in human disguises. The seal was broken. Now...you shall know them by their fall. And you shall know it is God by His warning."

Rebecca pulled Stephen out of the car and they made their way onto a side street, Stephen insisting that they find a vantage point so they could see the roadblock.

They saw Casey handcuffed and arrested. One of the policemen looked around, scanning the perimeter for others. "Get back!" Stephen said to Rebecca. "They didn't see us."

As they continued to watch, another police cruiser pulled up. Casey was put into the back seat with two officers and the cruiser pulled away quickly.

Astonishingly the officers dispersed quickly, forgetting about the roadblock. Casey had accurately predicted what would happen. He had spoken of going home, of rejoining *his family*. Rebecca remembered and told Stephen: "He spoke of his people, he spoke of walking to and fro, meaning back and forth from heaven to earth, from time to eternity, and he said that the ships over the desert—"

"Ships over the desert?" Stephen interrupted, straining to understand. "Look, all I know is that in my studies, the disks, or UFOs or whatever, were always considered evil. Demonic. I mean, what if this Casey guy is a demon?"

"And the visitations? I saw them too, Stephen," she said. "I was afraid, and they told me what was to come. They entrusted Casey to me, and they said he was not of this earth. When he proved it to me, I was filled with the Holy Spirit, just as he said I would be— and I changed. I forgave—"

"But you made that stupid phone call. I should have stopped you."

"He wanted me to, Stephen."

They looked in each other's eyes, and time slipped away. Stephen did not see Cynda, the atheist-scientist he had seen before. He did not see the person who might have been his enemy. He saw a beautiful woman, a woman he would desire, a woman he wanted to protect. When he hugged her, he knew she was the one God had told him about in his prayers, and that he would be safe, he would be a survivor and would one day have a family. "Trust in this, son," God said, "and you will serve me in gladness and joy."

They prayed together and boarded a bus to get out of the area. The bus driver looked at them and said, "I've been expecting you." Then he winked.

The bus was empty, and they were not afraid this time because they were being soothed, and they knew there were many on the ground. "It's a battle and we're just human; how can we make a difference?" he whispered to her.

"Don't worry," the bus driver said without turning around. "We have to save them for God."

Stephen tapped him on the shoulder, but the bus driver would not turn around. He slowed down somewhere in the San Fernando Valley, and Stephen said: "No, man. We need to get to Hollywood, I need to find someone."

"Who?" Rebecca asked.

The bus driver advised: "Forget her, son."

The man looked older than a bus driver, with his white hair and chalky cheeks.

Stephen touched him again, to see if he were indeed real. "Get out and go your way—they'll find you," the bus driver said.

thirty-five

Dear Mr. Parker:

In answer to your question, the answer is, unfortunately, yes. There is a judgment to come quickly, and I am to show it to you. It is a warning.

I have prayed and supplicated and fretted, hoping for this not to come to pass. And yet, though I may not understand fully, He is always just in judgment, and any man who disagrees with God is wrong. This I found true, especially in my later years, when I could look back and reflect upon things I had questioned God about. We read in the Scriptures that Heaven rejoices when the false church is destroyed, saying *Alleluia* over the utter failure of mankind to solve any of his problems, through any means of his own. Through this failure, many would give up and come to the Lord, realizing the truth, that He alone is our God, that He alone is sovereign, that He and not us, is the author of our destiny, and that all creation is for Him alone, and not us.

Every man has a choice about whom he will serve. The angels rejoice at the humbling of man because this is the heeding of many. Heaven rejoices, not *because* of man's failure, but because of the glory of God to act out of love, and not hate.

What I am about to write has been sanctioned by Him who called me. This is the record of His perfect judgment. This is a record of the events that are not to be confused with the Great Tribulation, as described in the Book of Revelation.

As I have been ill of late, I have worried that I have caused this record to be held back. I pray that it is not too late for you to receive it. I thank you for supporting me during this tumultuous time. Your generosity has kept me in good stead. I humbly send a prayer of thanks, since you sustained me that I might live long enough to complete this work and deliver it to you.

As you have seen, others might see also.

If, for any reason, I am found in error, I pray that this work be stopped and destroyed, rather than be another voice of deceit, another false record, another false prophecy. Over millennia we have had false interpretations of the prophecies found in our glorious and infallible Bible, mainly as they relate to *time*. Some believe that the things of the end have already happened, some believe that they are about to happen, and some believe that they are happening now.

Here is a key, given to me by the Holy Spirit and no longer sealed in the Book of Daniel, the prophet: *all three* aspects of time are correct. It is also correct to say there will be an end, that the Bridegroom will come for His Bride, that the wedding feast shall be a time of peace, and after that the end shall come, and there shall be a new heaven and a new earth.

Indeed, the judgment that you will soon witness is terrible, but at the same time glorious, because many will be saved. I have learned this. We shall never know what time we are in; the agreement is clear in our Bible. The beginning of wisdom is when you ask questions like, "Why doesn't God just end evil and create miracles and call all to Him instantly?" Or, conversely, "Why doesn't Satan just overrun the world and get rid of the Bible and all believers if the world is truly his?"

Both questions point to a truth, to a *limitation* that is, by space, by time, perhaps by contract, made clear in the Scriptures. Or, to look at it another way, humans are in the middle of a supreme test. Can they find their way back to their Creator, through their Redeemer, with the stumbling blocks of blindness, infirmity, temporality and evil? Especially with false teachings that pretend God to be everything and everyone, omnipotent but distant, not involved in the affairs of men, not watching our every move, not efficacious to solve our problems, not worthy to surrender to. Suffice it to say, we do not understand His ways, and the way of the world is only of God, because He created it. And so "they" say: we had better make this world the best it can be for future generations, since it is up to us to bring world peace, world health, world prosperity, to end world hunger, global warming, environmental abuse, and overpopulation. We need to be tolerant of all ways of life, and open-minded to evolving cultural mores, artistic freedom, and public use of funds. We are to accept the world as our beginning and our end, and we are to share its resources with all equally, as that is only fair. Their argument being that if God were real, He would have made sure this was already a reality.

This is nothing new. The Lord says to this scribe, quoting the prophet Ezekiel, chapter 3, verse 18: *"When I say to the wicked, 'You shall surely die,' and you give him no warning, nor speak to warn the wicked from his wicked way, to save his life, that same wicked man shall die in his iniquity, but his blood I will require at your hand."*

So I must warn even if it causes my own death. If souls are saved, then it is my glorious reward.

As I write you now, Mr. Parker, I struggle to understand, but I cannot, as I have never known a time in my life where decisions for Christ had to be made, and made *immediately*. Like others in Christ, I have only known our Lord to be patient and loving, gentle and kind, bestowing grace to all who would accept

Him. Tribulation and persecution far outweighed the glorious treasures of His Mercy.

While serving my prison sentence, I realized He was a God of Mercy. I knew Jesus as the Christ and when He sent His Spirit to fill me for the first time, I heard Him speak! To me. Even me. I had made sure I could not ever be forgiven. I had judged everything according to survival and comfort, according to hysteria as my discernment; and I hoped death would come as my death was to be a joy, a final end to a cruel joke, as the wave of iniquity done by me and to me were insurmountable.

But His Spirit raised me from the dead. Christ lifted me into reconciliation, a new life that was for the first time real, something I had not experienced in pursuits of things religious in my younger years, as there was no chanting, no figurehead, no fancy robes and no false words of transcendence. Nothing I could say accurately describes the glory of His Presence, and the Holy Spirit must teach us the greatest mystery of all.

As I am telling you, I have told others. He changed me, and as a loving Father, he corrected me and brought me up as a new man. My sins fell away as he lifted me from the mire. Though I am an ordinary man who is fallible and who still sins, even this is forgiven by His ever-reaching Blood. So I keep a short list and repent often, and my fruit is the fruit of change, no longer a slave to sin, but seeking to live for Him at each and every moment, and that is my joy. I tell you all this as a prelude to extreme urgency.

For now, there are things of mystery, which have been told to you in the Bible. There is little time to come boldly to His Throne, little time now to repent and receive forgiveness through the Blood of the Lamb, and little time to fully understand the enemy.

His Word has occurred, is occurring, and will occur again—in other words, His Word is as vital today as it was yesterday and tomorrow. True prophecy stems from the Scriptures, is taught by the Holy Spirit, and reveals things for each one specifically to God's plan for us individually, a mystery that no man can fathom intellectually.

It is true no man knows the time of these things, and nothing need be added to His Word, as throughout the ages, the wicked have been cut down. Let Him guide you into understanding of the mystery. I humbly pray that through these words you will understand, and not turn away, but even though you die of the flesh, you live in the Spirit.

For death will cover the earth as has never been seen before. It is again as in the days of Noah.

Mr. Parker, you have been generous to me, and I thank you for the supplies. The Day of the Lord is coming, but before that day, so I have received, God will pour out His judgment and much destruction will take place, before the time that the book of Revelation describes, and indeed, possibly a prelude to the end.

Indeed, I have been shown these mysterious beings referred to as angels, and I am learning about their purpose in exacting God's will. They have names and they have faces; they are described throughout the Bible, and sometimes they are disguised in flesh. I must admit I am as perplexed as you are about my learning their names and their individual purposes. But the Holy Spirit is accurate. Though I have been shown what is to occur, I pray that it is not so.

Suffice it to say, Mr. Parker, in the case of the angel you asked me about, despite all the security, all their surveillance capabilities, he escaped their scrutiny. He is powerful, and he makes war for God. And he, whose name I do not understand, was said to be the fulfillment of what all the visionaries, all the so-called "ascended" Masters and enlightened gurus and all the off-world Intelligences believed to be the sacrificial lamb of the New Age. One whose blood could be transmuted and transmogrified into the Holy Grail, the "Blood of Christ," which would sustain the world for the next millennium, at least. They did not know, despite evidence of supernatural capabilities, that he was anything but a child of God, a human to be exact. Indeed, he had to be human, and he had to be a specific person, according to their "religion." What is incredible is that they did not sense danger, and they did not see God was moving on them through this being, whom I have no way of verifying as anything other than an angel, to be sure, disguised in human flesh, despite, or because of, having been born into a womb of a human and made for this specific purpose.

For now, Mr. Parker, I thank you for your fellowship and support. I hope this answers some of your questions. You were correct in sounding a note of alarm. You thought it a work of fiction, when indeed it is not. The Lord hides it, and indeed, He uses *code*. Those who need to know will know; those who are chosen to act will be activated.

Lord help us. We are part of something that every human being on earth will soon know of. Faith will be tested, heroes will be born, and the wicked will flee for a time.

If for any reason you need to contact me further, please use the regular box, and I will be able to get it quickly. Please send my regards to your family, as it has been good for me to hear of their lives. I will be sending the rest soon. Please be patient.

May He richly bless you, sir.

Mountain

• • •

Cal was arrested when Spruug and his family went to see the burned church. He would not talk, he would not move. He was locked in a typical interrogation room. He was not alone for long, as a young woman was thrust into the room with him, and she laughed at him.

Cal said nothing, and when he was strapped on the gurney he

said nothing. He lived in a dark space and was shown the extensive footage of the five thousand who were killed on the island, and then he screamed for mercy.

He remained in the darkness; he heard tones and saw colored lights, and the woman spoke softly. She was Sally Anne, his wife, in the prime of her life. "Caleb, how I love you. Please do what they ask, and live with me forever."

They walked on the beach, and the sun hung low and beautiful over the vast ocean. He was home. "You're a pilot, and your flight is almost ready," she told him.

"Sally Anne, I have found the Lord," Cal said. "He is glorious, and He is coming back. I've seen that His judgment is righteous."

She gripped his hand, and he saw in the reflection of the pool of water that he was not old, indeed, he was young again as well. "There is no Jesus," she said. "It was a myth. The world has its own way."

"Sally Anne," he insisted, "You don't speak as yourself."

"I do," she insisted, kissing him all over.

When she took him to bed, he pulled away, not trusting her. "What's wrong, honey? Don't you know I love you?"

"No!" he said, and pulled away. He saw that she was not Sally Anne.

"Who are you?" he asked.

She laughed, she was a beautiful young woman with dark hair cropped around her perfect face, and her liquid eyes shone as the beauty he had lost forever. "You can have me. You can have anything you want."

"Get away from me, whore!" he said.

She laughed again. He could not break free of his bonds. "Who do you think you are? Do you really think you can stop the god of this world? You, a pathetic fool? I'm young, I'm beautiful, my body is gorgeous, and it will love yours, and I will renew you. And if you don't make love to me right now, I will kill you."

He looked away, and when he looked back, the demon was sitting on his chest. She removed her mini-dress and he looked away. "NO! Never! I saw the Christ! He's my Lord and Savior! I'm saved!" he screamed.

He shut his eyes as she punched his face with her fists.

Whether he blacked out, whether time passed, whether he had already gone to hell, it did not matter. "Dear Father, help me, please. Without you I will perish, and if that is your will, let it happen; know that I am with You, no matter what. In Jesus' name. Amen."

The next morning Cal found himself in a hotel room. He looked around; was it a dream? Were they setting him up again? Once in, could a man like Cal ever get out?

A voice came to him: "You're forgiven, Caleb. Do as they ask of you, and trust in the Lord."

He opened the drapes. He was overlooking the Los Angeles International Airport. Planes were landing, taking off. There was a bustle of traffic along the boulevard.

He turned to the television for the news. The latest on FEMA and earthquake relief. He watched trucks and National Guard vehicles entering a high school football field, as tents were lined up in neat lined rows, all trenched for water drainage. The news anchor reported: "Relief efforts have been greatly enhanced by the semi-private trust, Resource International. Los Angeles is grateful this morning that the relief effort has had such a positive impact on the city. The president and founder of Resource International, Jordan Star, is being lauded by the President of the United States for the foundation's quick action, primarily in the San Fernando Valley, in setting up tent communities on all local high school grounds, and especially for their food-relief efforts. Mr. Star stated that his foundation was simply better prepared because of their prior efforts in Bosnia and in the recent quake in Bolivia."

When Star's face filled the screen, Cal was stricken by nothing less than unbridled fear. Well-dressed, mild mannered, a celebrated man throughout the world, there was nothing unusual about Star, except the way Cal felt when he saw his image. When Star spoke, everything was reassuring, just the opposite of what Cal saw. Cal discounted his first impression.

Star went on: "I have worked with the President and the United Nations to bring relief efforts and spiritual comfort to the victims of the last quake. We will be there with food, shelter and clothing. In addition, we have ministers at every site to offer spiritual comfort."

"Mr. Star," the heralded reporter asked, "is it true that the religious program you offer is non-denominational, or what would you call it, sir?"

Jordan Star smiled winningly. "We offer non-denominational counseling, based on the sharing of the world's resources. We believe that is what Jesus taught so long ago. We have rehabilitated many into our ministry and outreach programs and had great success in recruiting them for the worldwide ministry."

He looked so believable as he stood in front of the long row of tents in the parking lot of a church, which had been burned to the ground. Construction crews were clearing away debris, and food lines were moving swiftly. Then he saw Spruug! He and Isabella and their children, including the miraculous eight-year-old who the strange man had brought into Spruug's home.

Spruug wasn't limping; he was walking. As he looked into the camera, his lips moved. Cal thought he said, "Cal—don't believe it. Cal, do not believe anything you see here."

Did he really see that? He couldn't have seen that—he must have *thought* it. Throughout his life he had not known reality as a rock on which he could place himself—to him there was no difference between installed reality and reality itself. But now he had a rock, more solid than any scheme they might try and inject in his formerly fractured psyche. He had received a miraculous healing, and the rock he came to know was Jesus the Christ, as he had accepted Him alone as Savior and received His Holy Spirit, which was guiding him easily through what had heretofore been a labyrinth.

He used the shower, shaved off his beard—all the toiletries were provided—and donned a fresh set of clothes, khakis and a work shirt. Room Service brought in a continental breakfast, though he had never called.

He had turned the television off, but the screen went bright white, then red, and then an image filled the screen. The point of view of the camera was on the beach. The ocean had receded so far that it was no longer visible. Islands rose from dry land. Only puddles remained, and the ocean bed itself was dry.

A multitude of people was on the shore, watching, perplexed, as the ocean floor became a desert. He tried to turn the television off, not in the mood for a movie, and he convinced himself that this was what it was. But the television would not cooperate. He could not reach the power cord behind the armoire, so he sat back on the bed, riddled with fear and sickness in the pit of his stomach. "Help me, Lord," he said as a towering endless wall of blue approached in the far distance.

"What is that? What is *that*?" he said to himself. "Lord, is this you? Or are you trying to kill me, Ritali? Keep your mind-warping garbage away from me; I quit, General! You hear me!" he screamed at the ceiling, figuring that his room was bugged.

All he could see was a blue backdrop the size of the TV screen itself, and so he knew it must be rigged. The *blue background* came closer, and closer. The camera tilted up and what seemed like a backdrop now seemed alive. Then he could tell what it was, *a wave*, thousands of feet high. Oh, my God, he screamed in his mind, knowing what he was seeing (yet still cursing the General and all those in what he now knew was the shadow government and the mercenary community). "Right," he said, "scare me to death and implant me and hypnotize me and then maybe I'll kill. But I'm done killing, Jack! I'm done, you hear me!"

The wave rushed over all the people and took out the camera and the screen went blank. Yet the television was off.

• • •

Stephen and Rebecca had found their way to a small motel. They did not know their location exactly, but Stephen knew that Casey was either a demon or an angel, through the miraculous power of God that had led him to this point. Rebecca had become discouraged and distraught, and Stephen wondered whether he should call her by her original name, Cynda, though the name bothered him even saying it. "Cynda?" he began.

She snapped back at him: "Don't ever call me that again!"

She would not reveal the cause of her sadness. Stephen somehow knew that this whole mystery centered around Katarina and what had happened to the band's manager. Perhaps Rebecca, never Cynda now, could find a church or a group to take care of her while he conducted an investigation into what was either some sort of dream, or God Himself breaking into reality, along with His angels, to intervene, as He had in the past. He reasoned that not every intervention had been recorded in the Bible. Miracles and signs do occur and are not necessarily indications of the last days.

He wondered too if he had fallen into what was referred to as the End Times, and then discounted it. Then he reapplied that thought with the idea that the Rapture had occurred but he was left behind.

Neither discounting it or the Rapture theory proved adequate. He simply did not know, and yet they had turned Casey over to the authorities. According to Rebecca, he had not done anything wrong, had committed no crime. The Serin Institute was a government installation involved in the darkest of experimental manipulation of the human psyche, and worse, she had told him that even though she never saw this, they worshiped Satan. Or so Casey had said early in their relationship.

"Rebecca, please...just, let me help you."

"You can't. I turned him over. I knew better than to make that phone call," she said, her wavy hair now fringed and flattering to her soft round face.

He just kept looking at her; he had never felt the way he felt now. It made him forget the vision of the man in the cell who Casey had seen and called Michael. There was just no basis for this, Stephen reasoned.

The television was on while Stephen was in the bathroom, and he was relieved. The television worked, there were no further aftershocks, and Rebecca was starting to come around. After all, it was not her fault that Casey was taken. Not at all.

"Oh, my God! Stephen! Stephen!" she yelled.

He bolted back into the tawdry little room with the holes in the carpet and an ancient TV. "You all right?" was all he could think to say. He saw her open-mouthed expression and looked at the screen, where he saw a glowing being wearing a robe of linen and standing above the city, pointing to the ocean. The being's voice sounded like the *voice of many people*, but his face *appeared* to be Casey's, and he said: "A lamb was born into the womb of Satan, but the lamb was not of this earth, though they thought he was human. This lamb belongs to Jesus, like you. The difference is, this lamb is not limited to human form."

She said, "the Angel of the Lord."

The television snapped off. "What?" Stephen asked, now on his knees and trembling.

"Do you believe now?" she asked.

They both wept openly and cried to God to help them. "Lord, we don't understand. Help us to serve you. Oh, Jesus, Your mercy is beyond our ability to comprehend!" Stephen pleaded.

"Father help us," cried Rebecca.

He held her close and they clung for a long time before moving again.

thirty-six

The funeral for their wayward son was held at St. Anne's in Manhattan. Jackson Kincaid felt that now she was not only vindicated, she was a god. She was the one who knew how far the inner sanctum reached, and that membership constituted a series of tests throughout one's lifetime. Those on the plane were killed by "terrorists," and Jackson had been lucky to get away with her life. Those on the ground had been unrealistic, thinking somehow the outcome would be different. How the Brotherhood had underestimated her—of course she had been armed and ready! She had killed them all without a regret and had taken pleasure in proving her worth and her skills. They would *have to* cover her. The incident had been a supreme test, but she had passed it easily, as she had passed *every test*. She had wanted to photograph each and every one of their doubting faces when she walked away from the jet, bloodsplotched and smiling.

Glorious was this day, a few days before the High Holy Day!

"It's too bad Diane won't be here to participate," Arles said during the funeral for Jackson's son, searching her face for a reaction. But she would not let his comment affect her into giving anything away. Jackson knew she had now surpassed him.

"Jackson, you'd better have protection," Arles told her under his breath in the crowded church, as he tried for a slot on the already crowded track.

As the choir sang "Onward Christian Soldier" before the minister's words of solace, Jackson asked, "How many friends do you have here, Arles? You think one initiation, one test, makes you a star? I don't think you know yet what you're dealing with."

He turned and faced the minister, who ironically spoke on ethics and the need to let God work through the lives of those left on earth. "May the Lord bless you and keep you; may He make His face to shine upon you, and be gracious to you; the Lord lift his countenance upon you, and give you peace..."

She fought back the yawn, and turned to see her new friend and confidant, the owner of the largest satellite network in the world, Harry Summers. Fascinated with him, she had watched him play polo on Long Island and at Martha's Vineyard. She couldn't believe that she *felt* something ancient stirring within her. She wondered when the divorce from her husband would be final and whether her pathetic husband, now on the run for murdering Justin, their only child, would ever surface again.

"I am so sorry for your losses, Jackson," Harry Summers commiserated. "First, your husband murders your son, then the horrible attack on your plane. How did you manage to escape?" Before she could answer, he quickly added, "Did they ever catch the terrorists?"

"They hate us all—we should lock everyone up who believes in God," she replied. "It's all hate."

She dodged his questions of investigations, of why a press blackout had been set up, and any suggestive questions about security issues.

Summers was persistent: "The story is that the senator was in a traffic accident—how long—"

"Forever," she said. "Best you don't go asking any further questions."

Summers was taken aback as Jackson calmly sipped her tea at the reception, surrounded by wealth and overconfidence, people with names everyone knew but deeds no one would remember, the underhanded things they had had to perform to become prominent. Her knowledge about them was her amusing secret. Ah, life was sweet, she thought. "Thank you for your concern, Harry, you're so sweet," she said and kissed Harry gently on the lips, letting him know she cared but being discreet enough so that others could not detect she might not be in mourning. She was very much in mourning, but for herself, since the sharpshooter had missed Brand altogether.

In his dapper manner, smoothing his long gray hair away from his handsome face, he asked: "Are you sure you're...ready to date again, Jackson?"

"You looked so dashing on your horse," she said, avoiding the subject. "I haven't seen a man look that good in, well...you looked good." She admired the way his tailored black suit, blue tie and blue and white handkerchief set off his commanding physique. For a man of sixty, he seemed not a hair over forty-five. She answered his dating question with her embrace, and with her caressing hands.

He took in the beautiful brunette with her piercing eyes and lithe figure, and sacredness became open-mindedness. "Yes, we have all had to learn to accept our carnal duties, though our relationships are based on monogamy."

"Yes," she said. "The couple sets out to share in pleasures untold, pleasures that the unenlightened world could never know because of their hang-ups."

He smiled at her. He had no problem seeing her as the maven of power behind the new Serin Institute, which would be based in Zurich, with offices in New York and Washington, D.C. It would be a political force; the vacuum left by Senator Diane's untimely death would open the way for a few choice candidates.

"Fundraising is so important," Summers pointed out.

"Oh," she laughed. "I've been told our funding is now unlimited."

They both laughed heartily at the reception and drank the good wine upstairs at the club, where she sealed her intentions with a longer kiss.

"I am now Jackson Monsoret, not Jackson Kincaid."

"Ms. Monsoret, such a noble name," Summers told her while waiting for his Ferrari in the valet area of the exclusive club.

Harry did not know much about the hierarchy, and Jackson liked that. He was like many successful executives in the United States and Europe. They understood something was going on, they did a few favors, turned a blind eye and pretended they never saw certain things. They could marry and have their families, so long as they would perform what was asked.

Harry was no rebel, but he was a rogue. He liked the sting of battle; he liked destroying the competition, and yet he politely shied away from the Temple. She understood that—so many men were not...*spiritual*.

When Jackson was done with him, his personal accomplishments would not belong to Harry Brighton Summers; they would belong to the Brotherhood.

Jackson had become elevated into the inner circle of Jordan Star, and all because of a plane ride. Merits were always given out for extreme performance, and hers was the ultimate.

The funeral for Justin Kincaid was a social convention for the neighbors, Justin's friends from high school and those fans who had known and admired him. It had been arranged by the Institute, of which she was now the director, voted in by the board in the wake of her husband, now a fugitive for the murder of his own son, Justin. Construction would soon begin on a new building in Zurich, and it would not operate like the Arizona experiment, which Jackson knew the incompetent Brand had never understood. He had never gone to the five underground floors nor had he ever asked about their purpose or use. He was ignorant of the principalities that funded the operation. She knew that her idealistic if idiotic husband had always thought of the Brotherhood as The Brotherhood of the Light, connected to some Arthurian legend of a magnificent past which was ritualized in modern times.

Jackson Monsoret Kincaid never believed all the hysteria of a coming Judgment Day; she and others like her were to judge. How she marveled in her candlelight prayers, as her vanity had always been the altar. Every prayer had been quickly answered, unless it was against a man of God—how that frustrated her!

She loved to comb her hair and envision the fall and destruction of someone who had said an unkind word or deed. How magnificent was the god of the universe to grant her wish every single time. It was simply amazing how her enemies would crumble.

She would never attempt her negative wishes on those of superior stature, and that was why she had to move up. How the *unillumined* did not know about the hierarchy was beyond her—the world was simply not safe.

Jackson Monsoret had heard the Bible was true, and then thought about the hundreds of millions of years of creation, though at the last ascension she received the answer: *unfortunately, the Bible is literally true.*

Unfortunately, time is perfectly rendered, and completely misunderstood.

When she talked to Mr. Star about eradicating the Bible, he told her it was off-limits. He said it was enough that the public relations campaign against it had been so successful. "No one of any stature really *believes* the Bible anymore, and that is our great victory," he once said during an initiation ceremony she attended in Rome.

It was called Society. There were Rules. It required an agreeable Mind. And they worked on minds on all levels, from education to media, from religion to hysteria. It was Dictatorship. Serfdom.

And it was Freedom.

Jackson Kincaid was simply doing her duty in finally eradicating her embarrassment—the lame, the stupid, the ignorant...Justin. How his life became her supreme benefit! How her power doubled at the news of his *untimely* death!

And she was proud of it. Tonight she would revel in her newfound power with Harry Summers, a beloved uninitiated one, who made her feel *new* again.

• • •

Casey Burns Smith was kept in a cell in Bock Wiley's lab under armed guard. Wiley's scientific way of explaining Casey's delusion took into account Casey's past. Casey had been born to privilege— a privilege borne by satanic intervention several generations earlier, perhaps in his mother's bloodline. While they were skiing together, Casey's younger brother died in a skiing accident in upstate New York. The excruciating guilt and trauma on Casey's part had led to his accepting Christ, and then to his own inflated role as something "not quite human." At least this was Wiley's theory.

Wiley had well-known ties to the Serin Institute and he was involved with the destruction and "clean-up" of the Serin facility in Arizona. Some witnesses had seen Wiley's *torture-chamber* in full swing, with its sensory deprivation tanks where shrink-wrapped and implanted human subjects would be left and studied as they slowly died from suffocation and disease. He had set up the mind control studies; little children were programmed to shoot up a school and then kill themselves. The *uninitiated* did not know or ask the reasons for Wiley's activities.

But the earthquake, he knew, was no accident—it was the perfect cover-up.

"Isn't it curious no one asks why?" Bock commented to Arthur Reddick. "Indeed, it is better for them that they do not know why, and even the question of who benefits would be appropriate in this case. But they will never ask, and that's why they will live in relative peace."

Specifically, he was discussing Brand Kincaid with Reddick. "Kincaid's escape from the collapse of the Institute was a divine comedy. Didn't he know that he was simply a stooge without a clue? Doesn't he know he's an idiot?"

It was vital that Dr. Wiley intervene. He was their best candidate, the super-shrink who made his name supervising the development of *Rizac*, an antidepressent which, when used with Dr. Wiley's methods, could produce a human time bomb that was so accurate that one could literally set a watch to the event. The first time Wiley used the drug he was blessed with results within one week.

He recalled fondly the headlines in the *Denver Post*, which read: *MAN GOES BERSERK, SHOOTS 8 CO-WORKERS IN POST OFFICE. The news story related the resulting pandemonium as the man kept shooting until he ran out of bullets.*

He was a scientist, yet he attended the rituals when he was required. He knew the rituals were an excuse to delight in the taking of innocent life, an inherent human quality, combined with sexual release. He enjoyed this aspect of their torrid faith.

Wiley enjoyed watching hypocritical politicians appear on television, claiming things like: "We are utterly confounded that a child could be tortured and left for dead like this. We are instituting new laws that will protect children from their parents."

Dear Mr. Parker:

I must stop here and caution you, and any others who would read what is contained herein with the following caveat: Do not read on if you are not fit in the Lord. If this should ever reach a non-believer, stop reading now. Find someone strong and upright in the Word of God and ask him or her to help you. For those who question the validity of the supernatural events described herein as not in accordance with Scripture, I declare that every single event points to our glorious God, and to Christ Jesus. Now is the time to turn away for those who do not know the truth simply because of ignorance, social absorption, legalism, moral doctrine, doubt, skepticism, or misappropriation of spiritual instincts. Those of you who have had a laugh, those of you in the church who are pious but are non-believers in God's supernatural workings in the world and only see the Scriptures as lessons in obedience and not divine revelation or God's miraculous force flowing through the world; those who do not believe what the Scriptures say about angels, divine beings, and those who are not human, turn away now. To those skeptics in the church, you elders and priests and pastors who believe that any claimed miracle is the work of Satan, keep reading. For you shall deem my warning the same, and the blood will be on your hands. You who are so cautious about prophecy only being relegated to the preaching of the Scriptures and not to divine and accurate revelation of events to come, keep reading, for you will find fault with this letter, and will dismiss it, as that too is prophecy.

All of you who think that God will occasionally pour out his blessed judgment on those who have defiled His Name, take this message as your warning.

As the prophet said: *"But if the watchman sees the sword coming and does not blow the trumpet, and the people are not warned, and the sword comes and takes any person from among them, he is taken away in his iniquity; but his blood I will require at the watchman's hand.* (Ezekiel 3:18)

I pray, here in my seclusion provided by the Lord through His saints, that this warning, that this judgment will not take the lives of anyone. I have sought to follow Christ and have forgiven those who persecuted me, who tried to murder me time and time again, my enemies who celebrated my misfortunes. I have removed myself so that they would not further sin by attacking me, that they would hear the Lord and take heed, that they would even remember the miraculous communication from one whom God spirited away without even the memory of those around him, one whom God has placed with his best angels, who *are flesh and not flesh.*

All those who do not understand that miracles

are "covered-up" do not understand the holographic nature of God's reality. God can change history *and* the collective memories of all who observe history, and thus alter the past, present and future without so much as a hint that anything has changed.

I have seen a man healed with prayer and laying on of hands. The photographic evidence showed the hemorrhaging of a heart attack, and after the prayer, the next picture showed that that there had never been a hemorrhage, and the doctors were astounded. What happened was not healing, in human terms, but the *altering of reality as if it had never happened.*

There are saints God has called home who did not pass into death, but they were as our Lord Jesus said in Matthew 16:28: "*Assuredly I say to you, there are some standing here who shall not taste death till they see the Son of Man coming in His Kingdom.*"

Enoch was taken up with the Lord, and so was Elijah—the mystery of these things is sealed. The apologists say that these were men who still owe a death and will return as the two witnesses in the Book of Revelation. But that would be conjecture. The truth is that they do not owe death, just as those to be Raptured before the Great Tribulation will not owe death.

Many in Christ today who might try and beat death only fail to realize that they already have through His Blood. And there would be little profit in this. It is better that the Lord hides certain things from man, and the angel I have come to know is no exception. Not only did the disciples see Jesus transfigured, but they also saw Moses and Elijah in their glorified—eternal—bodies, but later they doubted what they saw. Today, should a person be caught up with the Lord, without dying, it is my belief that in some cases there is no memory of that person ever having been on the earth, much in the same way that man was healed of his "heart attack"—as if it never happened in the first place. This is simply my belief, and I have asked the Lord to search my heart and mind for error, and this belief of mine has not been challenged, nor has there been Scripture denouncing it. The Holy Spirit has validated it as true, and God has now demonstrated the validity by showing me something I will not reveal, as I was asked to seal this from men, as Jesus told his disciples in Matthew 17:9: "Tell the vision to no one until the Son of Man has risen from the dead." Similarly, the Lord told me: "Son, seal up what you have seen until after the warning and the judgment to come shortly."

You who worship the fallen angel have been deceived, for you do not know that Jesus is Lord, and you do not believe that the Word of God is perfect truth—all of which has come to pass, just as it is today, and will be again tomorrow. Your minds have been sealed up by the man of sin and there is no way for you to understand these words, or any other truth.

I invite you to read on, as you are written herein, and you may as well know what your enemies know now. Your intelligence operatives and *Echelon* devices and *Tempest* viewers will never be as glorious as the mind of God. Keep that in mind when you beam your burnt offerings into your temple of abomination.

I forgive you, and I pray for you now that you may see the error of your thinking and surrender, repenting before the Living God and accepting Jesus as your Lord and Savior now, while there is still time. For if you have heard, and you turn away or stiffen your neck, your death will mark the end of any option you will ever have for redemption. You will have blasphemed the Holy Spirit by misappropriation, by the use of mirrors and obelisks, by all kinds of trickery and sorcery. For you there is little hope, but I will pray for you because I know who you are, and I have not a bitter root against you. For this is what my Lord commanded of those who walk with Him, and when I learned this, I was released from a prison far worse than the one which housed me for twenty-seven years.

For those of you wishing for the Rapture and Tribulation, I have disappointing news for you; no one knows *that* time. Realize that God has poured out many judgments on the disobedient throughout history, from the days of Adam to the flood of Noah, to the Babylonian Captivity, to war without end, to the slaughter of innocents in famine, plague and earth changes. Indeed, His wrath is perfect and born from love; even if you do not understand this mystery, He is perfect love. You who pray for the Rapture day and night and forget your daily walk with our Lord, manifested in the small things, take warning: no matter how horrible you think the Book of Revelation is, this warning and judgment to come will compete mightily. Those of you who must perish for our Lord, your comfort will be everlasting life and, hopefully, a good crown for your faith and service to those in need.

Here is something to encourage you who continue to read on: the Lord chastises His own. The wicked sometimes abide lavishly for a long while because they are *not* the Lord's. When his wrath is poured out upon them, they are never ready because of its suddenness, and they wail and scream, "But Lord...Oh, Lord, don't you remember *me*? All the *good things* I did?"

He remembers them not. For no good work is worthy of Him.

May God richly bless you, Mr. Parker, for supporting this old man in his quest to tell the truth. I will pray for you and your family, sir.

May our Lord have mercy on us,

Mountain

• • •

Dr. Gerald Bockwaite Wiley was able to devise special and unrelenting programs for Casey Burns Smith, whom they deemed to have certain powers; among the first things planned would be the interview.

The plane flying Casey from California was piloted by Cal Wilson. Due to intense medication such as Secanol and Dilaudid, Casey slept heavily. Cal, who didn't know Casey was drugged, was flying the mission under duress; when he deposited Casey in Baltimore, he had a certain sense of finality. His thoughts were with Spruug and Jesus. He knew that Jesus was with him because the Voice had told him to do what was asked, to rebuke no one, to complain about nothing, since the Lord would be with him. That was all he needed to complete the mission as a glorified robot.

Casey was less fortunate, molested day and night with electrodes and even sexual attack, which he resisted easily for the most part, remaining asleep and inattentive, impervious to virtually all stimuli, much to the consternation of Bock Wiley.

"Tell me, young man, do you now sense that you are in trouble, and that the only way out of that trouble is to come clean and admit that your beliefs are wrong?" Wiley asked.

Casey sat back and told Bock the truth: "Look, Dr. Wiley, you are going to do what you have to do, and then you will turn me over and they will *attempt* to kill me."

Bock was horrified. "What about last night? Didn't someone attack you...I mean, you know, sexually?"

"What, the flesh? I am not my flesh, Dr. Wiley, and so there is no corruption of the flesh you could do to me—there is nothing you could do that would influence or corrupt my spirit."

"Spirit—there is no such thing as spirit."

"You *will* die, Dr. Wiley, and *they*, whom you serve, whom you hold so dear, will accomplish it."

"What do you mean *attempt* to kill you? Don't you think they will succeed?" Bock asked, determined.

"They will fail," was all Casey would say.

Wiley sat back, frustrated. He had never seen anyone behave in such a manner, and he knew, professionally, that this was no delusion. What it was he could not say, because obviously it was not what it seemed to be, it couldn't be. For certainly Casey knew nothing of himself or the world around him.

Casey sat back on his bunk, chuckling.

"What's so funny!" Bock exclaimed, now angry.

"You are. God is laughing at you—at your wickedness, how you think you're going to get away with it. You won't."

"Young man—"

"Isn't there *any* good in you?" Casey asked earnestly, his smile gone.

There was a long pause, and Bock did smile, now needing and hoping to go to his chamber of horrors. Torture would be the only way of reasoning with this foolish young rebel. Even though an admission of what Bock considered real would not prevent his dispatch to the temple.

It was research, and Bock had also verified to Arthur Reddick that he had never met such a young man before, *who defied human logic despite Bock's every effort to verify that he was a human being.* "He's an anomaly," he told Reddick, who seemed elated with that news, and hung up.

Bock tried everything. For days he implanted Casey's brain with electrodes, had various surrogates and aides attempt to sexually stimulate him, applied sensory deprivation, torture by sound, by electronic device, by movies, by everything he knew out of his mentor's playbook, written by the illustrious Dr. Malcolm West, an expert on Nazi mind control methods, methods guaranteed to fragment the personality so the facilitator could gain total control. No matter what Dr. Wiley tried, Casey would laugh and continued to laugh! Bock was prevented from scarring the young man or physically harming him because of the Brotherhood's future plans for the boy.

"Won't you take me to your temple, Bock?" Casey, who was in a silly mood, asked as he laughed and laughed.

After many days, Bock realized he was beaten. He was truly at a loss. He called Jackson Kincaid, who in turn called Casey's parents and told them if they wanted to *advance*, they should go to the Temple for the blood offering of their son, who was a very special child of God.

Casey reminded Bock about the spiritualizing of blood, which the Brotherhood planned to accomplish at the temple ceremony, its purpose to bypass God's judgment on the earth, in the vainglorious hope that the millennium would sustain them without end. Bock did not find it amusing to be reminded about it; it made him extremely uncomfortable to see anything he would deem supernatural at work.

It was gratifying for Casey to see these men toiling and scheming to find a way to beat God. If he were even younger, he might have been sad, but from his current perspective, it only amplified his love and delight in the Lord God.

One name he loved was *El Shaddai*, the Hebrew name for *God Almighty.* Though his Father conferred to him that He wished to be called *Father, Father God, Lord, Lord God*, or *God*. On rare occasion, *Jehovah*. And all the other names were to be considered, but not allowed in addressing Him verbally.

Darwain, Casey's progenitor or earthly father, arrived one day and pleaded with his son to accept defeat and graciously do what was asked. He offered his son a deal. He could save his life if he would denounce Jesus Christ and perform sexually in front of the congregation. They would accept that he was no innocent and could not possibly be declared a lamb worthy to be killed.

He would, however, have to witness another young man's death—that is, after having sex with him in front of the congregation...proof that Casey was carnal after all, a rather *confused lad*.

"Father, why did you go to the church on Sundays?" was all Casey would ask. "Did you not believe?"

"Why can't you talk like a...like a seventeen-year-old kid? Why can't you be the way you were? What did your mother and I do to you that made you so sick? All you have to do is a small thing, and you can live and bring happiness back to our family. Don't you at least want that? Don't you want your mother and me to be happy? Don't you want to be a good son?" Darwain pleaded.

"By raping a boy in front of an altar to Satan, then killing him? Would that make me a good son, Dad?"

Of course, Darwain was nonplussed and without excuse, nor additional words. How could he defend himself or his society now? Yes, it would have to be extreme if he were to save his son's life—but he would be accepted, if only he wasn't so...*pure*.

"I am *not* your son—I'm in disguise, Mr. Smith. God will show you who I am, a warrior for Christ, an exacter of God's will, to carry out His judgment on man along with others like me."

"Then what in the devil are you? You're evil," was all Darwain could manage to say.

"Yes, I can see how you would think that," Casey said.

"Then I will wash my hands of you—and you won't be my son!" Darwain said, with rising anger and wrath.

"My Lord is returning soon to judge the whole world. Before that happens there will be the most terrible warning, a judgment the world has never seen, so you know God means business. You and your kind will either repent and seek forgiveness for your sins, or you will try again to make the world in your image, but many of you will die in your sin now and go to eternal hell. Think of it,

Father: eternity without God."

"You are sick! You're not my son! You're not! You're an evil little brat! We gave you everything and you shame us like this? You deserve to be killed. All they want is a *commitment*. Everybody has to commit—otherwise they are cast out! How do you think we got our money? Who do you think paid for that fancy prep school where you learned nothing! SOMEBODY HAD TO PAY! Oh, you had no problem accepting all the gifts that I sacrificed to earn, did you? Who do you think got you accepted into the best college, which you will never go to now? Casey, listen! I DON'T KNOW YOU, I DON'T KNOW WHERE YOU COME FROM! BUT IT'S NOT ME, IT'S NOT HERE!"

"I was hidden under your nose. You gave birth to a monster. Lord have mercy on your soul. I forgive you, Father. Please repent now; we'll pray together. Ask Him for forgiveness; admit your sins, Father, or you will die. I love you, and God will forgive you. God is love, Father. He is your Father."

"Just call me *dad* like you used to," Darwain said, dejected now and sad.

"*I am not Casey.*" He rose from the bunk and appeared in the mirror.

Every night afterward he appeared in Darwain's dreams; everywhere Darwain looked, there Casey would be. Darwain could not escape his terrible role and knowledge of the abominable things he had done in order to achieve acceptance, financial well-being and a future. He had renounced the Lord Jesus Christ; he had participated, marginally, in their satanic rituals and temple practices, and he knew about the inner sanctum.

• • •

Bock had failed. In his office he scanned the so-called secret writings of the Brotherhood again. There was nothing important there, only advice on how to be a good citizen so that all people would hold Brotherhood members in high regard; there was nothing about the truth. He was trying to discover whether the Brotherhood acknowledged that there was a God, and whether Jesus Christ was His Son.

Bock and his entire world of the Brotherhood served a god called "the one," and also called "the savior of humanity." There were references to charities and trusts around the globe that served this god and thus were seen as charitable, which was very important.

The writings of the Brotherhood told how members could tap into the true power of the one, being the Almighty God, and use it for what they wanted. Advice about eating to live and not living to eat was included, as well as an admonishment to be a good citizen above all else and to keep fit. There were references to sexual practices, and phone numbers for weight loss clinics and plastic surgeons. Gyms and health food stores were listed. "God has provided everything for your happiness. We are nothing short of God ourselves," the pamphlet said.

When Bock Wiley went home to the lavish house they had provided for him while he was in Baltimore, he was greeted by his wife and two dogs. His children, Stacey and Jimmy, were both in graduate school, in biology and philosophy; he knew Jimmy would get over this philosophy kick, become an atheist and serve his own needs.

Was it real, he wondered as he punched up the television news? He got his answer when he had not just a vision, but a full-blown hallucination of Casey delivering the newscast! He indulged himself in what he knew was a fantasy, in what he understood all too well was fallout from the amphetamines he'd taken to keep working. He'd have to calm down, and so he watched television while sipping a single malt and avoiding Mrs. Wiley, who had just come home from her tennis tournament at the club.

Marianne, the housekeeper who spoke only French, brought in the next single malt with light rocks in the Lismore tumbler. He turned to the Secret Codex of the Brotherhood and then saw the esoteric rite of Easter: an inverted cross with urns to catch the blood of the crucified lamb—*Lamb* was their term. The next chapter explained alchemy and reversing the Resurrection of Christ as described in the Bible.

He had to ask himself: If Jesus was a crackpot, why go to all this trouble to reverse something that had no efficacy in the first place?

On television Casey said, "Because it's real. Jesus is Lord, Dr. Wiley."

He flipped the channel and Casey was all the international satellite stations—in the movies, the subject of documentaries...everywhere. He tried to turn it off, but Casey's face filled the screen; the fantasy had dislodged, and he was becoming a victim of his own mind control techniques.

"Don't you understand? God laughs at you. He allows you to think you discovered a rule, a principle, and then He will take it away and drown you in His disgust. Repent, Dr. Wiley. Accept the truth."

"Why are you torturing me!" Bock cried out.

Marianne looked into the den from the hall. Noise traveled easily in the Georgian colonial. As she watched, tears flooded her eyes, and she hid herself behind the crack in the door. "Merci, merci," she said.

Bock could not hear her. He began to see the images of what had transpired in Los Angeles. Casey showed him one after another: the burning of the Faith Church, the sniper killing young Justin, the deaths of the five thousand virgins on St. Lucy, the massacre at Waco, TWA 800 going down, jets into the World Trade Towers, the bombing of civilians in Bosnia, and a cacophony of little children screaming, "We are the law, we are the law!"

He showed Bock the crushing of each and every worker at the Serin Lab in northern Arizona, then the screen was filled with the Pyramid on the Giza plateau in Egypt.

He was shown the children with limbs removed, laughing, the men who were eunuchs screaming, "Praise God!"

He saw the robots he had made—those once referred to as students—shoot each and every classmate, in close-up. He knew their names: Sally, Jesse, Timothy, Michael, Lionel, Tony, Jake, Mary, Heidi and Martha—the same at each high school.

He could not breathe; he was gasping, crawling on the hardwood floor, tears flooding his face. "Stop it! Stop it!"

Casey tapped him on the shoulder and stood him up. "Now, look, you're going to have to be a man about it."

When he turned, he saw Marianne. "I see him too," she said, attempting to muster her best English.

He looked at her twenty-year-old face, her long curly hair and blue eyes. He had bedded her, and she bore the guilt. "I was a virgin," she said in French and he understood.

"I'm sorry," he said.

"Dr. Wiley, you will go through with this," Casey told him.

When Wiley looked around, Marianne was gone. He thought he looked ugly in the mirror over the fireplace. No amount of possessions—the Italian clothes, the Porsche or his Rolex could erase what he saw. Even if he did not engineer all of this for the world, the world was what he served. "I based my entire life on helping other people," he said feebly.

Casey replied, "You mean by doing what was asked of you. But you never believed in them."

"Why won't you just go away?"

"Because you are guilty, and God's justice will be done. That is all I am here to do, exact God's will. That is all I can do." Casey sat in the easy chair in front of the empty fireplace. Spring had come and in a short while there would be the sacrifice. Casey was the candidate, he was still seventeen, and his birthday was Easter. He was a virgin, despite all best efforts to the contrary, and he had powers—of God—because he was pure, a lamb. But Bock did not know for sure what all this meant.

He kept him under military guard at the Maryland lab.

"From now on," Casey told him, "You'll do what you're told. Watch."

Bock Wiley sat, and not even his Golden Retriever could help him. On television the detonation of a nuclear bomb ended the Manhattan skyline—all the ships, the Statue of Liberty, all the buildings, all the people—everything reduced to fire and ash. Gone.

And then it happened: Paris, London, Baltimore, The White House, the Chicago skyline, San Francisco Bay, and finally Miami—nuclear judgment, the culture, in fifteen minutes...vanished.

Life, as Bock Wiley defined it, was permanently and geographically over.

These scenes were duplicated on the laptop on his desk, where he spent many hours in the study, writing and developing his theories.

It was duplicated in his mind so he could not look away from the screen. He saw that the audience in the medical theater where he had presented paper after paper on the human psyche and the need for social control through behaviorism were not his fellow colleagues, but were all children, applauding wildly. "Hooray for the Lord," they said in unison, "He's coming back to judge the whole world."

Even in his office, he would have the same vision—nuclear devastation and the children. The vision included the children he had programmed for destruction, even the ones who had died. They were very much alive, cheering and laughing, restored.

"Don't you want to get out of this cell?" he remembered saying to Casey one day when he was thinking that this was all some sort of fantasy on his part. Then he saw himself on the sidewalk, dead from the ten-story fall.

"No, *not even one* will be spared," Casey said.

"Fine, I guess we've got nothing more to do here," Bock Wiley said, and without hesitation he transferred him to the care of Reddick's people.

Arthur Reddick called him, "Go ahead, take your vacation in Provence. We've found you a wonderful country chateau, it will be good for you."

He looked at his surroundings and then boldly asked Arthur, "Is it real?"

"I don't know what you're talking about, Bock. Is *what* real, specifically?"

Wiley paced around his office, took off his lab coat and slipped into his silk summer blazer, popped a couple of single-grain codeine pills, chasing it with a snort of cognac. "Hello? You there, Arthur?"

"Who's been talking to you?"

"No one. I just, well I was reading the Codex and I never thought much of it...I'm a scientist, and you know I'm an atheist. It's all the human psyche, we can make ourselves see or feel anything."

Arthur said, "So you've been talking to no one?"

"I just asked if you thought it was real?"

"Whether *I thought* it was real, or whether *it is* real?"

"I don't know, Arthur."

"How do you think you soared so high above your colleagues. Did you see them witness the things you've seen?"

Arthur's voice sounded strained, cautious, and it caused alarm, so Bock backed away. "Wish I could see you. I'm headed over to Jeff's boat for the party." There was no response. "Hey, hello, Arthur?" To hell with him. Such a nervous old man.

Casey told Bock, "You will go to the party, and you will find the answer to all your fears."

thirty-seven

hey would all be there, at least most of them, Bock Wiley thought, as he arrived in his bright yellow turbo Porsche to Dock 18, where the thirty-cabin yacht cruiser was being fueled. When he boarded, he found the usual scene—celebrities, the women. He was a scientist of renown, had written the seminal work on behaviorism, on social control through image control, as well as a book for parents to help their kids achieve success in scholastic endeavors. But such an irony never sought refuge in Wiley's mind.

There were the Hollywood elites, hungry for more money for their flailing production budgets. Lance Stendahl and Steven Pearl, a bevy of actresses, one of the great opera singers of the world, Donati, television news anchors, and even the Vice President of the United States, as well as the vice prime minister of England. There were three bands playing one after the other, and the music varied. It was no secret that the cocaine and other exploits would go on below, through a door guarded by men in black suits with machine guns.

Security forces were massive. Each person was frisked. They had to have the same invitation that Bock had, and ID to prove it. It was truly an international affair. He saw his old friend, Wayne Jorvelle, the African dignitary, who was a supporter, as well as the nobility of the UN. There were two four-star generals, as well as a coterie of prostitutes who were *prime du jour* for later in the evening.

The owner of the yacht, Jeffrey Sorenson, knew that raising money for candidates was no easy thing. Commanding with youthful vigor, the affable Sorenson projected the idea he could accomplish anything. His smooth, smiling face made him look like he had never had a trying time, a bad day, or a financial problem. He inspired confidence and especially gratitude, yet he could blackmail with the best of them. He knew that he needed money, and lots of it. Every single person on the guest list had been hit up for hard cash. They would have had to at least gotten their foundation to kick in, anonymously of course, to obtain enough "clout" to insure good social status and a *seat at the table.*

As the ship set sail for a chilly Spring cruise (the deck was replete with overhead heaters everywhere), all the guests were in good spirits. Jordan Star was particularly dapper in a white jacket, adorned with a red handkerchief and matched with black trousers; his short-cropped blonde hair shot through with gray was slicked back evenly and perfectly. He was eloquent and spoke directly to the cameras: "Ladies and gentlemen, we are here to ask for your support in the clean up of Los Angeles, and in restoring the lives of its citizens, many of whom became homeless after the quakes. The increase in earthquakes makes it vitally important that we have the funds ready and willing to reach all corners of the globe if necessary. We do not want anyone to suffer needlessly."

"Hear, hear," said Sorenson.

The Vice President echoed with muted approval no one could hear, and all applauded.

Down below, in the room used for the inhalation of substances, Wiley had a change of plan. He used it for a briefing. "He is the one," he told Jordan Star's special guest. "And he's looking forward to it." Wiley waited for a reaction but there was none.

Star's friend said: "I must leave you now, and I thank you for finding him. Our people have seen him too."

Wiley felt crazed and worried. Star's "guest" had arrived while the ship was docked just outside the Baltimore harbor. Those driving him seemed like military or intelligence operatives; they did not smile, they did not look around or away. They helped the man below and the boat slipped away without notice.

Things were certainly hopping—hundred-million-dollar movie deals, political fund raising, charity drives, and sex, down below. There were a string of rooms reserved for such practices, everyone knew, and no one needed encouragement. The two virgin girls performed as Bock expected they would, and all seemed to enjoy the spectacle, one way or another.

He saw no ritual, no candles and no altars on the ship and Wiley was glad of it. In the restroom he saw Casey's face staring back at him in the mirror, saying: "You can eat the cow dung instead of human waste. The prophet said it like this: 'When your wares went out by sea, you satisfied many people; you enriched the kings of the earth with your many luxury goods and your merchandise. But you are broken by the seas in the depths of the waters.'"

"Leave me alone!" Wiley screamed, holding his ears.

Cal had now descended 10,000 feet. He knew he was in sin, he knew he was disobedient, but he could not help himself. Perhaps the only good thing he had done was to take off without a crew. As he looked over the Baltimore harbor, he could see the ship, festooned with lights and thronged with guests. He passed over and turned off the radio. He had orders to land at the airport and fly several dignitaries back to Los Angeles for another celebration. He prayed to be a good soldier and to be rid of the programming; he remembered those who died at his hand and it spurred him on.

The tower had already called the police and the military, as the plane was not only off course, but without crew and circling the harbor without authorization. "Well, Sam," he said to his trusty parrot, perched right on his shoulder as always, "Looks like we're heading on to greener pastures!"

The parrot seemed happy and content, as he had on every flight Caleb Wilson ever flew. Closer now, he could see the festive array of lights on the massive yacht, nearly a cruise ship by any standard.

The crowd cheered as they saw the blue and red jet tipping its wing overhead. Jackson seemed worried for a moment—as she recognized it as one of theirs—but this was a strange sight. "What I want to know," she asked Jordan Star, "is where is Arles? He is supposed to be here, and he is supposed to support me, as I supported him."

Jordan looked at the jet and smiled. "Incredible."

"What!" she said, "what's incredible?"

The jet circled around again.

Cal was never happier, even as a child in his mother's arms.

Wiley had grabbed his ears and was yelling, forcing one of the security people to escort him into a room where he could settle down. Most of the guests went back to their frolicking and carousing as the jet went into a kamikaze dive.

"Oh, no!" screamed Jackson. "Oh, no!" She was too stunned to move.

"You have had a good life, and now you will pay for it," Star said.

"What do you mean, what do you mean!" She started to climb over the ship, but her dress caught on the rigging, and she looked up at a machine the size of the universe.

The band played on, and below deck they were eating the cake in the shape of the great pyramid at Giza in Egypt.

Cal was singing "Glory, Hallelujah!"

He could see them in shock and celebration, every single twitch in every single eye. "All glory to you, my Lord. Thank you for letting me serve you, thank you for giving me the chance to make something right!" The security forces had all drawn their weapons, both sub-machine guns and side arms and fired uselessly at the oncoming passenger jet.

Now skimming the water, nose on the ship.

The explosion was seen for miles. Arles, who watched it on the news, was shaken and trembling—a true terrorist attack! Still there were haters in the world, who must be eradicated once and for all. Arles' use of Muslims on the Trade Towers was one thing, but an independent attack—it was enough to make him want to kill every single Christian on earth, and in a hurry!

Arthur e-mailed Arles: *Contact me by secure means.*

Arles knew what it meant but could not believe it.

At the Rescue Mission, Spruug saw the explosion on television, and he feared that Cal was involved. But he did not understand.

No one understood, except for Kincaid, who knew his wife was on the ship and knew there were no survivors.

The President of the United States issued a message to the terrorists involved, and Caleb Wilson's image was splayed across the screen as a "right-wing Christian terrorist." A hate campaign went out around the airwaves, rioting broke out in various cities, and churches were burned.

Christian groups around the country and the world quickly denounced the terrorist act as "cowardly," "misguided," "ungodly," and "un-Chrisitian-like."

Spruug would say, "He disobeyed God, and he sinned. Let's forgive him."

No one else, and no Christian, was in a forgiving mood.

The President wanted to quell the anti-Christian fervor that suddenly swept the world like a plague: the headlines reading:

Christian Terrorist Slams Jet Into Yacht

Arles was elevated above the status of the deceased Diane Mitchell, and his former friend, the deceased Jackson Kincaid. He would now be needed and would have a seat on the (Brotherhood) Council, which was a division of the (Brotherhood) Covenant. The Covenant was cousins of the (Brotherhood of) Light Foundation and had roots into everything from Freemasonry to Egyptian religion, though these groups were factionalized and would sometimes war with each other.

"What was Star?" Arles asked Arthur.

"He will live on forever."

Arles knew not to ask anything else.

The high-rise in downtown Los Angeles proved to be immune to the earthquake, though Arthur had arranged to move everything to his Omaha headquarters as soon as he heard from his superiors which plan to follow. Los Angeles was his experiment, and he had helped shape and influence the city in virtually every way. He had been a donor to the colleges and universities and received several honorary doctorates for his efforts, and his name appeared on medical wings at private as well as community hospitals. Arthur Reddick had been given the modern equivalent of a world capital, and he was able, at will, to shut it down or cinch it in. Arthur's power extended far beyond Los Angeles; he was already the shadow governor of New York, Paris and London.

"What we know now," said Arthur, while sipping his own label of brandy, "is that we have the one for the rite."

"Why is he so important? He's just a...a kid, isn't he?" Arles asked ignorantly.

"Just as we have transitional beings, so do they. We will find out what he knows, and allow him to communicate. As long as he remains in custody, then obviously he can't be any threat. We will do the same thing we did the last millennium and further exemplify that God is nothing more or less than a force to be *used*."

"My men told me that he's very polite, that he's confident."

"He's *evil*!" Arthur blurted out. "You will come with me to the base in Colorado—the top command is in shambles and needs organizing. We have lost dozens of good men in the last week, many to suicide."

"Why?" Arles asked, zipping up his jacket and concealing his weapon.

"Our intelligence has picked up on a situation right here in this city, where one of Bock Wiley's...how should I say—*experiments*—found out everything, either through Casey, or maybe some angelic host, I don't know."

"Sir, is this some kind of test, are you testing me?" Arles asked.

"I'm quite serious. We have been at war for centuries, for eons, forever in earth terms. And we have been successful, do you know why?"

"No, sir," Arles replied, nervous and fearing for his life.

"Because we have kept the being they call God from fulfilling the Covenant."

Arles knew where this conversation was going, but he never believed it, to him it was all about the military and power begetting power. He was lost beyond hope at this point. But Arthur was a man on a mission, invigorated. He removed his wig and his mask, and Arles was astounded when he saw a young man of only thirty. Arles was in fear of his own shadow, and the depth of this fear was staggering. Arthur—*a young immortal man!*—stuck his hand through the wall and pulled it out again. He laughed as Arles cowered. "You can have what I have, Arles, both *immortality* and *mobility*. But only if we can get the blood back. You see, we must put the genie back in the bottle, or lose all. Look," he said and pointed up to the sky.

Arles saw what looked like hovering helicopters, surrounded by bright, unnatural lights, beautiful in color. When he looked back, Arthur was again in "costume," gruff as ever and buttoned up in his suit.

"The rules are that the blood of Christ, the Holy Grail, can be inverted and appropriated to keep Jehovah God's judgments from occurring, not just in the Book of Revelation, but all the judgments that we ourselves do not impose on humans. For example, we should have been blown to bits by nuclear war; it was prophesied by our greatest visionary as God's judgment, but we staved it off, you see, with the blood. Get it? Catch up now, lad. As you can see, we took God's power of *translation*, since our angels were the same. *Everything they have, we have*," Arthur went on. "But if we slip, then it will affect every single being out there—all our angelic hosts, our serpent brothers, our Nephilim friends, and our *Ascended Masters* who are every bit as holy and forthright and charitable as the saints and are the true stewards of this universe, the sustainers of all that is physical. If for any reason the blood covenant is restored, then every one of us is dead and gone. The experiment is over. The material world will be lost. That is why, my young talented warrior who is fit to go against the mightiest one, we must have the right son, and on the right day, we will undo the damage that has been done by our carelessness. By the *evil one* known as Jesus. Do you understand?"

Arles was completely still.

"Now I want you to meet Harry Summers at his office in New York. There is something you must do for us, before the Easter ritual."

"That's only a week away, sir. Shouldn't I be—"

"You should do what you're told and someone like you need not ask questions. Suffice it to say you will attend. You know what that means—no turning back now."

Arles vomited in the bathroom, fear gripped him like the jabbing of so many knives. His thoughts raged. He was in too deep, he was being set up—he knew that much for sure. He knew he had already been mind controlled but did not know it at the time. That is how Arthur made him see such unbelievable things. What was he trying to say? That those things in the sky—the UFOs—they're ours? Are part of the Brotherhood? And what is the Brotherhood? How far does it reach into the heavens? Was it everywhere? If so, why worry about Jesus?

He had heard of a secret space program, but that was *us*. Yes, he had heard about some base on the moon, but that was *us*; okay, sure, he had heard that we were on Mars, and had been for decades, but that was just a rumor, and that too, was *us*; and yes the disinformation campaign, and of course the cloning, and the public was wrong about all of it, and now, suddenly, *some of it is true?*

He was being set up and he knew it, and there was nothing he could do about it now.

thirty-eight

"I know Cal flew that plane," Spruug told Bauman at the dining bench. He ate another piece of donated turkey and looked at Bauman again, wondering about what had happened. "The television showed footage of my apartment, with me and my wife and kids and the new girl with...the miracle. But that man was not in the footage. How did they get the footage?"

Bauman laughed as he slurped up his soup and rice. "You know, Joe, for an out-of-work sales executive, you seem pretty naive. What are you doing for Easter?"

"We're worshiping...I guess at the new church on Roscoe."

"That's great," said Bauman. "I'm still on the job. Getting close, you know. It's very gratifying work—got leads, don't need much sleep, gives me time to work."

Spruug looked around nervously and said: "We have to leave this city. That's what...the....what I heard, okay?"

"Sure, we should all get out of this cesspool," Bauman said. "But we're homeless, in case you haven't noticed, and we're dependent on the food bank."

Spruug ignored reality and said: "I saw him on television, the young man, or whatever he is. The older men told me he would come."

"What older men?"

"I think...I believe we're supposed to get as many people out of here to higher ground as possible, to save the remnant," Spruug said nervously.

Bauman dismissed Spruug. He just couldn't fathom leaving Los Angeles when he was still on the case. Marta and his wife Sheila had already returned to the condominium, as there was little damage there and the repairs were underway. He glanced back at Spruug: "Listen, if I don't see you again, God bless you, and thank you for sharing the Lord."

"But—" was all Spruug could say in the vacuum of Bauman's once occupied space in the makeshift homeless shelter/mess hall.

Fred and Louis headed up the prayer lunch with songs and festivities. The Rescue Mission had done its job, and FEMA had provided, as promised, the necessary services: food, clothing, shelter, and especially, money. They would be able to pay subsistence wages to their staff, just plain folks too who had, through circumstances, fallen on hard times and then found the truth in Jesus Christ.

Big Willy had gone back to his job at the storage facility, and the others, Shep, John the Apostle, and their band of Christian homeless had disappeared, preferring, it would seem, to live the way they had, on the street. Louis and Big Fred did not trust Bauman at all at this point. He was dangerous, clearly was hearing and speaking to the voices in his head, and they had seen this behavior in many who had come to the mission and many whom they had cared for on the streets. They felt Bauman shouldn't have let the voices take over, and they doubted very seriously that it was the Holy Spirit.

Sheila and Marta had deserted Bauman, at Big Fred's suggestion, and planned to reunite when Bauman had received counseling.

Spruug, who was caring for an undocumented girl named Soledad, was their other main concern.

"Do you wish to adopt her?" Fred asked as he looked over at the little girl who was playing with the other children.

Spruug wanted desperately to watch the news, the follow-up on the terrorist attack blamed on Cal Wilson, the man who had accepted Christ when a man who clearly was not human and claimed to be named "Michael" appeared in the condo and at the Mission. "Do you remember Michael?" Spruug asked.

Big Fred unstrapped his guitar and turned the PA system off. He surveyed the room full of beds and tables and wounded people— it was just too much for one man to handle. "No, Spruug (everyone called him that except Bauman), I do not remember anyone like that."

"We have to leave here. Will you pray with me?"

"Where are your wife and kids?" Big Fred asked, always trying to help.

"Dear Father God," Spruug prayed, ignoring him. "Please help Fred, Louis and the rest of the staff here understand what's going on. Please give us transportation and a place to relocate these people."

Fred interrupted Spruug's prayer, unable to validate this man as anything but in a state of shock. "Son," Big Fred said warmly, "life is just what it has always been. A battle between the forces of good and the forces of darkness. God used this earthquake to test all of us. Perhaps He wants you to work here with us. We could use you. You wouldn't make what you made selling industrial equipment, but—"

"—Fred! Listen to me! We were warned! The old man, Daniel, he told us that! Does this mean anything to you?"

Fred put on his best Scripture to refute what was an obvious form of demonic possession. "Second Timothy 4:2: *Preach the Word. Be ready in season and out of season. Convince, rebuke, exhort, with all longsuffering and teaching.* Spruug, you need rebuking. Beware of false prophets, and those doing signs and wonders."

"Don't you believe that countless angels are walking to and fro? Don't you think that angels exact God's judgments?" Spruug asked frantically.

"Today, we have the Word of God, and that is sufficient. We needn't be concerned with misinterpretation—it's dangerous."

"When Moses led them to the Red Sea, it appeared that he was deluded, you know? The enemy was right there, trapping them against the sea. And then—"

"Okay," Fred reacted. "Satan's battlefield is the mind, and he uses hallucinations, wrong thinking, false prophecy, and maybe even images on television—the enemy is always around us. Let's pray," he said, and put his hands on Spruug's shoulders. "In the name of Jesus, under the blood of the New Covenant, with the victory at Calvary, I ask you to place extra battalions of *Your* angels around Joe Spruug, and around his wife and children, and around little Soledad, that she might find a new father and a new life. He is a man of talent and responsibility. Bless him and keep him. Make your face to shine upon him and comfort him that he may be vital to the needs of our suffering people today."

Spruug wept. "Fred, it's true anyway. There are angels, and we see them occasionally."

"You *do not* see angels! You want to attend church this Sunday in honor of His glorious resurrection, and if you go in there talking like this, they will do two things. One, pray for you, as I am doing now. And two, an elder or two will rebuke you for not being Scripturally sound, and if you continue, you will not be allowed to corrupt the body. Now, I've got to take care of these people. I ask you to join me."

Spruug smiled. Here was proof, he thought. "Fred, the man who crashed the jet and killed all those people on the yacht was at my house, and little Soledad saw him, and so did my wife and children. So did Michael. And he showed us the face of a young man who was one of us, who is a harbinger, who is God's will, in addition to the Holy Spirit that we all received when we accepted Christ, which those who are not in Him can never know."

Fred was trembling at a concrete fact that he would have to verify. "You say the man, Cal Wilson...flew the plane? He was at your house?"

"He got arrested there...I mean, not by police, just guys, like undercover cops or something—they took him away. Next thing you know his picture is blasted all over the TV set claiming he was a terrorist, but he wasn't. He just came to Christ that night, the night before they took him away," Spruug said.

A woman, who was a newcomer, entered the mission alone. She was silent. Fred went to help her, found her a cot to lie down on. All she said was that her name was Rebecca, and that, "It's all true."

When he looked for Spruug again, he was gone.

• • •

Bauman was led right to the warehouse in the *borrowed* car. He had to follow Ricky, and Ricky had led him to a chop shop, or so he thought. He would not forget Alice Garcia, even if the Department wanted to. Shep and John the Apostle were with him, and they said they had never been in that part of town.

The Voice told Bauman to look at the sky—it had an orange haze that did look different from the normal haze of spring. Daniel, who was not Daniel the prophet, but Daniel the old man, pointed at the warehouse and blocked Bauman from entering. "If you go in there, you won't come out again."

"I don't care." He brandished his weapon but it wound up in

Daniel's hand, and he hid it so that Bauman could not possibly retrieve it from him, as it was not anywhere on his person.

"You have a wife and daughter. Better you prepare to evacuate your family. They will try and kill him, he who is one of us, even if you can't remember what you saw in your mind and on television. He will appear at the Mission. Lead them out," said Daniel.

Bauman ignored the warning, and sneaked in with Shep, who wasn't going to listen to somebody he could not remember or even see. John the Apostle stood guard and prayed. He had thought they were rid of Bauman, but they went with him out of concern. They couldn't desert him now.

The two of them entered through the back, along a dark corridor, then climbed the scaffolding on a narrow wooden stairway. When they found a safe perch, they looked down and did not see a chop shop, a drug or weapons dealing ring, but a large pentagram, the sign of Satan, drawn in a circle, and several children tied and gagged, who were seated at the center. Several cameras surrounded the scene. Vehicles were parked neatly on the other side of the building.

"Shep, what do we do?" whispered Bauman. "They killed my partner, I have to do something."

Shep left Bauman alone, because he was afraid.

Bauman watched as they drew guns and prepared to shoot the crying children. If he would lose his life, now was the time. From the perch he screamed for all he was worth, and all the lights went on. They held their fire, shouted a flurry of expletives, and one of them, a man in a suit said: "You don't know what you're doing, Stranger. We're filming a movie—it's not real," he said. "Come on, you can check if you want."

"I'm staying right here—I'm a cop."

"Hey, man, we like cops," said the fellow that seemed like a producer, not a criminal.

But Bauman remembered what Daniel had said.

"Don't make me have to come up there and get you."

Another man, also in a nice jacket and tie, warned: "If we don't get this done, we'll miss the window."

"Officer," the first man said, looking up at him. "We're on a tight production schedule, and..."

"This kind of thing is going to stop!" Bauman yelled. "What's *he* doing with you?" Bauman was referring to Ricky, the drug dealer, who shrank from the light. "What is he doing with you?"

Suddenly, the lights went out. The building started shaking—an aftershock, Bauman thought. It was almost pitch black. The scaffolding gave way and Bauman fell into the darkness, collapsed on the floor and could not get back up again. The building was still shaking slightly. He could see the door open in the corner, as a shaft of light rained in on his eyes, which he fought to keep open.

He heard sirens, turned and looked up at a man whose eyes were so dark he could see no pupils, who held a gun at his nostril, who could have killed Bauman. When he smiled, his teeth shone like plastic, but Bauman would find it hard to remember him because he could not stay awake. Later he would know that he had seen nothing of the natural world.

thirty-nine

Stephen had been warned by God Himself, had been instructed time and time again never to pursue any personal vendetta, lest it become your burden also. He'd learned to forgive in prison. In his prayers he had been warned not to leave his bride-to-be, but under the exigent circumstances, the Mission would have to care for her in his absense. He had walked with angels and knew it. He had been blessed by God to be a leader and was told he had an urgent duty in Los Angeles, to lead the remnant out. He had seen Casey Smith revealed as one of God's stealth angels, Metatron, who was to end, along certain predetermined and legal rules that he did not know of, the World Order, under no uncertain terms.

He sought and found Katarina, but it was almost too easy. She had dressed for the occasion, and he stirred a bit at her innocence. He had been referred to her location by Rick Lowie, and it seemed to him that she knew he would come to her. He would know later that this was not the case. He would regret seeing her again, especially after receiving his gift—a bride-to-be. It was not lust he was after, but truth. After all, she framed him for murder didn't she?

At her condo in the Hollywood Hills she was surrounded with every amenity a successful person would want: new car, new clothes, new friends, which were presented in framed pictures on the window sill; perhaps a new club scene, and definitely new secrets. Her drug habit seemed to him under control in the sense that she was not crazy. While he was there, he noticed how beautifully stylish she was as she sniffed something in a vial and drank a little white wine. "You look different, you've really changed," she told him.

"Did you set me up or what?" he asked her pointedly.

"Let me touch you."

"No," he told her firmly.

"Oh, right," she said, "your faith." She primped in the living room mirror and took her shirt off, revealing an expensive lacy bra. He immediately averted his eyes and sat on a leather chair facing the view of the Los Angeles basin. "First of all, Stephen, I did not turn you in or testify against you. In fact, the case was dropped and I went with the band."

When he had to use the bathroom, he found gifts of perfume and cards from admirers and hundred dollar bills in a tray. When he checked the closet on the way to the john he saw men's slacks and shirts and shoes and jackets. It looked as if she were shacked up with someone. But there were so many different sizes.

"You have a lot of admirers," he said in the kitchen, sipping an espresso while she stared at him and touched his muscular arms.

"I admire you. You took it like a man and now you're free. Well, you're not really free, if you know what I mean." She put a Strange Muumuu CD on and grooved a bit to the beat.

"Do you have to do that?" he said.

"Don't you want to know how he died?"

"His father killed him, right? That's what the papers said."

"True, but I think it was God."

"What are you talking about?" he asked, fitting into the leather jacket she brought out of the closet for him. "Thanks," he said. "But...you sure?" Yes, he could use a jacket, he could use pants and he could use money.

"I want to help you. Look, I'm not doing badly. One good turn deserves another."

"You hooking again?" he asked matter-of-factly as they sat in the breakfast nook with their coffees.

"No, I mean, I'm dating. What I have to tell you is wonderful. I want to tell you why you're not free."

"I'm listening," he said, dreading what would happen next.

"Well, what I meant was...I mean it's everything you're against. There's a meeting next week, and..."

"I'm not interested, Katarina."

"Or I have to turn you in."

He'd finally gotten the truth. He got up, threw off the jacket and stuffed himself back into his compromised T-shirt, and then bore down on her. "Because I'm on the other side, and you went over, isn't that it, Katarina? Isn't that why Justin died—don't you know what he did—look!"

He grabbed her and shoved her against the window, forcing her to watch the city. Down Sunset Boulevard there were military vehicles and patrols.

"It's only because those stupid idiots are looting, probably a lot of your friends, Stephen."

He was now terrified for Rebecca, his true love he had left so he could pursue nothing. And nothing was in him, as everything relied on God, and God clearly was not here. He looked out the window again. "So...people can come and go."

Just then, the power went out.

"Oh, man," she said, "not again. I'm starting to think another city might be better. New York's so violent now, after the bombings."

Just as quickly the power came on again. Her alarm tripped and she shut it off. "See?" she said. "Everything's returning back to normal. No big thing, you handsome devil."

He walked her to the television set, sat her down on the leather sofa and put on the news channel. She liked this kind of attention from him; it was difficult to contain her smile.

"The replay of the explosion, see, and the picture of Caleb Wilson, a Christian extremist, they call him, right? The incarceration of church pastors across the country, all potential terrorist cells. Don't you think that's a little extreme?"

"That's what you people deserve. You're so filled with hate."

Stephen knelt on the floor in front of the television, and he could see her rolling her eyes in the reflection on the screen. "Dear Heavenly Father, he began, let us see him again, Your angel. In Jesus' name I pray. Amen."

He looked at her with tears in his eyes, "It's a judgment. You killed Justin, who was a key. He gave his life, and then the Angel of the Lord—the Judgment Angel. Or something like that—that's what—"

"What, you're into all this supernatural gobbledy-gook? Who's this angel—I thought it was against your religion to talk to angels?"

"He's an angel of God. He's here to destroy."

"You're insane, Stephen, admit it. You need help. I can help you. Just...look at me more." She offered her vial of white powder. He refused.

"Don't you know they'll kill you? They're everywhere," she said. "This isn't about you and me anymore."

Stephen J. Petchick thought about his mother and wondered what she would think of this situation. *What would Jesus do?* she would ask him. He pondered about the convicts he knew, wondered what Preach thought at this very moment, if God was moving within the prison. But here, nothing was stirring. She kept smiling seductively at him, and he felt he could not compete with her.

"You people are the reason all these earthquakes and insane problems are happening. You hate everything that's good. One big mind trip—all this hysteria. I mean," she lit a cigarette and blew it at him, "you're so funny. This world goes on the way it always has. There are terrorist threats; there is a new Cold War, why? Because of all the Christians in government. They're ruining it, that's why."

Behind him, on the screen, the funeral for the Vice President of the United States. She continued, "They should kill everybody associated with that. I mean, there were top people at the party—Dinko, the designer, Anabelle Frazare, the diplomat to Italy, and Stone Mason, the singer for *Death*. There were really cool artists and, oh, yeah, the head of the museum. Did they all deserve to die? What did they ever do to you?"

He turned to face her: "Vengeance belongs to the Lord."

"Oh, but this is a war."

On the screen was the face of Sergeant Phillip Bauman, accused of being the head of a satanic ring that tortured children. The reporter said, "Sources tell us Sgt. Bauman is part of a right-wing Christian extremist group out of the San Fernando Valley."

"Sick," Stephen declared.

"The real thing is so much better," she said.

He couldn't understand what she was saying, as her words became garbled in his mind.

"You have to be free—let people love you, Stephen, and show them love in return." She tried to unzip his pants and he pulled away. But he was weak, she had beaten him, and she knew it.

"My friends are into loving, not hating," she said. "You want to hate us and the world, and everything about life here? Is that what Jesus told you to do? I thought he told you to love all."

She put on some lipstick, and she removed her red skirt. This time he could not look away. He was roiling in his confusion, weakened by the hypnosis of her words, and her big, innocent-looking eyes. She had her hair the way he liked it, dark brown and cropped around her face. But Rebecca, who was betrothed to him by God, did not deserve abandonment, not now. He had disobeyed everything, and now God was no longer speaking to him in the form of the Holy Spirit. There were no further visions of Casey; there was no vision at all. "Please forgive me, Lord. Please help me. In Jesus' name I pray. Amen."

"He can't hear you. Your God doesn't exit. It's just a big mind game, Stephen, my beautiful boy."

While she seduced him, Casey's face appear on the television screen, though he did not see. He did not see the picture of the beach, with no ocean either. But it was there, a message—but he had turned away.

"I want to help you," she said. "I want to make you whole again. I want to restore your soul, don't you understand?"

He felt the arousal he did not want. He felt her loving hands the way he did not want.

"You can be one of us, Stephen, and all will be forgiven."

He managed to say one last thing in his losing struggle against his own possessed flesh: "By what authority do you speak, Katarina?"

She turned away from him, that question moved her across the room from the sofa he was trapped on. He zipped up his trousers and tucked in his shirt.

She would not look at him. She stared out the window. In the background the broadcaster on the TV said: "US and UN forces are on high alert after a US F-A 18 downed a Russian Mig over Iraq today. In further news, the Louvre in Paris was closed and surrounded by the French army. An extremist Muslim group is threatening to take out all museums of idolatry, as, and I quote, 'most of the art is blasphemous and against God.' Christian spokesman Gerry Archer commented that he was not surprised, since museums have celebrated man's sinfulness and not, as he called it, 'the anointed art' that glorifies God and not man. His comment was denounced as the cause of all the hatred flaring up in the wake of the jet crash last Sunday night. A private jet flew kamikaze style into a private yacht and tragically killed 300 people and 150 crew members. Those dead included the Vice President as well as some of the world's most renowned politicians, artists and international celebrities. Extra security measures have been taken for general transportation purposes in Washington, D.C. as well as in Hollywood, California. Since the market collapse after the suicide jet crash, many of the world's wealthy are on guard. Some left-wing groups are calling for religious extremists to be documented and incarcerated. The President denounced this as hysteria. Now for the weather..."

"Katarina," he said, "don't you see?"

She turned and instead of the face he had seen, it was the face of a stranger, and she hissed in a voice that was not her own. "You vile creature! I hope you die tonight! Get out! Get out!" she screamed. Her skin looked pale green and her eyes glowed; the inside of her mouth was deep red, and her voice was not human. "Who do you think you are, Stephen? Do you really think someone as insignificant as you can bring down our whole society? You idiot, you pervert, you're a disease. Nothing you do or think will ever make a difference. He is powerful, and he protects us, and *we* own the world, not you!"

Her voice was so loud it alerted some pedestrians to stop and look up.

"Not me, but my Lord God—"

"Shut up!" she said, back to her human self. "He's not going to ruin my world now that I'm finally *living* for a change. You're dead and I'm alive. You don't care about people, you'd like the whole world to suffer, wouldn't you?"

"No, Katarina," he said as he made his way to the door, though the pull of guilt gripped him. He would have to make his case, and she would have to listen, wouldn't she? He felt weak and fell back down to the floor, devastated. "It's a judgment. He's perfect and His wrath is perfect," he said.

She laughed, suddenly seductive and beautiful again. "I'm sorry, Stephen, I've been so tired lately. Will you just hold me?"

forty

*P*astor Ted appeared outside the building referred to as the Mission. He went to Big Fred's office in the building adjacent to the new bunkhouse.

"Come in," said Big Fred automatically, and when he looked up, he could see it was the pastor. He immediately asked, "How's your wife and kids?"

Pastor Ted was with three disciples, now co-workers for Christ: Apple, Darnelle, and Bob Orly, the paraplegic on crutches. He had made good on his promise to get them out of the hospital, and they had been sleeping with some friends that he used to know when he pastored the Faith Church.

Ted introduced his three disciples and Fred only saw three more homeless victims of a harsh society. "I understand they're going to rebuild the church—you going back?" Fred asked.

Ted ignored the question, "Apple is a prophet, and he likes to be called Apple, so his name is Apple."

Fred closed his eyes; he was too tired to move.

Darnelle helped Bob Orly into a chair, and she looked around Fred's humble surroundings and smiled at him. "Hi. God is here," she said.

"Praise the Lord," Fred said, seeming much thinner to Ted, which meant he had been working around the clock. "You living at home, Ted?"

"No, Sarah and the kids are there now. We're in touch."

"That'll change. Let's pray right now," said Fred. They all held hands and knelt around Bob Orly, the paraplegic. "Father God, please restore Pastor Ted to his congregation. He's one of yours, Lord—"

"Amen," Apple interrupted.

"Shhh," Darnelle gently nudged him, and he quieted down.

Fred went on: "He's one of Yours, Lord, and this community needs him to be strong, sane, and serving. Place all your best angels around him right now because I too need his help. Restore his reliability and his ministry. When two or more are gathered together in His name, it shall be done. Lord, restore his new friends on the road of faith, service and hope, and return him to his beloved wife, Sarah, and his children. In Jesus' name we pray. Amen."

Apple laughed so hard he fell to the floor and started screaming. Ted picked him up and Fred said, "It's sad there isn't treatment available anymore. But now, with the curfew and government agencies breathing down my neck, I'm limited in what I can do."

"Apple is a prophet," Ted said again.

"Yes," Fred replied. Louis and Fred's wife, Billie, entered the room and surrounded the potential troublemakers. "It's okay," Fred told the new arrivals calmly, "Ted's working the streets now. We should arrange a meeting with his wife soon."

"It's a judgment!" Apple screamed.

"Hey!" ex-brain-surgeon Louis Small said, "don't yell in here."

Billie, Fred's skinny wife, full of fire for Christ, said, "It's okay—they can come with me."

"No, we have to say something," Ted said. "I came back, and I started preaching about regeneration, and I tried to tell you what was going on, but no one listened. So I brought my godchild with me to tell you."

They saw that Ted had not been restored. Not in the least. They saw that Ted was in danger of being thrown out of the Mission, of which they were in charge, and they did not want him to sin or blaspheme his way into total destitution—especially for the sake of the children he was with.

"Speak, Apple. Now you sit down and listen, Fred. My God, you are dense sometimes, brother," Ted said with such insistence that everything froze. As if on cue, the power went out, and the Christian posters advertising various Easter ceremonies around the Los Angeles area were invisible.

"I speak. I speak! You hear?" the young man called Apple asked. He too seemed thinner than in the hospital, Ted thought, but his authority grew years on him that Ted had not seen but took as proof of God's super nature. "I speak," Apple went on, "I speak—that there are angels here, and their names are not those they say, but they are visible and then you forget what you saw. And then the truck drivers are dropping people off and recording everything in the big computer. It's a judgment, it's a judgment...."

Louis and Fred and Billie exchanged terrified looks—their eyes betraying their thoughts. Should we let him go on? Should we send them back to the hospital? Should we find shelter for them? Is there a halfway house that could help?

Apple would not stop, convincing them with his overpowering manifestation of the Holy Spirit, Ted knew. "It's water," Apple continued. "Remnant, remnant—get all to busses and go into mountains. God wants *remnant*...."

"That's what Spruug was talking about," Fred said, puzzled, beginning to be alarmed.

"God killed the boat, and God will kill all here. War will break out, and museums will crumble, because they defile the name of God. Ishmael does some of this, and He uses earth to warn the whole world. The dollar bill that blasphemes the Holy Spirit is gone. Satan will have time to put it all together again, but many will come now because this is God calling in His own. The *lamb* is reversed and Casey's the Angel of God, and you will see big signs because God wants you to get all the busses and evacuate this place because He wants a tear here, a tear there. Many are coming in the busses over the first mountain." Apple fell to the floor in an epileptic seizure. Darnelle helped him, but the missionaries were astonished and afraid because they saw two more in the room, and they did not remember them entering.

Apple got up and continued: "Not the whole earth, *not the whole earth!* I am the law living in the word! The whole world is warned! A judgment, *a judgment*, understand? Do you understand?"

"I do, son," said Ted, tears streaming down his face.

"NO, I understand, I understand," Apple went on. "You, why are you non-believers! Why don't you believe that God is supernatural? Why don't you see all the angels? They make me fall down and I get up. Look at them, look at them, look at them—look, look, look!"

Apple was smiling at them all. Rebecca was smiling through tears as she watched them too.

Then Fred said: "My God, my God, I see them—*I see somethin'!*"

"This is crazy, this is nuts!" Louis said.

Billie ran out of the room, and Fred followed her.

 • • •

Stephen J. Petchick stood on what used to be the Sunset Strip in Hollywood; it was now was a riot zone, full of broken windows, and roving bands of kids who would scatter every time a police truck came down the road. He didn't have to wait long. A nondescript van pulled up and a young blond man, who was very slight, got out and handed him a yellow slip of paper with writing on it, then got back in the van.

Stephen knew that Katarina had set him up, it was obvious. When he read the note, he quickly understood that it was not evil. But the van had gone and he needed friends right now. He had left Rebecca and Katarina had finished with him. Casey had been real, though Stephen did not know his true name. He knew it could not be lowly, since he had never known an angelic being, but now he wondered if Casey was some sort of plant.

He looked at the note the man gave him, and it said: "For this angel is the highest, and he makes the way for the Lord."

Whether this note could be true or not was beyond him. He was no scholar, he was a sinner, a lowly car thief and mechanic, who knew nothing until he read the rest of the note. He had diminished into weakness, sitting at the bus stop while the police rousted others, but left him alone. The rest of the note said, "We are many. You have seen the truth for God's purpose. He is disguised in flesh. He belongs to God."

"Oh, my Father, forgive me—I am a stupid man!" Stephen cried out as chills went up and through him. "It's real! My God is real!" he yelled at the police, who ignored him from their trucks, from their patrol cars, "My God is real!" he yelled to troops patrolling on foot, but no one paid attention to him.

A man in a dark coat stood at the signal, and his outline in the sun was shimmering. He smiled mightily at Stephen, then he was sitting on the bench with Stephen, but Stephen had not seen him move toward him. Stephen would not look at him, with his head in his hands, he was trembling, crying and shaking his head. He could see up and down the boulevard. The sky was orange and the earth reeked of sewage.

"Come, son, let me care for you now," the being said.

Stephen reclined into the arms of something he did not understand. "When God moves, we all move with Him. We have been with you forever and will never leave. I love you, Stephen J. Petchick," the being said in a voice that changed with each word, so that there were many sounds, but one language—a being with many voices but one word, made of shimmering light but not visible to anyone except Stephen.

"I've let you down," Stephen said. "I left the woman you provided me. Forgive me, my Lord."

He felt himself yanked to sit up, and the glowing man said, "I am your brother."

"Are you evil?" was all Stephen could manage to say.

"No, Stephen, I am not evil, but now is the time for such things. A man such as you is chosen for this time, in this place, and now is your time to prove your faith to the Lord God, who is, and was, and will be forevermore. Hold my hand and we shall pray the prayer."

Stephen held a hand that did not feel like skin, nor was it hot or cold. He had no reference for what it was.

"Dear Heavenly Father, we thank you for the time to bring your will to the earth again. I pray for my earthly brother, Stephen J. Petchick, a worthy son who has served our Lord Christ Jesus nobly, and I beckon you for his crown in heaven. Please let him see us without fear; please allow him to serve without confusion, for many souls are at stake and he does not see who he is and what he is, as we do. We thank you, Heavenly Father, for this glorious time to exact Your perfect justice, Your perfect love, and Your perfect beneficence on this earth, as our leader, Your Angel, is in the midst of the ocean of eternity, against the one who shone above us all, who fell to perdition and sin and now seeks to destroy all. Deliver us, Oh Father, in this day before Your Son's glorious ascension. We thank you for everything, and I thank you for my fellowship with my fellow servant, Stephen John Petchick, whose mother we have welcomed into the heavenly place, which to Stephen is close and far. I beseech You to deliver him from confusion, and make plain that he has seen the evil one in the flesh, and he walked many miles with her. Please let him know that we cheered him when he won! Hallelujah! We praise You, Lord."

Stephen joined in, "Praise you, Lord. We thank you, Jesus. How I love you, my Christ."

"And we humbly ask for Your blessing. In the Lord's name we pray...Amen."

"Amen. Amen, brother," Stephen said and hugged the being. Stephen felt the being did not quite occupy the clothing he was wearing.

"You know what I am," he said.

"Here, eat," the angel said.

The angel gave Stephen some globular objects of a beige color to eat, which had a sweet taste, and yet it was something he had never tasted. When he looked at the face of the man he now believed was an angel, his face had changed. His skin was brown and shimmered, and then it would become as white as snow. Then it was black, like a silhouette, and his eyes were blue and purple, yellow and red and orange. Then he looked like Stephen's best friend from prison, Preach.

It was Preach!

He cried and the angel stopped him and said, "I can't show you myself, or you would not see me."

When the angel stood, he was covered with white raiment, the robes that Stephen had read about, and his face was a light-source, and he was beautiful. He did not have wings, and he did not stand on the ground, but above it. Even though Stephen was conversing with this being, neither the crowd of pedestrians, nor the military troops, nor the police saw him.

"Come with me," he said. Stephen took a step. "Hold onto my hand," he said.

The light around the angel was so bright Stephen could not see, but he felt himself rise into the light. A light that cast no reflection or shadow as Stephen twisted up with his friend, whom he did not know, higher and higher.

• • •

Apple continued, "I am the voice, He's using me as the voice, God is the voice in me now. I talk to you and you listen!"

"Go ahead son," said Ted, as Fred and Louis and Rebecca tearfully watched the floating balls of light in the room.

Apple said: "I have appointed My servant, My Angel, as prince and chief to conduct my warning. For he knows everything about them, he knows the science of the celestials and the terrestrials, and I instruct him," Apple fell to the floor with another debilitating seizure. He screamed and Rebecca comforted him, while Darnelle and Bob Orly, who walked into the light, stood motionless and confused and afraid.

The one named Daniel stood in the corner. Pastor Ted introduced him, "This is my gardener at the church."

"Oh, praise God!" Fred exclaimed and fell to his face in prayer. Louis joined him and then all were on their faces in the tiny office that magically expanded several times its size to accommodate all the glorious appearances.

Daniel was now a bright light, and no one could see his silhouette. "It's time to take your Mission away from the city," he told them.

Then they could see him, a humble old homeless man with a long beard and a thick mane of gray hair, wearing blue jeans and a blue jean shirt. "We need to transport them out to a safe place. The call went out and the Holy Spirit guides us."

Louis and Fred could not look at each other, nor could they look at the one called Daniel, who was not the prophet Daniel from the Bible.

"So, what is your name?" Ted asked.

"I am one who serves and I can't tell you my name. None of us will. Understand—the wall is down, but it goes back up. You will tell no one of what you have seen, and even if you do, they won't remember, even if they have seen."

"Why?" asked Fred. "Why can't we have a miracle from the living God whom we serve with our hearts and minds?"

"Because you are human, because it is God's will. The wall of separation only comes down when God moves, then we seal up all the memories, and no one knows."

"So why the name Daniel?" Ted asked.

"Your officer who is now in jail called me that."

"Did Bauman do what they said on the news?"

"No," Daniel answered. "They lied. The enemy has never been more evil, and that is why this place will be no more."

"What about all the good people?" Fred asked. "Is God going to kill everyone?"

"Those in Christ will be home, those who are wicked will die, and those in the remnant will be the remnant, and the warning will be heard in hell as it also is in heaven. They will be awakened by him who was hidden in flesh, the Angel of the Lord, and many who were lost will come to Christ. Many who were worshiping the False One because of his cleverness will come—and those in power will be made as dust."

Fred was outraged. "This is the City of Angels. Why would God destroy all—"

"Why war, why floods? He is calling home His own now. This is a warning, a judgment that is righteous and true and borne of love, not hate.

"How many are going to die, Daniel?" Louis asked.

"More if you don't start getting them on busses and shipping them out."

"We don't have busses! We don't have the means. The power's out, lucky we have our generator, but we—"

A rumbling sound suddenly shook the walls and they all ran out. Bob Orly hobbled out on crutches, even though he had walked for a brief moment. They saw a line of school busses and tour busses arriving, with Stephen J. Petchick in the first tour bus. Others parked behind him, but there were no drivers.

Stephen got out and Rebecca fell onto him. "I know, I know," she told him.

Fred looked at all he was responsible for, all the reasons he could not fail. He could not stumble now. He knew something in that moment beyond his faith. His faith had to be stretched now, beyond any bounds he had ever imagined. He knew God was merciful and answered prayers. Believe, his still small voice was saying.

Yes was all he could answer in his mind.

forty-one

*T*he conference on World Religions was held in Bermuda. Every major figure from Buddhism, Hinduism, Jainism, Sikhism and about every *ism* imaginable, leaders from the coalition for Environmental Understanding, from the primitive culture religions and pagan religions such as Wicca, and leaders of the so-called secret societies such as Rosicrucians, Knights Templar and Freemasons were in attendance.

The idea was to conference about the escalating Cold War between the United States, China and Russia. The idea was to end terrorism once and for all, to end the population explosion before the resources ran out, to fellowship about global warming and sharing resources. One of the teachers was talked about as Christ-like, and he spoke of sharing the resources. He spoke of love and kindness and compassion and unity. Arles had seen him before, the man with the turban who seemed to *disappear through a wall.* When he spoke to the crowd, he said things like "verily," as Jesus had, and he was taken seriously.

Three groups were missing from this *coterie d'apologia*—Christians, Jews and Muslims in official capacities. Some were there as representatives, but mainly, this gathering was to be an association of the more agreeable religions, the tolerant traditions, the non-violent traditions, as this conference was, if anything, a conference for peace and global unity.

There were men of the cloth and they were welcomed, as all traditions and faiths were welcome. Many different speakers were gathered and the themes were always about being more loving and tolerant of all people, not simply labeling behaviors or traditions as sinful or wrong in the eyes of God. The consensus was that God loves all people, even though some traditions did not believe in a God, per se, but all believed it was man's responsibility to save the earth and bring peace.

There were conferences, seminars and lunches, dinners and world music celebrations. A document was signed by nearly all the religious leaders involving equitable distribution of the world's resources, and financial help to small countries who could not repay the massive debts they had accumulated to the large nations of the world, namely the United States. Bankers and politicians graced the scene, and they spoke of sustainable development and the United Nations peace initiatives.

There were games and volleyball competition and friendly exchange—it seemed a truly spiritual event, full of love and peace. The most celebrated man of all was the head of what was to be a new world religion of sorts. Several leaders of various traditions had signed a document for global spirituality whereby the best aspects of each tradition were stressed and combined, such as the belief that God dwelled inside all people. Human values were stressed and improvements in the quality of life were to be made. The conference proclaimed that this new religion would help to unify the globe. It was to be an understanding that all people were God's children, and all people needed to come together in love, and not hate, in order to solve the world's problems. To this end, Jesus, Gautama Buddha, and Gandhi, Martin Luther King, the Dalai Lama, and others were quoted and celebrated.

Some thought the man who embodied all these ideas and who organized the conference was an avatar, or God dwelling in a man on earth. He was revealed to be the major force in ending world hunger, strife and economic deprivation. His name, *Sunyasin*, was not a name at all, but meant *renuncient* in Sanskrit; he had renounced all worldly goods and gain and dedicated himself to God, and through obvious compassion was now dedicated to healing the planet. When he spoke, the wind whistled through the palms on the Bermuda shore, and suddenly the sea became bold and started lapping at the shore. Some were afraid. But soon, the sun shone directly on him and nowhere else. Some who had visited his website claimed to have seen visions of him in their hotel rooms, and some saw him walking on the water. He was from India and his background escaped many of the reporters. He had just popped up on the scene, and he healed several little children whose parents had brought them—one with cancer, the other a victim of polio. All were not only healed but restored. Word of this healing spread throughout the island. He had handlers and security around him, but he did not hide behind bulletproof glass.

His last speech was met with several bowing down in worship, tears and shouts of praise, and these responses came from well-to-do professionals, who were usually conservative and careful in their proclamations, like diplomats, or politicians, and especially the clergy from the various traditions, including Christianity.

Some said, "Christ has returned!"

Another said, "He is the Christ. Truly, he is."

It was said in every language, and then hushed. But all were amazed because each seemed to have a personal relationship with him, the new world teacher.

His last speech opened with a prayer. He stroked his beard and smiled. The crowd cheered. He looked them all over, adjusted his turban and held his hands out, as if to receive God's blessing. He proclaimed: "The lord god blesses you, all of you. As god dwells in me, I give to you my blessings, and each of you I know by name. Not the name you were given by your parents, but the name god knows you as. This is a time of peace, may you love each other, and more abundantly. Verily I say to you, the economic collapse that has just occurred is a blessing—as we will rebuild the world based on fairness and sharing of all things." He continued to the enraptured crowd, and many of the Hollywood dignitaries and celebrity musicians were weeping for joy.

As he continued to outline a prayer for the world, in a form that seemed to speak to each one, and not just the group, a man in a priest's collar appeared at the side of the stage. He was at first hidden from the crowd behind a large PA speaker. Then he moved toward the man called Sunyasin. Several thousand who were on the beach, sitting in the sand, or standing or sitting on beach chairs, saw the priest, who looked out of place, banal compared to the holy men in their white robes, long beards and turbans that surrounded the Holy One, Sunyasin.

Some surmised that he was a local priest because he was a black man, but others thought he was just out of place. A woman singer laughed and said, "Preacher, give it up—this is the real thing!"

The priest smiled and waved. Sunyasin acknowledged him with

a nod because he was standing inappropriately on the stage. Yet the security guards did not remove him. "Welcome, my son," Sunyasin said. "I give you my blessing, god sends his blessing. May we all love one another and tap the true god in us all."

To that he smiled and waved at the crowd—it now looked like part of the routine of bringing unity where there was separation, to bring a Christian preacher together with a Hindu or tribal tradition. Sunyasin went over to him and gave him a hug, as he had a portable mike, so that he could continue speaking: "My Brother, you are most welcome. Come, let us stand together." Sunyasin put his hands in the air and welcomed the spirit moving "in us all."

The famous singers and politicians did not see what he was doing—they could not see the minister's eyes behind the dark glasses and they could not see his face due to the neat-cropped beard.

They did see the shiny object as Sunyasin said: "It does not have to be a time of famine, of lack, of pain and suffering. We do not have to be shackled by the bonds of old things. Love whom you love, who brings god out from inside you. Put away jealousy and animalism. Share each other as you share your wealth. This is not the age of materialism, but spiritualism. I bring you a new covenant, one of—"

BANG!

Confusion struck, two security guards grabbed the priest, as Sunyasin fell to the stage. Blood hosed the crowd momentarily from the bullet hole in his forehead. Reporters thronged in with cameras to catch him bleeding.

The crowd, crying and angry, became despondent and had to be subdued.

They wrested the gun from the priest and took him to the local police station where he was accused of killing Sunyasin, the speaker who announced the new world religion.

He was quickly transferred into the hands of American intelligence operatives, or so it seemed. He was an American, and the reporters were given this story:

CHRISTIAN PRIEST shoots and kills Sunyasin, claims him to be the antichrist

Immediately, the conference was shut down. Word went out about the intolerance displayed by Christians—on the Internet and the airwaves. As Arles removed his false beard and glasses and hairpiece, he was gratified that he had done as Arthur had asked, and now would look forward to Sunday's ceremony in Egypt.

He was to be flown to France, where Casey Smith was being "prepared."

Arles' new girlfriend, Gwendolyn, met him for drinks and spoke about her eldest son, and he knew that her husband had been the pastor of the church Arles had been initiated in, which burnt to the ground. He had met her at his initiation, had made love to her in a ritualistic fashion, and now would be wed, all according to plan. She was younger than his deceased wife, and her son had already been sent to the proper boarding school for re-training. There was no jealousy, and she would support his every lust, his every desire. She would aid him in obtaining everything he desired, and was happy when he would turn to her, but the trip to France would be without her. She would wait in Washington, D.C., in the mansion that he had called home, where he was seen not as a warrior, but as a lobbyist for certain causes of a corporate nature.

• • •

Casey had baffled them all, as they watched him in seclusion, not moving, not sleeping, not anxious. He was given luxurious food, and offered every kind of indulgence. Arthur Reddick was very much looking forward to spending quality time with the one who would *renew the blood*, and hence their ruling power over earth.

Arthur had appeared to Casey as a young man, then as a creature of light, and then with reptilian scales—but no matter, Casey always met him with respect. "Mr. Reddick, you are what you are. Even if you were cast out forever, you should know that you will not prevail," Casey said.

"Mr. Smith, young man, please indulge me. I am trying to dissuade you, in your last minute, as it were, on earth, from believing the lie of Jesus Christ," he said. "If you renounce Him, and do what we ask, you may live."

With that Casey stood, meekly. "I forgive you. I serve my Lord, the Christ. Praise God, for we will celebrate his ascension and victory over you and your kind!"

"But you can't believe that," Arthur said. "Look, He's not helping you right now, is He?"

"You have no idea," Casey said with a smile.

"So is this what putting on Christ is all about? Letting us kill you?"

"You won't kill me. You know, Mr. Reddick, I am not allowed to tell you anymore—you have had your chance. You saw me, you got a glimpse. I told you what I was, and you do not understand—you still think that you have some power over God, and that is amusing."

"You are confident," said Arthur, "they said you were confident. Because you're young, you were hurt, you lost a brother, I understand... You blamed yourself and you went into denial. You thought you were something special, that God had chosen you for something, indeed, that you were not really even human."

"Correct, but I did not lose a brother—thank the Lord God who took him before they destroyed his life."

"So hateful, aren't you?"

"No, sir. Even with all the powers you've amassed by magic and manipulation, I scare you."

Arthur was amazed that this adolescent could know what he was thinking. He certainly did not know what Casey was thinking. He had a block. He had never had a block before, not in business, not in knowing the mind of the earth, not in any door of the flesh he had ever wanted to enter, not since his last initiation into the galactic, not since living on the soul-energy of the multitudes sacrificed on the altar and in the field.

"But really, it's the soul, you're after, isn't it? The Brotherhood lives on the moon, and you make a big white tunnel of light for all the dead to find their loved ones. It feels warm and cozy and they go into the white tunnel of light willingly, truly lambs to the slaughter. Because then you steal their souls and use the life-force to animate your forms, your ships and your lives," Casey said while lying on his bunk and throwing a rubber ball monotonously toward the ceiling.

Arthur said to Arles, "You must get him to renounce Christ before tonight or you're finished here. The Ritual cannot be complete unless he renounces Christ. We tried to bribe him with the idea that he would live if he did so, but he outsmarted us. He is trouble, and the sooner this mission is accomplished, the better for all of us, indeed, for the whole earth," Arthur said.

It was a threat, and Arles had never before been threatened by Arthur. Even though he knew it was a set up, and that the world outside the remote and bucolic chateau had decidedly fallen into darkness, he had never heard desperation in Arthur's voice. They had been working on Casey non-stop for a couple of weeks, and Casey continued to tell his tormentors what *they* were thinking or doing, Yet neither Arthur or Arles had seen any supernatural activity to explain Casey's powers. Nothing they did to him, even misbegotten attempts to molest him through seduction, corrupted him. Arles did not understand why they just didn't force the boy sexually, but one of the Brotherhood's rules stated it had to be of the child's own free will.

Everyone at the chateau was ready for the helicopter transport to a nearby church near the tomb of Charlemagne, who, Arles was told, was the purest link to the bloodline of Jesus. Arthur told Arles to be a soldier and not ask too many questions, because he was not yet one of them.

"Arles, you could be one of us," Arthur told him, "it's simple genetics. When this is finished, and the world agrees to our global order in exchange for peace and prosperity, you will be given that chance. It's not bloodlines; it's genetics, just as the grail, the blood of Christ, is spiritual—a spirit-line, not a bloodline." Sipping a 200-year-old Bordeaux with enthusiasm as he and Arles sat on a park bench watching several small children happily playing with make-shift swords, Arthur added his bombshell, *"We make the blood."*

• • •

"I see him! I see him!" exclaimed Stephen, while loading up supplies into the first bus. He saw other beings with Casey, who no longer resembled Casey at all, but was a glorious being of light with a face of fire—pointing to the ocean with one hand and to heaven with the other. He saw the wave in the distance, and the angel he had seen before was looking at Stephen, and he said: "This is the judgment of the Living God on the world. This is a warning."

The question arose again: "Do you have to kill them all? Even the good?"

There was no answer, but Stephen knew the role angels played in the world—they would carry out the judgments of God on men.

He knew that God's judgment was always perfect, even though he could not always understand. Such a small remnant, he thought, but his friend whom he did not know, said, "There are many others who have an ear, and many who are called home to be with the Lord, and they shall not see pain. But those who had stiffened their necks and those who will stand aghast at God's judgment will wish for death but it will not come, and those who wish for more life, will only find death. You have had many warnings, human son. They have had their chances."

He watched as the sun moved in front of the bright light in the sky, and he saw that those loading the busses were seeing the light in the sky as well.

"Tell no one what you have seen, brother," the angel said.

Stephen did not feel afraid, for there was another with a message who passed in a van. This was a man in tennis shoes and a golf shirt, very clean cut with piercing dark eyes and a youthful countenance, a glorious smile and an innocence that was pleasing and attractive. He said nothing, handing the note to Stephen, which read: "You shall marry."

He knew that getting married to Rebecca was too much of a rush, but the circumstances warranted that things be put in order, and quickly. He admired her, and he thanked God for every moment of his life. Everything about her attracted him, the way she moved, the way she laughed with the children, the way she gave herself so completely to the Lord. He watched her memories fade away, and he watched the peace well up from deep within. He knew she had had the baptism of the Holy Spirit, and that she was saved immediately.

She knew herself as Rebecca and never spoke about her previous life. She said she had given it all to Him and had repented for a misspent life. Since she was broken beyond repair, she not only fell in submission to the Lord but completely gave her will to him. Only someone who is truly in Christ would understand this, he thought. He thanked the Lord again for the chance to fellowship and minister to so many the Lord wanted.

They loaded a couple of thousand people in busses, and he was told that others were also packing up and moving. No one questioned the need to evacuate, as if it had been planned for months! This changing of the total reality, the true miracle-working of God, was something Stephen could see, but others could not. The angel told Stephen he was to be God's witness, and was to shepherd the flock along with Pastor Ted, Pastor Fred, Pastor Louis, and Spruug, who might become an elder of the new church on the mountain.

"The world blames us for everything," Fred said. "The city is dark, and we have a retreat in the mountains." Suddenly it was all Fred's idea that the busses had been ordered, and no one spoke of angels or miracles. Even Rebecca was working with the children as if this had always been her job!

Stephen wondered why he had the memory of the supernatural, of seeing the brightest lights and the heavenly spirits. Of seeing the planets and stars whizzing by while traveling in some sort of vehicle that emitted white light, of walking in a place where he could see glowing beings communicating without talking? Of walking through a door and into another realm where Casey was sitting and telling him that he was to carry out the judgment? Of disappearing from Katarina's apartment without exiting the door? He realized he was to be God's witness of the supernatural, and that events like this occurred from time to time, without the world being aware. The world did not remember because reality was altered in its totality.

He understood immediately, however, how God used Stephen's talent of hot-wiring the busses. He repented and was pulled up by the angel he had seen and told, "Please do not repent for your actions."

Spruug had reconciled with his family and they were to set out on Easter Sunday for the unknown. They were assured that because of a benefactor, there was money, and there was a job waiting to raise money for the new church to be relocated in the mission retreat in the mountains above the city.

The next quake occurred at 3:00 P.M. exactly, a big one of at least 7.2. The city continued to be dark. Those on the busses feared that a line of cars already leaving the city would prevent them from using the highways, that the overpasses might have collapsed preventing their escape, or that the city, under marshal law, would be sealed off.

They boarded the busses for a night jaunt to the mountain retreat, which Fred had not seen but had been presented by a benefactor, or so he remembered. The map was clear—it was a Christian retreat that everybody now seemed to suddenly know about. Fred had a letter, which he claimed to have had for awhile now, inviting all of them to a feast and describing living facilities, which would be available for those traveling on the twenty busses.

"Twenty busses! We need a thousand busses!" exclaimed John the Apostle, who said he did not want to go.

There could be no more broken glass than there already was, and the next aftershock only drew cheers. There were more supplies and people to load up. When they finished, they took a single file approach to the freeway, which was clear for them, and they could move toward their intended direction. Sitting in their bus seats, all of them were excited to be getting out. Oddly, it was as if none of them had a memory of who they were, what they had been doing before, or history itself. Pastor Ted would catch himself and say, "Wait a second. How is all this happening? Why are we doing this?"

They had no idea that their destination would be temporary, and that they would have to move on again. Pastor Ted was reconciled with his wife and daughters, who were excited because he would be one of the pastors at their new home. Even though they didn't remember it, Pastor Ted's family had no home to return to—it was just a hull with no power and full of broken belongings.

Little Beth said: "If we stay here, we'll die."

"How do you know that, honey?" he asked her.

Sarah stood by, fighting back tears, consoled by Carole, who, like her younger sister, was excited to be going on a trip.

Beth answered her father: "I know that because He told me that." And she pointed towards the sky.

Bauman walked out. So did about two thousand other prisoners. The county lock-up building collapsed with the quake, and the guards had all gone to be with their families. Each and every criminal that Bauman saw he warned to go with God, to believe in Christ, that it is only through Christ that a person can come to the Lord and receive another chance, a new life. "Say, Julio!" Bauman said to his cellmate. "Vaya con Dios, eh?"

"Thank you, my friend," Julio answered.

"Why don't you help me solve the case I'm working on?" Bauman asked.

Julio stopped, thought about it, and surprised Bauman when he said, "Sure man, I got nuthin' else to do, homes. I'm down with you, man—down with Jesus too, man."

They walked and they "borrowed" a vehicle for police purposes, Bauman insisted, and they headed out.

Bauman found Shep and John the Apostle, re-recruited them,

and they agreed to stay on to solve the case. "I have some extra help here. Julio, meet John the Apostle and Shep, my boys."

"Hey, whassup, man?" Julio said.

"Now you boys go back and get on the bus. I've got all the help I need."

"We don't want to go—it's not for us. We want to help too."

"Okay with you, Julio?"

John the Apostle said, "So what happened in jail?"

"God let me out," Bauman replied.

"Me too man, and I don't even deserve it," said Julio.

"You will," Bauman said, in a more serious tone. He tucked his County shirt in and said, "We need some clothes."

"The police are everywhere, man, but I can arrange it," Julio said.

John the Apostle said: "This isn't the end, you know, it's the beginning of the end."

"How do you know that?" asked an angry Bauman.

"Because he knows things like that, Bauman," replied Shep defensively.

"Okay, alright," Bauman said.

"Look, we would have come to see you, but—things, well look at everything—it's crumbling every second," said Shep, and John the Apostle placed his hand over him, comforting him.

John said: "May the Lord bless you and keep you; the Lord make his face to shine upon you, and be gracious to you; the Lord lift up His countenance upon you, and give you peace...that goes for all of us. In Jesus' name. Amen. That's what the priest said to my mother when she was dying. And I liked it."

"Whoa, that was some heavy prayer, man," Julio said. "It was like, beautiful."

"You will deserve it, Julio," Bauman said assuredly.

"Look at them all—too many," said Shep, tears in his eyes.

"I'd rather be back in County, man. It's like Hell on earth out here with no power, no food, the military—I think this is real trouble."

"Just starting. It will never get better, unless you're in Christ."

"How do I do it?" asked Julio. "Just like say a Hail Mary a few thousand times or what?"

"John, tell Julio that he can't be saved unless Jesus wants him to be."

"That's a very hostile way to put it, boss," said John the Apostle.

"Yeah, well you're John A, from now on."

That quieted him down, for he only wanted to be called John the Apostle—anything else was an insult.

Bauman felt bad, but drove on anyway, because The Voice was telling him more about the case. "Oh, wow, the mayor even knows about it!" he blurted out, as if reporting from the scene.

• • •

Dear Mr. Parker:

Another communication has arrived. I was grateful to receive it, for it was an answer to my prayers. It pertains to prophecy and *coding*, which is a glimpse into the mind of God. This letter comes from someone who claims to know an angel, whom he does not identify.

I will tell you now, I am afraid, not for my life, as I am old and have had a life dedicated to Christ since my conversion in prison twenty-five years ago. This letter, which is from a reliable source, has become evidentiary to my own research and prayer. Now it appears that God's judgment or warning is a reaction to the growing presence on earth of what the author of the letter refers to as the reptiles or serpents, and the *Watchers*. These are two distinct groups of fallen angels: those cast out of heaven forever, and those who have access to the Throne of God, such as the greatest angel of all, Lucifer. *The Watchers*, as the *Book of Enoch* apparently referred to them, are beautiful creatures. They still have an angelic appearance though they are fallen, and they took human women as wives, as shown in the Book of Genesis, Chapter 6. They are angels who sinned and created an offspring known in the Bible as *nephilim*, the principal reason for the flood of Noah's day. The other group, the serpents or reptiles, belong to Lucifer; they are his angels and have become reptiles, as described in Genesis. The letter tells me that these two groups also make war with each other, though I cannot verify any of this. The Watchers and Nephilim appear holy, sensual, and beautiful; they are connected to the so-called *ascended masters* and are the chief architects of the New Age movement on earth, and also the authors of the Hindu Vedas. The other race appears as they are: demonic, reptilian. Both are spiritualized, that is, have control over matter. Both use space travel and apparently tell humans that they are from other planets and are interested in peace on earth.

He has sought to fill me in, though I have to admit as I write this to you, I am not sure any of my efforts will be in time, as we are months beyond the transformation of that one lamb I told you about. My friend, you will see and sense the *code*, which means things that come to your attention. What you see on television, glimpses of magazines you read or conversations you overhear, and visions in dreams. It simply means you are keyed into a frequency where God is communicating through material forms. The ultimate code is the Bible, which means it is true for all times and in all seasons.

I want you to know how grateful I am to you. You have kept me hidden for a time and sponsored me; even this communication has become part of the last warning, as I now know it to be called the Wave of Iniquity, the Wave of Judgment and the Wave of Perdition.

From here on, dear Publisher, the truth regarding the lie is divulged, and I am sorry it has come so late, though I am gratified that our God is a great God. How happy I am to learn that He is sovereign *always*. Even though my faith has been tested, as of late, He has proved Himself again, though this writer does not need further proof.

My contact divulged to me that his people are worried, because the *clock* had started again last July. It was as if the opening salvo of the terrorist strike against Sorenson's ship and the killing of the Vice President of the United States had put them on alert, but the collapse of the stock market and the currency, the growth of unemployment rolls, the global

riots in the streets, and nuclear terrorism has un-
raveled all their global plans. They had almost com-
pleted their task of unifying the world—they almost prevailed, as they almost always do—and then
something happened.

A lamb, a little lamb, could bring down an entire
empire. In other words, God is on the side of innocence. Someone got away, I am told, and this caused
what we might call a chain reaction involving the
whole world. With all their efforts at monitoring
every conversation, every deed, every tax return,
documenting every single child, promoting every
work of art, or movie, or symphony, or regulating
traffic, social security numbers, satellite surveillance—they felt they had achieved omniscience. Every human endeavor had been regulated by them, *belonged* to them. Yet they failed.

The programming that Arthur Reddick instituted
over all children in the Western educational system was based on secrecy and fragmentation of the
child's personality, and then of course, discredit-
ing anyone whose programming had worn off, been
compromised, or broken through. Kincaid was instrumental in all of this, and somehow, within his own
house, bred the traitor of traitors in his son. This
led to the uncovering of his son, Justin, as a lamb,
as a lamb without recourse, as a time bomb against
the realm—because he knew, and then rejected, his
high societal calling. He knew the truth, was indoctrinated, and then turned to God, and Daniel's clock
began to tick. Why *him* you may ask? He was the only
one, and he was fully human. There is apparently some
agreement between God and Lucifer as to the conditions for God to move in a mighty, wrathful way. No
one had been in Justin's position for over one thousand years. The prophet told me: "Then God was free
to exercise His wrath."

He would not tell me who he was, except that God
told him that I was His scribe and that one would come
to my house, as he did through a letter, of which I
cannot divulge the contents, under the terms of our

agreement. But I can tell you this: he proved to me that he was not of this earth. He would not tell me who he was. He was gracious enough to tell me about the greatest disaster which will ever befall the satanic realm, except for being removed forever from heaven and the judgment written in the Book of Revelation, where Satan and his minions—including the Nephilim and the Watchers—are cast forever into the lake of fire and brimstone (which to me means a world cut-off from God forever and ever).

Here is the next secret, which the world does not know. The secret is *not* in the bloodlines, as so many have surmised. The secret is *not* in the soul, as so many have misappropriated and thus stolen to the realm of the dead prematurely, so that the demon or fallen angel—or *serpent being*—could possess the human and operate as if under mind control. The secret is *not* mind control. As you will see, Mr. Parker, there is no such thing as mind control, there is soul-exchange, and it has always been like that.

Here is their big secret: *harvesting innocence*, those deemed God's own. It goes like this: they are violated sexually, violently, and sometimes through supplication of the body, which is *not* to Lucifer, or in praise of Lucifer, as the uninitiated believe, but in *trans-substantiational holography*, where time (T) is frozen. What is substituted is *their* time, and so by this method, using off-world science, they believe that they postpone the last days and God's judgments, as per Lucifer's agreement to have "a little time" to operate on earth. A loophole, Mr. Parker, in time. That is their big secret.

The being then told me that they were wrong, that they had made a mistake, an error in their science. That mistake gave rise to another loophole in favor of God—if one of His returned, if one of His—sanctified and separated—survived, one who had been indoctrinated, then God was free to move. Then time not only began again, *it became as if it would have always been had no agreement ever been in place.*

That is why the end-time prophecy will now occur quickly, but not before a terrible judgment on the earth, which is a warning to all peoples and nations. And believe me, everything I told you will occur, as stated.

Thank you for helping me during the editing process. As I believe, Mr. Parker, you are part of this process. Thank you, also, for the supplies.

God bless you.

Mountain

forty-two

*I*t was scheduled for Sunday night. Casey had been transported to Egypt and was incarcerated in an underground chamber beneath the pyramid at Giza. Arthur knew this was their last chance to again sustain the earth, which had been in a state of suspended time for two thousand years. No one was to know the key to the mystery of the pyramids, which had always been used for *sacrificial death*.

The Brotherhood was not surprised that Casey knew everything; they were not surprised when he said: "Repent and come to Christ, before you do yourself and a lot of people harm. God's judgment will pour out on the whole earth, *because of what you do now.*"

They believed just the opposite would occur.

Casey stopped short of saying who he was, that he, as an angel, *would execute that judgment*.

When the appointed hour approached, Casey was strapped upside down to a cross resembling the crucifixion cross of Christ.

Arles lied to Arthur that Casey had renounced Christ. No one could get a word out of Casey, from the time he was incarcerated at Charlemagne's tomb. Five hundred seers verified that he was a lamb of God, an innocent of Jesus, related through his unique spirit, and therefore he was the only one on earth. Not bloodlines, but spirit-lines. Casey Smith was, according to their visionaries, the only one presently on earth who could fulfill the *non-Resurrection, the non-covenant, the undoing event*—the holographic ceasing of time. Not in earth terms, in *spirit* terms.

The auditorium under the pyramid was accessible from Cairo by underground tram from Cairo, which was vacuum driven. Every month there were offerings, as the Brotherhood liked to call them. Arthur knew they were not offerings at all, but transmogrifications to mark time, genetic manipulation of God's ideal, to be one with the Grail, the Blood of Christ. The great pyramid was indeed their clock, built by the Watchers. By altering the paradigmatic universe, the physical universe would alter itself without detection by the human populace, the hosts for the takeover and implementation of the galactic order, which is based on harvesting souls and selling them to various enterprises so that demonic beings could continue to live. Arthur Reddick was the perfect example of the Brotherhood's idea of immortality. Arthur would say, "This world, of course, is inferior to the *real* thing, but the real thing is denied to us forever. So we make the best of what we've got, until we can find a way to make it seamless."

Arles was dressed in traditional black for the ceremony; he and everyone else would wear an ankh, the universal symbol of Satan, around their necks. The pyramid at Giza, like all pyramids, was used for special ceremonies involving space, time and the afterlife. The elite would be in the special chamber, adorned with walls of crystal backed with pure gold. The Altar of Eternity was placed underneath a machine that would literally change its dimensions with proper ritual. Just as most of the devotees were able to access other dimensional realms, which Arles had been shown, the reversal of the blood of Christ could only be taken once every thousand years. Every intelligence operative, both off-world and on the earth, had verified that Casey was the one. Arles took his seat amidst dignitaries from across the globe. He had truly arrived, for this was the highest inner-circle on earth. This was the *inner sanctum*.

Casey had smiled when he told Arles on the plane that he was looking forward to eternity. Arles hid the secret that Casey had *never* renounced Christ, but since Casey hadn't spoken, Arles simply assumed early on that it was not necessary for Casey to do so.

"Arles Dubailles," Casey proclaimed, "you and your kind will perish, as there was One before me, and now the seal will be broken and He will return. He will come as a Conqueror, no longer a lamb, a mystery you cannot possibly understand."

Arles gagged Casey so that he could no longer utter a sound, and felt great pleasure as Casey was attached to the cross upside down, which was enhanced when the music swelled and the lights dimmed. Urns for his blood hung under his feet and hands. The ceiling was vaulted, and Arles thought he could see faces or beings floating around. He thought he could see scaly faces under the hoods of those draped in black robes; they were the reptiles he knew were representative of the prince himself.

Cameras beamed the ceremony up to satellite and then around the globe. Every major corridor of power throughout the world would see and celebrate the *Event*.

War would then be declared and waged, and the terror of the populace would be theirs to enjoy.

Within minutes all went black, except for the torches which illuminated the frightful stage. Four men in black robes hammered nails into Casey's feet and hands. Casey Burns Smith hung upside down, and his life's blood drained into the urns. Arthur Reddick stood on the stage announcing: "Welcome, children, to the celebration of our race."

Arles, who was seated on the side of the altar, wondered whether this would mean immortality, as he assumed the rest of them were ageless, timeless and of infinite potential.

"We will glorify our god. He is in us, and we are in him. We are to spread across all reality through our manifest destiny, to civilize all the known worlds and a myriad of other worlds, all created by the blood of the fallen one, who was called Christ, Jesus, Yeshua, Immanuel, Rabbi, Teacher, and Master."

One of the men took a sword and pierced Casey's abdomen, but Casey did not lose consciousness or show any sign of pain. The crowd assumed it was temporary, and the congregation began chanting in a dialect that Arles did not know. Then someone slit his throat, and Arthur, now in the form of a youthful being emitting pure light, took a golden chalice, climbed up the crystalline staircase, drained Casey's blood into the cup, and drank heavily.

"It is accomplished!" he said, knowingly intoning the last words of Christ on the cross.

The blood from the urns was poured out into this chalice and given to each member of the audience to drink as they stood in front of the altar. Casey's body hung pale and still on the inverted cross, illuminated for all to see. But his eyes were open, and they appeared to be watching.

"Drink, my brothers and sisters, and you will receive eternal life, and a world that is to be our heaven below," *young Arthur exclaimed!*

Arles had understood the purpose of the ceremony and his fear subsided—but he was barred from drinking the blood by several tall men in robes and hoods. He stood by, waiting to see some miraculous sign, but none came. The men with the handheld cameras zoomed in and out and covered the rather simple and uneventful ceremony. Arles wondered if the blood would work since Casey had never renounced Christ.

The earthquake startled everyone. They panicked—pushing and shoving, knocking over the urns—but then it went still again. Standing on the altar with several hooded priests, Arthur looked extremely worried. "Brethren, please calm down—it's just a little—"

White light beamed out from the empty cross. Casey smiled, as he suddenly appeared in front of the congregation in pure white robes. The blood drinkers pushed frantically toward the exits, but the doors remained shut.

Casey had become a bright glowing being. All eyes were upon him and all were very much afraid. "You have to kill me, Arthur," the transformed being said. "But you can't, because I am like those you serve, only I serve the Lord."

Some of the frightened audience actually begged for mercy and started to worship the being, whose eyes were full of fire. Clothed in white linen and suspended in air, his image vibrated between that of the boy named Casey and the glowing angelic being.

"You are all witnesses," he said as he appeared as the boy they had drained of blood. "You have opened up heaven, which will pour its judgment upon the earth. You cannot comprehend the Lord God—he will move on the earth and nowhere will you find peace. A great sentence has gone against you. Every single act of blasphemy, tyranny and sin, which you have delivered to the children of men, will mark you and you shall receive no relief or mercy," said the glowing being.

The congregation trembled and frantically trampled over each other as they forced open the exit doors and streamed out to the tram.

Arles tried to make it out, but he was stopped at the small train and without fanfare shot in the head by one of the security guards. As he lay dying, Arthur stood over him. "You will not find rest, even in Hell. He was supposed to renounce Christ—he is an angel of God, you fool! And not just an angel, he is The Angel of God—the chief of all angels. Mr. Dubailles, I will find you in the realm of the dead, and then you will pay for destroying our world."

Outside, the security forces locked down the site, but they fled when they saw the being standing on the top of the pyramid, becoming its glowing capstone—which was now a glowing star. When he spoke, some of the security forces fell to their faces and prayed.

• • •

Bauman didn't know what Ricky was talking about, until they got inside the church in Pasadena on Saturday night. They were able to access it from a basement underground hallway that led from the bookstore building next door. Once inside, it was too late. Several people, who had been drained of blood on an inverted cross, were dead around the "pulpit." Bauman didn't seem to notice the man who had been driving the Cadillac SUV, the very same one that kidnapped and murdered Alice Garcia.

John the Apostle and Shep kept Ricky in handcuffs in the back of the car, while Julio functioned as Bauman's aide. The city was in a state of curfew, but there were no police, no security forces, no National Guard or other military patrolling the area. Bauman had not seen any police since the last earthquake—and the City's power was still down. They did not even see the usual bands of roving hooligans intent on grabbing loot. Something had transformed the City of Angels, something caused it to become inert, something beyond Bauman's Voice, or mind.

The only security, the only lights and the only death were in the lavish church. Julio took Ricky's .38 Special. Bauman was armed with the gun he found on the broken floor when they escaped County—a Glock 40 cal. with extra-large capacity clip.

Julio, reacting to everything he had seen in the church, said: "Bauman, man, we need to get outta here, homes—this is like the Bible or something—David and Goliath?"

"But we have God on our side—except we can't kill, we can only defend."

"Bauman, what we saw, the babies, the women and that boy...I'm sick, I feel sick," Julio said, as he had finally seen something. When they approached the altar again, they saw an inverted cross with a young boy on it, drained of blood. The blood was all over the pews, the floor, the walls—and the smell was dank and fetid. Julio ran for the back exit, to get the car while Bauman waited just down the black street. When Julio came around to get him, Bauman said the tall guy was still standing outside.

Flames burst out through the windows, as the church was enveloped in fire. The conservatively but expensively dressed congregation on the street watched as they waited for the final parade of limousines to take them away. It was as if this fashionable group of people were out for Sunday church service.

After seeing and recognizing the tall man (the same one who kidnapped Alice Garcia) join a young woman in the back seat of a limo, Bauman and his friends followed him. Julio drove.

He, Bauman, would solve his elusive case—he was very close now. Closer than he had ever been.

forty-three

Brand had snuck into Arthur's room in Cairo in the darkness of predawn *disguised* as a doctor. For a time he held Arthur captive; he had no intention of letting him go. When Arthur transformed into a vibrating, pulsing being with scaly skin, Brand shot him in the abdomen. Arthur fell to the floor and was himself again. "I destroyed so many people," Brand said sadly. "All for you."

No one came to the room, as Arthur had expected. The phone line was dead, and it appeared, even from the bay windows overlooking the pyramids in the background, that the streets of Cairo were much like those in the City of Angels—deserted. News of the strange appearance of an angel had gone out to the world and many fled.

"I now know what my wife had been up to, that my son was the one you did not expect, and that Casey is an angel of God," said Brand, who shocked Arthur with his knowledge.

"How do you know this?" Arthur said, as he lay dying.

Brand poured himself a whisky and looked for an explanation in the blistering sun. "Though I accept Christ Jesus, I am a sinner, since I have come to take your life," he said to Arthur. He threw the small pistol out the window. "But I will not kill—I will repent for this."

Arthur said, "Disguised as an angel?—that's a myth. It's not even in your Bible...you do believe the Bible now, don't you, Brand? It's not too late, you can always come home to us. God won't accept you after what you've done."

"He prepares the way for the Lord's judgment—that's all I know. He left us all alive to witness this. I love God, and I believe that Jesus died on the cross for our sins—our fallen condition, our hopeless condition—that there is not one among us who is sinless or blameless before the Lord—and that when Jesus Christ was resurrected on the third day, all was accomplished. We were saved, all of us who believe in Him."

Arthur said, "You don't believe that. Look, that's all subject to debate. In fact, our people created the whole story of Jesus to control the masses—don't you get it? That was the best form of mind control. Look, this is *our* world—our lord is sovereign over it. Come home, son—be on the winning side—you need us, you can't prove that Jesus is Lord."

Brand laughed, "I accept Jesus as Lord of all—God saves the day, it's time for us to celebrate. But I am weak, and I can't live with what I've done, and though He offers me forgiveness, I don't think I deserve it."

Kincaid casually and fearlessly leaped out the window and fell to his death. Arthur smiled and watched as the body lay alone and unattended many floors below. He, on the other hand, was healing quickly—*supernaturally.*

And then he glanced up toward *his icons*—the pyramids.

They were gone!

All great and small pyramids everywhere—gone!

It would be blacked out—all traffic would be stopped in and out of Cairo because the pyramids had been *swallowed up,* they thought.

Arthur was nonplussed but not surprised, not completely. They had lost, and this unleashed The End.

And as his wound healed magically, he still felt renewed, because there was still more to come. Much more.

There were reports of angelic or bright glowing beings wearing slick black jumpsuits, leaping to and fro around the pyramid area of the *now empty* Giza Plateau. They were *killing with light,* the paper would say. An exotic weapon, perhaps emanating from space, causing hallucinations, they would say.

The *warriors* appeared human, and what emanated from their palms were what appeared to be lightning bolts—pure light, pure energy. Every person who came into their field of view was instantly disintegrated—every single person around the pyramids and on the streets. The people fled Cairo and headed out into the desert, to their idea of safety perhaps.

When Bauman arrested the tall man, he laughed for joy.

The prisoner's name was William Raines, a known movie producer no less. He told Bauman: "Lucifer is the god of this world; you will never get what you are after. What are you going to do with me? Take me to the police station? They'll arrest *you*, not me."

Bauman and Julio drove to the San Fernando Valley Rescue Mission with William sandwiched between John the Apostle and Shep. When they got there, Daniel had commandeered a van, and Shep, John the Apostle, Spruug, Julio and *the prisoner named William* got in. William started screaming and yelling, so they tied him, gagged him and let him lie on the floor behind the passenger seats.

Spruug drove, as his wife and children had gone ahead in the busses.

And as they drove out to the desert, they saw only a few cars. A church along the way was thronged with participants in Christ's resurrection. The sign of the church said, "God will wipe away every tear from every eye. There shall be no more death, nor sorrow, nor crying. There shall be no more pain, for the former things have passed away. Revelation 21:4."

forty-four

When dawn sprawled over Washington, D.C., there was no more *Washington Monument*—the symbol of Satan. Like the pyramids, *it was as if it had never been.*

It had not crumbled. There was a flat foundation of dirt, dirt fertile enough to plant! The reflecting pool was filled with a red viscous liquid that looked like blood.

Needless to say, everyone was in a state of shock and disbelief. Extra security forces gathered in Washington, as well as military. Offices were closed, and the President issued a message: "We have witnessed something that is unexplainable—let us pray. Dear Lord, please forgive us for what we've done, for how we have failed to follow your commandments. We are not worthy, *but we place our trust and lives in the hands of your son, Jesus Christ,* who is ascended today."

His prayer was met with hostile media barbs, accusing right-wing Christian extremist groups around the world of using explosives to rid the world of symbols and iconography that was priceless.

The President was removed from office and locked under military guard. Standing orders went out to round up Christians.

forty-five

Dear Mr. Parker,

I have let you down, for if I were to tell you all the things God will do through his angels in the coming days, or just how powerful angels like the one disguised as Casey truly are, then it would convince the world that God is serious about punishing sin and restoring His Presence on this earth. Besides Casey, who I believe is the powerful angel named *Metatron*, which ancient Jewish lore equates with Enoch, who did not die on this earth, but was taken by the Lord Himself. In Genesis 5:21, we find the following, heretofore mysterious passage: "And Enoch walked with God; and he *was* not, for God took him." Enoch did not owe a death because he was not human, in the sense that he did not have a human soul (though he was flesh, and lived on the earth for 365 years. He was a prophet, though his book was not incorporated into the Bible canon. Yet his son, Methuselah, who came after, and Jared, his father, who came before, possessed human souls, and thus owed—and gave—deaths).

Casey Burns Smith walked with God, though born into the womb of Satan, whose generational inheritance was Satan. He was recognized through their intelligence operatives as a lamb, meaning he walked with God and was therefore worthy of sacrifice for the purpose of keeping time timeless, as a mode of blocking the returning of our Lord and Savior, Jesus Christ. As you have seen, this was done through sorcery, and the transmutation of the blood, mixed with a substance that they believed was the blood of Christ. The pyramid, the central clock of their cosmos, was the holographic point between all dimensions, from which all time had flowed, *or would not flow*, as is now the case.

It was built by the fallen angels, whom Enoch called the Watchers, and synchronized on nearly every major planetary body, for the purpose of creating reality through time—to somehow usurp God's will, or so they thought. They discovered that they were incorrect, as God had delivered to them his most mighty angel, Metatron, who was Enoch, and who was even above Gabriel, Michael, Raphael and Phanuel. I will not elucidate here the nature of these beings.

It is my belief that God waits for His time, and He chooses it at the foundation of the world, that somehow this was all to come to pass, and He is firmly established as Lord of all that He created.

Here is the secret for those who have an ear to hear: all of their sacrifices are moot; all of their power is subject to God's will, and therefore is moot; every intention, every victory, every institution, and every body they have exalted will be destroyed by God. Every nation on earth will be destroyed now. Yes, they will rebuild, but then they will only hasten the return of our Lord. Amen.

Just as a child of God cannot be nurtured by a poisoned well, so God will end the lives of the wicked and even their offspring, who may not have yet been initiated into their sickness of maladaptive purpose to destroy humanity in order to supplant the realm of the dragon, which is the same in every country.

Just as this book is coded and this book is a warning, many will come to Christ out of fear for their very lives—and that is a good thing. You asked me how you would verify that these things shall come to pass, and I said what God told me to say: "You shall know them by their fall."

I am to witness that our God is holy, and righteous, and true, and full of perfect mercy, justice and goodness. He will protect His own, and to do that He will destroy much on the earth, taking many innocent to heaven, and leaving the remnant to witness to the lost. May the Lord help us be strong now, as the horrors of God's judgment may turn those who are not His against Him, let it not turn us against Him. Instead, let it edify and strengthen our faith in Jesus Christ, who sacrificed Himself so that we, unworthy sinners, could be made worthy under the Blood of the Lamb, which was, and is, and will forever be acceptable to God. And let us agree that God paid for us, that we had nothing in ourselves, or in our works, or in our thoughts, or in our intentions that would ever be payment enough— that He alone paid the price by sending His son, crucifying Him in our place, as sinners, so that we could be reconciled, by faith alone, to God the Father—and that the only God of this Universe, indeed all there is, is faithful and true, in the form of Father, Son and Holy Spirit.

Mr. Parker, I am not well, as you know, and all I ask is that you do not divulge that there are codes herein, as they may be misused by fortune tellers and the like, who are fallen and are in need of salvation through Christ, lest all of them be cast into hell along with their hate-filled spiritual father, Satan, who is the dragon, and whose leaders are as serpents in nature, who has deceived them. Let them know that God kills to save His own, and He will always save the day.

Tell them to fear the Lord God, before they perish. Blessings be to you and your wife and children. I stand in awe of God's perfection, and I stand in gratitude for that which you have done in hiding me so that I could make this communication complete.

Sincerely, in Christ
Mountain

forty-six

*T*hey celebrated Easter at the Camp up high on the mountain, which was between the desert and the sea. Tents and cabins were already on the site. More people were streaming in hourly, as the city below had grown dark. Many who were not with Fred's mission had also been called to come to what looked like a training park for military or firemen. The barracks housed a few hundred, more were housed in tents. Fred and Louis and other missionaries from across the City of Angels went right to work, first putting up painted signs of crosses out on the deserted highway, then unloading the food bank, which was one of the "borrowed" tour busses.

Pastor Ted prepared the Easter sermon and delivered it late in the afternoon on Easter Sunday. "Do you know that angels helped Jesus? Yes, angels were there at his birth, and they were there after he was resurrected. When Mary Magdalene stood at the empty tomb weeping, two angels in white were at the sepulcher, and they saw her weeping. They asked her, 'Woman, why do you weep?' And she said to them, 'Because they took my Lord from me, and I don't know what they did with the body.' And when she turned to leave in utter grief, Jesus stood right in front of her, in his glorified body, the same that was shown to the apostles, and Jesus said to her, 'Woman, why do you weep?' She thought he was a gardener!"

The gathering laughed.

Ted laughed a bit, and said: "And Mary said to Jesus, and remember, this was her living Lord, as she had devoted her life to him—she said to him: 'Sir, you took him, where'd you hide the body?' There was a long silence, and he looked into her eyes. She was thrown by the stranger, especially when he called her by name, 'Mary.' When she recognized him, she said, 'Master,' and he told her to touch him not, because he had not yet ascended to His Father, John 20, verse 17. Then, look what happened! He says, 'I am not yet ascended to my Father, but go to my brethren, and say unto them, I ascend unto my Father, and your Father; and to my God, and *your* God.' He did not say, *my* Father and *not* your father. He did not say *my* God, and *not* your God. He said *your* Father! He said *your* God! He's *our* God, beloved! Because of what He did. But wait, look. He said, 'Don't touch me, for I am not yet ascended.' And he made glorious appearances to the disciples, and he preached to them. Look at John 20, at verse 21: 'Then said Jesus to them again, Peace be unto you: as *my* Father hath sent me, even so send I you.' Verse 22 now: 'And when he had said this, he breathed on them, and saith unto them, Receive ye the Holy Ghost.' Did you get that? He *breathed* on them, and from his breath came the Holy Ghost, that's the Holy Spirit, which lives in all believers. When we take the communion, we experience the entire life of Christ, the fellowship with our Lord and the one who saved us and brought us the Holy Spirit. If you think earthquakes are anything new, I have a little something to say about quakes, look at Matthew 28, verse 2. 'And behold, there was a great earthquake: for the angel of the Lord descended from heaven, and came and rolled back the stone from the door, and sat upon it.' Verse 3: 'His countenance was like lightning, and his raiment white as snow,' verse 4, 'And for fear of him the keepers did shake, and became as dead *men*.' Are you getting the idea that God's supernatural power can do *anything*? And do you see the connection between the earthquake and the angels? Listen, beloved, I know that in the past most preachers would not talk about the angels of the Lord, or the evil angels, except as it related to the mind, to spiritual attack or persecution. Beloved, *there are angels*. How many of you have seen or talked with angels?"

The rabble, sitting under the pines in the clearing surrounded by buildings on all sides, were relieved and delighted at Pastor Ted's sermon, and every single hand was held aloft.

"How many of you have seen the wave?"

About half the hands went up.

"In your dreams?"

Nearly every hand went up.

"The Holy Spirit speaks the truth, and this is a judgment, beloved. We are the remnant. We are not a cult; we are survivors. We have to pull together to see this through, because it's bound to get worse. How many of you had no choice but to come up here with the missions?"

Every hand went up.

"How many of you are broken, confused, sad, and in a state of shock?"

On that one, Sarah, the pastor's wife, looked on with fear.

But no hands rose.

"All right, how many of you can solve your own problems right now?"

No hands of the 2500 refugees rose.

"How many of you want to give it to Jesus? You think He can solve our problems?"

Every hand went up and the crowd began to cheer. He continued to tell them about the resurrection, about the reconciliation of man to God, of the price that was paid, and what the Spirit could do.

Stephen and Rebecca slept in separate sleeping bags. Stephen told the leaders about his experience and that *in the Spirit,* he had heard the name *Metatron,* and they all re-read the Bible section about how Enoch walked with God and how "God took him."

"We want to get married, in fact, our Lord insists on it," Stephen and Rebecca told Fred.

Fred and his wife, Billie, met with Rebecca, to see if that was indeed what was in her heart, as she had been silent, then sometimes weeping, then wailing to her Lord in the middle of the night. Billie said, "Honey, you've been through so much—"

Rebecca interrupted, "Billie, we're going through so much more now...It's real, Billie. It's real. It's *all* real. The Spirit tells me what's going to happen, and it happens. I was the last witness to the angel of the Lord, to see him. He was in my care and I tried to kill him! Oh, God!" She wept and held back her tears again. Rebecca continued: "But he, Casey, took me to Lord Jesus—all he ever did was point to Jesus, his whole life is wrapped up in serving Jesus, but he's a warrior angel. He's not here to make peace, he's here to carry out the judgment of the Lord and to make the way for Jesus to return."

"Yes," Billie said, teary over the passionate and lovely young woman. "You were changed. It's a miracle. Do you miss your family?" she asked.

"I'm sorry. He called me Rebecca and told me to walk forward—

like a lot of us who came to Christ, and then those who had forsaken me started to fade. But I feel sorry for them, I want them to come to the Lord—I want everyone to know our God, *their* God."

That was the correct answer, and Billie had no further objections to marriage, because the young lady was in perfect mental order. She was modest, good with the children, always reading them The Word and patiently explaining it to them. Stephen was a good man, though he was questioned by the new elders as to why he would hot-wire all busses and not repent for it.

He replied: "The Lord told me not to repent for taking the busses—who do you think drove them all to the mission anyway? Those weren't people."

The miracle stood, and Stephen was exonerated.

Apple would only prophesy in the private office quarters for the missionaries.

Fred commented to Louis: "If anyone knew the way it really was, they would *all* come to the Lord. If the social workers or cops ever saw the way it really was, they would lock us all up as criminally insane."

They all shared a laugh until the final prophecy came.

Apple, with his belly hanging over his new, direct-from-the-mission jeans and too-tight T-shirt, endearingly non-self-conscious, totally absorbed and happy in the Lord, told that night why there was a worldwide news blackout. "They tried to do it upside down—reverse it to become timeless so God wouldn't come back and destroy them."

Ted knew what he meant, and Stephen said: "Metatron?"

"*Metatron was Casey*," Apple said.

"Yes!" Stephen said, amazed at God's gift in action.

"They didn't know it. They took him to be reversed, to reverse Jesus, so they could have more time. Instead they broke the seal, and now God will do to what he did to Noah, because the world is that corrupt, and he will do it with fire." Apple fell on his face laughing and everyone was afraid.

"It's good news, right Apple? I mean, they messed up, right?" asked Ted excitedly.

Apple rolled onto his back and spoke up into their faces, and the candlelight danced about the cabin.

In a somber tone, Apple said: "God will call many of His home. They will die with the wicked. Metatron marked them, and all the other angels, millions of them, marked them all to be *taken* first, and then some will die, but they will go to heaven and live there forever. And they shall have no pain in death." When he spoke this, his eyes rolled back in his head, and Billie and Rebecca tried to catch him before he fell back.

No one wanted to ask the question, but Stephen blurted out: "Is the wave real?"

"He needs rest," Billie said, and Rebecca helped her remove him to one of the tents.

"Praise God," Fred said. "I'm with you, Lord. We praise you, Jesus—do what You will! Amen!"

All the men fell to their knees in fervid prayer, led by Fred, who remembered the angels he had seen throughout his life. He knew why they were hidden from his memory-view for so long until now, and he knew that he and the others would all need rest. Eventually, he knew, they would have to elect leaders, and they might have to fight off the forces of evil, whether by mind, land, or air.

• • •

"What did I do wrong? Serve the god of this world? You know the military will kill all of you, every single one of you, because they work for me, not you," said the tall, slender man that Bauman, Julio, John the Apostle and Shep had arrested, or kidnapped. They had lost their way up in the mountains and had to break into a deserted cabin.

"Look, I've seen, The Voice in my head tells me that you should witness all of this," Bauman said, wondering about his wife and daughter.

Julio made a fire in the cabin, and they had blankets. One would have to stand watch, one would sleep, and two would guard William, the stranger.

"The floor is fine with me," said Julio, "it's better than jail—but I have to go back tomorrow," he said. "My family is down there."

Bauman said, "Lord Jesus Christ is the only way, the Voice says."

John the Apostle found a Bible and Shep was crying uncontrollably. "This is the end, the end," Shep kept saying.

"John, comfort us, will you?" asked Bauman.

John turned at random to a passage in Numbers 6 and read from the Bible. "Dear Holy God," he said, "please bless us and keep us, please make your face shine upon us, and be gracious to us. Lord, lift up your countenance to us and give us peace.

"You always say that same prayer," said Bauman.

John started to become uneasy, and then he said: "It's a good prayer."

The long night ensued, but they would not understand just why they were there until later, when they awoke and had a panoramic view from their 4400 feet elevation of the entire basin of Los Angeles, all the way to the distant sea.

That night another earthquake rocked the cabin, and the stranger named William escaped.

It did not matter, as they would make their way to the Mission, somewhere higher up on the mountain. The next morning they all noticed that the sea had disappeared, or in the distance it looked exactly like the land. It could not be explained. "Maybe it's a different color because of the sun," Shep said, terrified.

Fred found some extra batteries that night, and was able to listen to the short-wave radio. Terror had been unleashed on the world. Either Christian or Muslim terrorists had destroyed the pyramids at Giza, but it was unclear, so said the Voice of America, whether explosives were used. Spruug, Stephen, and others had come to Fred's tent to listen to the radio, as no one could sleep.

"We have also a report that the Louvre, in Paris, has been bombed. We have no further information, except that multitudes of Parisians were reported outside the walls wailing in mourning, and some have become completely disoriented. There was one report of ten university professors standing naked in the streets in protest. Two of them committed suicide by hurling themselves in front of military transports. The good news is that the President delivered a speech explaining there was no coup, and that he is very much in control of US forces, though this seemed insincere, since the background was not the American flag but a blank wall. The UN Security Council, however, blamed the United States, the President in particular, for waging war against all non-Christian targets by voting no on the resolution to condemn all Christian extremists. Curfews are in effect, and the US is on high alert for nuclear attack. Citizens are encouraged to take shelter and cooperate with government authorities. FEMA is very much in control and is in charge of housing those displaced by the earthquakes and also incarcerating dissidents across the country..."

"That means us," said Fred. "We have to fortify ourselves."

When the dawn came, they heard a report of an imminent tidal wave in Los Angeles.

Casey appeared to Rebecca and took her hand. "Rebecca, it's a judgment—those in Christ will go to heaven. Our God is a glorious God, full of mercy—His judgment is borne out of love, and not hate for His own."

forty-seven

Dear Mountain,

The pages you sent me are of an alarming nature, and I feel as though I must include some of our correspondence for the reader's sake. Though I have trouble understanding, I have the feeling you are who you say you are, and I am inclined to let the chips fall where they may, as it were. I am an editor, having worked in publishing all my life, and now, of course, I am the publisher and editor-in-chief of our company, which houses several imprints.

If you are correct about any of this, I am simply gripped by fear. I am sure you notice I do not use your name but your code name, respecting your wishes, which is prudent for your safety. I am personally afraid. I have children and an extended family—my mother, bless her soul, is ninety-eight-years-old. I remember how she used to warn me about the judgment of the Lord, or the Day of the Lord, but I suppose I never thought it was true. I just never believed her—most people, in all honesty, believed as I did. I am safe in assuming that, at least. My mother went to church every week, and I just thought it was Old Testament stuff. Can you send me something to comfort me? Please forgive my candor with this letter. My entire career now seems to be a waste of time—nothing makes sense anymore. Tell me more about Jesus, would he want to harm those who didn't know about all this? Would God seriously destroy us, even those who didn't know any better? Mountain, it doesn't seem fair, if you know what I mean.

The last pages have made me wonder what good life is. You mean to tell me that if I accept Jesus, I'll be saved? But I'm not sure I want to be saved by a God who would destroy so many. I feel that leading a good life, taking care of those in need, following laws, working hard, being kind to others, especially the meek in our society—that these attributes are to be lauded. Help me, Mountain—as my words cannot describe what I'm feeling. I don't even want to go home tonight. I'm not sure where I can go.

I await your response and hope you understand my lack of business demeanor in writing this.

Sincerely,

Crossley Parker
Editor-in-Chief and Publisher
Braithwaite Books

Dear Mr. Parker,

Let me start by saying that I am praying for you.

Your question, to paraphrase: Why God would harm those who are not wicked, if they do not worship Christ, but are good people nonetheless? The answer is that man's nature is sin, inherited by us because of the fall of Adam. God is holy and cannot accept sin. He sent his only Son to die for our sins because He loves us, and wants to redeem us—we have to voluntarily come "home," so to speak. Those who are in Christ do not need to worry about perishing, because they will be with our Lord in heaven; others are to be judged individually—those who have heard the truth and turned away, even if they led so-called "exemplary lives." They will not measure up.

Mr. Parker, nothing we do, no act of kindness or charity or philanthropy, or love or beneficence or gratitude is worthy of Him who is holy. That is why He sent his only son to die, to pay the price for our sinfulness, to reconcile us. God is no respecter of humans; He is to be feared. When the world does not fear him, He tends to destroy that which is corrupt before His own become corrupt.

It is clear from your letter that you need help. There are good people who can help you in Manhattan; I will e-mail you a list.

Sir, God is not "fair"—He is perfect. His ways are not ours, they are higher than ours. Indeed, those who do not understand and turn against Him are simply wrong. And they will pay the price. Death is no escape from judgment, as the Bible tells us that every single person will be judged. All those not in Christ as well as those who are in Christ will be judged, but those in Christ will not lose their salvation or eternity with God. I told you before that hell is being cut off from God, forever and ever. Please forgive me if I am not encouraging you in the right way.

Suffice it to say that most people feel the prophecy in the Book of Revelation is next, and I admit, the stage appears to be set. But that does not preclude God from casting judgment upon the earth before this, if He chooses to. He has done it before with floods, with invading armies, with disease, pestilence and famine. He gave me the gift of communication and prophecy, sir, and I am warning the people of the earth as the Holy Spirit instructs.

He wishes me to be His witness, to know that what He does is just—is perfect justice, is perfect righteousness, borne from love, only love for His own. Can you understand that?

May the Lord be with you, and keep you from evil.
God bless you and yours, sir

Mountain

Dear Mountain,

Thank you for your concern, and your kind words.
I am back and in thoroughly good stead. I finally
feel at peace. Please forgive me for going on as I did
in my last letter. Please note that, though I disagree
with you, I respect what you are writing about. I believe all religions are valid, and that those of faith,
in every tradition, are to be respected.

What God tells you may not necessarily be what
God has told others, though I admit, the things you
told me privately last year came true one hundred
percent.

I look forward to the concluding pages since we
will meet our production schedule, after all.

I hope all this secrecy will end when the book is
published, as I would like to meet you someday.

Sincerely,

Crossley Parker,
Editor-in-Chief and Publisher
Braithwaite Books

fin

*T*hey saw it in the morning light. Everyone was warned to stay in their homes. The Pacific plate shifted and the ocean did not cascade over the City of Angels and neighboring regions—it went the other way, out to sea. The quakes and aftershocks subsided, and many people, though they were warned, ran out and played amidst what had been buried under the sea. There were many dead, decaying human bodies and fish of all types. The sight was something to behold, a person could walk all the way to the islands off the coast.

The city was still under curfew. The only people who were wanted by the police were those from the Mission, and especially those who conspired in the theft of the busses. Spruug, who was named on television as the leader of a Christian terrorist cell with ties to both Muslim fundamentalists and certain orthodox Jews, had supposedly conspired to destroy the museums in the world because of anti-Semitic art.

Arthur Reddick took the initiative to help the United Nations identify those terrorist organizations who had "defiled or destroyed some of the world's great treasures." He appeared on national television representing the Global News Organization, and made a call for "all reasonable people to enter a dialogue of peace and unity."

The prices of commodities had risen so high that hoarding laws were immediately passed by an outraged Congress. Private foundations involved in feeding the hungry were to be inspected and their members scrutinized for ties to terrorist cells.

Bauman could hardly believe the news. Many in the camp wanted to return to the city. They had been buzzed by helicopters, which appeared to be conducting some sort of surveillance. Pastor Ted, Fred and the others prayed for guidance, but nothing came, until the third day after Easter.

Several glowing orbs of light hovered over the camp and over the city. Not UFOs, but balls of light. Many children said they were angels.

Over the radio they heard that people had seen a figure standing above the highest building downtown, pointing to the ocean with one hand with a sword pointed to the heavens. He was illuminated at night, and when they went to arrest him, he was found hovering above them, suspended in mid-air. They shot at him, sent jet fighters after him, but nothing worked, as all bullets and even the planes flew right through the glowing being.

Apple said, "They are going to execute the Lord's judgment. Oh, God help us."

Casey appeared to Rebecca in her tent, and said: "Do not fear, for the Lord wishes you and your people as a remnant and some of you are witnesses."

The next earthquake destroyed the cabins in the camp. No one had ever experienced anything that powerful—they could not stand, they could not move, and the quake lasted for at least thirty minutes.

In the bright daylight, the angel that Stephen knew as Metatron stood over the city—he was a giant, perhaps a thousand feet tall. The same being as reported on the radio. He pointed to where the ocean had been, which had subsided beyond the offshore islands.

Only a few were on lookout that day at the lower camp, where the city was visible. But they could see a wall of water, like a storm front or a fog, but this was blue, clearly water, moving evenly for the shore.

Then it started to crash and even from their vantage point, many miles away and thousands of feet up, they could see the force of the wave breaking.

"Lord, have mercy on us all," Bauman declared.

Apple cried and Stephen grabbed his head. Julio and the others were wailing, "No! No!"

"I love you, Lord, for your ways are righteous and true," said

Stephen.

The heavens opened up, all the angels were in attendance, and the sky grew dark.

Stephen saw his mother waving from the sky, and he was glad his new wife was tending to the children.

"Behold," the angel, who sat with Stephen between the two boulders and away from the others, said. "The Lord's will be done."

Flocks of doves, seagulls, hawks, falcons and every kind of fowl blotted out the sky as they flew overhead, away from the cascading beauty of nature.

It was a rushing wall of blue and white that was higher than the highest building. It made everything shimmering blue; it made everything beautiful again. It rushed in and no one could see death and things quickly ended—that is, life ended.

And death was everywhere below—the City of Angels was no more, and the mountains became islands, and silence roared with the screaming wind.

Not a building was left, only a lake; its shore was about half-a-mile down the mountain. The waters began to subside, but still covered everything that was inhabited only a few moments before.

Casey stood before Rebecca and Stephen, and said: "I want you to understand, I have executed the will of the Lord. They will not cause Christ to become *un-resurrected*, they will not blaspheme the Holy Spirit, and they will not create the abomination of desolation until the appointed time when the antichrist will occupy the reconstructed temple in Jerusalem. Now all are warned, now all institutions and countries and principalities brought low by war, famine and *natural* disasters will have to be rebuilt—but many will come to Christ. For only a moment they will see that their roots and spells and magic rituals and space ships and portals and all their feeble creations are all subject to God's will and not their own. Let no one say He can direct God this way and that, and let no one ever say again that God is *in* us, or *is* us—He is holy, and separate from us, except through Christ Jesus, and we serve Him day and night, forever and ever. Amen."

Bauman worried about his prisoner who had escaped. The Voice told him to take care of his wife and daughter.

There were no more helicopters, and Apple prophesied that the entire camp, the little remnant, would move eastward, to further mountains, as the judgment had not yet ended.

They would make trips to help the survivors; they would see it was about the taking of innocent life for a purpose that would forever elude them. Others would say that there is only one Lamb—Jesus, the Lamb of God. Later, the memories of angels would fade.

Apple screamed: "All of our brothers and sisters are with Jesus now—hallelujah!" He convulsed on the ground, and many had to console him.

The refugees would be safe for now, for the world was in an utter state of shock. The world would say at first it was God's judgment; later they would deny it. The television blackout would not stop the angels from appearing on every single television with the face of every young man that had ever been a sacrificial lamb for a family who gave in to what was called "the truth" so they could have a better life.

Every single boy and girl who had ever lost their innocence because of those who would betray them, the serpents and those who would be aliens, invaders, and dragon worshipers; every single person who lit a candle for the black prayer was, for a time, broadcast throughout the airwaves of the world and held in a blazing white light so that every single person who had harmed an innocent one would be known by *all*. Every single name of every single one given over to the wicked side would be known by all.

Would be held accountable.

Would be cursed forever.

Metatron, Michael, Gabriel, Raphael, Phanuel and a myriad of angels did their work around the world, and all would know that the City of Angels was the City Of Sorrow, the Hall Of Flesh, Queendom Of Narcissus, Township Of Murder, Stronger Preying On Weaker, Home To The Perverse And Mistaken, Prison To The Kind And Pure, Where Innocence Died, A City No More—no, not of God.

As Sodom was also slain.

Those in authority who saw that their monuments removed were in mortal terror—they would hide their faces and hide their bodies, but all knew *who they were* now.

An angel spoke to them on all media throughout the entire universe. His countenance was glowing white, his hair was as wool, and his robes were of fine linen; and all knew him as an angel of the Lord, a servant of the Christ. "My Lord Jesus spoke to you when he was with you, and you were warned, but none of you believed He would ever judge you. None of you believed when he said the following in your Bible, the Word of God, in Matthew 18:6: 'But whoever offends one of these little ones who believe in Me, it would be better for him that a millstone were hung about his neck, and he were drowned in the depth of the sea.'

"And now you have your answer," said the angel, in the voice of all creation.

CPSIA information can be obtained
at www.ICGtesting.com
Printed in the USA
FSHW01n0800050818
51172FS